GW00808862

# Jacqueline Wilson

# girls

# 3-in-1

## Illustrated by Nick Sharratt

incorporating GIRLS IN LOVE,
GIRLS UNDER PRESSURE
and GIRLS OUT LATE

CORGI BOOKS

GIRLS 3-IN-1
A CORGI BOOK 0552 548804

This collection first published in Great Britain by Corgi,
an imprint of Random House Childlen's Books

Corgi edition published 2002

1 3 5 7 9 10 8 6 4 2

Copyright © Jacqueline Wilson, 2002

GIRLS IN LOVE
Copyright © Jacqueline Wilson, 1997
Illustrations copyright © Nick Sharrat, 1997

GIRLS UNDER PRESSURE
Copyright © Jacqueline Wilson, 1998
Illustrations copyright © Nick Sharratt, 1998

GIRLS OUT LATE
Copyright © Jacqueline Wilson, 1999
Illustrations copyright © Nick Sharratt, 1999

Papers used by Random House Children's Books are natural, recyclable
products made from wood grown in sustainable forests. The manufacturing
processes conform to the environmental regulations of the country of origin.

Set in Bembo by
Phoenix Typesetting, Burley-in-Wharfedale, West Yorkshire

Corgi Books are published by Random House Children's Books,
61–63 Uxbridge Road, London W5 5SA,
a division of The Random House Group Ltd,
in Australia by Random House Australia (Pty) Ltd,
20 Alfred Street, Milsons Point, Sydney, NSW 2061, Australia,
in New Zealand by Random House New Zealand Ltd,
18 Poland Road, Glenfield, Auckland 10, New Zealand
and in South Africa by Random House (Pty) Ltd,
Endulini, 5a Jubilee Road, Parktown 2193, South Africa

THE RANDOM HOUSE GROUP Limited Reg. No. 954009
www.kidsatrandomhouse.co.uk

A CIP catalogue record for this book is available
from the British Library.

Printed and bound in Great Britain by
Bookmarque, Croydon, Surrey

# girls
# in ♥
# love

# Nine Dedications!

1. Stephanie Dummler and Year Nine Venus (1995), Coombe Girls School.
2. Becky Heather and Year Nine Chestnut and Beech (1995), The Green School for Girls.
3. Jane Ingles and the pupils of Hillside School.
4. Claire Drury and the pupils of Failsworth School – especially Jackelyn and Rachel.
5. Sarah Greenacre and the pupils of the Stoke High School.
6. De Reading and the pupils of St Benedict School.
7. Angela Derby.
8. Becki Hillman.
9. To all the other schools who made me so welcome in 1995 and 1996.

# Nine Major Resolutions

1. Stay best friends with Magda and Nadine.

2. Draw every day – and come top in Art.

3. Try not to come bottom in all other subjects!

4. Go on a diet and STICK to it.
   (No more Magnum ice-creams, sob sob.)

5. Do something with my hair. Anything. Grow it.
   Or cut it right off. Dye it??? 

6. Get some sort of paid work the minute I'm fourteen
   so I can...

7. Buy some decent clothes.

8. Go clubbing. Seventh Heaven

9. GET A BOYFRIEND!

# One Girl

The first day back at school. I'm walking because I missed the bus. *Not* a good start. Year Nine. I wonder what it'll be like.

Number nine, number nine, number nine . . .

It's on that classic Beatles White album, the crazy mixed-up bit at the end. I've always felt close to John Lennon even though he died before I was born. I like him because he did all those crazy little drawings and he wore granny glasses and he was funny and he always just did his own thing. I do crazy little drawings and I wear granny glasses and my friends think I'm funny. I don't get the opportunity to do my own thing though.

It's half past eight. If I was doing my own thing right now I'd be back in bed, curled up, fast asleep. John Lennon had lie-ins, didn't he, when he and

Yoko stayed in bed all day. They even gave interviews to journalists in bed. Cool.

So, if I could do my own thing I'd sleep till midday. Then breakfast. Hot chocolate and doughnuts. I'll listen to music and fool around in my sketchbook. Maybe watch a video. Then I'll eat again. I'll send out for a pizza. Though maybe I should stick to salads. I guess it would be easy to put on weight lying around in bed all day. I don't want to end up looking like a beached whale.

I'll have a green salad. And green grapes. And what's a green drink? There's that liqueur I sipped round at Magda's, crème de menthe. I can't say I was that thrilled. It was a bit like drinking toothpaste. Forget the drink.

I'll phone Magda though, and Nadine, and we'll have a long natter. And then . . .

Well, it'll be the evening now, so I'll have a bath and wash my hair and change into . . . What should I wear in bed? Not my own teddy-bear nightie. Much too babyish. But I don't fancy one of those slinky satin numbers. I know, I'll wear a long white gown with embroidered roses all colours of the rainbow, and I'll put a big flash ring on every finger and lie flat in my bed like Frida Kahlo. She's another one of my heroes, this amazing South American artist with extraordinary eyebrows and earrings and flowers in her hair.

OK, there I am, back in bed and looking beautiful. Then I hear the door opening. Footsteps. It's my boyfriend coming to see me . . .

The only trouble is I haven't *got* a boyfriend.

Well, I haven't got a Frida Kahlo outfit or a bedside phone or my own television and video and my bed sags because my little brother Eggs uses it as a trampoline whenever I'm not around. I could put up with all these deprivations. I'd just like a boyfriend. Please.

Just as I'm thinking this a beautiful blond boy with big brown eyes comes sauntering round a car parked partly on the pavement. He steps to one side to get out of my way, only I've stepped the same way. He steps to the other side. So do I! We look like we're doing a crazy kind of two-step.

'Oh. Whoops. Sorry!' I stammer. I feel my face flooding scarlet.

He stays cool, one eyebrow slightly raised. He doesn't say anything but he smiles at me.

*He smiles at me!*

Then he walks neatly past while I dither, still in a daze.

I look back over my shoulder. He's looking back at me. He really is. Maybe . . . maybe he likes me. No, that's mad. Why should this really incredible guy who must be at least eighteen think anything of a stupid schoolgirl who can't even walk past him properly?

He's not looking up. He's looking down. He's looking at my legs! Oh, God, maybe my skirt really *is* too short. I turned it up myself last night. Anna said she'd shorten it for me, but I knew she'd only turn it up a centimetre or so. I wanted my skirt really short. Only I'm not that great at sewing. The hem went a bit bunchy. When I tried the skirt back on there suddenly seemed a very large amount of chubby pink leg on show.

Anna didn't say anything but I knew what she was thinking.

Dad was more direct: 'For God's sake, Ellie, that skirt barely covers your knickers!'

'Honestly!' I said, sighing. 'I thought you tried to be hip, Dad. Everyone wears their skirts this length.'

It's true. Magda's skirt is even shorter. But her legs are long and lightly tanned. She's always moaning about her legs, saying she hates the way the muscle sticks out at the back. She used to do ballet and tap, and she still does jazz dancing. She moans but she doesn't mean it. She shows her legs off every chance she gets.

Nadine's skirts are short too. Her legs are never brown. They're either black when she's wearing her opaque tights or white when she has to go to school. Nadine can't stand getting sun-tanned. She's a very gothic girl with a vampire complexion. She's very willowy as well as white. Short skirts look so much better with slender legs.

It's depressing when your two best friends in all the world are much thinner than you are. It's even more depressing when your stepmother is thinner too. With positively model girl looks. Anna is only twenty-seven and she looks younger. When we go out together people think we're sisters. Only we don't look a bit alike. She's so skinny and striking. I'm little and lumpy.

I'm not exactly *fat*. Not really. It doesn't help having such a round face. Well, I'm round all over.

My tummy's round and my bum is round. Even my stupid *knees* are round. Still, my chest is round too. Magda has to resort to a Wonderbra to get a proper cleavage and Nadine is utterly flat.

I don't mind my top. I just wish there was much less of my bottom. Oh, God, what must I look like from the back view? No wonder he's staring.

I scuttle round the corner, feeling such a fool. My legs have gone so wobbly it's hard to walk. They look as if they're blushing too. Look at them, pink as hams. Who am I kidding? Of course I'm fat. The waistband on my indecently short skirt is uncomfortably tight. I've got fatter this summer, I just know I have. Especially these last three terrible weeks at the cottage.

It's so unfair. Everyone else goes off on these really glamorous jaunts abroad. Magda went to Spain. Nadine went to America. *I* went to our damp dreary cottage in Wales. And it rained and it rained and it rained. I got so bored sitting around playing infantile games of Snap and Old Maid with Eggs and watching fuzzy telly on the black-and-white portable and tramping through a sea of mud in my wellies that I just ate all the time.

Three meals a day, and at least thirty-three snacks. Mars bars and jelly beans and popcorn and tortilla chips and salt and vinegar crisps and Magnum ice-creams. Gobble gobble gobble, it's no wonder that I wobble. Yuck, my knees are actually wobbling as I walk.

I hate walking. I don't see the point of going for a walk, lumbering along in this great big loop just to get back to where you've come from. We always do so much walking in Wales.

Dad and Anna always stride ahead. Little Eggs leaps about like a loony. I slouch behind them, mud sucking at my wellies, and I think to myself: This is *fun*??? Why have a holiday cottage in Wales, of all places? Why can't we have a holiday villa in Spain or a holiday apartment in New York? Magda and Nadine are so *lucky*. OK, Magda was on a package tour and they stayed in a high-rise hotel and Nadine was only in Orlando doing a Disney, but I bet they both had brilliant sunshine every day.

In our little bit of Wales it's always the rainy season. Black clouds are a permanent fixture, like the mountains. It even rains *inside* the cottage because Dad thinks he can fix the roof slates himself and he always makes a total botch of it. We have buckets and bowls and saucepans scattered all over upstairs, and day and night there's this drip-tinkle-splash symphony.

I got so utterly fed up and depressed that when we paid the usual visit to this boring old ruined castle I felt like casting myself off the battlements. I leaned against the stone wall at the top, my heart still banging away like crazy from the awful climb, and wondered what it would be like to leap over into thin air. Would anyone seriously care if I ended up going splat on the cobblestones below? Dad and Anna had a firm grip on Eggs but they didn't make a grab at me, even when I leaned right over, my head dangling.

They actually wandered off hand-in-hand with

16

him, mumbling about Bailies and Boiling Oil. They are overdoing the involved-parent act. I doubt if Eggs can spell castle yet so he's certainly not at the serious project stage. Dad never did all this stuff with me when I was little. He always seemed to be working or busy. When we went on holiday he went off sketching. But I didn't care. I had Mum. Then.

Thinking about Mum made me feel worse. People don't expect me to remember her still. They're mad. I can remember so much about her – heaps and heaps of stuff. The games we used to play with my Barbie dolls and the songs we'd sing and how she let me put on her make-up and try on all her jewellery and her pink silk petticoat and her high heels.

I want to talk about her so much but whenever I try with Dad he goes all tense and quiet. He frowns as if he has a headache. He doesn't want to remember Mum. Well, he's got Anna now. And they've both got Eggs.

I haven't got anyone. I started to feel so miserable I mooched off by myself. I walked to the other side of the battlements and found a crumbling turret. The entrance was roped off, with a warning. I ducked under the rope and climbed up all these dank steps in the dark. Then I put my foot on a step that wasn't there and tripped, banging my shin. It wasn't really that painful but I found I was crying. You can't really climb when you're crying, so I sat down and sobbed.

After a while I realized I didn't have a tissue. My glasses were all wet and my nose was running. I wiped and sniffed as best I could. The stone steps were very cold and the damp spread through my jeans but I still sat there. I suppose I was waiting for Dad to come looking for me. I waited and I waited and I waited. And then I heard footsteps. I sat still, listening. Quick, light footsteps. Too light for Dad. Too quick for me to get out of the way in time. Someone tripped right over me and we both screamed.

'Ouch!'

'Ooooh!'

'I'm sorry, I didn't have a clue anyone was sitting there!'

'You're kneeling on me!'

'Sorry, sorry. Here, let me help you up.'

'Careful!' He was hauling so vigorously we both nearly toppled downwards.

'Whoops!'

'Watch out!'

I struggled free and stood with my back against the damp wall. He stood up too. It was too dark to make out more than a vague shape.

'What were you doing, sitting in the dark? You haven't hurt yourself, have you?'

'I wasn't hurt. I might be now. I still feel very squashed.'

'Sorry. I keep saying that, don't I? Though it *is* a bit crackers to crouch like that in the dark. Next time you might get a whole troop of boy scouts hiking over you. Or a coachload of American tourists trampling you with their trainers. Or . . . Or . . . I'm burbling. It's difficult making conversation when you can't see. Let's go on up to see if it gets any lighter.'

'I don't think you can. The steps seem to give out.'

'Oh, well. That figures. Let's go back down then.'

I hesitated, having a quick wipe of my face with the back of my hand. There wasn't much point sitting there any longer. Dad and Anna and Eggs had probably forgotten all about me. Gone right back to the cottage. They'd suddenly snap their fingers three days later. 'What's happened to Ellie?' they'd say. And shrug. And forget about me again.

The boy seemed to think I was timid. 'I'll hold your hand if you like. To help you down.'

'I can manage perfectly, thanks,' I said.

Though it was a bit hairy feeling our way down. The steps seemed more slippery, and there wasn't any handrail. I stumbled once, and he grabbed me. 'Careful!'

'I'm *being* careful,' I said.

'I bet you there's an attendant waiting for us at the bottom to nag us rotten about the danger,' he said. 'That's the trouble, though. The minute I see something roped off I have this desperate urge to explore inside. So consequently I'm forever in a fix. Dopey Dan, that's what my family and friends call me when they're narked. I'm Daniel. But I'm only called that when they're really really really going ballistic. It's plain Dan most of the time.'

He went on like this until we emerged blinking into the daylight. Plain Dan was perfect. He had wild exploding hair and a silly little snub nose

19

that he twitched to hitch his glasses into place.

I blinked through my own smeary specs and focused properly.

'It's you!' we said simultaneously.

His family had another equally damp and dilapidated holiday cottage about half a mile down the valley from ours. We saw them in the village Spar buying their groceries and they were often in the pub in the evenings too. My dad and his dad sometimes played darts together. Anna and Dan's mum sat and made strained conversation. They looked like they came from different planets, even though they were both in jeans and jerseys and boots. Anna's jeans show off her tiny tight bum and her jersey is an Artwork designer sweater and her boots have got buckles and pointy toes. Dan's mum has a bum much bigger than mine. Her jumpers were all too tight, too, and one of them was actually unravelling. Her boots were serious walking boots caked with mud.

The whole family were serious walkers whatever the weather. We'd see them setting out in a downpour in their orange cagoules, and hours later we'd spot these mobile marigolds at the top of a dim distant mountain. There were five children, all earnest and old-fashioned. Dan was the eldest, about my age, a good inch shorter than me even though I'm little. He had a fat guidebook about castles sticking out of his cagoule. Typical.

'We made it!' he said, as if we'd just returned from outer space. He tried to jump the rope in triumph but tripped.

'No wonder they call you Dopey Dan,' I mumbled, as I skirted the rope.

There was still no sign of Dad and Anna and Eggs. Maybe they really *had* gone off without me.

'What's your name?' Dan asked, brushing himself down. 'Rapunzel?'

'*What?*'

'Well, I found you languishing in a tower, didn't I?'

I had sudden memories of a little Ladybird fairy-tale book. 'Are you into fairytales?' I said.

I intended it as an insult, but he took me seriously. 'I don't mind them actually. Some. My dad gave me a copy of *The Mabinogion*, seeing as we're in Wales.'

He could well have been speaking Welsh for all the sense he was making.

'It's old Welsh fairy stuff. Dead romantic in parts. I'll lend you the book if you like.'

'I don't think it sounds my sort of thing.'

'So what is your sort of thing, eh? What do you like reading? What's that little black book you've always got with you?'

I was surprised. He must have been watching me carefully. I usually kept my book hidden in my jacket pocket. 'That's just my little sketchbook.'

'Let's have a look then,' he said, patting my pocket.

'No!'

'Go on, don't be shy.'

'I'm not the slightest bit shy. It's *private*.'

'What sort of thing do you sketch? Castles?'

'*Not* castles.'

'Mountains?'

'Not mountains either.'

'Then what?'

'God, you aren't half nosy.'

He wrinkled his snub nose at me cheerfully.

I gave in. 'I don't sketch. I draw. Stylized pictures. Cartoons.'

'Oh, great. I love that sort of stuff. Do you ever do comic strips? I love Calvin and Hobbes. And Asterix, I've got all those books. Look, I've even got Snowy on my socks.' He hitched up his jeans and straightened his socks, which were all bunched up in his Woollies trainers.

'Very cute,' I said.

He grinned. 'OK, OK. I know my clothes aren't exactly hip.'

He was dead right there. If I was home I'd be terrified of being seen talking to him. But he was kind of fun in a silly lollopy way, as persistent as a puppy. He didn't even seem to mind my being so snappy with him. I wouldn't normally have been anywhere near as sharp. It was just I was getting seriously bothered about my stupid family.

*His* family were all down in the grounds, peering knowledgeably at little heaps of stones. One of his sisters looked up and spotted us. 'Hey, Dan! Come on down, we need your castle book!'

All the other little marigolds waved and shouted.

'I'd better get cracking. They won't stop now they've started,' said Dan. 'You coming?'

I followed him down. Dad and Anna and Eggs weren't anywhere. Maybe I'd have to join up with the marigolds. I was getting so desperate that it began to seem an attractive idea.

But guess who I came across strolling round outside the castle walls. Dad and Anna and Eggs. They didn't look the slightest bit concerned.

'Hi, Ellie,' said Dad. 'Hey, have you made a friend? Great.'

Dan grinned. I glared.

'Where have you been?' I demanded.

'Well, we were showing Eggs the way medieval people went to the loo in the castle – and then he needed to go himself so we had to trail right over to the toilets. Oh, poor Ellie, were you getting worried?'

'No, of course not,' I said sulkily.

'See you around . . . Ellie,' said Dan.

I did see him around a few times after that. Mostly with the marigolds. And Eggs. One day we joined up for a picnic. It even drizzled that day so we ate damp sandwiches and soggy sausages and mushy crisps. No-one else seemed to find this depressing. Dan was especially good at keeping all the little ones amused. Eggs *adored* him. I got sick of all this clowning around and went and sat on a wet rock and drew.

I was doodling away when a shadow fell across my page. I snapped my book shut.

'Let me see,' said Dan.

'No.'

'Meanie. Go on, special favour. Seeing as it's the last day of the hols.'

'Thank God.'

'What?'

'I can't stick this dump.'

'You're mad. It's fantastic. And anyway, who wants to go back home? School on Monday. Yuck yuck yuck. I wonder what it'll be like – in Year Nine.'

'You're not going to be in Year Nine,' I said. I'd found out that Dan was only *twelve*. Not even a teenager yet.

'Yes, I am.'

'Rubbish. You'll be in Year Eight. With the other little boys.'

'I *am* going to be in Year Nine. Honest.' Dan looked unusually embarrassed. 'I've been put up a year, right?'

'Oh, God. Because you're so brainy?'

'You've got it.'

'Trust you! I should have sussed you out for a right swot.'

'You ought to be pleased you're going out with a boy of mega-brainpower,' said Dan.

'We're not going *out*, idiot.'

'I wish we could.'

'What?'

'I like you, Ellie,' he said seriously. 'Will you be my girlfriend?'

'No! Of course not. You're just a baby.'

'Don't you fancy having a toy-boy?'

'Definitely not!'

'Can't I see you sometimes?'

'You're nuts, Dan. You live in Manchester, I live in London, right?'

'Can we write to each other then?'

He nagged on until I gave in and scribbled my address on a page torn from my sketchbook. He's probably lost it already, knowing Dan. Not that I *want* to know him. He won't bother writing even if he's still got the address. And even if he does I don't think I'll reply. There's no point. I mean, he's just this irritating little kid. I suppose he's OK in small doses. But he's not exactly boyfriend material.

Oh dear. If only he were five years older! And not all nerdy and nutty. Why can't he be really cool, with fantastic fair hair and dark brown eyes???

I wonder if I'll see that blond boy again tomorrow. I slow down, going all dreamy just thinking about him. Then I catch sight of my face in a shop window. I look like I'm brain-dead, eyes glazed, mouth open. And then I see the clock at the back of the shop and it's gone nine. Gone nine! It can't be. It *is*!

Gone nine, number nine, my first day in Year Nine – and I'm going to be in trouble before I've even started.

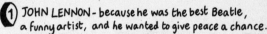
# Nine Heroes and Heroines

1. JOHN LENNON - because he was the best Beatle, a funny artist, and he wanted to give peace a chance.

2. FRIDA KAHLO - because she produced amazing paintings lying flat on her back in terrible pain.

3. ANNE FRANK - because she wrote a wonderful diary hiding in that annexe in Amsterdam during the war.

4. VAN GOGH - because he was such a great artist and went on painting even though he never sold a single canvas.

5. ANNE RICE - because she writes about vampires and has a huge house full of life-size china dolls.

6. MAURICE SENDAK - because his drawings are incredible, especially "Where the Wild Things Are."

7. JULIAN CLARY - because he's so outrageous and I think he's ever so good looking.

8. ZOE BALL - because she's so bubbly and I used to like watching her art programme. ART ATTACK

9. NICK PARK - because Wallace and Gromit are fantastic!

# Two Best Friends

It's weird walking along the corridor to Mrs Henderson's room. We *would* have to have Mrs Hockeysticks Henderson as our class tutor in Year Nine. What *is* it about Games teachers? She's always picked on me right from Year Seven.

'Come *along*, Eleanor!'

'Missed *again*, Eleanor.'

'You're not even running, girl, get a *move on!*'

I developed strategic tactics, suddenly stricken with appalling migraines or agonizing periods at the start of every Games lesson, but she soon got wise to me. She made me run six times round the hockey pitch for malingering and blew her poxy whistle at me whenever I tried to slow down.

I can't stick Mrs Henderson. I've always hated PE. Magda sometimes hangs about with me and acts like she's useless too. She doesn't like games either. She hates to get her hair blown about and she won't try to catch a ball in case she breaks a nail. Yet if she's forced to participate she can run like the wind, shoot six goals in a row at netball and whack a hockey ball clear across the pitch.

At least Nadine is even more hopeless than me. She looks graceful but when she's forced to run her arms and legs jerk out at odd angles and she totters along like a broken puppet, her head hanging.

I can't *wait* to see Magda and Nadine. I haven't seen them for weeks. We only got back from that stupid crumbling cottage yesterday. But somehow my feet are going more and more s-l-o-w-l-y as they squeak along the newly polished corridor. They look so hideous too, regulation brown school shoes, you've never seen such rubbish, your actual Clarks clodhoppers, when at any other school girls can wear whatever they want – heels, trainers, Doc Martens . . . Oh, there are these seriously wonderful sexy shoes in Shelleys! OK, they've got heels, *high* heels, but they're this amazing shiny bronze colour. Now bronze is brown. Well, brownish. I begged Anna to let me have them for school but she wouldn't give in. It's so unfair. Just because she wears those boring Sloaney little pumps all the time. She's one inch taller than Dad and ever so self-conscious about it.

'Eleanor Allard?'

Oh, God. It's Miss Trumper, the deputy head. She's even worse than Mrs Henderson. School's only started five minutes and she's already on the warpath. It's pathetic. Why can't these old bags get a *life*?

'What are you doing lurking in the corridor, Eleanor?'

'Nothing, Miss Trumper.'

'I can see that for myself. Whose class are you in this year?'

'Mrs Henderson's,' I say, nodding at the door right in front of me.

'Well, why are you just standing there? You don't mean to tell me you've been sent out the classroom in disgrace *already*?'

'No! I haven't even gone in there yet.'

'Well, do so, Eleanor. At once!'

I seize the door handle. I can hear Mrs Henderson in full flow inside, giving the class an introduction to the 1001 rules that must never be broken in Class Nine Neptune. Oh, yeah – all the years are divided into these pathetic planets: Venus, Mars, Mercury and Neptune. Funny how they never pick Uranus. We're Neptune and we have this little trident thing on our badges. It's all so boring. None of us want to be in Neptune anyway. Magda fancies Venus and Nadine wants to be in Mars because she likes the chocolate bars and I want to be in Mercury because I've got a soft spot for the late lamented Freddie . . .

'Eleanor!' Miss Trumper has paused halfway along the corridor. 'Have you gone into a catatonic trance?'

Dear goodness, they think they're so *witty*.

'No, Miss Trumper.'

'Then go into your classroom!'

I take a deep breath and turn the handle. In I go. And there's Mrs Henderson, sitting on her table swinging her legs. She's wearing a yucky pleated skirt to show she's being class tutor, but she's got bare legs and ankle socks and tennis shoes so she's all set to bounce off down to the gym when she's finished giving everyone an earful first lesson.

I get two earfuls. In fact she gets so aerated that my poor ears expand to Dumbo proportions. Stuff like *First Day*. And *Idleness* and *Attitude*. And *Just Not Good Enough*.

I bow my head and act like I'm in the depths of despair just to disconcert her. Under my hair I peer round for Magda and Nadine. Great, they're right at the back! Magda's grinning at me. Nadine gives me a little wave. They've saved me the seat in between them. And *eventually* Mrs Henderson draws breath and lets me slide off to the back. Magda whispers 'Hi, babe,' and Nadine gives me some chewing gum and I settle down and school is started. At least old Henderson didn't give me a detention for being late the first day!

First days are always so bitty. There's all the new timetables and notebooks and each and every teacher starts in on their own little lecture about Now You're in Year Nine. Then at morning break Chrissie shows us all these photos she took in Barbados during the holidays and then Jess has us all in fits telling us about this action holiday she went on where she did this bungee-jumping and she keeps trying to demonstrate – so we don't have a moment's peace to be just *us*, Magda-Nadine-and-Ellie, until after lunch.

We saunter off to our special place on the steps that lead down to the Portakabins. It's where the three of us have always sat for the last two years. But there's a whole bunch of drippy little new kids hanging around doing handstands up against the wall, skirts tucked into their brand-new regulation ghastly grey school knickers.

'Per-lease,' says Magda. 'Can't you kiddiwinks go and wave your legs somewhere else? It's just too distracting, dearies.'

They straighten up, giggling foolishly, and then scatter when Magda flaps her hands at them.

'Right,' she says, seating herself carefully. Her skirt is a good six centimetres shorter than mine. She has to position it with extreme accuracy or else *she'll* be the one showing off her knickers. Which are definitely *not* regulation.

Nadine sits beside her, kicking off her battered school shoes. I can see her black pearl toenail varnish through her tights.

I nudge up beside them, feeling a sudden warm rush of love for both of them.

Nadine's been my friend ever since nursery school, when we stirred bright green dough in the Wendy House and played we were poisoning all the dollies. We stayed staunch friends all through primary school, playing Witches in the playground and Mermaids when we went swimming and Ghosts when we spent the night at each other's houses. We vowed we would stay best friends for ever and ever, just the two of us. But the first year of secondary school we weren't allowed to sit where we wanted. We had to be in alphabetical order. I found myself sitting next to Magda.

I was a bit scared of Magda at first. Even when she was only eleven she had a proper figure and she arranged her hair in a very sophisticated style and wore a thick coat of mascara so that her eyes looked knowing. She had finely plucked eyebrows that she raised when she took a second look at you.

She hardly spoke to me that first week. Then one time in class I was doodling on the back of my new school roughbook, drawing an ultra-hip cool-cat Magda. I made her a real pussycat with sharp whiskers and a fluffy tail. I drew me as a little fat mouse, frightened of Magda, all twitchy nose and scrabbly paws. Magda suddenly leant over me to see what I was doing. She worked it out at once. 'Hey, Ellie! That's *great*,' she said.

So I drew some more stuff and she liked that too. We were friends after that. She wanted me to be her *best* friend.

Only of course I had Nadine. And Nadine didn't like Magda at all at first. But when Magda invited me over to her place one day after school I forced Nadine to come too. I wanted moral support more than anything else. I imagined Magda living this amazing cool independent existence. I couldn't have been more wrong. She's got this lovely noisy inter-fering funny family. Magda's the baby. Everyone's pet. She acts like a cute little kid at home. Anyway, she invited Nadine and me up to her bedroom and she gave us both a full make-up job. I loved it. She actually made me look like I had big dark eyes behind my specs and she did this subtle line each side of my face so it looked like I had cheekbones. It was the first time I'd ever worn make-up and I thought it was wonderful. Nadine was a bit sniffy. Magda said it was her turn. She gave Nadine a real gothic look, chalk-white face and truly black lipstick and astonishing outlined eyes. When Nadine saw herself in the mirror she smiled all over her amazing new face and wanted Magda to be her friend too.

So we've been this best-friend threesome ever since, right through Years Seven and Eight. Now we're Year Nine, thirteen – well, Magda's nearly fourteen, and Nadine is fourteen in December, but I've got to wait all the way round till next June.

It's irritating. I really look the youngest now, because I'm still so small and roly-poly with these revoltingly chubby cheeks. I have *dimples*, for goodness' sake. I'm used to Magda looking older, especially now she's highlighted her hair. But Nadine used to look really young for her age with her heart-shaped face and her long black hair tumbling round her shoulders like an Alice in negative. Now she looks . . . different.

'Come on, then, I haven't seen you both for ages! What have you been up to?' says Magda, but she doesn't pause for breath. She tells Nadine and me all about her Spanish holiday, and how all these waiters kept waylaying her and this guy at the pool kept picking her up and throwing her in the water and this other much older guy kept trying to buy her drinks at the poolside . . . This is the standard Magda stuff and I don't always concentrate because I'm watching Nadine. She doesn't look as if she's listening either, bending forward so that her hair hides her face like a black velvet curtain. She's inking a tattoo on her wrist with a black felt-tip pen, a careful heart with an elaborate inked frill. This is a change for Nadine. Her tattoos are usually skulls or spiders.

'What about you, Nadine?' I say the second Magda shuts up.

'*What* about me?' says Nadine. 'You mean my hols? I saw you after. Before you went to your cottage. It was hell. Relentlessly cheery. And you had to queue for hours and all the kids had Mickey Mouse ears and there were all these giant cartoon characters *waving* at everyone. It was all so bright. It made my eyes ache.'

'Crawl back to your coffin, Ms Vampire,' says Magda, laughing. 'I bet Natasha loved it.'

Natasha is Nadine's little sister. Nadine and I have never been able to stand her, but Magda is extraordinary, she actually likes little kids. She's even fond of Eggs. She's always going on about how she'd like to have little brothers and sisters herself.

'Natasha ate four ice-creams and then was very sick all down her brand-new pink Minnie Mouse T-shirt,' says Nadine. She painstakingly inks a name across her heart.

I lean forward to read it. 'Liam?' I say.

Nadine blushes. Nadine *never* blushes – she doesn't look as if she's got enough blood – but now

I can see bright pink beneath the fronds of black hair.

'Liam?' says Magda. 'I didn't know you were an Oasis fan.'

'Not *that* Liam,' says Nadine.

Magda looks at me for enlightenment. I shake my head. We both turn back to Nadine.

'So who's *this* Liam then?' Magda asks.

'Oh,' says Nadine. A tiny pause. 'He's my boyfriend.'

We stare at her. 'Your *boyfriend*?'

I nearly tip over backwards down the steps. Nadine has a boyfriend. I can't believe it! How come Nadine's got a boyfriend before me? Before *Magda*? Magda has loads of guys fawning all over her – well, so she says – but she doesn't actually go *out* with anyone yet.

'A *real* boyfriend?' says Magda, and she sounds just as shocked as me.

'But you don't even *like* boys, Nadine,' I say.

'I like Liam,' says Nadine. 'And he isn't a boy anyway. Not really. He's seventeen. At college.'

'So where did you meet him?' says Magda, sounding suspicious. 'How come you've never even mentioned him before?'

'Yes, you didn't say a thing about this Liam in your letters, Nad,' I say.

I wrote lots of letters to Nadine and Magda when I was cooped up in the cottage. Magda never bothers to write back properly. She just sends postcards with 'Love and Kisses, Magda' on the back – which is sweet, but not exactly informative.

Nadine is a much more satisfactory correspondent

– several pages in her carefully printed italic script, with little showers of star and moon sequins scattered inside the envelope. But all she wrote about was this weird new band she's keen on and how she's trying to teach herself to read the Tarot and a whole long moan about her family. Her dad's forever on at her to work harder even though she's always in the top three at school. He can't see why she can't come top in everything, which is crazy because Amna is always way in front of everyone and she's got this mega IQ, like she's a total genius and no-one could ever beat her no matter how hard they tried. Then her mum hates Nadine's clothes and make-up and hairstyle and wants her to smarten up and wear these chichi clothes and smile like an American cheerleader. And Natasha is just Awfulness in Ankle Socks, acting the Angel Child whenever Mummy and Daddy are around but being the Brat from Hell whenever Nadine is forced to look after her.

*So*, there was all the usual stuff but not a single line about a Liam. I can't help feeling outraged. Nadine and I always tell each other *everything*. 'Why didn't you *tell* me?' I say. My voice cracks, almost as if I'm going to start crying.

'I've only just met him,' says Nadine, stretching her arm out to admire her completed love-token tattoo.

'Ah!' says Magda, her eyebrows arching. 'So he's just this guy you've seen around, right? Not an *actual* boyfriend?'

'An "I wish" boyfriend,' I say, cheering up

considerably, getting all set to tell them about the blond guy I saw coming to school this morning.

'No, no. Liam and I went out together Saturday night,' says Nadine. 'We met in Tower Records that morning. I was sorting through the indie section and he was too, and we were both looking for the same band and there was just the one CD so he said I could have it.'

'And then he asked you out, just like that?' I say incredulously.

'Well . . . we chatted a bit. *He* did. I couldn't think of a thing to say, actually. I was just standing there dying, wishing I could come out with something, *anything*. Then he started asking me about this other group who had a gig at the Wily Fox that night and he said did I want to go. So I said yes. Though I've never been to the Wily Fox. Well, *any* pub. You know my mum and dad, they'd go crazy if they ever found out, so when I got back I said you'd got back from the cottage early, Ellie, and we were both going round to Magda's for this little party, and then your dad was going to take me home. I had to say that, because I guessed I'd be back really late from the Wily Fox. I hope you don't mind.'

'So you went there on your own?' I say, astonished. I still can't believe it. Nadine's always so quiet. She generally stays shut up in her bedroom playing her loopy music night after night. She never goes anywhere.

'And he turned up OK, this Liam?' says Magda.

'I didn't think he would. I was so scared of going

in there by myself. I was sure they'd chuck me out for being under age,' says Nadine.

'Why didn't you phone me? I'd have come with you,' says Magda.

'Yes, but it might have put him off. Or he might have liked you better than me,' says Nadine.

Magda nods.

'No, I thought I'd just put my head round the door and have a look and then I could always run home if I wanted. But he was there before me and he paid for us to go into the back room where the band were playing and then he took me home after. Well, to the end of the road. I didn't dare let him come further in case my mum and dad saw. And then I'm seeing him again *next* Saturday so can I say I'm spending it with you, Ellie?'

'Yeah. Sure,' I say, still stunned.

'So what's he *like*?' says Magda.

'Oh, he's really cool. Dark hair, moody dark eyes, hip clothes.'

'Did you tell him how old you are?' I ask.

'Not at first. I made out I was fifteen. And he said "Nearly old enough",' says Nadine, giggling.

'Oh, God,' says Magda.

'Yeah, OK, but later I was talking about you two, and I said I'd been friends with Ellie for ever and friends with Magda the two years we'd been in secondary school, and then I realized what I'd said. And Liam twigged – but he just teased me a bit. He doesn't mind that I'm only thirteen. Well, nearly fourteen. He says I act old for my age, actually.'

'I see,' says Magda. 'So. Did you snog?'

'Yes. Lots.'

'Did he open his mouth?'

'Of course,' says Nadine. 'He's a truly great kisser.'

My own mouth is open. Nadine and I have frequently discussed French kissing and we both thought it a squirmily revolting idea, someone else's sluggy tongue slithering around your fillings.

'You said—' I start.

Nadine giggles. 'Yes, but it's different with Liam.'

'It's great, isn't it?' says Magda, who has given us frequent accounts of her own amorous encounters.

Nadine is looking at me almost pityingly. 'You'll see, Ellie,' she says. 'When you get a proper boyfriend of your own.'

That's it.

My mouth stays open and starts talking. 'Oh, don't worry, I've *got* a boyfriend,' I say, before I can stop myself.

Nadine stares at me.

Magda stares at me.

It's like I've nipped out around my glasses and *I'm* staring at me too.

What have I just said???

What am I doing?

How come I started this?

But I can't stop now . . .

# Nine Wishes

1. I wish I really had a boyfriend.

2. I wish I was a stone lighter. No - two stone.

3. I wish I was six inches taller.

4. I wish I had long blond silky hair.

5. I wish I had a leather jacket.

6. I wish I had new shoes from Shelleys.

7. I wish I was eighteen.

lighter

taller

older

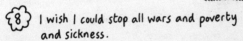

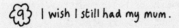

8. I wish I could stop all wars and poverty and sickness.

9. I wish I still had my mum.

# Three Boyfriends

I hear this voice going on about a boy on holiday in Wales. A boy I kept seeing – but I didn't get a chance to talk to him until we met up in a romantic ruined castle one wild and windy day. 'We literally fell into each other's arms!' I say.

Well, it's sort of true.

I tell them he's called Dan. They immediately ask how old he is.

'He's not as old as your Liam, Nad,' I say.

That's true too.

'So how old *is* he?' Magda insists.

'He's . . . fifteen,' I say.

He *will* be, in three years' time.

'What does he look like? Is he dishy? What sort of clothes does he wear?' Magda persists.

I abandon all attempt at truth. 'He's very good

looking. Blond. His hair's lovely, it sort of comes forward in a wavy fringe, just a little bit tousled. He's got dark eyes, a really intense brown. He's got this way of looking at you . . . He's just a real dream. His clothes are very casual, nothing too posey. Jeans, sweatshirt – still, that's just what he was wearing on holiday. It's so unfair, we didn't meet up properly until right at the end, and yet somehow when we started talking it was like we'd known each other for ever, you know?'

'Did he kiss you?' Nadine asks.

'We didn't get a chance to kiss, worst luck. We were with my stupid family nearly all the time. We *did* manage to steal off together at a picnic, but just as Dan was getting really romantic, Eggs came chasing over to us and started pestering us and that was it! *Honestly!*'

'What are you getting all passionate about, Eleanor?'

Oh, God, it's Mrs Henderson in her tracksuit, jogging off to the gym.

I look down at my lap, going all pink, trying desperately hard not to giggle.

'Her boyfriend!' says Magda.

'Surprise, surprise!' says Mrs Henderson. She sighs. 'You girls seem to discuss little else. You've all got one-track minds. Many thousands of determined intelligent women fought battles throughout this century to broaden your horizons, and yet you'd sooner sit there babbling about boys than concentrate on your all-round education.'

'You said it, Mrs Henderson,' says Magda. Unwisely.

'Well, you three are going to have to curtail your cosy little chat and do a detention tomorrow, because you've been so carried away by your enthralling conversation that you've failed to notice the bell for afternoon school went five minutes ago. Now get to your lessons at *once*!'

We jump to it. We get told off all over again when we get to English. It isn't fair. I quite like English. It's about the only thing I'm any good at, apart from Art, but now Mrs Madley glares at us and goes on and on and on and we get divided up and I have to sit right at the front.

We're doing *Romeo and Juliet* this year. Everyone thinks it's dead boring. Privately I quite like Shakespeare. I like the way the words go, though I don't understand half of it. Certainly the beginning bit's dull – but when I flip through the book and find the first Juliet part it gets much more interesting. Juliet is only thirteen, nearly fourteen, so *she'd* be in Year Nine too. As far as I can work out her mother and her nurse are keen for her to get *married*.

I sit wondering what it would be like to be married at thirteen in Juliet's day. It would be fun as long as you were rich enough to have someone pay the mortgage on your Italian mansion and loads of servants to spruce up your medieval Versace frocks and deliver your pizzas to your marital fourposter . . .

Mrs Madley suddenly shouts my name, making me jump. 'You not only come to my lesson ten minutes late, Eleanor Allard, but you obviously

44

aren't paying the slightest attention now you're here! What on earth is the matter with you?'

'She's in love, Mrs Madley,' says Magda. She can't *ever* keep her mouth shut.

Mrs Madley groans in exasperation while the whole class collapses.

It looks like I'm in serious trouble *again*. I stare wildly at the page in front of me. I spot a line at the top that looks dead appropriate ' "Under love's heavy burden do I sink",' I quote, sending myself up.

Mrs Madley is wrong-footed. She even looks mildly amused. 'Well, take care you don't sink too far, Eleanor. Look what happens to these star-crossed lovers at the end of the play. Now, girls, settle down, and let us *all* concentrate on Shakespeare.'

I decide I'd better concentrate too – so I don't really have time to plan what on earth I'm going to say going home from school with Magda and Nadine.

In Maths last lesson there's no point my trying to concentrate because I can't figure any of it out, so I sit nibbling my thumbnail, worrying about this boyfriend situation. When I was little I used to suck my thumb a lot. Now when I'm ultra-anxious I find I have to have a little weeny suck and chew just to calm myself. I wondered if smoking might have the same effect – not in a classroom situation obviously – but when Magda shared a packet of Benson's with me I felt so sick and dizzy by the time I lit up my second it's put me off for life.

I have to sort out what I'm going to say about Dan. I think of his blond hair and dark brown eyes . . . Only that's the boy I saw this morning on the way to school. I don't even have a clue who he is. I just started describing him when Magda and Nadine asked all those questions. I couldn't tell them what the real Dan looks like or they'd crease up laughing.

Oh, God, *why* did I open my big mouth? I was like some demented Fairy Godmother waving a wand over nerdy little boy Dopey Dan in Wales and turning him into the Golden Dream I saw this morning.

Magda and Nadine believe it all too. *I* practically believe it. I've always had this crazy habit of making things up. It was mostly when I was little. Like after my mum died . . .

It was so horrible and lonely that I kept trying to pretend she wasn't *really* dead, that if I could only perform all these really loopy tasks like go all day without going to the toilet or stay awake an entire night then suddenly she'd come walking into my bedroom and it would all be a mistake, someone else's mother had died, not *mine*. Sometimes when I was lying awake holding my eyelids open I'd almost believe she was really there, standing by my bed, leaning over ready to give me a cuddle, so close I could actually smell her lovely soft powdery scent.

Even after I gave up on those daft tricks I didn't give up on my mother. I felt she still had to be around for me. I talked to her inside my head and she talked back, saying all the ordinary Mum things, telling me to be careful crossing the road, and to eat up like a good girl, and when I went to bed she'd chat to me about my day and she'd always say 'Nightie Nightie' and I'd whisper 'Pyjama Pyjama'. I did that long after Dad married Anna. She said some of that stuff too, but it wasn't the same at all. I used to hate Anna simply because she wasn't Mum. I'm older now. I can see it's not really Anna's fault. She's OK, sometimes. But she's still *not* my mum.

So what would Mum say? This is the awful bit. I can still make Mum say all this stuff to me, but it's the *old* stuff that I needed to hear when I was little. My made-up mum can't seem to get her head round the idea that I'm big now. Big enough to want a boyfriend. Only I haven't *got* one and yet I've told my two best friends I have.

'Tell them the truth, Ellie,' Mum says firmly, her voice suddenly loud and clear.

She sounds so real I actually look round the classroom to see if anyone else can hear her.

I know Mum is right. In fact I even work out how to do it. I shall say I was just teasing them, playing a silly joke to see how much they'd swallow. I'll say I did meet a boy called Dan on holiday but I'll say what he's *really* like. I'll even tell them about the gorgeous blond bloke on the way to school. I'll draw a cartoon for them, the real Dan and me with my wand turning him into the Dreamboat. They'll think it's funny. Well – maybe more funny peculiar than funny ha-ha. But they're used to me being a bit weird. They'll still *like* me, even though they'll think I'm nuttier than ever.

I'll tell them on the way to the bus stop. Then it'll be over and everything will go back to normal. Except Nadine really *has* got a boyfriend. This Liam. Unless . . . could *she* have made him up too? Nadine and I used to play all these pretend games together. She was always great at making things up, that's why I always wanted her for my friend. Oh, what a hoot if Nadine's been fibbing too! I really wouldn't put it past her!

But when we come out of school at the end of lessons and Magda is asking me more about Dan and I'm all set to say my piece, though my throat's dry with nerves and I feel incredibly silly, Nadine suddenly stops dead and gasps.

'Nadine?'

We stare at her. She's blushing. I can't get used to seeing Nadine's snowy skin shine salmon-pink.

'Nadine, what's up?' I say.

Magda is quicker than me. She's seen what Nadine is staring at. Not what. *Who*. 'Wow!' says Magda. 'Is he Liam?'

Nadine swallows. 'Yes! Oh, God, what am I going to do? I'm in my school *uniform*.'

'Well, he knows you go to school.'

'But I look such a berk in uniform. I can't let him see me like this!' Nadine dodges behind me, ducking right down. 'Walk backwards into school, Ellie!' she hisses.

'Don't be so nuts, Nadine,' says Magda. 'Look, he's seen you anyway.'

'How do you know?' Nadine mutters, still hiding behind me.

'Because he's waving like crazy over in our direction. And he's not waving at me. Worse luck. He's really gorgeous,' says Magda.

He is. He's tall and he's got dark hair and very dark eyes and he looks hip in his skimpy black top and black jeans. He's the sort of guy who seems totally out of our class. Like my blond dreamboat. But Liam isn't pretend. He's real and he's still waving at Nadine.

She steps sideways round me, pink and pretty. It's as if she's a whole new person who I hardly know. She waves back, an odd little waggle of her fingers, her elbow tucked into her side. Then she runs over to the wall where he's waiting.

'I can't believe it,' Magda mutters. 'He's so yummy. What does he see in Nadine?'

'Magda! Don't be such a bitch,' I say primly – but she's only saying out loud what I'm thinking.

I feel as if I've been in a race with Nadine and I always thought I'd win, but now she's forged ahead and left me behind.

'Come on, Ellie, let's go and say hello,' says Magda.

'No! We can't butt in.'

'Of course we can,' says Magda, shoving me sharply in their direction. She runs one hand through her hair, fluffing it up, and undoes the top button of her school blouse. 'Hey, Nadine,' she calls, wiggling across the playground towards them.

I stand foolishly, not sure whether to follow. I edge towards them as if I'm playing Grandmother's Footsteps. Nadine is sitting on the wall beside Liam.

Magda is standing in front of them, one hand on her hip. She's chatting away like crazy but it doesn't look as if Liam is paying her much attention. Nadine isn't saying much. She's looking down, hiding behind her hair.

'Oh, and this is my other friend, Ellie,' she mumbles when I get near.

What's wrong with her voice? She sounds all wet and whispery.

'Hello,' I say awkwardly.

Liam gives me a curt nod and turns back to Nadine. 'You look cute in the uniform,' he says.

'I look *awful*,' Nadine protests. 'What are you doing here anyway?'

'I finished early at college so I thought I'd see if I could spot you amongst all your little schoolgirly chums. So come on. Let's go for a walk or some-thing.'

'OK,' says Nadine, swinging her legs over the wall.

Liam raises his eyebrows and she giggles stupidly.

''Bye then, Nadine. 'Bye, Liam,' says Magda. She waves. He doesn't bother to respond.

'Well!' says Magda, staring after them. 'So we're the little schoolgirly chums, eh, Ellie?'

'She's so different with him,' I mutter.

'He doesn't exactly get ten out of ten in the charm stakes,' says Magda. 'I hope Nadine knows what she's doing. He's ever so old for her.'

'I don't like him,' I say.

'Neither do I. Though if he'd liked *me* more I might feel more positive,' says Magda, laughing.

That's one thing about Magda. She might be a real scheming bitch at times but she's always honest about it.

'Oh well, Ellie, I'll walk with you to the bus stop, eh?'

She links her arm in mine. There's a whole crowd of Anderson boys at the bus stop. Our school is Anderson High School too, but they're entirely separate, across the road from each other on different sites. One school for girls, one school for boys. Twin schools for separate sexes. Only most of the Anderson boys are so awful it's depressing. The little ones are just like animals, yelling and kicking and bashing each other with their schoolbags. Their idea of sophisticated humour is farting. Come to think of it, the Year Nines go in for that a lot too. They are all revolting, each and every one. The Year Tens and Elevens are almost as bad, though I suppose there are a few possibles.

One of these possibles is at the bus stop. He's Greg Someone. I suppose he's quite good looking but he's got red hair that he hates, so he puts heaps of gel on it to make it as dark as he can. If you were ever in a clinch with Greg and you ran your fingers through his hair it would be like dabbling in cold chip fat. *Not* a happy thought.

Magda's never given him a second glance before, but suddenly she bounces up to him. 'Hey, Greg. How's things? Did you have a good holiday? Pretty dire having to come back to this old dump, eh? And look at all this homework first day back, can you believe it! See how heavy my bag is.' She thrusts it at Greg. He staggers, blinking rapidly. It's not the heaviness of Magda's bag. It's the heaviness of her approach. I don't think she's ever said one *word* to him before.

He turns almost as red as his hair and looks totally idiotic. Magda gazes at Belisha Beacon boy as if he's a Keanu or a Brad. She sighs and stretches her arms, making out they're aching. This action has an amazing effect on her school blouse. The buttons strain. Greg positively *glows*.

A foul little gang of Year Eights are ogling too, nudging each other and making disgusting comments. Magda shakes her head at them. She makes a pithy comment that indicates they have been exercising their own arms more than somewhat. Then she looks back at Greg. Her blue eyes have a positively lighthouse beam. 'You're not any good at Maths, are you, Greg? I'm *useless.*'

She's not, actually. I'm the one who can't even add up correctly using a calculator. Nadine's not much better. Magda is always the girl who does *our* Maths homework, but now she's acting like she's got candy floss for a brain.

'I'm OK at Maths actually,' says Greg. 'What's the problem then?'

'Oh, it's ever so complicated,' says Magda. 'And look, isn't that the bus coming? I don't get on the bus, I'm just here with my friend. Look Greg, do you ever go to the McDonald's near the market?'

'Sure I do.'

'Well, how about if we meet up there? Half seven, something like that? And I'll bring my stupid Maths with me and see if you can make me understand it, OK?'

'Yes, sure,' said Greg. 'Half seven. Right.'

'It's a date,' says Magda, retrieving her schoolbag and giving Greg a dazzling smile. She turns to me – and winks.

So now Magda's got herself a boyfriend too. In less than five minutes.

Greg waves after her as he gets on the bus. I wonder if he might sit next to me as I'm Magda's friend, but he barges straight past and sits with some other Anderson boys who have already got on. He's talking rapidly, obviously showing off that he's scored with Magda.

I sit all by myself. I am starting to feel seriously depressed. So. I didn't tell Magda and Nadine I was making it all up. I didn't get a chance, did I? And Nadine has got a real boyfriend. And now Magda has got one too, just like that. Why can't *I* chat someone up the way she can?

I gaze round the bus in desperation. There are two nerdy Year Ten Anderson boys sitting across the way from me, earnestly discussing some stupid sci-fi stuff. They look like beings from another planet themselves but I'm so desperate I'll try anything.

I bare my teeth at them in a big cheesy grin. They reel back as if I'm a rabid dog about to bite. I cover my teeth and cower in my seat. It's no use. I'm not like Magda.

Oh, God, I feel so fed up. I'm never ever going to get a boyfriend. No boy in the entire world is ever going to fancy me.

No. I am wrong. When I get home there is a letter waiting for me.

# Nine Things I **Hate** About School

1. It starts too early.

2. The teachers - ESPECIALLY Mrs Henderson and Miss Trumper.

Oh, I'm sorry Eleanor and Magda. Is my assembly disturbing your conversation?

3. Maths - yuck.

4. PE - even yuckier.

5. The sarcastic way the teachers tell you off.

6. The bitchy way girls whisper behind your back.

bitch bitch

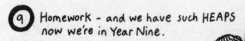

7. Having to rush everywhere and getting all sweaty.

8. The worry about the pale grey school skirt the first day of your period.

9. Homework - and we have such HEAPS now we're in Year Nine.

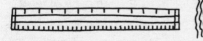

# Four in the Family

Dear Ellie,

Hello! It's me, Dan. Sorry this is such jiggly writing.
I'm scribbling this going home in the car and various
sprogs keep jogging me and my mum is driving and she's
a total maniac – she does a ninety-mile-an-hour dash
down the motorway and then when one of the kids starts
screaming for a wee she screeches to a halt on the hard
shoulder in seconds so that we practically hurtle through
the windscreen.

This is not romantic subject matter for a love letter.
OK, shall I try to be romantic? I should make up a super
romantic fable about a fair maiden languishing in a tower
being rescued by a handsome knight. A Welsh fable, set

in a Welsh castle. Like THE MABINOGION. That's
those old Welsh tales I told you about. They're written
down in a White book and a Red book. Well, this isn't a
book, it's a scrappy letter, and you're not fair, you're
dark, and I'm not handsome. You can say that again. I
know you think I'm all nerdy and nutty. Well, I'm wordy
as well as nerdy. And OK, who cares if I'm nuts? I'm
nuts about you. I wish we didn't live so far away. But
you can come on a visit to my place any time. If you
don't mind being surrounded by all my stupid siblings.
Or I can come and visit you??? Hint hint!

Love from Dan

P.S. It was truly great meeting you.


Honestly. He *is* nuts. If *only* he were older. And not
so daft. And good looking.

'Who's it from then?' asks Anna, stirring soup at
the stove. She tastes it delicately. 'More pepper,
Eggs. Carefully.'

Eggs likes cooking. He even helps make Eggs
Benedict, his namesake. Well, he's called Benedict,
Anna's slightly poncey choice, but no-one's ever
called him that. He started off as Baby Benny and for
the last two years he's been Eggs. Possibly Pickled.
Sometimes Scrambled. Often *Bad*.

'It's just some silly scribble from Dan,' I say,
stuffing the letter into my pocket.

Anna raises her eyebrows. 'I *thought* you'd made
a hit there.'

'For God's sake, Anna, he's only *twelve*. Don't be crazy.'

'I like that Dan. Oh, great, is he your boyfriend?' Eggs burbles, shaking pepper enthusiastically.

'Careful, Eggs. Just a *pinch*,' says Anna, catching hold of his wrist.

'Pinch pinch pinch,' Eggs giggles, pretending to pinch her arm.

'Idiot boy,' says Anna fondly, turning him upside down and tickling his exposed tummy.

'I'm going to do my homework,' I say.

I usually hang around the kitchen for a bit first but I don't particularly enjoy watching Anna and Eggs together. It always makes me feel weird. Like I was jealous or something. Not that I want to play about with Eggs in the slightest. And I certainly don't want Anna tickling me! She'd fall flat on her back if she tried to pick me up anyway. I weigh much more than her already, even though she's heaps taller.

Anna never tried any romping, tickling, cuddling mumsie stuff with me. I'm too old and she's too young. Of course there's far more of an age gap between Anna and Dad. He's nearly old enough to be *her* dad. He teaches Art and Anna was a student at his college. Dad didn't teach her. She did textiles. She used to work part time as a design consultant but that firm went bust so she's been looking for a new opening for ages. Dad still teaches at the college. The students haven't gone back yet but he's out at some college meeting nevertheless.

'Hang on a tick, Ellie,' says Anna. 'I don't know when your dad's going to get back. You know what

58

he's like. But I'm supposed to be starting this Italian evening class tonight, so you wouldn't be an angel and put Eggs to bed for me?'

'Look, like I *said*, I've got all this homework,' I whine. For a while. And then I change tack and point out that other girls get paid for being a babysitter.

'Cheek! I'm not a *baby*,' Eggs intervenes. 'Why is it baby*sitter* anyway? They don't sit on the baby, do they?'

'Shut up, Eggs, or I'll take great delight in sitting on you,' I say.

I do agree in the end. Very very reluctantly. Though I can't see why Anna's making such a point of starting up this Italian evening class. It's not as if we're going to romp in Rome or flourish in Florence. We will get wet in Wales, as always.

She gets Eggs all bathed and ready for bed after supper, so all I'm supposed to do is supervise his last wee and stuff him into bed. Ha ha.

He starts capering about like a monkey and whenever I catch him he screams and giggles and squirms. When Dad comes in at last Eggs runs down the hall to him yelling at the top of his voice.

'Hey, hey! Why aren't you in bed, Mr Eggs-and-Bacon?' says Dad. He looks at me reproachfully. 'You shouldn't get him so excited before he goes to bed, Ellie, he'll be too worked up to sleep.'

Like it's *my* fault!!! That's the thanks I get. And it's dead annoying because Eggs does quieten down with Dad. He snuggles up on his lap and Dad reads him a Little Bear story. Eggs smiles angelically and gently strokes each picture of Little Bear with his finger.

They're *my* Little Bear books actually. I can't ever remember Dad reading them to me. Not when I was all sleepy and snuggled up like that.

'What's up, Ellie?' Dad says suddenly. 'Are you sulking?'

'No, I'm *not* sulking. I'm just sitting here. There's no crime in that, is there?'

'*Read*, Dad,' Eggs insists. 'Don't talk to Smelly Ellie.'

'Eggs!' says Dad – but he chuckles.

Suddenly I can't stand either of them. It's suffocating even being in the same room as them. I stalk off to my bedroom and put on some music. Loud.

I suppose I ought to make a start on all this horrible homework but I catch sight of myself in the mirror and my hair looks awful, sort of exploding in all directions, so I have to brush it into submission and experiment with different hairstyles. I can scrunch it up into a little top-knot so it looks neater – almost OK – but then it makes my face look so much fatter. Oh, God, my face *is* fatter. It's like a huge great white beachball, and I'm getting a spot on my chin, and there's a little one on my nose too, a pink-and-white polka-dot beachball. I can't *stand* spots. Anna says I should never ever touch them but it's OK for her, she's got this incredible English rose skin, I don't think she's ever had a spot in her life.

I have a little squeezing session. It doesn't help. I feel so ugly. No wonder I haven't got a boyfriend.

No-one will ever want to go out with me. Apart from Dan. And he's so short-sighted even *he* would probably run away from me screaming if he polished up his specs and saw me properly.

I pick up his letter and read it again. Dad suddenly comes barging into my room.

'Dad! You're not supposed to come into my room without *knocking*!'

'I *did* knock. You just didn't hear me because of that awful row. Turn it *down*. I've just put Eggs to bed.'

Eggs Eggs Eggs Eggs Eggs. I see him as a row of Humpty Dumptys sitting on a wall. I tip them off one at a time, smash smash smash smash smash.

'Oh, of course, we mustn't disturb the boy wonder,' I say, switching off my CD player. 'OK? Happy now? Total silence so his little lordship can nod off in peace.'

'I didn't say you had to turn it off altogether,' says Dad. 'What's *up* with you, Ellie? You're so prickly all the time now.' He comes closer, tugging at his beard the way he always does when he's worried. 'Hey, what have you done to your face? It's bleeding.'

'I haven't done anything,' I say, covering my chin with my hand. 'Now would you mind leaving me alone so I can get on with my homework?'

'That's not homework. It's a letter. Who's it from, eh?'

'It's *my* letter, Dad,' I say, crumpling it up. Not quite quickly enough. He sees the end bit.

'Love from Dan! It's a love letter!' he says.

'No, it isn't!'

'So who on earth is this Dan? When did you get yourself a boyfriend, Ellie?'

'I haven't *got* a boyfriend! Will you just mind your own business, *please*,' I say, stuffing the stupid letter in my skirt pocket.

When Dad's gone I sigh deeply and put my head in my arms. I think about crying but actually fall asleep. I wake up with a stiff neck. I find I can't sleep when I go to bed.

Dad puts his head round the door when he comes upstairs to bed himself. 'Are you asleep, Ellie?' he whispers.

'Yes.'

'Anna told me about the boyfriend. He's that weird brainy kid in the anorak, right?'

'Wrong wrong wrong. He is *not* my boyfriend. Oh, God, I'm getting so sick of this,' I say, putting my head under the pillow.

'OK OK. Calm down. Sorry. Anna says I shouldn't tease you. Ellie?'

I stay underneath the pillow. There's a pause. Then I feel a slight pressure as he bends forward.

'Nightie nightie,' Dad whispers, kissing the pillow instead of me.

I wait. Then I whisper, 'Pyjama pyjama.' I take the pillow off my face. But Dad's gone out of the room already.

I still can't sleep. I hang on to the pillow for something to cuddle. I wish I'd kept some of my cuddly toys from when I was little. I had this blue elephant called Nellie and when I was Eggs's age I always had to lug her around with me. I talked to her constantly as if she were real, so you didn't just get me then, you got an Ellie-and-Nellie package.

I also had a panda called Bartholomew and a giraffe called Mabel and a big rag doll with orange hair called Marmalade.

I had really grown out of them all by the time Eggs was born, apart from Nellie. When Eggs started crawling he ignored all his own new cuddly toys and always wanted mine.

We once had a fight over Nellie. Eggs was screaming and screaming and wouldn't give her back. I could see it was a bit ridiculous a girl like me wrestling with a toddler over a dirty toy elephant with a wonky trunk – but I wouldn't give up. And then Eggs was suddenly sick all over Nellie. I insisted he'd done it on purpose. I said Nellie was spoilt for ever. My mother had made her for me when I was little. I bawled like a baby.

Anna sluiced Nellie down and put her in the washing machine. She ended up a rather naff pale mauve and her stuffing went lumpy. She was still Nellie but I insisted she was spoilt and I threw her in the dustbin.

I wish I hadn't. I wished it almost the minute the dustmen carted her off. I know it's totally mad but I still sometimes think of her now, lying amongst rotting Chinese takeaways and soggy teabags on some stinking rubbish tip, her trunk crumpled in despair.

I threw all my other toys out when I redecorated my room, wanting to change everything, to stop being that sad silly dreamy fat girl. I wanted to remodel a new shiny hip version of Ellie to match my new room. I painted it bright blue with red furniture and yellow curtains, primary colours for a very secondary style. I tried to be bright and snappy and cheerful to match but I couldn't keep it up. In fact right now I feel so dark and dreary and dismal I feel my matching habitat would be down a drain.

I clutch the pillow close. When I was younger I used to have Nadine sleep over at my house at least once a week. We'd never bother with campbeds and sleeping bags, we'd just snuggle up together in my bed. Nadine's not the cuddliest of girls, her elbows are sharp and she's very wriggly, but it was great fun all the same. We'd make up ghost stories so gross and gory that I'd have nightmares when we eventually got to sleep, but that was OK too because I could hang on to Nadine and feel the knobs on her spine as I cuddled up against her, her long hair tickling my face.

Only now Nadine has got Liam to cuddle. I still can't believe it even though I've met him now. I wonder how she got on with him on their walk. And Magda with Greg. Nadine and Liam, Magda and Greg, Ellie and no-one at all . . .

I drift off to sleep at long last. I dream. Ellie and Dan. Not the real Dan – the pretend boy, the one with blond hair and brown eyes. He waits for me outside school and we go off for a walk together down by the river. He holds my hand while we're walking along the street but when we get to the secluded riverside he pulls me close, his arms go round me, he whispers lovely things, he lifts my hair and kisses my neck, my ears, my mouth, we're kissing properly, it's so beautiful, we're lying on the mossy bank, entwined, I am his and he is mine and he whispers that he loves me, that he loved me from the moment we first set eyes on each other when he dodged round the parked car and we nearly collided, and I whisper that I love him too.

'I love you,' I whisper, and I wake up. I've never had such a vivid dream. I can still see the dappled sunlight on our skin, smell the honey musk of his chest, hear the beat of his heart, feel the warmth of his body . . .

That is where I am, where I want to stay. I'm a stranger in this banal world of bathroom and breakfast. I won't say a word as I sip coffee and spoon cornflakes. We sit at the table, Dad, Anna, Eggs and me. Four sides of the table, four members of a family, but they don't seem to have any connection with me whatsoever.

Dad is saying something to me but I'm not listening. It seems so strange that the only reason I'm sitting at this table is that the eight pints of blood in his body are similar to mine. He's just a plump middle-aged guy with an embarrassing haircut and beard way too old to wear that silly T-shirt. That small boy with the yelping laugh choking on his cornflakes has even less to do with me. The calm woman in her white shirt nothing at all.

She's saying something about me missing the bus if I'm not careful, and she's right. It's there at the stop when I'm only halfway down the road. I could try running, but I don't want my skirt to ride up even further, and besides, maybe I don't really *want* to catch the boring old bus. I can always walk to school. Just in case . . .

So I walk, past the bus stop, down the street, round the corner. The parked car's not there, he's not there either . . . YES HE IS! That's him, right down at the end. Walking towards me!

My dream is still so real it's as if I know him, as if we went for that walk together and were in each other's arms down by the river.

He's getting nearer, wearing a blue denim shirt today. It looks great with his colouring. He's looking straight ahead. Is he looking at me? Looking *for* me? What if he dreamt about me too? What if he somehow dreamt the very same dream?

I walk on and he walks on too. I can see his features now, his brown eyes, his straight nose, his sweet mouth, he's smiling, he's smiling at me. I shall smile too, a deeply significant smile to show that we share a secret . . .

'Hi,' he says, a few paces away.

Hi! To *me*? Is he really talking to me? He *can't* be. My head swivels to see if there's someone standing behind me. No-one. It's me. Oh, God, I feel such an idiot. I try to say Hi back but my throat is a sandy Sahara, so dry it comes out as a croak. Then he's past, he's walking on, I've lost it, I've lost my chance. He must think me a complete fool, only capable of frog-talk.

I am late for school again. Mrs Henderson gives me a detention. Another one. Two in two days. Mrs

Henderson suggests that I seem to be going for some sort of record.

'Not a wise move, Eleanor,' she adds threateningly.

I don't know what to do. I'm not fussed about old Hockeysticks Henderson. It's me. I think I'm really going mad. Because now I'm in school and I'm breathing in the familiar smell of rubber trainers and canteen chip fat and Body Shop scent and Clearasil my dream is fading fast. I was starting to *believe* the dream was real, that the blond boy and I were really involved.

I've got to stop this fast. I've got to tell Nadine and Magda that I made it all up.

But I still don't get a word in edgeways, not even at lunchtime on our steps. Nadine goes on about Liam, Liam, Liam. She's inked a whole series of lovehearts all the way up her arm. She'll give herself blood poisoning if she's not careful. It's as if she's dyed her brain with his name too, because he's all she can talk about. Not that *they* seem to talk at all. He's barely said anything to her so far. They just skive off and snog, basically. Which is a little *too* basic, if you ask me.

'Well, I didn't ask you,' Nadine snaps.

Magda says that Greg does too much talking, he never stops. He showed her how to work out the Maths homework although she already knew perfectly well how to do it. And then he started giving her tips on Science into the bargain.

'How about a few tips on Human Biology?' Magda suggested on their way home.

But he was too thick to take up her offer. He might be dead brainy but he's brain-dead when it come to physical relationships, obviously.

'It's not necessarily obvious,' Magda retorts. 'I've just got to give him time. Redheads are *known* for their tempestuous natures.'

'You're ever so picky about Liam and Greg,' says Nadine. 'What's bugging you, eh, Ellie?'

'Nothing's bugging me.'

'You're not feeling just the teeniest bit left out?' says Nadine.

'Certainly not!'

'Well, she's probably fed up because her Dan is so far away and she can't see him,' says Magda.

'If he even exists,' says Nadine, staring at me very intently.

I feel my heart pounding underneath my blouse. Nadine knows me so well. I hate the way her green eyes are gleaming.

'Oh yes, he's a figment of my imagination,' I say, staring at them both. I pause. Then I feel in my skirt pocket and produce my crumpled letter. 'A figment of my imagination who somehow miraculously has managed to write to me,' I say, flashing the letter in their faces.

I cover up most of the words but I show them the important part: *Love from Dan*.

# Nine Dreams

1. THE BEST DREAM: The blond boy and me down by the river.

2. THE SADDEST DREAM: I see my mum in a crowd and I struggle to catch up with her and I can't so I shout and scream but she doesn't hear, she just walks on until I can't see her any more.

3. THE SILLIEST DREAM: Magda and Nadine and I are still thirteen but back in nursery school and we have to make little dough people and mine won't go right, it keeps going back into a lumpy little ball.

4. THE MOST EMBARRASSING DREAM: I'm walking to the bus stop with lots of Anderson boys around me and they're all sniggering and when I look down I see that my skirt has ridden right up to my waist and I'm showing all of my knickers.

5. THE STRANGEST DREAM: I'm flying, but only just, skimming up and down the staircase, not quite clearing the steps so that I keep scuffing my shoes.

6. THE MOST TERRIFYING DREAM: There are robbers and they're in the house and they're going to kill me and I can hear them coming, and then just as they get to me I wake up and I run into Dad and Anna's room but I haven't REALLY woken up and the robbers are in Dad's bed and they leap out at me.

7. THE MOST BABYISH DREAM: I'm in a cot and someone is rocking me and it's lovely but the cot's very small so my head is pressing hard against the top and my legs are poking right through the slats and hanging in mid-air.

8. THE DAMPEST DREAM: I'm in a ship sailing up and down and the water is sparkling so I dive off the side and start swimming and the water is so warm and so wet. (I used to have this dream when I was about Egg's age. Sometimes with disastrous consequences.)

9. THE MOST FREQUENTLY RECURRING DREAM: I'm very late for school and I can't find my uniform and I can't get my bag packed properly and I miss the bus and I'm in serious trouble when I eventually get to school. This happens enough in real life, so it feels very unfair that I have to dream it too!

# Five Alive

(but only just, and all dying of embarrassment and boredom!)

There's no way I can ever tell the truth now. So I'm stuck. Treading in treacle, superglued into silence.

I write back to Dan. Mostly because I need him to write back to me again so I can show off his letter to Nadine and Magda. Which is so mean.

He writes back. And I write back. And he writes back. And so it goes on. They're just silly letters. He goes on about school and stuff and things he's reading and he tells a lot of corny old jokes. He puts 'Love from Dan' at the end each time, but they're not *love* letters.

Dad says we're like Elizabeth Barrett and Robert Browning and sniggers. They are dead poets. I mutter something ultra-unpoetical along the lines that I wish Dad were dead too. Dad hears and gets narked and says I've completely lost my sense of humour. Anna surprisingly takes my side. She says Dad's crass and insensitive and she's sick of it, so goodness knows how Ellie feels. Both Dad and I blink at her a bit. She doesn't usually rush to my defence. I think maybe she and Dad have had a row. I heard a lot of angry whispers last night after Anna got back from her evening class. I don't know what's going on with them. I don't know what's going on with *me*.

I haven't even seen the dream Dan again. I caught the bus for a bit because Mrs Henderson was giving me so many detentions it was getting like I'd be stuck at school for a full twenty-four hours. But I chance walking today. I even hang around a second on the street where we met. Longer than a second actually. More like fifteen minutes. And I still don't get to see him. *And* I get another detention.

It's quite companionable actually because Nadine is doing a detention too. It's just the two of us. Mrs Henderson makes us write out *lines*, would you believe? I had to write out: I MUST PULL MYSELF TOGETHER AND TRY TO BE ON TIME.

I write it one hundred times. I don't feel pulled together. I feel as if I'm flying apart. And I tried to be on time to see Dream Dan. I couldn't try any harder if I wrote it out one million times.

Nadine's line is shorter than mine so even though she writes in an elaborate twirly way she still gets finished first. One hundred times: I MUST NOT BE INSOLANT.

72

She came to school with this amazing love-bite on her neck, a big blotch that looked impressively purple on her white skin.

'For God's sake, your Liam must have a mouth like a vacuum cleaner,' said Magda.

'Well, Nadine's always had a thing about vampires,' I said, trying to sound funny and flippant.

I couldn't stop staring at Nadine's love-bite. When we were little we used to experiment, sucking on each other's arms to see what it felt like. When we got older we agreed love-bites were *gross*. And yet now Nadine had one right at the front of her neck so that it wasn't even hidden by her hair. I tried not to think of Liam doing it to her but I couldn't help it. It made me feel so weird. I couldn't work out which I felt most, disgusted or envious.

Mrs Henderson's feelings were more straight-forward. 'I think you need to go to the medical cupboard for a sticky plaster, Nadine,' she said coldly. 'I don't want to look at that stupid mark on your neck. Surely you realize how silly it is to let someone do that to you. It's not exactly treating you with respect, is it? Let alone risking serious infection.'

Nadine scowled. 'Bet you're just jealous,' she muttered.

Not quietly enough. She got her detention too.

Mrs Henderson leaves us to finish our lines while she goes off to supervise a hockey practice.

'Well, I've done my stupid lines so I don't see why I can't go now,' says Nadine, fidgeting.

'She said we had to wait till she came back.'

'It's ridiculous. She's got no right to comment on what I do out of school hours,' says Nadine, fingering the plaster covering her bite.

'What on earth did your mum and dad say when they saw it?

'Don't be mad! I wound this scarf right round my neck, right? I tell you, if they found out about Liam they'd go seriously bananas.'

'Nadine?'

'What?' She doesn't bother to look up. She gets a magazine out of her schoolbag and starts flipping through the pages.

Nadine used to despise teen mags. She just read weird fanzines about her favourite bands and horror stories. But now she's reading this problem page as if her life depends on it.

'What's it feel like? You know – the love-bite?'

Nadine shrugs.

'Did you want him to do it?'

'Well, he wants to do a lot *more*.'

'And . . . do you let him?'

Nadine wriggles. 'Well, *some* things.' She hesitates. 'Look, keep this a secret, right? Don't even tell Magda.' There's no-one else in the room but she still leans forward and then whispers.

'Nadine!' I say, stunned.

'Well, what's wrong with that, eh?' says Nadine. 'Honestly, Ellie, you're such a baby.'

'No, I'm not.'

'Everyone does that with their boyfriends.'

'Do they?'

'Well, I take it you don't do it with Dan.' Nadine looks at me sharply.

I try to imagine such intimacy with both my Dans. I think of doing it with the dream Dan and the blood starts beating in my own neck. Then I think of doing it with the real Dan and I practically crack up laughing.

'What are you grinning about?' says Nadine. 'So you *did* fool around with your Dan.'

We'd certainly make fools of ourselves! 'Chance would be a fine thing,' I mutter. 'We don't see each other, do we?'

Dan (real, of course) has been nagging me to go and stay with him or invite him down to London. I keep putting him off with elaborate excuses, but it's getting a bit awkward. The whole situation is so difficult I let out this long sigh.

'Do you really miss him, Ellie?' says Nadine softly. She puts her arm round me, crumpling her magazine.

I snuggle into her, though I feel guilty. 'It's just . . . Oh, I wish I could explain properly, Nad,' I whisper.

'I know,' says Nadine – though she doesn't. 'Look, things are a bit difficult with Liam and me too. We had this sort of row yesterday.'

'Yeah?'

'Because I won't, you know, go the whole way. I just don't feel ready to. And the magazines say you shouldn't do it till you *are* ready – look.' She reaches for the magazine and shows me this letter.

'Bla bla bla, "so don't let your boyfriend do . . ."

Ooh! "And if he complains that his tackle . . ."
What's his *tackle*? Like in *fishing rod*?'

We both get a fit of the giggles.

'No, you nutcase. It's his . . . *you* know.'

Oh. Yes. Even *I* can work it out now. I carry on reading the letter. 'So does your Liam get all narked with you like the guy in the letter?'

'He did yesterday. He said he'd been ever so patient. And didn't I love him enough. And I said I loved him desperately but I still didn't feel ready, right? And he said if I wasn't ready now I never would be, and what was the matter with me, didn't I want our relationship to develop.' Nadine's not giggling now, she's nearly in tears.

'Oh, Nad. He's acting like a right . . . *tackle*!' I hope she'll laugh, but a tear drips down her cheek.

'No, I can understand, Ellie. I mean, it's so frustrating for him—'

'That's *rubbish*! Look, you don't have to do anything with him. You're only thirteen, for goodness' sake. It's against the *law*.'

'Yes, but nobody takes any notice of that. And all his other girlfriends have always done it, no bother.'

'There you are! You don't want to be one of a whole long *line* of stupid girls. Honestly, Nadine, where's your *brain*?'

'I have often been tempted to ask that question myself,' says Mrs Henderson, walking through the door.

Nadine shoves her mag under her desk and bends her head so that her hair hides her tear-stained face.

Mrs Henderson approaches. She's actually

76

looking *concerned*. 'What's up, mmm?' she says, in a different sort of voice altogether. 'I know you girls think I come from another planet – but maybe I can still help. What's the problem?'

Nadine fidgets behind her hair. I look down at my lap.

'Nadine?' says Mrs Henderson. 'Are you upset about a boyfriend, is that it?'

I suppose it's a reasonably obvious guess, with Nadine's neck still purple.

Nadine keeps quiet.

'It does help to talk things over, you know,' says Mrs Henderson. 'And no problem is unique. I'm sure I've had similar problems myself.'

I immediately get this amazing image in my head of Mrs Henderson doing this particular thing to Mr Henderson. I have to bite the sides of my cheeks to stop myself shrieking with laughter. Nadine's shoulders shake. She's obviously got the same mental image. Thank God Mrs Henderson doesn't twig the trouble.

'Don't cry, Nadine,' she says gently.

Nadine gives a little gasp.

Mrs Henderson interprets it as a sob. 'Oh, come on, now. Well, I can't force you to confide in me. But don't forget, I'm always here. Now. How far have you got with your lines?'

Nadine hands her page over, her head still bent.

'"I must not be insolant." One hundred times. Oh dear, I really ought to give you another hundred: "I must learn to spell:" In-so-*lent*, Nadine. But never mind. Off you go now. And you too, Eleanor.'

I hand in my own page, hoping she won't count the lines as I'm still only at seventy-something. She scans them quickly, raises an eyebrow, but waves me away.

Nadine and I hold our breath till we're safely down the corridor, and then we let out great *whoops* of laughter. At least it cheers Nadine up for a bit. But she still can't seem to see any kind of sense at all.

The next day I have a private word with Magda.

'She's totally mental,' says Magda.

'I know. But there's no way I can get through to her,' I say.

'I'll have a go,' says Magda.

'Well. Do be ever so tactful. And don't let out that *I* said anything, eh?' I say, but Magda isn't listening to me.

'Nadine! Come over here! Ellie says you're going to do it with Liam, you silly cow.'

Practically every girl in the playground looks up and gawps.

'Magda! You and your big mouth!' I say.

'I think it's you and *your* big mouth, Ellie,' says Nadine. 'Thanks a bunch.'

'Hey, don't be like that,' says Magda, rushing over to her and putting her arm round her neck.

'Get off me, Magda!'

'I just want to talk to you, Nadine.'

'Yeah, but I don't *want* to talk about it, OK?'

'We're mates, aren't we?'

'But this isn't about you and me and Ellie. It's just to do with me and Liam. So you keep your nose out of it, OK? And you too, Ellie,' says Nadine, and she stalks off by herself.

'Shall we go after her?' says Magda.

'We'll be wasting our time,' I say miserably.

I know Nadine too well. She'll never listen to either of us now. I feel I've really blown it. I've betrayed Nadine's confidence – and I haven't helped her in the slightest.

She barely talks to either of us all day. When school is over she goes rushing off to meet up with Liam, who's waiting for her by the wall.

'So let's have a word with him, eh?' says Magda.

'No! You can't! And Nadine would kill us,' I say.

We don't get the chance anyway, because Nadine and Liam hurry away. It's cold, so Liam is wearing this incredible black leather jacket.

'That is a seriously sexy jacket,' Magda says wistfully. 'He might be a pig but he sure looks good. Why can't Greg wear a leather jacket? He's got this naff zippy thing that is practically an anorak.'

'How's it going with Greg, anyway?' I ask.

'Well . . .' says Magda, and sighs.

'*He* doesn't want you to . . .?'

'Per-lease!' says Magda. 'Greg??? No, he's OK, he's quite sweet actually, but all we seem to do is talk homework and hang out at McDonald's. Ah! Which reminds me. One of Greg's mates, Adam, is having a party this Saturday. His parents are away for the weekend so they're planning a serious rave-up. Want to come?'

I stare at her, heart beating.

She mistakes my hesitation. 'Look, I know you

and Dan are an item and the last thing you want is to meet someone new at a party. I mean, you've *got* a boyfriend.'

Oh, Magda! If you only knew. A party. I've never ever been to a party before. Well, of course I've been to *parties* – the little-girly balloons-and-birthday-cake kind. But I've never been to a party with *boys*.

'Please come, Ellie. It should be a laugh, if nothing else. Maybe *I'll* meet a new boyfriend. Greg is OK, but he's seriously lacking when it comes to street cred. His mates might have more potential.'

I don't know what to say, what to do. A serious rave-up. No parents. And boys, boys, boys.

It sounds incredible.

It sounds incredibly scary. I think drink. I think drugs. I think bedrooms.

I want to go. Maybe I'll meet a *real* boyfriend. One of Greg's mates. Although perhaps they'll have girls already.

'Are you sure it won't be just a couple party?' I say.

'*No*, that's the point. This Adam is inviting along half Year Eleven at Andersons, and most of them are totally *un*coupled. They're desperate for more girls. Greg practically begged me to ask some along. I was thinking – who else shall we ask, eh?'

There doesn't seem much point in asking Nadine. Magda asks Chrissie, but she's already going to a party that night. She asks Jess but she says it's not her kind of thing, thanks. She asks Amna who says she'd give anything to go but her dad would go bananas.

'Maybe *my* dad won't let me,' I mumble.

'Rubbish. Your dad seems really cool to me,' says Magda.

Dad always makes a fuss of Magda when she comes round to our house.

'I'll ask him for you if you like,' says Magda. 'OK?'

I don't really want her to. I don't know if I really want to go to this party. What will I wear? What will I say? What am I expected to *do*?'

'What's up?' says Magda. 'He knows you're going out with Dan so you won't let any other boy try it on at the party – so he can't object, can he?'

Oh help. I'll have to keep Magda away from Dad at all costs. Dad thinks it hilariously funny that I write so much to the real Dan. He'll talk about him to Magda and she'll twig what he's *really* like.

'No, leave Dad to me, I'll handle him,' I say firmly. 'OK, I'll go to the party with you, Magda.'

'You won't regret it, I promise,' says Magda.

I regret agreeing almost immediately. I tell Dad about the party, practically hoping he'll say no way. Anna is very doubtful, and asks straight away if the parents are going to be there and what about the drink/drugs situation and suppose there are gate-crashers?

'Look, I don't want to be rude, but I wasn't asking you, Anna, I was asking Dad,' I say. Though I'm secretly glad she's pointed out all these objections.

I hope Dad will take them all on board and agree it's out of the question.

But he doesn't. 'Come off it, Anna, you're sounding positively middle-aged,' he says. 'This is just some tame little party at a schoolboy's house. Why shouldn't Ellie go? And she'll be fine if Magda's going too. That kid knows what she's doing all right.'

'I don't give a damn about Magda. It's Ellie. Does she know what *she's* doing?' says Anna.

'We've got to credit her with some sense. You know enough not to do anything stupid, right, Ellie? You go to your party and have fun.'

'I don't think you're being a very responsible parent,' says Anna. 'But then you're not famed for your responsibility, are you?'

'What's that supposed to mean?' says Dad.

'I think you know,' says Anna.

'I don't have a clue,' says Dad.

I don't have a clue either but I leave them to have a row while I go up to my room. I get out all my clothes and try on every single item. I look a mess in everything. Fat. Babyish. So utterly uncool that I despair.

I'm still despairing on Saturday evening, even though Magda arrives early and gives me advice.

'Dress down. You'll look as if you're trying too hard if you dress up. Wear your jeans. *Not* the cruddy ripped ones. The black.'

OK. So that's my black jeans, even though they're so tight I shall be cut in two if I sit down.

'You won't be sitting down, babe. You'll be dancing,' says Magda. She looks at my boots. 'Well, lumbering.' She sees my face. '*Joke*, Ellie!'

I don't feel like laughing. I feel so fat I select my biggest baggiest T-shirt to wear with the jeans.

'No no no,' says Magda. 'Dress down but also dress sexy.'

'But I'm not.'

'You don't have to *be* it. Just look it. Something little and tight on top. For God's sake, Ellie, yours are Wonders *without* the bra. So if you've got it, flaunt it.'

I've never felt less like flaunting in my entire life. But I do as I'm told and put on an old purple T-shirt I wore when I was practically a little kid. It strains across my embarrassing chest. I look as if I'm wearing a giant rubber band but Magda insists I look fine. She makes me up with purple shadowed eyes to match the T-shirt and fusses that we haven't got deep purple nail varnish too.

Dad is giving us a lift to this Adam's house. (Magda is meeting Greg there.) Dad winks approvingly at Magda, who is looking ultra-cute in a little black skirt and a black-and-white top so short she shows her tiny waist whenever she moves. Dad stops winking and blinks when he sees me. 'Ellie!' he says.

'What?' I say, trying to sound surly and defiant – but my voice cracks.

'Mmm. Well. You look very . . .' He looks over at Anna. 'Maybe this party isn't such a good idea after all,' he says. 'I didn't realize it was going to be so . . . grown up.'

Anna raises her eyebrows. Eggs jumps up onto the armchair. 'Look at me! See how tall I am! I'm a grown-up. I want to go to the party.' He jumps up onto the arm and slips.

Anna is kept busy quelling his yells and rubbing his sore bits. Dad sighs and offers us an arm each. 'Allow me to escort you, ladies,' he says.

He fusses in the car, grilling Magda about Greg and the other boys. He asks all Anna's questions about parents and drink and drugs and insists that he will be waiting outside at twelve to take us home.

'Like Cinderella. Only ball gowns aren't what they used to be,' he says, giving my T-shirt another nervous glance.

He looks a little reassured when we draw up outside Adam's house, one of those cosy mock-Tudor jobs with a little goldfish pond and a garden gnome in a little red plaster cap and matching bootees. There's a car parked in the drive.

'Ah. At least his parents *are* at home,' says Dad.

'Cool subterfuge,' Magda breathes in my ear.

But guess what? It's not subterfuge at all. Adam's mum comes to the door, in a pastel sweater and leggings, holding one of those big plastic plates with little sections for nuts and crisps and twiglets. 'Ah! You two are . . .?'

'I'm Magda and she's Ellie,' says Magda faintly.

'And you're friends of Adam's?'

'Well, I'm a friend of Greg. And he's a friend of Adam,' says Magda. 'And Ellie's *my* friend.'

I don't *feel* like being Magda's friend, not after tonight!

This is not a rave-up. This is a terrible embarrassing non-event. Adam is a boy who looks almost as young as Dan even though he's in Year Eleven. He's a little weedy whatsit with an extremely protruberant Adam's apple (appropriate), which bobs up and down when he talks.

For a long terrible while it's just Adam and Magda and me in the living room, with Adam's mum bustling in and out offering us party nibbles and some ghastly punch that's got about one tot of red wine to every gallon of fruit juice. Damp shreds of maraschino cherry and tinned mandarin lodge against my teeth whenever I try to take a drink.

Adam hisses that his parents decided against their weekend break because his dad has a shocking cold. We hear frequent explosive sneezing from upstairs. I don't think there are going to be any heavy bedroom sessions tonight somehow.

Greg turns up eventually. Magda gives him a hard time, whispering furiously in his crimson ear.

One more boy arrives half an hour later. He's clutching a can of lager and boasts that he's had a few already. He keeps belching. Adam finds this funny and swigs from the can too when his mum is out of the room.

I would sooner go out with Dan than these two.

I would sooner go out with *Eggs*.

Why doesn't anyone else come???

After endless awful ages there's another knock and it sounds as if there's a whole crowd of boys outside but when Adam's mum goes to the door there's a whole load of spluttering and mumbled excuses and someone says they've come to the wrong house and they all charge off.

So we are left. Five of us. We are the party. And

I don't drink and I don't take drugs and I don't dance and I don't go up to a bedroom with a boy. I don't even *talk* to a boy.

I just sit there at the first and worst party of my life.

# Nine Parties

1. IDEAL 'I WISH' PARTY: just me and Dream Dan...

2. MY BEST LITTLE-GIRLY PARTY: when my mum was still alive and she fixed a rainbow party with red strawberries and orange juice and yellow bananas and green jelly and blue-iced birthday cake and indigo blueberry crème brûlée and violet cream chocolates and there were rainbow balloons and she hung crystals up at the windows so there were rainbows all over the room when the sun shone.

3. MY BEST BIG-GIRL PARTY: my twelfth birthday when I had an ice-cream party with all different varieties, and ice-cream soda and a big ice-cream birthday cake.

4. NADINE'S BEST PARTY: when I stayed over on her birthday night when we were little kids and we played Vampire Barbie and smeared red Smartie dye all over our Barbies' mouths and made them manically attack all baby Natasha's fluffy toys.

**5. MAGDA'S BEST PARTY:** when her mum and dad took us all to Planet Hollywood and then to a Brad Pitt movie.

**6. FUNNIEST PARTY:** Eggs's Christening party, when he wouldn't stop screaming and Dad said, 'Let ME hold him,' and he patted Eggs on the back and Eggs was amazingly, copiously sick all down Dad's posh suit.

**7. WETTEST PARTY:** the picnic party in Wales when it drizzled most of the time, and then positively tipped down in stair-rods. Dopey Dan looks even less fetching with his anorak hood up!

**8. NEXT-TO-WORST PARTY:** my birthday party just after Dad and Anna got together and I kept arguing about the games and hated the birthday cake even though Anna had made it in a special blue elephant shape and I started flicking bits of it about and got told off and I complained and then I cried in front of everyone.

**9. WORST PARTY:** Adam's party!

## Six Letters

Dear Dan,

I went to a great party on Saturday night. A real rave-up.

I danced.

I drank.

I socialized.

I didn't get home till dawn.

Dear Dan,

I am a liar. You should see my tongue. We always used to say when we were little that you got black spots on your tongue if you told a lie. Mine is black as coal all over. It was a truly terrible party if you really want to know. So mind-bogglingly awful that I phoned my dad to come and get me early.

I felt so STUPID. There are all these long

fussing articles in the papers about the teenagers of today and how they're all into drink and drugs and snogging everything in sight. Well, I am leading the most dull dreary demure life imaginable. And it's dead boring.

I feel sort of OUT of things. Like I don't belong anywhere. Do you ever get that feeling? Of course you don't. You're a boy, you obviously don't know what it's like. You don't ever have to worry about how you look and what you wear and whether you're popular.

I don't know why I'm writing all this rubbish. It's just it's late at night and I can't sleep and I'm feeling so fed up and there's no-one I can really talk to, so hard luck, Dan, I'm rabbiting on to you. I've always had my two best friends, Magda and Nadine, to talk to – but it's sort of different now. I'm still friends with Magda but she's such a jokey lively fun sort of girl she doesn't always understand if I'm feeling depressed. And she's got this boyfriend Greg who she's seeing quite a lot of. She's not THAT keen on him — but he's OK. They were at this awful party but it was all right for them because they could just sit in a corner by themselves and snog. Magda initiated the embrace. She just pounced and Greg was powerless. But he didn't seem to mind. Well, he wouldn't. Magda is a pretty stunning girl.

Usually if I'm feeling low I confide in my other friend Nadine, who is a naturally gloomy sort of girl. Nadine and I have been best friends ever since we were tiny tots. We even used to dress alike and pretend we were twins (which was a little dopey as I've always been small and round with frizzy hair and Nadine is tall and thin with dead-straight hair, but we never let that deter us.) But now... she's got this boyfriend Liam and he's much older and Nadine thinks he's so cool and yet I think he's a creep because of the way he treats her, expecting her to do all sorts of stuff — well, YOU know — and Nadine told me all this and I told Magda and Magda told Nadine she was an idiot and Nadine stopped talking to us and she still won't make it up and I'm dead worried about her. And I'm worried about my dad and my stepmother because right this minute they're having an argument in their bedroom. I can hear them even though they're whispering. I don't know why they're having all these rows. They used to get on so well together. In fact when Anna first came to live with us I used to hope they WOULD fight, I used to do my best to wind Anna up and kept telling tales on her to Dad. Not because I absolutely hated her. In fact, she's OK, really. Well, most of the time. But she's my stepmother and I never wanted any kind of substitute mum, because mine was the best in the world.

I'm not going to write about my mum because it might make me cry. ANYWAY, I've sort of got used to Anna now, it's like we're friends. Not GREAT friends, just OK, ordinary friends. She's always been so calm and quiet and happy which is just as well because I can get ever so stroppy and moody sometimes and my little brother Eggs is a right pain most of the time as you know only too well and my dad is the worst of us all for going ballistic but Anna's always known how to handle him, she's always calmed him down. It's always been like he's this great growly dog and she knows just the way to give him a firm word and then a pat so he drools all over her like a puppy. But she's lost the trick now. Or maybe she's got fed up playing that game, I don't know. She seems to want to be her own person more, especially now Eggs has started school. She's tried to get back into doing design work, only there aren't any jobs going at the moment, which is a bit depressing for her, and then she started this evening class and last Tuesday there was a great ding-dong because I was going round to Magda's and Dad had promised to be home to look after Eggs so Anna could go to the class only something cropped up at my dad's college and he didn't get back in time and Anna couldn't go to her class and when I got back I could see Anna had been crying. I can't see why going to this evening class should matter so much to her. It's Italian conversation and we're never ever going to GO to Italy, just

92

boring old wet Wales. (Do you REALLY like it???) Mind you, I'd give anything to go to Italy because I want to see all the Art, and Magda says the ice-creams are mega-fantastic. And Italian guys are meant to be the sexiest guys in the world. I suppose Anna likes Art because she did go to Art School but she won't touch ice-creams, she's far too fussed about keeping her figure. And Anna isn't into sexy Italian guys because she's got Dad. Unless...

Oh, God, I've suddenly thought of something. Maybe Anna's got another bloke. A sexy Italian. Or is she just using the evening class as an excuse, and she's off meeting some mystery boyfriend somewhere? I've always wondered what on earth she sees in my dad as he's so much older than her, and she's pretty stunning to look at, and Dad's got this pot belly though he sucks in his stomach whenever he looks in the mirror and insists all his flab is solid muscle, and he wears jeans and denim jackets like he's young only he isn't, and then there's his awful beard and his long hair and those terrible sandals he wears in the summer. And it's not as if he's got the easiest personality—

I'll say! Dad just got up to go to the bathroom and he spotted my light on and he said, What on earth are you up to, Ellie? and he's switched my light off so I expect my

writing's going up and down all over the place
and you won't be able to read a thing but
anyway it doesn't really matter because I
don't think I'll be sending you this letter
anyway as it's just a load of rambling rubbish
and you'll think I've gone completely nuts.

Love, Ellie

Dear Ellie

You're not nuts at all. I'm so glad you sent your letter.
It was the best letter I've ever had. It was as if I've
seen through a little window right into your head.
I've read it over and over. I carry it about with me.
Well hidden, naturally.

I was just so amazed and bowled over to realize
you can get so bothered and fed up and stuff. Me too,
me too, me too! You are entirely WRONG about boys
not knowing what it's like, though. I don't EVER feel like
I belong anywhere. I feel as if I've been zapped here
from my own special Planet Dan and now I'm plodding
around totally alien territory and all the Earthlings are
laughing at me. Absolutely wetting themselves. And
even more now, because I'm reacting to alien air by
erupting into loathsome pimples all over the place, yuck
yuck yuck, and even though I anoint my spots with all
sorts of junk Mum buys in Boots it doesn't help much.
My entire body seems to be going berserk. I am not

going into details but girls have NO IDEA AT ALL how embarrassing it can be. I wish I could hide inside a special spaceman suit with a fishbowl helmet and not have to make contact with anyone else ever. Except you.

   You wrote 'Love Ellie' for the first time. That's the best bit of your letter. I've read those two tiny words over and over, so many times it's a wonder the ink hasn't worn right off the page, such is the ardour of my laser-gaze.

LOTS of love,

Dan XXX

Dear Dan,

   I didn't mean to post that last letter! I just shoved it in an envelope in a tearing rush in the morning and put it in the letter box as I ran for school and THEN I remembered some of the stuff I'd said and I was so embarrassed. I even ran back to the letterbox and tried to wriggle my hand through the slot. Then this police panda car slowed down and I thought, Oh, my God, I'm going to get arrested for attempting to steal the Royal Mail. I wriggled my wrist free and sort of grinned sheepishly at these police guys and they just laughed at me.

   MOST people laugh at me. I like the idea of wearing a spacesuit. I'd like one too. Only how can one communicate in a fishbowl helmet? You couldn't go shopping unless you did some serious miming to show you wanted the latest indie album, leaping in the air in manic mode. Come to think of it, you wouldn't be able to HEAR it. And what about talking to your friends? (Though one of my best friends still isn't talking to ME.) And school??? Though I'm not a brainbox like you obviously are, so I don't do much communicating with the teachers at the best of times.

This is the WORST of times. I feel seriously fed up. Oh, God, I'd better stop now or I'll write ANOTHER long rambly rubbishy letter. I didn't really put 'Love Ellie' last time, did I? I don't remember. I don't ever put Love to anyone, not even Luv or Lurve. I just put me.
                                                          Ellie.


Dear Ellie,

   You did So put 'Love Ellie'. I have your letter here, beneath my heart. Well, that sounds poetic but it's not anatomically accurate. I don't have any pockets up at chest level. I've got your letter in my trouser pocket. So your words of Love (not Luv, not Lurve, LOVE) are actually rubbing against my thigh, only that sounds embarrassingly intimate and I don't want this letter to develop into one of those porny pervy jobs some of the guys at my school write to girls. No, their letters are probably not TO girls, they're just ABOUT girls.

   I don't want to think of you like that, Ellie. Not that you

aren't absolutely wonderfully attractive etc, etc, etc. It was love at first sight like I said. I knew you were the girl for me. I think about you all the time. I've never been in love before. I suppose I love my mum and dad (though they do go ON a bit, and act all silent and reproachful if I want to do anything normal like watch RED DWARF or BOTTOM or play computer games or go to a football match – because they just want to read books and listen to classical music and wear Oxfam and recycle everything and lead a life as Green as Grass they think I should too). I love my brothers and sisters a bit too (though like your brother Eggs they are Right Pains – no, Excruciating Agonies, especially when they come barging into my bedroom and read all my private stuff and mock my new hairstyle). I am trying to turn myself into a dead cool guy so you will look at me and decide you'll follow me, your Lord, throughout the world. I haven't suddenly gone nuts – well, nuttier than I am already – it's something Juliet says. Are you doing ROMEO AND JULIET too? It's quite good though it's murder doing it at my school because we're all boys so some poor sap has to be Juliet when we read aloud. I was the original poor sap actually, and everyone fell about and I could see this was NOT going to improve my street cred among the lads so I had to camp it up and do Juliet in a silly high-pitched girly voice which got me into trouble

97

with the teacher – shame, as he's quite a decent bloke really and he's lent me some of his books – but it made everyone think I'm a nut instead of a nerd, only I don't want to be, and there's nothing I can do about my weedy physique or lousy complexion and I can't even earn any hard cash for cool clothes till I'm fourteen BUT I did think a haircut might help. Mum normally just chops bits off here and there. NOT a pretty sight. So I badgered her to let me go to a proper barber and I said I wanted a radical new hairstyle, one that would last. Until I see you: WHEN WILL THAT BE??? You can come and stay for the weekend any time but our house is ever so crowded with kids' stuff. All the flannels in our bathroom are currently growing mustard and cress and you can't eat off the table in the living room because it's covered with a giant jigsaw puzzle and there are ducks swimming in the bath (generally just the plastic variety but you never know!) and if you sleep in the only spare bed that means my sisters Rhianne and Lara will be in the bunk bed opposite and Rhianne sings all the time, even when she's asleep, and Lara climbs into bed with you at four in the morning, bringing her entire soft toy menagerie with her. So you would be ever so EVER SO welcome but not extremely comfortable. So how about if I stay with you? I have this cousin who is going out with a girl at London University so he drives down most Friday nights and says he doesn't mind giving me a lift, which is brilliant. So what about next weekend? Although maybe I ought to wear a space helmet for real. Made of black ambulance glass. Because the new haircut might just be a bit of a mistake. My mum shook her head and sighed deeply when she saw me. My dad got all worried that I'd joined some skin-head gang. My brothers and sisters fell about laughing. Which was NOTHING compared to the reaction of the guys at school. I am certainly well established as a nut now. You will also get a right laugh when you see me, Ellie. So ... next week, yes? I'll be arriving between eight and nine, depending on traffic. See you S-O-O-O-O-N!

Lots and lots and lots of love,

Dan

Dear Dan,

No, don't come next weekend! I'm sorry, but it's Magda's birthday, and we're hanging out there Saturday and then will be going out celebrating somewhere, but it's girls only, I'm afraid, so I can't ask you to come. In actual fact I don't really think it would be a good idea if you came at all because our spare bed situation is pretty chronic too. (Eggs broke the springs on the guest bed so it's just a camp bed, the sort that suddenly springs shut when you're inside it), so let's wait until we meet up again in Wales, right? Do you go there at

Christmas? We do, it's completely crackers, we all have to wear six jumpers and it snows and there's frost INSIDE the windows, let alone outside, but it's becoming a loopy family tradition, worst luck. Still, if you're there too we could play Sir Edmund Hillary and Sherpa Tensing.

L. Ellie

Dear Ellie,

I can't wait till Christmas! I'll come the next weekend AFTER the next weekend!

Lots and lots and lots and LOTS of Love,

Dan

# Nine Unexpected Odd Facts

1. Dopey Dan writes good letters.

2. Cigarettes look cool but feel hot.

3. Cheese smells foul but tastes good.

4. Eggs looks sweet when he's fast asleep.

5. One titchy little chocolate bar contains 350 calories. → CHOC

6. The hippest deadliest rock stars have the mumsiest of mums.

7. An outfit that looks truly great in the changing room becomes hideous the moment you get it home.

8. Likewise, new shoes that fit perfectly in the shop rub and pinch the moment you step into the street.

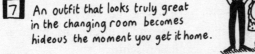

OUCH!

9. A boy can be mega-brainy but very s-l-o-w to catch on.

Seventh Heaven

'O f course Dan can come and stay the weekend after next,' says Anna. 'Oh, Eggs! Watch your juice. You're spilling it *all*.'

'No! You weren't *listening*,' I say. 'I don't *want* him to come.'

'I thought you just said you did,' says Anna, stripping Eggs stark naked and stuffing his pyjamas straight into the washing machine.

'I'm all bare. Look at my willy, Ellie,' says Eggs, practically waving it at me.

'Yuck. Can't you stuff him in the washing machine too, Anna?' I say.

She's on her knees, sorting through the dirty clothes basket, juggling little balls of socks.

'You just wish you had a willy too,' says Eggs.

'Attaboy, Eggs,' says Dad, finishing his coffee.

'You've got these women sussed out. Right, I'm off.'

'Why are you going so early?' says Anna. 'Can't you wait and take Eggs to school?'

'No, there's someone I've got to catch,' says Dad, scooping up Eggs with one arm and giving him a kiss.

'Who?' says Anna, her fists clenching.

'Oh, for God's sake. Jim Dean, the graphics guy. Anna, don't start.'

'It's not me that starts things, it's you,' says Anna. 'OK OK, you go to work. Just make sure you come home on time. I'm not going to miss my Italian class again.'

'You and that wretched evening class. You go on about it as if it's the most important thing in your life,' says Dad as Eggs wriggles free.

'What else have I got in my life?' Anna says bitterly. She holds out an armful of smelly socks. 'My life is so full and so rich and so exciting. Here I am, sorting your dirty socks. Wow, I can barely contain my excitement. Why can't you smooth them out straight for a start? Why should I have to unravel them all? Why can't you put them in the machine? You keep kidding yourself you're still a young man. So why don't you act like a *new man* and do your share of the chores?'

'Why can't you act like the young woman you are instead of a bitter old nag?' says Dad, and he walks out.

Anna bursts into tears as the front door slams.

'Mum?' says Eggs. 'Have you hurt yourself?'

'Get *washed*, Eggs. And put your clothes on,' I say, steering him towards the door.

'Mummy do it,' says Eggs.

'Don't be such a baby. Mum's tired. Now off you go. I'll take you to school.'

'I don't want *you* to take me to school. Dad takes me.'

'Listen, Squirt. You wash. You get dressed. You do as I say. And then I *might* tell you the Egg story on the way to school.'

'Oh, wow. Right. OK,' says Eggs, whizzing off. He pauses at the door. 'Mum? Isn't it getting better?'

'Yes. Mmm. I'm fine now,' says Anna, sniffing. 'Go on, go and get washed, lickety spit.'

Eggs rushes off, mumbling 'Lick and spit, lick and spit, lick and spit.'

'Thanks, Ellie,' says Anna.

'Anna. You and Dad . . .?'

'Oh. It's – it's just a bad patch.'

'Anna . . .' I stand still in the quiet kitchen. 'Anna, there isn't anyone else, is there?'

Anna's head jerks. 'Someone else?' she says. She's staring at me, her face very white. 'Why? What makes you say that? What do you know? Ellie?'

'I don't know anything. I just wondered . . . Well, Dad can be a right pain at times, and if you've met someone else at your Italian class, well, it's scary because it's horrid with you and Dad arguing like this, but I do understand. I know I always used to take Dad's side but now I'm older – well, I wouldn't *blame* you if you had an affair, Anna.'

Anna is staring as if she can hardly believe what I'm saying. Then she shakes her head, half laughing, though she's still got tears in her eyes. '*I'm* not having an affair, you chump,' she says.

'Then . . .?' I suddenly *realize*. 'Is *Dad*?'

'I don't know. He says he isn't. I say he is. Sometimes I think he's telling the truth and I'm just paranoid. Other times I'm sure he's lying,' says Anna, hurling the socks into the machine along with all his other stuff.

'Who do you think it is?'

'Some girl in his Art class. I don't know her name but I saw her hanging on his arm in the town. Very young, very pretty, with a lot of blond hair.'

'Well, couldn't they just have been walking along together?'

'Maybe. But I saw the way he was looking at her. The way he used to look at me.'

'Oh, Anna.' I hover helplessly.

'I'm sorry,' says Anna, shutting the door of the washing machine and getting to her feet. 'I shouldn't have said anything. It's probably all my imagination anyway. It's just when I get started I can't stop. It's just . . . I love him so.'

That's the weirdest bit. I think about it as I take Eggs to school. I'm busy making up this daft serial story he likes about the Eggstremely Ovoid Eggles – there's Mama Eggle, Papa Eggle, Grandma and Grampy Eggle, and hundreds of eggy little Eggles, Edward, Edwina, Edith, Enid, Ethelred, Ethan, Evangeline . . . and they all sleep in an Eggidorm which has a big bed with oval segments for the eggles to snuggle in and then when they get up in the morning they wobble to a hole in the floor and whizz down this slide to get their breakfast in the kitchen down below. They only ever eat cornflakes – they hate and detest cooked breakfast. And then there are their cousins the Chockies who only visit at Easter and they hate hot weather . . .

I go on and on and it gets sillier and sillier, but Eggs adores it. After a while my mouth takes over and tells the story while my mind thinks about Anna and Dad. How can she still love him like that? I suppose *I* love him, but he's my dad. I couldn't *stick* him as my partner, especially if he started playing around. Anna must have got it wrong. Why on earth would any pretty young student fall for my dad? And yet Anna did exactly that. I can't understand it. Dad isn't even good looking as old guys go. Why don't they want someone young and gorgeous like . . .

Oh, God, it's him! My Dan! The dream one, with the blond hair and the brown eyes. I haven't seen him for ages. I gave up on him and started getting the bus every day. But now he's walking towards me, getting nearer. I think he's looking at me, he *is*! Oh, what shall I do? I look away. Oh, please don't let me blush. I'm getting hot, he's getting nearer still—

'Ellie? Ellie, what's up? Go on with the Eggle story!' Eggs demands, tugging at my arm as if it's a water pump.

'In a minute,' I mutter.

'*Now!*' Eggs demands. 'You promised.'

He's right in front of me. I look up and he's smiling, he's really smiling. Then he shakes his head at Eggs. 'Little brothers!' he says to me.

I nod, dumbstruck.

'See you,' he says, and he walks on.

'See you,' I whisper, dazed.

'Ellie? Who's that man?' Eggs demands.

'Shh!' I hiss. 'I don't know.'

'Why have you gone red?'

'Oh, God, have I?'

'Ever so. Go on with the Eggles story, *please*.'

I blurt out a few dumb Eggle incidents, inventing a new egg who is made of solid gold, so gleaming yellow that he dazzles everyone.

I deliver Eggs to his primary school and dawdle off in the general direction of my school. I'm going to be late, of course, but I can't possibly dash. I need to savour this moment. He said 'See you.' He really did. I didn't make him up. He was there, he spoke to me, and he said 'See you.' Which means, See you again! Or even, I *want* to see you again!

Oh, I want to see *you* again, so much.

All my problems with the insistence of the real Dan seem unimportant. I can't even worry too much about Dad and Anna now. This is one of the most magical moments of my life. I feel like . . . Juliet.

I wish I dared bunk off school and drift around all day hanging on to this feeling. But I trudge there eventually and get seriously told off for my pains. Nadine is still being all cold and huffy and when we do PE we see another love-bite, lower down this time. Magda and I can't help boggling at it as Nadine hurriedly pulls on her games shirt.

'What are you staring at?' she says.

'Nadine! Isn't it flipping *obvious*?' says Magda. 'Can't you get Liam to eat a decent meal before he goes out with you? He seems to want to slurp great gobbets out of you all the time.'

'Just mind your own business, OK?' says Nadine.

Magda shrugs and saunters out of the changing rooms. I hang back. Nadine knows I'm still here but she bends down, fussing with her shoes. Her hair swings forward and I see the startlingly white scalp at her parting. I remember when we used to play hairdressers and how I loved to brush Nadine's long soft rustling hair, so different from my own mass of wire wool.

'Naddie–Baddie,' I say softly. I haven't called her that since we were in the infants.

She looks up and she's suddenly herself again. 'Ellie-Smellie,' she says.

'Oh, Nad. Make friends, eh?'

'I didn't ever *break* friends.'

'Yes, but you've been all cold and narky.'

'Well, you started it, gabbing to Magda.'

'I know, I'm sorry. I could have bitten my tongue off for telling her. Look.' I stick my tongue out and mime biting it. I'm a little too enthusiastic with my demonstration and my teeth sink in before I can stop them. '*Ouch!*'

'Oh, Ellie, you are a nutcase.' Nadine gives me a quick hug. 'We're friends, OK?'

'I'm so glad. I can't stand *not* being friends with

you,' I say, sucking my tongue. 'Are you going to be friends with Magda too?'

'Well, only if she stops giving me grief about Liam. She's just jealous anyway, because he's so dishy, a hundred times better than that Greg of hers.'

'Cheek!' says Magda, who's come running back to see what's happened to me. Then she laughs. 'But certainly partly true. Greg isn't a patch on Liam when it comes to looks. When I first saw your Liam I *was* dead jealous, I admit it. But now . . . Oh, Nadine, can't you see, he's just using you.'

'No, he's not. He really cares about me. He can barely leave me alone when we're together,' Nadine says.

'Yes, but that's just sex, Nadine. That's all he wants. He doesn't even take you out properly. Just gets you to go off on all these walks.'

'He does *so* take me out. We're going to Seventh Heaven on Saturday night,' says Nadine. 'He's got these freebee tickets from a mate.'

'Wow! Seventh Heaven!' I say. It's the newest and baddest and best club. Everyone's desperate to go there. None of our lot has made it yet.

'But what about my birthday?' says Magda. 'I thought you guys were coming round to my place, right? And we would go out all girls together?'

'Oh, God,' says Nadine. 'I forgot, Magda! And these tickets, they're just for Saturday night. Oh, what am I going to do?'

'It's OK,' says Magda. 'You go. Who'd want to pass up a chance to go to Seventh Heaven? Hey! Ellie, how about if you and me go too? I'll get my dad to cough up the cash. Don't worry, Nadine, we won't cramp your style. We'll keep well away from you and Dracula.'

'Dracula indeed!' says Nadine, but she laughs.

It's OK at last. We're all three friends again. And we're going to Seventh Heaven!

I wonder if the blond dreamboat Dan ever goes clubbing???

Nadine is telling her parents she's spending Saturday with Magda. I really *am* – but of course I'm not telling Dad and Anna we're planning to go to Seventh Heaven. My dad loves to act laid back but I know he'd never let me go there in a million years because there's been all this stuff in the local papers for weeks about the fights at four in the morning and girls being rushed to hospital with drug overdoses and all this other seriously heavy stuff. I just tell them Magda's having this little party and I'll sleep over at her place and come home some time on Sunday.

'What are you going to wear to this party?' Dad says. 'Not that T-shirty thing again?'

He's home half an hour *early*, so Anna's all set for her evening class. Dad's trying to act as if the row this morning didn't happen.

'Maybe it's time you had some new clothes, Ellie. Here.' He hands me twenty quid. Then realizes it's not enough. He fumbles in his wallet. 'I haven't got enough cash. Look, why don't you go shopping with Anna, use the credit card?' He looks at Anna. '*Both* of you buy yourself something new, eh?'

Anna looks tense. I'm scared she's going to

start another row, start on about guilt money or something – and then *I* won't get my outfit after all. But then she shrugs. 'OK. Sure. So, Ellie – we'll go late-night shopping tomorrow.'

'Can you get home early again and look after Eggs, Dad?' I say. 'He's such a pain to take shopping.'

There. I've fixed Dad now. He can't stay out late and play around. Anna gives me a little nod of acknowledgement.

It turns out that we have fun shopping together. It's almost as if Anna is Magda or Nadine. We wander round Jigsaw and Warehouse and River Island and Miss Selfridge and Anna tries on all this mad stuff and when I see her slinking round the changing room showing off her navel in this really raunchy gear I just fall about laughing and she gets the giggles too and it's like we're two girls together. I dare squeeze into some of the sexier stuff too but it's a BIG mistake. I am the mistake. I am big. Well. F-A-T.

'You're *not* fat, Ellie. For God's sake, you're just perfectly normal size,' Anna insists, although she's Ms Stick Insect herself so she's OK. I'm Ms Big Bumblebee – with the emphasis on the Bum.

'What am I going to *wear*?' I say, after I've tried on 101 outfits and discarded them all. 'I want something hip and cool and now – and yet I look positively indecent in all this stuff.'

'You're just a bit curvy for current fashion,' says Anna. 'You don't want these tacky tops or skimpy little skirts.'

111

'So what else am I going to wear? A black plastic rubbish bag?'

'We'll find you the perfect outfit, Ellie, I promise,' says Anna.

And she does! There's this long tight stretchy skirt that I'm scared might be a bit frumpy, but there's a sexy slit up the back – and then she finds a satin shirt to go over the top and I try it on and it's like – wow! – I'm not me any more. I don't look like some stupid podgy little kid. I look much older. Fifteen. Maybe even sixteen.

'Oh, Anna, it's great!' I say. 'But the two together are going to be ever so pricey.'

'So what?' says Anna. 'Let's go mad.'

She buys a little short bright skirt for herself that is *so* different from her usual check-shirt-and-jeans young-mum style. Anna doesn't look older. She looks much much younger.

'Let's buy some tarty shoes too,' she says.

We strut around in these silly heels, both of us staggering. Then we go for identical black suede shoes with little buckles.

'You have them, Ellie, it's OK,' says Anna.

'No, it's not fair. You saw them first. You have them, Anna.'

'You two are very sweet to each other for sisters,' says the assistant, laughing at us.

'We're not sisters,' says Anna. 'Though it feels like we are sometimes.'

'We're . . . friends,' I says, and it's true. For the moment, anyway.

We both get a pair of black buckled shoes and we

dance down the road in them, though we've both got blisters by the time we get home.

Anna's being so sweet I feel bad about telling her lies but I know the moment I mentioned Seventh Heaven she'd morph into strict stepmother mode and say No Way.

So off I go to Magda's on Saturday and we have a fun time with her family. You should see the birthday presents they gave her! It's not as if they're rolling in money either. She gets a VCR for her bedroom and a satin blouse a bit like mine but much more clingy and a huge cuddly bunny and a lacy nightie and a big box of chocs and posh lipstick and nail varnish and lots of CDs and scent and a necklace and a great big basket of smelly stuff.

Nadine sends her a Forever Friends card to show she really wants to make up, with a pair of ultra-sexy black knickers inside. I give Magda a cartoon card I drew myself, with Magda up on a pedestal being worshipped by all these different males, not just Greg and his mates and poor sappy Adam, but people like Mr Lanes the History teacher who is quite dishy in a mature sort of way, and I add all her favourite film stars and rock stars too. It sounds like showing off, but she really loves that card – and my present too. That's home-made as well. Anna helped me make it last night. Magda's always liked the Cookie Monster in *Sesame Street* so I baked her a whole batch of different cookies, chocolate and raisin and cherry, and then when they were cool I put them in a special tin. It's airtight so the cookies can keep, but as we spend most of Saturday afternoon in Magda's room mucking around and watching videos we keep stuffing cookies one after the other, so there aren't many actually left now.

It's a good job my new skirt has an elasticated waistband because Magda's mum gets together this incredible birthday cake and crème brûlée and tiramisú and banoffi pie – *and* all the poached salmon and quiche and chicken and little-sausage-on-stick stuff.

'We'd better watch what we drink at Seventh Heaven or there's going to be a serious chucking-up situation!' Magda whispers.

I'm starting to feel a bit sick actually when we set out. Not because of all the food. Because suddenly Seventh Heaven is the very last place I want to go to. You have to queue up to get in and this awful bouncer guy at the door eyes you up and down and if he thinks you're too young or too wet or too boring he won't let you in.

I don't want to go – but it would still be terrible to be turned away!

'Come on, Ellie! What are you hanging back for?' Magda asks.

'My shoes hurt,' I say – which is true. And the slit in my skirt isn't that big, so my knees are a bit hobbled. 'Magda . . . what if we don't get in?'

'We will. You leave it to me,' says Magda.

'We don't know anyone that goes there.'

'So? We'll be part of this great new crowd,' says Magda. 'And anyway, we know Nadine, don't we?'

It's seriously weird when we get there and join the queue. There are some very tall glam girls with very tarty clothes and lots of make-up who make me feel very small and mousy.

'Clock all those trannies!' says Magda, giving me a nudge.

I blink and take another look. Magda's right, they're boys under all the blusher. And there are ordinary gay guys too, in tight T-shirts and fantastic tight leather trousers, showing off their muscle tone. There are girls too, giggling together, with cropped hair and nose studs.

'I think it's a gay night,' I hiss. 'Oh, Magda, maybe we're going to look stupid if we try to get in tonight.'

'Relax, babe. It's *everybody's* night,' says Magda, nodding at a crowd of guys further up the queue. 'Wow, they look pretty tasty. Now they're not gay, I'm sure of it. And look, there are loads of straight couples too. Can you see Nadine and Dracula?'

I can't see them at all. I just see lots and lots of cool clubby chic people and I feel smaller and sadder every second. We're working our way up the queue now and I'm so scared the guy will yell 'You must be joking, you don't belong here, you silly little schoolgirl,' and then I'll literally shrivel up in my suede shoes and die here and now.

But Magda winks at him saucily and he grins at her and nods us both in, just like that. I can't believe it!

It's so great, seeing inside Seventh Heaven. It's midnight-blue with luminous stars and incredible strobes and the music is so loud and the smoky-cloud stuff pumping all over the place is so strange that I stop being me, Ellie, I'm this new cool clubber and I'm here to have fun. Magda and I have a quick tour round to see if we can spot Nadine but she's not here yet. Magda takes me by the wrist and we get onto the dance floor. I'm not too bad at dancing but I generally worry in case anyone's looking at me and noticing my fat bum but now I just get into the rhythm and leap around like part of the crowd. I *am* the crowd. We're *all* the crowd and it's truly fantastic.

Only we get tired eventually and go to get a drink. Magda orders two vodka and cranberry juices at the bar, but the barman tells her to dream on. So we have the juice without the vodka. It's more refreshing that way.

Then this older guy comes up and starts hitting on Magda, leaning over and whispering in her ear. My heart starts hammering, because what am I going to do if she gets off with someone? – but then Magda shakes her head and he goes away.

'What was he saying?' I ask.

'Oh, he was pushing E and whizz and all that junk,' says Magda.

'*Really?*' I say, staring after this real live drug-pusher.

'It's OK. I made it plain we're not into drugs.'

There are lots of other kids who obviously *are*. As it gets later lots start crashing about, their eyes huge and staring. A girl near us suddenly sits on the floor and starts weeping.

I stare at her, wondering if she's all right. Suddenly Seventh Heaven doesn't seem quite such a glittery place after all. I still can't see Nadine anywhere. Maybe she isn't going to turn up.

Magda and I dance again, and I have to take my shoes off, but I don't dare put them down in case they get kicked away so I dangle them by their straps, which is a bit awkward. I'm starting to get ever so tired. I think Magda is too.

Then way off at the other side of the club, right at the back, I think I see this blond head. My dream guy! Well, maybe not, I can't see properly. Heaps of guys have that amazing fair hair, though I think it really *could* be him, only now there's a whole load of other kids in front of him.

'Let's go over the other side for a bit,' I suggest, trying to sound dead casual, though I have to yell in Magda's ear before she can hear me above the music.

We're edging our way over when we spot Nadine at last. She's dancing wildly, her dark hair flying, her eyes very big, very black, very staring.

'What the hell is she on?' says Magda.

Liam is with her. It's horrible the way he's leering at her.

'Hey, Nadine!' Magda yells, charging over to her. 'You look ever so hot. I think you maybe need a drink. Come to the ladies' room, eh?'

Liam tells Magda to get lost. Magda takes no notice. '*Nadine.* Come on.' Magda takes hold of one arm, I take the other, and we pull her away.

I glance back once but I can't see any blond head now. Maybe I was mistaken anyway.

Nadine is all sweaty and stares at us blearily, practically out of it.

'What has that pig got you to take, eh?' Magda says fiercely. 'You'd better have a drink of water. Several. You're dehydrated. Only not *too* much,' she says, as Nadine bends over the washbasin in the ladies' and starts slurping straight from the tap. 'Honestly! You're like a baby. It's a good job Ellie and I are here to keep an eye on you.'

Magda finds a paper cup and we give Nadine a couple of drinks. Then she staggers off to the loo.

A whole little gang of girls come into the ladies'.

'It's OK, we're not in the queue, we're just waiting for our friend,' Magda tells them.

'She's not the dark-haired girl with that Liam, is she?' says one of the girls.

'So?' says Magda.

'Well, she wants to keep clear of him. He used to hang round this girl at our school, really young, just in Year Eight, or maybe she'd just started Year Nine.'

Magda and I keep stum.

'He has this thing about really young girls. He says if you go with virgins you don't have to bother about safe sex because you can't catch anything off them.'

'*What?*' I say.

'I don't *believe* it!' says Magda.

'It's true. He's done it with lots of girls, but he gives them the elbow the minute they start to put out. This girl at our school, she got pregnant from this one time, but he just told her to get lost, he didn't want to know. He said she was a slag anyway, saying if she'd do it with him then she'd do it with anyone.'

Magda and I stare at each other, horrified. Then we look at the cubicle where Nadine is. Surely she must have heard? She stays in there until all the other girls have gone. After a few minutes we hear her crying.

'Come out, Naddie,' I whisper.

'Yes, come on, babe, it's just us,' says Magda.

Nadine comes out, tears streaming down her face. She heard all right.

'We're going to go home,' says Magda, putting her arm round her. 'We'll sneak out the back, leave him standing there. I've got the cab fare. You come back to my place and sleep over with Ellie and me.'

So that's just what we do. And when I wake up at dawn and hear Nadine sobbing in the spare bed I slip over and get in beside her and cuddle her close.

# Nine Favourites

1 FAVOURITE BOY: Dream Dan.

2 FAVOURITE GIRL: Nadine and Magda -
can't choose between them.

3 FAVOURITE CLUB: Seventh Heaven. OK, it's the
only club I've ever been in, but it's definitely the best.

4 FAVOURITE MEAL: pizza with extra toppings
of everything,
especially pineapple.

5 FAVOURITE SNACK: Magnum ice-cream.

6 FAVOURITE ANIMAL: elephant.
Girl elephants stay with their
mothers all their lives - true fact.

7 FAVOURITE COLOUR: purple.

8 FAVOURITE FLOWER: pansy.

9 FAVOURITE TV PROGRAMME:

The X-Files   Friends   Sesame Street

# Eight till Late

Dear Dan,

I'm ever so sorry but you really CAN'T come and stay at my home. I did ask, but Anna my stepmother won't allow it. I don't think you realized this on holiday but she's really really strict and right at the moment she's dead annoyed with me because she found out that I went to this amazing club with a serious reputation so now I'm grounded for the rest of the TERM and she says I can't have anyone at all to stay, so I'm afraid it really will be Christmas at the cottages before we see each other again. I do hope you understand and don't feel too mad at me.

L. Ellie   x

My tongue is black all over. It's a wonder it hasn't cracked at the roots and crumbled into cinders in my mouth.

I feel so mean saying all that stuff about Anna. She's been really super to me. And she's never said anything about the night of Magda's party. I came home from Magda's as good as gold on Sunday and said we'd just had this super birthday meal that had lasted practically all evening, but when I kicked off my killer shoes Anna saw my tights were all holes because I'd been dancing so much. She's been an absolute sport and it's especially unfair for me to say she won't let anyone come and stay because next weekend she's letting Magda and Nadine stay over Friday night.

We're all going to Stacy's birthday party. It's going to be great if everyone starts celebrating their birthdays in style – we'll be raving right through the year! Not that Stacy's party is going to be a *rave*. We wondered why on earth she'd asked us to her party because she's not our particular friend, we hardly know her, but it turns out she's asked the entire form, and a lot of girls in Year Nine in the other forms too.

'My mum and dad are hiring the hall at the community centre and there's going to be a disco and a finger buffet and we've got an extension so it's going to be eight till late,' Stacy burbles.

'Wow!' says Magda, but Stacy doesn't twig she's being sarcastic and just grins gratefully.

'Yeah, isn't it fabulous? Well, see you there, you three.'

'We're really looking forward to it . . . *not*,' says Magda, the minute Stacy's back is turned.

'Shut up, she'll hear,' I say. I always feel much more worried about damply enthusiastic girls like Stacy who are so terribly uncool. If I didn't hang around with Magda and Nadine and try really hard to be hip I could so easily be one myself.

But Magda can be caring too. She's looking at Nadine, who hasn't said a word. She's barely spoken since the Seventh Heaven night when she walked out on Liam. She just drifts round after us like this pale little ghost. The purple marks are fading on her neck but it's going to take her much longer to get him to fade from her mind.

'Oh, I don't know, Stacy's party could be a laugh, I suppose,' says Magda. 'We could stick together, us three, and have a bit of a bop. I quite fancy a girls' night out. OK?'

'OK!' I say. 'Right, Nadine?'

I have to nudge her twice before she nods.

But it turns out it isn't going to be a girls' night out at all.

'You can all bring a boy,' Stacy announces. 'My boyfriend Paul is coming. This is going to be a *proper* party.'

'I like *im*proper parties,' says Magda.

'I can't come then,' says Nadine. 'I haven't got a boy. Not any more.'

'Oh, don't go all droopy again, babes, I can't bear it,' says Magda. 'Of course you're coming.'

'Yeah, with me. I haven't got a boy to bring

either, have I?' I say. 'Seeing as my Dan is stuck up in Manchester.'

'I can always ask Greg to bring along two of his mates,' says Magda.

'No way! Not again!' I say very firmly indeed.

It turns out *Greg* won't agree to go to Stacy's party. Magda can't believe it.

'The *nerve* of it! He says he won't go to a stupid Year Nine baby birthday party because his mates would give him stick about it if they found out – after he made *me* go to that night of Ultimate Embarrassment at that nerdy Adam's place! I told him where to get off. Or words to that effect.' Magda grins. 'So now I haven't got a boy either, Nadine. We're a right pathetic trio. One totally absent boyfriend, and two exes.'

'Well, we'll go to Stacy's party just the three of us, like we planned originally. Let's make it a real girls' night out,' I say. 'You two come back to my place and sleep over afterwards, yeah?'

Magda agrees enthusiastically. Nadine doesn't look as if she agrees at all, but she can't summon up the energy to argue.

'I am seriously worried about Nadine,' Magda whispers to me in class. 'Ellie . . . how far did that Liam get with her?'

'I'm not sure. I know he made her do all sorts of stuff, but I'm not sure about actual sex.'

'You don't think . . .? She couldn't be pregnant, could she?'

'Oh, Magda!'

'She looks so pale.'

'Well, she's always pale.'

'Yes, but now she looks like *death*. And she's so droopy.'

'That's because she's missing Liam.'

'How *can* she now she knows the truth about that creep?'

'Maybe she's missing him even so.'

'*What?* Look, I don't get all this moping-around lark. I've just given up Greg and yet I'm not an old droopy-drawers.'

'Yes, but you were never really that gone on Greg, were you?'

'How do you know Greg wasn't the love of my life, the passion of my girlhood, the flame of my bosom, the fire of my loins—?' We are both shrieking with laughter by this time.

Nadine stares over at us but she doesn't even ask what we're laughing at. I look at her tense white face and the dark circles under her eyes. I start to get scared. Could Magda really be right? What if Liam has got Nadine pregnant, just like that other girl?

I know there isn't any point asking her outright, not at school. I'll have to talk to her privately, without Magda.

So after tea this evening I tell Anna I need to borrow a textbook for homework off Nadine. Anna's in a bit of a flap herself because Dad's late home again.

'He'll be in a meeting. Or helping some student with a project,' I say. 'Don't worry, Anna. I'm sure he's not . . . He'll be in any minute, you'll see.'

I feel mean leaving her but I have to go round to Nadine's. Nadine's mum asks me how I am and her dad calls me Curlynob as always, but there's something guarded about their welcome.

Natasha is her usual prancy poisonous self: 'Hi, Ellie! Look, do you like my new knickers? They've got frills, see?'

I can't help seeing as she's got her dress hoiked up to the waist. Why are all little kids such exhibitionists? If we carried on like that we'd get locked up – and yet *we're* the ones who're meant to be sex mad.

'Natasha, darling!' says her mum fondly.

'Where's your brother Eggs then, Ellie? Why didn't you bring him round to play with me? I like Eggs,' Natasha gushes, making her eyebrows waggle.

'You little saucepot,' says her dad, pretending to smack her frilly bottom.

Nadine says nothing at all through all this. She stays hunched on the sofa, barely looking at me.

'Nadine! Aren't you going to offer Ellie a drink of Coke or a juice or anything?' her mum hisses.

'It's OK, thanks. I've only just had my tea. I've really just popped over to borrow that History book for homework, Nadine,' I say awkwardly.

Nadine stares at me, as we don't even have History homework this week.

'Let's go up to your bedroom,' I say.

Nadine gets to her feet like it's a huge great effort.

'For Heaven's sake, buck yourself up, Nadine,' says her mum. Then she looks at me. 'I'm sorry, Ellie, but I'm really going to have to stop Nadine going out with you and Magda so much. I think you girls must stay awake half the night when you're sleeping over at each other's houses. Nadine's been like a limp rag just recently and it's really not good enough. Just look at the state of her!'

'Yes, I know, I'm sorry,' I mumble.

When we're out in the hall Nadine raises her eyebrows apologetically for using me as an alibi. I follow her upstairs. The midnight tone of her black walls and gentle spiral of her hanging crystals make her room a soothing bolthole from the aggressive rose wallpaper and pink Axminster on the landing.

Nadine flops down on her bed. I sit beside her, fingering her black quilt. She's sewn it with silver stars.

'Nadine?' I delicately trace the star shapes with my finger, trying to get up the courage to come out with it.

'What?'

'Naddie, look, I wanted to see you, just you and me. To ask . . . to ask how you are.'

'You can see how I am,' says Nadine, turning on her side.

'Well. I know you're feeling pretty fed up.'

'That's the understatement of the century.'

'I'm sorry. I'm making a muck of this. It's just – oh, Nadine, I can't stand to see you like this. We thought, Magda and me, that maybe . . . maybe . . ?'

'Maybe what? I wish you and Magda would quit discussing me. Aren't you both happy now?' Nadine says bitterly. 'You can both say I told you so because you've been right all along about Liam and I've made an utter fool of myself.'

'Oh, Nad, we don't think that. It's just you said you did all this stuff with Liam and I couldn't help wondering – well, if you went the whole way with him and if you could possibly . . .' I lower my head so I'm whispering right into her ear. '. . . possibly be pregnant.'

Nadine lies still for a moment. I hold my breath. Then she looks up. Her eyelashes are spiky with tears. 'No,' she says. 'No, I didn't. And no, I'm not. I wanted to, just to show Liam how much I love him, but whenever he tried to I was suddenly too scared and I went so tense we couldn't. So he said I was frigid.'

'Oh, for God's sake! *Nadine!* That's the oldest and dirtiest trick in the book.'

'I know. But I just wanted to please him. So on Saturday he gave me this stuff to relax me. We were going to go on to his mate's place afterwards, where we could have a proper bed, because Liam thought it was maybe doing it out in the open that was bugging me. But then you and Magda came over. And then I heard those girls . . .'

'Well, I know it must be awful for you, but at least you know what he's really like now.'

'But – but I got to thinking – I mean, what if those girls were talking about some other Liam?'

'You have to be joking. They saw him. *Your* one.'

'Or maybe they were making it all up because they were jealous because they wanted him them-selves.'

129

'Nadine, you can't believe this crap!'

'Well, that's what I started telling myself. So I thought I ought to see Liam just to find out.'

'No!'

'And so yesterday after school I went looking for him, and when I found him with a whole crowd outside the video shop he wouldn't even speak to me properly. He just said he never wanted to see me again after walking out on him like that in Seventh Heaven. He said I was a tight bitch, so cold that going with me would be like bonking a bag of Bird's Eye frozen peas, and all his mates laughed, and this girl started hanging on his arm and cuddling up to him and sneering at me . . .'

'Oh, Naddie, Naddie!' I put my arms round her and held her tight.

'Don't tell Magda, will you?'

'I swear I won't.'

'I feel so stupid. And ashamed. He was so awful to me, and yet – yet I still feel I *love* him. Do you think I'm completely nuts, Ellie?'

'No, of course not. It's *him* who's the really vicious nutter.'

'I wish it wasn't all such a mess. If only I had someone who really loved me back. Someone romantic. Something like your Dan, writing to you all the time.'

I take a deep breath. 'Nadine. About Dan . . .'

Nadine looks up at me. 'What about him?'

I open my mouth. The words are there, buzzing in my brain. I just have to trigger my tongue into action. Say it, Ellie. SAY IT!

'I made him up.'

I say it so quickly it comes out as one weird word: *Imadimup*.

Nadine blinks, not quite getting it at first. Then – 'Ellie! You made him *up*?'

'Well, sort of. There was this boy on holiday, but he wasn't . . . and then there was this *gorgeous* guy, and he *did* talk to me once, but he's not called Dan, the other one is.'

'What are you *on* about?'

'I don't know. It's all a muddle. The thing is, my Dan isn't mine and he's not even called Dan. So if there's anyone who's completely nuts it's me, saying all this stupid stuff about a boyfriend when I've never ever had one, not a proper one, anyway.'

'I just can't get my head round this! I *did* wonder, just at first – but you were so *convincing*. Hey, have you told Magda?'

'No! I couldn't bear it if she knew. She'd have such a laugh at me. You won't tell her, will you, Nad?'

'I promise I won't. Oh, God, Ellie, we're a right pair, aren't we?'

'You're telling me.'

'We're a right pair.'

'You're telling me.'

'We're a . . .'

'You're telling . . .'

We're laughing so much we can hardly speak. It's an age-old routine we used to spout when we were about seven and it wasn't really funny then. But it feels so good to giggle like crazy. We both roll on the bed, helpless – and we're truly back to being Best Ever Friends.

Nadine's still dead depressed about Liam, of course, but she's not in quite such a zombie trance.

I tell Magda there are no worries on the pregnancy front.

'You're sure, Ellie?'

'Positive. They never actually did it.'

'Well, at least that's something. Though it still beats me how Nadine can have been *mad* enough to go with a guy like that.'

'Well, we all do crazy things sometimes, Magda,' I say uncomfortably. 'Let's stop going on about it, eh?'

Magda is happy enough to change the subject because she's found out that Stacy has this older brother Charles who's going to be keeping an eye on things at the party, and apparently he's really quite tasty looking, with blond hair.

'How old?' I ask.

'About eighteen, according to Amna. She's been to Stacy's house for tea.'

Stacy's got big brown eyes.

'Are his eyes brown by any chance?' I say, though I know it's a chance in a million. Well, there aren't a million people who live in our town. Ten thousand? But that's everybody. How many halfway good-looking boys of eighteen are there? The odds are whittling downwards. A thousand to one? Maybe even a hundred to one?

'I don't know about his eyes, Ellie. You'll be

asking me for his inside leg measurement next! Ask Amna. Ask Stacy.'

I'd feel a right fool asking Stacy about her brother's eyes. I decide I'll just have to wait and see for myself. Of course he might not even deign to come to this party. But it's getting quite famous now and all sorts of extra people are going. A whole crowd of Year Tens who go to Stacy's dance class are going to be there, and several of them are going out with Year Eleven boys.

Greg is waiting for Magda after school.

'What do *you* want?' she says, linking in with me and Nadine.

Greg scurries along behind us. 'About this old party on Friday night, Magda,' he puffs. 'Hey, wait a minute. I want to *talk* to you.'

'Well, I don't want to waste my breath on you, Greg, so why don't you just push off?' Magda sings over her shoulder.

'Don't be like that. Look, I've changed my mind. I'll go to the party with you, Magda. OK? That's what you wanted, isn't it?'

Magda sighs. She stops. 'That *was* what I wanted. God knows why. It's certainly *not* what I want now. I'm going to the party with my girlfriends. Right, girls?' Magda smiles at us. We smile back, and the three of us walk on, still linked.

There's a pause.

'Well, see if I care,' Greg yells. He's obviously trying hard to come up with something ultra-crushing. 'You girls. You're just a lot of *lezzies*.'

We burst out laughing.

'Poor Greg. He's history,' says Magda. 'I like the sound of this Charles. I just have a feeling. Maybe Stacy's party is going to be a key event in our lives, even though we started off thinking it the naffest non-event of the year. Maybe we'll all have a dream encounter there. Are you listening, Nadine? And maybe you'll meet your dream guy too, Ellie – or are you too involved with Dan to be interested?'

I hesitate. I don't dare look at Nadine. I mumble something about always being interested and then change the subject as quickly as I can.

But as the three of us get ready round at my place to go to Stacy's party on Friday evening I can't help hoping that Magda is right. Maybe Stacy's brother might *just* be my dream Dan. I haven't caught a glimpse of him since he said See you.

'*Please* let me see him tonight,' I say over and over again inside my head as I put on my new shirt and skirt and the killer shoes.

I think I look pretty cool, but when I see Magda I feel depressed. She's wearing a brand-new raunchy red number and she's got this new glossy red lipstick that makes her mouth incredible, a shiny scarlet Cupid's bow.

'Want to borrow my lipstick, Ellie?' she says.

I have a go but my lips are too big and my face too fat. I look like a little girl who's been at the strawberry jam. I sigh and rub it off and start again.

'What about you, Nadine? Want to add a bit of colour to your old chops?' says Magda.

'Colour!' says Nadine, shuddering. She's

powdered herself chalk-white and outlined her eyes with kohl. Her own lipstick is such a dark purple it looks black and she's done her nails to match. She looks pretty stunning in a black skirt and a black lacy top and black pointy boots.

'Nice to see you looking your own deathly vampire self again, Nadine,' I say.

I wonder if the dream Dan might go for Nadine's gothic glamour or Magda's sexy scarlet. It seems very very very unlikely that he'll plump for me instead. Plump being the operative word.

But when we get to Stacy's party her brother Charles doesn't go for any of us.

He's not my dream Dan. Well, I knew it would be *way* too much of a coincidence. He *is* pretty tasty though, in a sort of floppy-haired posey kind of way. Stacy is charging about in a flouncy fancy frock, shrieking and squeaking in batty birthday-girl mode, so it's left to big brother Charles to welcome us three into the party and show us where to leave our jackets and stuff.

'So glad you could come,' he says, smiling, looking at us with big blue eyes. (*Not* as distinctive as brown, but pretty devastating all the same.)

I go all girly and Nadine manages a smile and Magda is in Total Vamp mood, her red mouth wide open as if she's about to gobble him up. But then this other girl comes up to us, also smiling. She's taller, older, even glossier than Magda's lipstick. Charles puts his arm round her. She's his girlfriend.

'Oh, well, never mind. Let's hope there are plenty

of other spare guys,' says Magda, her eyes darting round the already crowded room.

'Honestly! I thought this was our big girls' night out,' I say to Nadine. 'Look at Magda, eyes on stalks, desperate to pull.'

'Oh, well. *I* don't want to meet up with anyone,' says Nadine. 'I don't want to go out with another boy for ages. If *ever*.'

Nadine looks much better but it's obviously going to take months before she's completely over Liam.

But at least she's been out with someone properly, even if he was a right pig. I feel so pathetic that the only boyfriend I've ever had is a pretend one.

It's not such a bad party. The music is OK and there's lots of fancy food and that red wine punch they always give you at teenage parties when they don't want you to get drunk.

We have a glassful each and then we have a dance and then a laugh with some of the girls in our class. I suppose it's a good night out, but I can't help feeling depressed when I see that even Stacy has a reasonably good-looking boyfriend and lots of the other girls are with their boys, and though there *are* a few spare boys none of them so much as glances in my direction.

They do quite a lot of glancing at Magda, of course. And Nadine gets her fair share of attention too. But there's no-one here for me. No-one interested in me. No-one at all.

'Ellie?' Stacy suddenly comes rushing over. 'Ellie, there's this boy, he says he knows you. He wants to come to the party. *Do* you know him?'

She points over to the door. I peer through the blurry lenses of my glasses, wondering if it could possibly somehow be my dream Dan.

It *is* Dan.

Not the dream one.

The *real* Dan . . .

# Nine Most **Embarrassing** Moments

1 Dan turning up at Stacy's party. **SURPRISE!**

2 Wetting myself up on the stage at primary school.

3 Going swimming in a bikini and the top coming unhooked.

4 Starting my period one night when I was staying over with Nadine, so that I got blood on the bedclothes.

5 Hearing what my voice really sounds like when Magda and I sang during a karaoke session.

6 Trying on clothes in a changing room full of beautiful girls who only weigh about six stone.

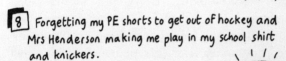

7 Getting a boil on my bum and having to show the doctor.

8 Forgetting my PE shorts to get out of hockey and Mrs Henderson making me play in my school shirt and knickers.

9 Making such a fool of myself whenever I meet Dreamboat Dan.

I stare at him. It *can't* be. It *is*.

But how? I told him not to come. So what the hell is he doing here? How did he know where I was?

He hasn't seen me yet. Oh no. He has. He's grinning. Waving. At me.

'What on earth?' says Magda.

'Who *is* he?' says Nadine.

Everyone's looking. Everyone's staring. Oh, God, he looks worse than ever. *His hair!* It's not even a skinhead cut any more. It's sticking straight up for three centimetres, like he's permanently plugged into a live wire. And he's wearing a totally nerdy huge white T-shirt with a silly message and his jeans are showing his ankles and he's wearing ancient Woollies trainers. They squeak as he crosses the polished floor. Squeak, squeak, squeak at every step. Nearer and nearer. And everyone's still staring, whispering, giggling.

'Who *is* this berk?' Magda says, giving me a nudge.

'I don't know,' I mutter madly.

'Hi, Ellie!' Dan shouts above the disco music.

'Well, he knows you!' says Nadine.

'Oh no,' I say, and I turn, desperate, wondering if I can make a run for it.

'Ellie? Hey, wait! It's me, Dan!'

'*Dan?*' says Magda.

'*Dan?*' says Nadine. 'How can it be Dan? You said you made him up.'

'Well this guy looks all too real,' says Magda, giggling. '*He's* your boyfriend, Ellie?'

'No!' I insist, but he's got to me now, trampling past everyone in his awful trainers, a silly grin still ear to ear.

'Hi, Ellie. Surprise!' he says, as he lunges forward.

I'm so terrified he's going to put his arms round me in front of everyone that I step back sharply and spear Stacy with one of my killer heels. She squeals.

Dan's arms are stretched out. They stay empty, clutching at air. The grin fades from his face. He swallows. He doesn't know what to say, what to do. And everyone's still staring. He's going red right to the tips of his ears. They stick out so with his new silly haircut. His glasses are starting to steam up. His eyes look agonized. Oh, poor Dan!

'Hello,' I say weakly. 'Meet my best friends, Magda and Nadine.'

They are still staring at him as if he's just arrived from Planet Nightmare.

'This is my friend Dan,' I say.

Magda and Nadine give him a little nod, both struck dumb.

'So . . . what are you *doing* here?' I say.

'I wanted to surprise you. I'd set it all up for this weekend, and even when you said your stepmum wouldn't stand for it I thought I could maybe just turn up and sort of sweet-talk her because I thought she was really nice on holiday and she *is* nice, she said she didn't mind a bit if I stay the weekend, even though it's going to be a bit of a squash with your friends staying too. And your dad gave me a lift here and so . . . here I am.'

'Yes. Well. You've certainly surprised me,' I say.

'Shocked, more like,' says Dan.

'I hope you realize you've just about crippled me, Ellie,' Stacy says, still rubbing her foot.

'I'm sorry.'

'So. Is this your boyfriend?' Stacy says, and her eyes are gleaming.

'No!' I say.

'Yes!' says Dan.

Oh, God. Stacy isn't half enjoying this. So is everyone else. No-one's even dancing now. They're stopped for the cabaret. The comic turn. Ellie and Dan.

'Well, is he or isn't he?' Stacy persists.

'Dan's a boy. And Dan's a friend. That's it,' I say. I look at Dan. 'Come and get a drink, eh?'

We walk over to the drinks table together. I go

tock-tock-tock in my killer shoes. Dan goes squeak-squeak-squeak in his tatty trainers.

'Everyone's staring at us,' Dan says.

'I know.'

'This maybe wasn't such a good idea,' says Dan.

'Well . . .'

'I bet you're wishing I hadn't come. I'm showing you up in front of all your cool mates,' says Dan.

'Don't be silly,' I say – but I don't sound very convincing.

'You'd better kiss me quick,' Dan says.

'*What?*'

'Then I'll unzip my frog-suit and step out this hip handsome prince,' says Dan, running his fingers through the lethal stubble of his hair. He tugs at it ruefully. 'The new hairstyle doesn't help, does it?'

'You said it,' I say. 'Well, what are you going to drink? There's not much selection actually. Coke. Or red wine punch.'

'My favourite tipple,' says Dan. 'I'll grab some sandwiches too, I'm starving. We drove straight down south, no stopping at any motorway caff. I was just so desperate to see you.'

'Oh, Dan.'

'True. I might be the last boy on earth you want as a boyfriend but I'd give anything for you to be my girlfriend. You look fantastic, Ellie.'

'Rubbish.'

'Look, I'm doing my best to be dead romantic. Like Romeo and Juliet. Only if I came to serenade you at night you'd come out on your balcony and tip a bucket of water all over me, right?'

'Probably.'

'I don't know. I'm at a bit of a loss as to how to impress you. Travelling long-distance to see you is a no-no. Sweet-talk turns sour. There's not much point trying to dazzle you with my brawny body.' He flexes his puny arm so that his baggy sleeve flaps.

'Did you say brawny – or scrawny?' I say.

'Cruel! OK OK, Arnie Schwarzenegger can relax for the moment. So – what about my ready wit?'

'Er . . . wit or twit?'

'Ouch. God, you've got a wicked tongue.' He raises his glass and drinks to me. Then shudders. 'What *is* this stuff? It tastes like undiluted Ribena.'

'I think it's the key ingredient.'

'Oh well. I'll have another slug or six to get up some Dutch courage before I dare ask you to dance.'

'Maybe it might be better to put that request on hold,' I say.

I'm proved right. Someone starts playing the naughty version of that old Alice song and everyone starts dancing again.

'Come on, let's give it a go,' says Dan.

*Major* mistake!

Dan has a whole new dance style all his own. Bouncy-bouncy in his squeaky-squeaky trainers. With head nodding, arms whirling. One arm catches someone on the shoulder, another on the chest.

'Sorry, sorry!' he shouts and moves away from them. Nearer me. He bounces again and lands straight on my killer shoes.

'Oh, God, I'm sorry, Ellie. Have I hurt you?'

'It's OK. I think I'm just crippled for life – but I'll

get used to it. So. Maybe we'd better sit this one out.'

We sit at the side, sipping our drinks, watching the others. Magda and Nadine are dancing together. They glance in our direction rather a lot.

'Your friends are very striking girls,' says Dan.

'I know.'

'Nowhere near as striking as you, though.'

'Come off it!'

'You're supposed to simper sweetly when I pay you compliments.'

'Simper – or whimper?'

'Look, you're the princess I released from the tower, right? You're meant to be in my thrall.'

'In your *what*?'

'Perhaps I'd better perform some other princely feat. Kill a dragon or two. Rescue you from a fate worse than death.'

'I don't think there's a clamouring horde queueing up to ravage me right now,' I say.

As I say it there's a sudden shout, raised voices, stupid laughter, swearing. People stop dancing, turn and stare. There's a whole crowd of guys over by the door. Strangers with real skinhead haircuts and real tattoos and real cans of Tennants in their hands.

Stacy's brother and her boyfriend and some of the other boys are arguing with them, trying to get them to go.

'Nah, we're staying, right? We've come to join the party, have a little drinkie, have a little dance,' says the biggest boy, tipping his can. He looks round, staggering a little, obviously already out of his head. His mates follow him, egging him on.

'So which bird shall I pick, eh? Where's the bleeding birthday girl?'

Stacy bobs behind her boyfriend, her face white.

The skinhead doesn't see her. There's only one girl not up on the dance floor. It's me.

'Hey, what are you sitting down for, darling? Little bit of a wallflower, are you? Come and dance with me,' he says.

I freeze.

'She's with me,' says Dan. His voice is as squeaky as his trainers.

'You what?' says the skinhead. 'Who the hell are you, creep? Now, come on, darling, dancie-dancie. He grabs me by the wrist and pulls me up. 'Woooaa! Up you get.'

'She doesn't want to dance with you,' says Dan.

'Yes she does, don't you, darling?' says the skinhead, hanging on to me. 'You come and have a little dance with me and my mates.'

'Are you deaf or something?' Dan says desperately.

'Dan! It's OK. Don't argue with him,' I hiss, because I'm so scared there might be a fight. They could have knives.

'There! She *wants* to dance, don't you, sweetheart?' he says, and he puts his arms round me, his horribly beery breath hot on my cheek. 'That's it – let's get cosy, eh?' he says, his hands on my bottom.

'Leave her alone!' Dan shouts, jumping up.

'Shut him up, eh, Sandy,' the skinhead says.

The heaviest of his mates lumbers over to Dan. There's a thud, a squeal, and then Dan is sprawling on the floor.

'Dan!'

'Shut up or you'll get it too,' says the skin. 'Did you pop him one, Sandy?'

'Help!' Dan screams, staggering up. His white T-shirt is stained dark red. 'He's stabbed me! I'm bleeding, look!'

Screams echo right round the room as Dan lurches forward and then sinks to his knees.

'What you done now, Sandy? Quick! Run for it!' the skinhead yells, shoving me aside and taking to his heels. The others follow him. No-one dares stop them.

'Dan!' I say, bending down, clutching him, trying to prop his head on my knees. 'For God's sake, someone dial 999, and get an ambulance!'

'It's OK,' says Dan, trying to sit up. 'I don't need an ambulance.'

'Are you *crazy*? You've been stabbed!'

'No I haven't,' says Dan, grinning. 'Those thugs have gone, haven't they? I thought they might run for it if they thought I was bleeding to death. I don't think that guy even had a knife. He just punched me in the stomach and I fell over.'

'But the blood!'

'Smell it,' says Dan, holding out his sopping T-shirt.

'Yuck!'

'It's the wine punch. I spilled it all over me.'

'Oh, you *idiot!*' But then I think about it. 'Though it *worked*. They did go.'

'That was real quick thinking, pal,' says Charles. 'It could have got really nasty with those louts.'

'Thank you so much, Dan. You've saved my birthday party from being an absolute disaster,' Stacy gushes.

'Yeah, well done, Dan.'

'Great thinking.'

'Really cool.'

'Hear that, Ellie? I'm *cool*,' says Dan.

'You're wet and sticky, I'll say that,' I say, shifting him off my lap. 'Get up then, I don't want wine all over my new skirt.'

'After I've seriously rescued you from a fate worse than death? I'm heartbroken. You were supposed to tell me you love me and beg me not to die,' says Dan, gingerly getting to his feet and rubbing his stomach.

'Dream on, matie,' I say, because I'm not going to say anything else in front of everyone.

I wait till later, when there's just him and me in a corner. Which is much *much* later, because everyone keeps clustering round, wanting to talk to Dan and congratulate him.

'Your head's going to be so swollen you're never going to squeeze out of the door,' I say.

'Just as well I've had my new haircut then,' says Dan.

'You are a nut,' I say, and I rub my hand over the bristles. 'But . . . you're a *brave* nut. You stuck up for me when they were really scary blokes.'

'They'll be pretty scared themselves, thinking they've murdered me,' says Dan.

'I hope they've really cleared off, and they're not hanging round outside waiting to get us,' I say. 'Lucky job my dad's coming to collect us in the car.'

'Hey, Ellie. Nadine and I were thinking,' says Magda, coming over. 'We'll go home to my place, right? You won't want us sleeping over with you if you've got Dan.'

'Ooh, am I sleeping with Ellie then?' says Dan, grinning.

'No you are not! I guess you'll be tucked up with my little brother Eggs, which serves you right. No, Magda, Nadine, *do* come back with me, *please*. It'll be fun.'

And weirdly, it *does* turn out to be fun. Dad arrives dead on twelve and when the four of us thank Stacy she's still being ever so gushingly grateful and she gives me a hug and then she gives Dan a hug too.

'Wow,' says Dan. 'This is definitely my night.'

'You certainly look as if you've been celebrating,' says Dad, taking in Dan's dramatically stained T-shirt.

'Dan's the hero of the hour,' says Magda.

'He fought all these skinheads to protect Ellie,' says Nadine.

'Well – not *exactly*,' I say.

'See, Ellie? All your friends appreciate me,' says Dan. 'Come on, Nadine and Magda, I'll squeeze in with you two in the back. Ellie can sit in the front with her dad. Then she'll maybe get all jealous.'

'You wish,' I say.

When we get back home Eggs wakes up even though we try to be quiet and he's ecstatic when he sees Dan. He runs to him and gives him a great hug and a slobbery kiss. When he realizes Dan will be sharing his bed he goes really bananas, leaping up and down until his pyjamas fall down round his ankles.

'Hey, no indecent exposure in front of the ladies,' says Dan, yanking his pyjamas into place and picking him up. 'Come on, little guy, let's go to bed.'

Anna has been great sorting out pillows and cushions and duvets and sleeping bags so we've all got somewhere to sleep.

'I'm sorry about Dan arriving out of the blue,' I whisper.

'It's OK. In fact he was tremendously sweet, arriving with a battered bouquet of flowers and a crushed box of chocs. He practically went down on his knees to me to beg to stay here. Almost as if he felt I was some utterly unreasonable ogress who had to be appeased.'

'I wonder what gave him that idea,' I say guiltily. 'Anyway, thanks Anna.'

'No problem. I like Dan, he's a sweet boy.'

And amazingly Magda and Nadine think he is too. We stay awake for ages, whispering and giggling. I have to tell the entire Dan story right from the beginning, explaining how I embellished the original Dan into this super dishy hunk based on the fair boy I bumped into on the way to school.

It's not really such a big deal telling them, though it maybe helps that we've all drunk several glasses of wine punch. It's dark too, so I can go as red as the wine and they can't see. Magda and Nadine say I'm seriously screwy, but don't act that surprised. Magda gets interested in the dream man.

'*He's* real, isn't he, Ellie? Is he really-really-really ultra-tasty? Maybe I'll walk your way before school to see if I can spot him.'

'Hands off, you! I saw him first!'

'But you've got the real Dan,' says Nadine. She adds wistfully. 'He's obviously nuts about you.'

'He's obviously nuts, full stop,' says Magda. 'What's up with his *hair*, Ellie?'

'I know, I know.'

'I thought old Greg was a bit dodgy, borderline Anorak Nerd – but Dan is Star Geek of all time. Though he *is* sweet, I must admit,' says Magda.

'You can have a good laugh with him,' I admit.

'Yeah, but what about a good snog?' says Magda.

I think of snogging Dan. Magda and Nadine are imagining it too. We all burst out laughing simultaneously, and have to dive under our duvets or we'll wake everyone up.

I don't surface until gone eleven in the morning. Magda and Nadine are still fast asleep. Magda's on her side, both arms wrapped round her pillow, her mouth in a sexy pucker. She is obviously snogging someone in her sleep. Nadine is lying on her tummy, her black hair a cloak across the pillow. I can't see her face at all but I can hear little sucky sounds. I think she's sucking her thumb.

I sit up and smile at my two friends, and then I pad off to the bathroom. I take my time getting washed and dressed because I want to look halfway decent. But when I get downstairs at last there's no sign of Dan.

Anna gives me a mug of coffee. 'Poor Dan. Eggs was wide awake at six o'clock and begging him to get up and play with him.'

'Where are they now? And Dad?'

'They've gone swimming. I don't know how Dan will manage for a costume. Your dad's old trunks will be far too big and yet Eggs's stuff is far too little. Maybe he'll just wear his underpants.'

'Please, Anna! You're conjuring up an all too graphic image,' I say, sipping coffee.

'So I take it you and Dan aren't going to be the romance of the century,' says Anna. 'And if your dad and I wanted to go out tonight, say, and leave you two here in the house, you're not likely to start up any X-rated bouncing on the beds?'

'I solemnly promise that Eggs will be the only one to bounce on the beds,' I say. 'So, you want Dan and me to babysit?'

'Your dad did wonder . . . There's this jazz concert up in town. And we could maybe have a meal out first. But it's a bit of a cheek asking you. You and Dan probably want to go out somewhere.'

'You go. You and Dad. Anna . . . How are things with you two?'

Anna crosses her fingers. Things certainly *seem* OK when she and Dad go off together at six. Anna is wearing her new skirt. Dad seems to appreciate it enormously. He gives her a little pat on the bum when he thinks I'm not watching. Yuck. Dad is a really sexist pig at times. He's offered to take her to an Italian restaurant so she can try out her newly acquired conversational skills on the waiters. This sounds a bit patronizing if you ask me. But Anna seems happy enough. Love is blind.

I am not in love. I see Dan all too clearly. Anna's washed his T-shirt for him so he's clean – but that's about the only positive thing I can say about his appearance. And the chlorine at the swimming pool has increased the scrubbing-brush tendency of his hair.

But so what? He's really quite good fun to hang around with. When he gets back from swimming and Magda and Nadine crawl out of bed at long last the four of us play a crazy game of Scrabble until Eggs tips up the board accidentally-on-purpose because he can't bear not to join in too.

We listen to my CDs for a while and Magda and Nadine are a bit scornful because Dan isn't very hip in his musical tastes. But then we get cracking on some of Dad's seventies stuff and Dan comes into his own. He does a brilliant Freddie Mercury imitation, prancing round the living room until we're all in stitches – and then we get going on ancient strutting Stones stuff, and then right back to Elvis. Dan teaches Eggs to flip a quiff of hair and wiggle his hips. Then the boys say it's our turn so I dig out my Beatles compilation. I sing 'With a Little Help from My Friends' (*with* a little help, etc.) and Nadine does her version of 'Lucy in the Sky with Diamonds' and Magda chooses 'All You Need is Love', and then we all sing 'Hey Jude' over and over and then 'Hello, Goodbye'.

Then Magda and Nadine say goodbye and Dan and I watch Wallace and Gromit videos with Eggs. Eggs badgers me until I make him his own plasticine Wallace and Gromit. Dan tries to make stuff too but his things go all hunched and lumpy so he says they're aliens from outer space. So we all make plasticine aliens. I make my alien very thin with sticky-up short hair and big ears. Dan laughs and Eggs plays with it so enthusiastically that the alien's legs fall off.

'Imagine your legs falling off!' says Dan, and then he keels over onto the sofa, pretending his own have done just that. Eggs squeals and jumps on top of him.

'Come on, Ellie!' Eggs yells.

'Er . . . no, thanks!' I say.

Eggs is still bouncing about, full of beans, when Dad and Anna set off for their night out. Anna's left all sorts of stuff in the fridge for tea and Dad's given us a tenner in case we'd sooner go to a McDonald's.

We decide on the McDonald's. We've got no transport and it's a good half-hour's walk, but maybe it'll help tire Eggs out at long last.

I get just a tiny bit tense wondering if there'll be anyone I know at McDonald's but it's still early and it's mostly families. Dan pretends we're a family too, Ma and Pa and Little Egbert, which makes Eggs chuckle. I hadn't realized you could play daft pretend games with boys. He's really great at it too. Nadine used to be good at imaginary games but she won't do it so much now we're older, and Magda's never gone in for that sort of thing anyway.

I see someone I do know on the way home. Well,

I don't *know* him. Though I've thought about him so much I feel as if I've known him all my life. I stare at him and it's as if the real and the pretend are all mixed up for a moment. Then they separate out, and I'm with the real Dan, and this is the dream Dan, though he's certainly not called Dan and it's even more unlikely that he ever dreams about me.

He's with someone. Not a girl. Another boy, almost as good looking, but dark, with blue eyes. Dream Dan's in black, the dark boy's in white. They look great together. And then I realize something else. They *are* together.

They're chatting and laughing, looking at each other – but just as they're going past the dream Dan sees me. 'Hi there!' he says.

'Hi,' I say, smiling wistfully.

The real Dan stares. 'Do you know him?' he says, when we're past.

'Yeah. Well. Sort of.'

'He's ever so good looking,' says Dan, and *he* sounds wistful now. He peers round at them. 'Is that his boyfriend?'

'It looks like it,' I say, sighing.

'Are you Ellie's boyfriend?' Eggs asks Dan.

'Definitely,' says Dan.

'Not even possibly,' I insist.

Dan *isn't* my boyfriend. OK OK, he's fun. And I have a good time with him. And I can say all sorts of stuff to him. And though he's a hopeless nerd he's also brave. And quick-witted. And imaginative. And it doesn't really matter one hundred per cent if he looks stupid. Anyway, I'm hardly some Pamela

Anderson type pin-up. He's not cool. But maybe the *truly* cool guy doesn't care if he's cool or not. But he's still not my boyfriend because I could never get *romantic* about Dan. Not in a Romeo and Juliet kind of way. I'm not too fond, like Juliet. No true-love passion.

Although . . .

We play Ma and Pa as we bath Eggs and put him to bed (which is a struggle, and takes hours). Then we settle down in front of the telly with Coke and crisps. We chat and crunch companionably. We laugh at something daft on the video and Dan rolls one way on the sofa and I roll the other way, towards him. And guess what? We kiss. My first real kiss. And it's not at all the way I imagined it. I didn't crack up laughing. I like it. Even though it's only Dan.

Maybe *because* it's Dan . . .

# Nine Romantic Couples

1. Romeo and Juliet.

2. John Lennon and Yoko Ono.

3. Queen Victoria and Prince Albert.

4. Kermit and Miss Piggy.

5. Julian Clary and Fanny the Wonder Dog.

6. Jane Eyre and Mr Rochester.

7. Elizabeth Bennett and Mr Darcy.

8. Morticia and Gomez Addams.

9. Ellie and Dan ???

# girls under Pressure

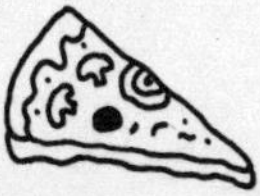

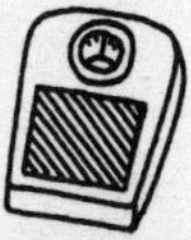

For Theano Petrou

# Chapter One

It's all my idea.

'Let's go Christmas shopping on Saturday,' I say to my two best friends, Magda and Nadine.

'Great,' says Magda, who lives to shop.

'Sure,' says Nadine, but she looks surprised. 'I thought you always made your own Christmas presents, Ellie.'

'Yes, well, I think I've grown out of that stage now,' I say hurriedly.

We've always had this silly tradition in my family. I'd think of a theme and then make everyone a present based on it. There was the year of the stripy hand-knitted scarves, the wobbly vases the year I joined the pottery class, the cross-stitched canvas purses . . . I made them for everyone, friends as well as family, and because people were polite I thought they really *liked* my loopy home-made junk.

I've known Nadine since we were both five so she's endured years of fraying dresses for her Barbie dolls and lumpy little felt mice. When we started secondary school I made Nadine a black and silver friendship bracelet. I made one for Magda in pink and purple. They seemed to like them. They both wore them for a while anyway.

Last Christmas I made special boxes for all the family, studded with beads and shells. I used liquorice allsorts for Eggs's box – but he tried to lick them through the glaze and hurt his tongue. Typical. Dad and Anna act like he's an infant prodigy but *I* think he's got the brains of a flea. I pondered long and hard over boxes for Magda and Nadine. In the end I made Nadine a silver box with a painted silver shell design. I did an identical one in gold for Magda. She opened hers as if she was expecting something inside – and then she asked if I'd be making her a gold necklace to go in it next year. She was joking – I *think*. I suddenly felt about Eggs's age.

'We'll go round the Flowerfields Shopping Centre,' I say firmly. 'We'll buy all the presents for our families, and then we'll split up for a bit and buy each other stuff.'

'And then we'll go to the Soda Fountain and have a milkshake,' says Magda, getting more enthusiastic by the minute.

The Soda Fountain recently opened up on the Flowerfields basement floor. It's like those shiny ice cream parlour places you see in old American movies.

It's become the in place to hang out now – rumoured to be great for meeting boys. If there's one thing Magda likes better than shopping, it's boys. Lots of them.

Nadine sighs and raises her eyebrows at me. She's seriously off the opposite sex at the moment, ever since she got heavily involved with this creep Liam who was just using her. She doesn't want to go out with anyone else now. Magda wants to go out with a different boy every night. I'm not sure what I want. And it's not like I get that many offers anyway.

Well. There's this boy Dan I met on holiday. He's my *sort-of* boyfriend. I don't see him much because he lives in Manchester. And he's younger than me. And looks a bit weird. He is definitely not a dream-boat.

I shall have to get him a Christmas present though. Goodness knows what. I've had this sudden brilliant idea of buying Magda and Nadine underwear from Knickerbox. Red satin flowery knickers for Magda. Black lace for Nadine. And then I could get Dad a big pair of Marks and Sparks boxer shorts and Anna some pretty prim white panties. Eggs could have Mickey Mouse knickers. I've been warming to the universal knicker present. But I can't give Dan *underpants*! Though I know exactly what sort, a wacky pair with a silly message . . .

I decide I'll have a good look round on Saturday and see if I get any further inspiration. I go over to Nadine's house around ten. Her dad's outside, washing his car. He's the sort of guy who worships his car, spending hours and hours annointing it every weekend.

'Hello, Curlynob,' he calls.

I force a cheery grin and knock at the door. Nadine's mum answers, in an old jumper and leggings, with a J-cloth in her hand. She is obviously dressed for serious house-cleaning.

'Hello, dear. Nadine's in her bedroom,' she says, sniffing disapprovingly.

'Hello, Ellie. I'm helping Mummy,' says Natasha, waving a feather duster from the living room.

Natasha is still in her cutsie-pie pyjamas and fluffy slippers. She's dancing round to some silly cartoon music on the telly, flicking her feather duster as she goes.

'Isn't she a good girl?' says Nadine's mum proudly.

I try to manufacture another smile.

Natasha rushes at me.

'You look dirty, Ellie,' she says. She prances round me, poking her feathers right in my face. 'There! I'm wiping all the dust off.'

'Oh, *sweet!*' says her mum.

'Ouch! Natasha, that *hurts*,' I say, my smile now very sickly indeed.

Natasha is the only six year old in the world *worse* than my little brother Eggs. I sidle past and run up the stairs to Nadine's room. It is wonderfully black and bleak after the glaring patterns in the hall. Nadine is looking glamourously black and bleak herself, her long black hair hanging loose, her eyes heavily outlined with black kohl, her face powdered white as

167

chalk. She's wearing a black skimpy sweater, black jeans, black boots – and as I come into her room she pulls on her black velvet jacket.

'Hi. What are those weird red marks on your face, Ellie?'

'Your delightful sister has just been seriously assaulting me with her feather duster.'

'Oh, God. Sorry. Don't worry. She wants a new Barbie doll for Christmas. I'll customize one. How about Killer Barbie, with a special sharp little dagger that whips out of her dinky stiletto?'

'Remember all our Barbie doll games, Naddie? I liked it when we turned them all into witches best.'

'Oh yeah, you made them all those little black frocks and special hooked noses out of plasticine. Wicked.'

We both sigh nostalgically.

'I used to *love* playing with plasticine,' I say. 'I still like mucking around with Eggs's little set, though he's got all the colours mixed up.'

'OK, then. That's your Christmas present solved. Your very own pack of plasticine,' says Nadine. 'I don't know what I'm going to get Magda though. She was hinting like mad about this new Chanel nail varnish but I bet it costs a fortune.'

'I know. I'm a bit strapped for cash too, actually.'

'It's all right for Magda. Her mum and dad give her that socking great allowance. My dad gives me exactly the same as Natasha, for God's sake. In fact Natasha ends up with heaps more because they're forever buying her extra stuff. It's so lousy having a sucky little sister.'

'Just as bad with a boring little brother. That's why Magda's so lucky, because *she's* the spoilt baby of the family.'

Magda certainly shows stylish evidence of spoiling when we meet up with her at the Flowerfields Shopping Centre entrance. She's wearing a brand new bright red furry jacket that looks wonderful.

'Is that your Christmas present, Magda?' Nadine asks.

'Of course not! No, I had a little moan to Mum that although my leather jacket is ultra hip it isn't really *warm* – so she had a word with Dad and we went on a little shopping trip and *voilà*!' She twirls round in the jacket, turning up the collar and striking poses like a fashion model.

'It looks fantastic, Magda,' I say enviously. 'Hey, what about your leather jacket then? Don't you want it any more?'

I've been longing for a leather jacket like Magda's for *months*. I've tried dropping hints at home. Hints! I've made brazen pleas. To no avail. Dad and Anna won't listen. I have to put up with my boring boring boring old coat that doesn't do a thing for me. It makes me look dumpier than ever. I *know* it's too tight over my bum. I'd have sold my soul for Magda's soft supple stylish leather – but now her furry scarlet jacket is even *better*.

Nadine fiddles at Magda's neck to have a deck at the label.

'Wow! *Whistles*,' says Nadine.

She bought her black velvet at Camden Market. It's a bit shabby and stained now, but it still looks good on her. Anything looks good on Nadine because she's so tall and thin and striking.

'Come on then, you two. Shopping time,' I say.

'Do you really want plasticine, Ellie?' Nadine asks, linking arms.

I wish *I* was made out of plasticine. Then I'd roll myself out, long and very very thin. I'd stretch my stubby fingers into elegant manicured hands, I'd narrow my neck and my ankles, I'd scrape huge great chunks off my bottom, I'd pull off all my brown wiry hair and make myself a new long blond hairstyle . . .

'Ellie?' says Nadine. 'You're dreaming.'

Yes. Dream on, Ellie.

'I don't really know what I want,' I say. 'Let's look round for a bit.'

'Shall we go and see the teddy bears?' says Magda. 'I think they're really cute.'

At Christmas time the Flowerfields Centre updates its mechanical singing teddy bear display. They sprinkle fake snow over the flowers, dress the teddies in winter woollies, turn the biggest teddy into Tubby Christmas with a red robe and a cotton wool beard, add a few parcels and presents and a glittery tree and change the tapes inside the bears. *Bananas in Pyjamas* and *Teddy Bears' Picnic* get a rest. The bears let rip with *Jingle Bells*. They jingle those bells over and over and over again.

'I had to stand in front of those bloody bears for

over half an hour last time I was here with Eggs,' I say. 'I can't take any more torture, Magda.'

'At least Eggs doesn't dance to the music,' says Nadine. 'Natasha waits till she's got a good audience and then points her toes and flits about. It's the most utterly emetic sight ever.'

'You're a couple of sour old bats. I want to see the teddies,' says Magda. She puts her chin down and pouts. 'Me want to see the *teddies*!'

'You *look* like a bloody teddy in your new jacket, Magda,' I say. 'Watch out the Flowerfields people don't plonk you down beside Tubby Christmas and make you sing *Rudolph the Red-nosed Reindeer*.'

But we let Magda hover around the Bear Pit for a couple of verses just to show willing. Nadine starts yawning and wanders off.

'Hey, what's going on? Up on the top floor?'

She's looking up past the fountains and bubble lifts and the giant Christmas tree to the top-floor balcony. I peer short-sightedly behind my glasses. There are crowds of people up there in a long queue.

'They'll be waiting to see Father Christmas – the real one.'

'You believe in Father Christmas, Ellie? How sweet,' says Magda, tapping her foot and clicking her fingers to *Jingle Bells*.

'The guy dressed up as opposed to the singing teddy,' I say.

'They're a bit old for Father Christmas, aren't they?' says Magda. 'They're girls our age. Lots and lots of them.'

A light keeps flashing up there, and an excited buzz circles the atrium.

'Is it television?' says Nadine.

'Wow, I hope so,' says Magda, adjusting her furry jacket and fluffing her hair. 'Come on, let's go and see for ourselves.'

There are too many people waiting for the bubble lifts so we go on the giant escalator. As we get nearer the top I start to focus. There're hundreds of teenage girls milling about up there, and big banners everywhere with the *Spicy* logo.

'*Spicy*, the magazine,' says Magda. 'Are they doing a special promotion? I hope they're giving out free goodies. Come on, you two, let's get in the queue quick.'

She dashes up the last stretch of the escalator, her patent boots shining.

'Come on, Ellie,' says Nadine, starting to run too.

'I think *Spicy* sucks,' I say. 'I don't really want any of their freebies.'

'Then you can use them for Christmas presents, right?' says Nadine.

So the three of us join the queue. It's so jam-packed and jostling that we have to hang on hard to each other. It's horribly hot at the top of the building. Magda unbuttons her jacket and fans her face. Nadine's ghostly pallor pinkens.

'Maybe this isn't such a great idea,' I say.

I'm squashed up so close to the girl in front of me that her long silky hair veils my face. Everyone's so much taller than me. I try craning my neck but the nearer we get to the front the harder it is to see what's going on. Lights keep on flashing and every now and then there's a squeal, but they're playing such loud rock music it's hard to hear what anyone's saying.

'Magda?' I tug her furry sleeve, but she's bouncing away to the music and doesn't respond.

'Nadine?' She's tall enough to see – and she's staring, transfixed.

'*What's happening*?' I yell at her.

She shouts something about a competition.

'Do we have to go in for it?' I say, sighing.

I don't think I'll be any good at a *Spicy* competition. I don't know much about music. I don't even bother reading *NME*. Nadine will do much better than me. Or maybe it's a fashion competition. I still haven't got a clue. Magda talks designer labels like they're all personal friends of hers but I don't even know how to pronounce the Italian ones, and I can never work out what all those initials stand for.

'Let's go and shop,' I beg, but there's a little surge forward, and suddenly Magda shoves hard, tugging us along after her.

We're almost at the front. I blink in the bright lights. There are huge *Spicy* posters and lots of promotion girls in pink T-shirts rushing round taking everyone's names and addresses. Each girl goes up in turn to a backdrop and stands there looking coy while a photographer clicks his camera.

There's a very pretty girl having her photo taken now: long hair, huge eyes, skinny little figure. She poses with one thumb hooked casually in her jeans.

She pouts her lips just like a real model.

The next girl's really stunning too. I look round. They all are. And then at long last the penny drops.

This is a *modelling* competition!

'Oh my God!' I gasp.

Magda darts forward and claims her turn. She takes off her jacket and slings it over one shoulder, her other hand fluffing up her bright blond hair. She smiles, her lipstick glossy, her teeth white.

She looks good. She may be too small, but she looks really cute, really sexy.

'Wow, get Magda,' I say to Nadine. 'Come on, let's get *out* of here.'

But Nadine is still staring. I pull her. She doesn't budge.

'Nadine, please! They'll think *we're* going in for this model competition crap,' I say.

'Well. We might as well have a go, eh?' says Nadine.

'What?'

'It'll be a laugh,' says Nadine, and she rushes forward to give her name to a girl in pink.

I watch Nadine stand in front of the camera. It's suddenly like I'm watching a stranger. I've always known Magda is seriously sexy and attractive. She looked pretty stunning at eleven that first day I sat next to her at secondary school. But I've known Nadine most of my life. She's more like my sister than my friend. I've never really *looked* at her.

I look at her now. She stands awkwardly, not smiling, with none of Magda's confidence. She's not really *pretty*. But I can see the girls in pink are taking a real interest in her, and the photographer asks her to turn while he takes several photos.

Her long hair looks so black and glossy, her skin so eerily pale. She's so tall, with her slender neck and beautiful hands and long long legs. And she's so thin. Model-girl thin.

'You're next. Name?' says a pink T-shirt, shoving a clipboard in my face.

'What? No! Not me,' I stammer, and I turn and try to elbow my way back through the huge queue.

'Watch it!'

'Hey, stop shoving.'

'What's her problem, eh?'

'Surely *she* doesn't think she could make it as a model? She's far too fat!'

Too fat, too fat, too fat.

Too F-A-T!

# Chapter Two

I run to get out of the Centre. I want to run right out of myself. I'm surrounded by all these perfect pretty posing girls. I'm waddling way down at their slender waist-level, the dumpy fat freak.

'Ellie! Hang on! Where are you going?'

'Wait for us!'

Magda and Nadine are chasing after me. I can't escape. I've got tears in my eyes. Oh God. I blink and blink.

'Ellie, what's up?' Magda says, catching hold of me.

'Are you *crying*?' Nadine says, putting her arm round me.

'Of course not. I just needed some air. It was so hot crammed together like that. I felt faint. Sick. I still do.'

Magda backs away a little, getting her new furry jacket out of vomit-range.

'Let's go to the Ladies room,' says Nadine. 'We'll get you a drink of water.'

'You haven't gone white,' says Magda. 'In fact, exactly the opposite. And what a shame you missed your turn to be photographed.'

'We can always go back and queue up again,' says Nadine.

'No thanks!' I say. 'I didn't *want* a turn. I didn't have any idea it was for a crappy competition. I mean, who wants to be a model?' My voice cracks. I don't think I'm convincing either of them.

'Oh yes, it would be such an ordeal!' says Magda. 'Think of all the money, the fame, the travel, the super clothes . . . *dreadful*! God, Ellie, don't be so stupid.'

'Lay off her, Magda, she's not feeling well,' says Nadine. 'Anyway, it's not like we've got any chance. There were heaps and heaps of really gorgeous-looking girls having a go.'

'Yeah, I reckon half of them were semi-professional anyway, which isn't fair,' says Magda.

They natter on about it endlessly. I listen hard when I go in the loo. Are they whispering about me? Are they raising their eyebrows and shaking their heads over poor plain plump Ellie? My eyes smart. Tears spurt down my cheeks and I have to take off my glasses and dab my face dry with loo-roll. I don't want to come out and face them. I don't want to face anyone ever again.

I could be Ellie the reclusive loo-squatter. I could set up home in this tiny cubicle. It could be quite cosy if I had a sleeping-bag and my sketch pad and a pile of books. In medieval times troubled young girls locked themselves away in tiny cells in churches and no-one thought it strange at all. Nowadays there might be an initial flurry of media interest: THE LASS LOCKED IN THE LADIES . . . SCHOOL-GIRL ELLIE STAYS SITTING ON THE LOO FOR THIRD DAY RUNNING! But eventually people would take it for granted that the end cubicle on the right in the Flowerfields Shopping Centre Ladies room is permanently engaged.

'Ellie, are you all right?'

'What are you *doing* in there?'

I have to come out. I try to chat as if I'm perfectly OK. I traipse all round the shopping centre looking for Christmas presents. It's no use. I can't make up my mind about anything. I could buy Magda the red knickers and Nadine the black, tiny wisps of under-wear, size small. They wouldn't fit me. I am not medium. Soon I won't even be large. I shall be outsize. Ellie the Elephant size.

I keep catching glimpses of myself in windows and mirrors. I seem to be getting squatter by the second. Magda drags us into *Stuck on You*, this new ultra-hip clothes shop that's just opened at the Flowerfields Shopping Centre. It's agony. I'm surrounded by skimpy little garments, skirts that would barely fit round one of my thighs, halter tops I'd have to wear as bangles. The assistants are staring at us. There's a six-stone girl dressed in black with short white hair and rings in her nose and navel, and a slender black guy with a diamond earstud in a tight white T-shirt to show off his toned body.

'Let's go,' I beg.

But Magda is eyeing up the boy and wants to try stuff on. Nadine is gazing enviously at the clothes and is happy to hang around too. So I have to wait for them both, feeling more and more like a guinea pig in a ferret's cage.

'Don't you want to try anything on too?' the white-haired girl asks.

That's what she says, but she's smirking as she says it. It's as if she's underlining the fact that nothing in the shop would fit me anyway.

'Hey, Nadine, Magda,' I hiss through the changing-room curtain. 'I'm going home, OK?'

'What? Oh, Ellie, don't go all moody,' says Magda. 'We'll only be a minute. Can you ask that guy if he's got these jeans in another size?'

'You ask him. I really have to go.'

'Are you feeling sick again, Ellie?' asks Nadine.

'Yes. I want to go home.'

'Well, wait, and we'll *take* you home,' says Nadine.

'I can't wait,' I say, and I make a run for it.

They're still in their underwear so they can't come after me. I rush through the Flowerfields Centre. Up at the top the lights are still flashing and the queue is even bigger and all around me there are girls much taller than me, much prettier than me, much much much thinner than me.

I really do feel sick. It's no better when I'm out in the open air. The bus going home lurches so much I have to get off several stops early. I walk through the streets yawning with nausea. I catch sight of myself in a car window. Yawning-Hippo Girl.

Thank God there's no-one at home. Dad has taken Eggs swimming. Anna's gone up to London to have lunch with some old schoolfriend. I go straight upstairs to my room and throw myself on my bed. The springs groan under my great weight. I rip my glasses off and bury my head in the pillow, ready for a long howl. I've been fighting back tears for hours but now I can cry in peace they won't come. I just make silly snivelling noises that sound so stupid I shut up.

I roll over onto my back. I feel my body with my hands. They mountaineer up each peak and descend each valley. I pinch my waist viciously to see if I can grab a whole handful of fat but my clothes get in the way. I unbutton my sweater and pull it over my head. I struggle up off the bed. I remove everything else. I can see my reflection in the wardrobe mirror but it's just a pink blur. I put on my glasses.

It's like I'm looking at my own body for the first time. I look at my round face with its big baby cheeks and double chin, I look at my balloon breasts, I look at my flabby waist, I look at my saggy soft stomach, I look at my vast wobbly bum, I look at my massive thighs, I look at my round arms and blunt elbows, I look at my dimpled knees and thick ankles, I look at my plump padded feet.

I stand there, feeling like I've stepped into a science-fiction movie. An alien has invaded my body and blown it up out of all recognition.

I can't believe I'm so fat. I've always known I'm a bit chubby. Plump. Biggish. But not *fat*.

I whisper the word. I think of greasy swamps of chip fat stagnating in the pan. I look at my body and see the lard beneath the skin. I start clawing at myself, as if I'm trying to rip the flesh right off me.

The girl in the mirror now looks crazy as well as fat. I turn away quickly and pull my clothes back on. My jeans feel so tight I can barely do up the zip. My sweater strains obscenely over my breasts. I brush my hair to try to cover my great moon face. I keep having one more look at myself to see if I might have changed in the last two seconds. I look worse each time.

I've never exactly *liked* the way I look. I suppose it was different when I was a little kid. I can remember my mum brushing my wild curls into two big bunches and tying them with bright ribbons, scarlet one day, emerald green the next. 'You look so cute, Ellie,' she'd say, and I *felt* cute. Maybe I even *was* cute in my dungarees and stripy T-shirts and bright boots to match the ribbons. I was cuddly, that was all. I was definitely cute, with my happy hairstyle and big dark eyes and dimples.

But then my mum died. Everything changed. I changed too. I felt empty all the time so I couldn't stop eating: doughnuts and sticky buns and chocolate and toffees. The sourer I felt inside the more I had to stuff myself with sweets. So I got much fatter, and then Dad noticed I frowned whenever I read and I had to wear glasses and Anna my new stepmother tried to dress me in conventional little-girly outfits that made me look like a piglet in a party frock.

I knew this but somehow I still stayed *me* inside. I could still *act* cute. People still liked me at school. They thought me funny. They wanted to be my friend. Even at Anderson High School I still fitted in. I wasn't the most popular girl in the class, I wasn't the cleverest, I wasn't the most stylish or streetwise, I didn't come top in anything apart from Art. But I was still one of the OK Girls. I wasn't a swot, I wasn't a slag, I wasn't a baby, I wasn't covered in spots, I wasn't fat. Not *really* fat, like poor Alison Smith in our year, at least fifteen stone, waddling slowly up and down the corridors as if she were wading through water, her eyes little glints inside the huge padded cage of her head.

I give a little gasp. Another stare in the mirror. I know it's mad but I'm suddenly starting to wonder if I'm actually as fat as Alison. *Fatter??*

If I don't watch out I could become an Alison. I'm going on a diet. I'm going on a diet right this minute.

It's lunchtime. Magda and Nadine will be sitting in the ice cream parlour sharing a chicken club sandwich with crisps and little gherkins, and sipping huge frothy strawberry sodas.

My tummy rumbles.

'Shut up,' I say. I punch myself hard in my own stomach. 'You're not getting fed today, do you hear, you great big ugly gut?'

It hears but it doesn't understand. It gurgles and

complains and aches. I try not to pay it any attention. I get out my sketch pad and draw myself in elephantine guise and then I pin the picture above my bed.

Then I draw myself the way I really want to be. Well, I *want* to be five foot eight with long straight blonde hair and big blue eyes, only there's no way this could ever happen. No, I draw myself the way I *could* be if I only stuck to a proper diet. Still small. Still frizzy-haired. Still bespectacled. But thin.

I wonder how long it will take. I'd like to lose a couple of stones at *least*. I went on this diet once before. It was all Magda's idea. The aim was to lose a couple of pounds a week. It's not going to be quick enough. I can't stand being so fat. I want to change *now*. If only I could unzip myself from chin to crotch and step out of my old self, sparklingly slim.

I wonder if Magda will go on a diet with me again? She was useless last time, she only managed a couple of days. So I gave up too. But then Magda doesn't really need to lose much weight at all. A few pounds and she'd be perfect. And as for Nadine . . .

I think of her standing there at the *Spicy* magazine competition, effortlessly, elegantly skinny. I don't know what I think about it. I'm pleased because Nadine's my oldest friend. I'm envious because I'd love to be that thin. And I'm angry because it's so unfair. Nadine often eats more than me. I've seen her eat two Mars bars on the trot. OK, she often skips meals too, but it's not deliberate, she just forgets because she isn't always hungry.

Not like me. I am *ravenous*. I hear Dad and Eggs

come back from swimming. There's a lot of chatter down in the kitchen. And then this smell. It wafts under my bedroom door, over to my bed, up into each nostril. Oh my God, Dad's frying bacon, they're having bacon sandwiches. I *love* bacon sandwiches. Dad's not that great at cooking but he does wonderful bacon sandwiches, toasting the bread and spreading it with great puddles of golden butter and crisping the bacon until there are no slimy fatty bits . . .

'Hey, can I have a bacon sandwich?' my mouth shouts before I can stop it.

I hurtle downstairs. Dad looks surprised to see me.

'I thought you were out somewhere with Nadine and Magda?'

I don't have to conjure up some convincing explanation because Eggs starts talking non-stop.

'I dived in, Ellie, a real dive, well, the first time was a sort of fall, I didn't really mean to do it, but then Dad said go for it, Eggs, that wasn't a fall it was a dive, so I dived again, I dived lots, guess what, I can dive . . .'

'Big deal,' I say, breathing in the bacon smell.

I can scarcely wait. I want to snatch it direct from the frying pan.

'*You* can't dive, Ellie, not like me. *I* can dive. I'm a good diver, aren't I, Dad?'

'Sure, little Eggs, the best. Though Ellie can dive too.'

'No, she can't!' Eggs insists, outraged.

'Can can can,' I say childishly.

'You can't, because you don't ever go swimming,' says Eggs, with six-year-old logic.

'She used to be a cracking little swimmer once,' says Dad, surprisingly. 'Remember when we used to go, Ellie? Hey, why don't you come one Saturday with Eggs and me?'

'Yes, then I can show you how I can dive. I bet you *can't* dive, well, not the way I can. I want the first bacon sandwich, Dad! *Dad*! *I* want the first one!'

'Pipe down, Mr Bossy,' says Dad, and he hands the sandwich over to me.

It's not often I get put before Eggs. I smile at Dad, and then wonder if he's just feeling sorry for me. Maybe all that snivelling has left my eyes puffy. In my great big piggy face.

I look at my bacon sandwich sizzling in splendour on the blue willow pattern plate. I pick it up, and it's still so hot I can hardly hold it. I raise it to my lips. There's a little fold of bacon poking out of the toast, glistening with goodness.

No, not goodness. Badness. Fat. To make *me* fat. How many calories are there in a bacon sandwich? I don't know, but it must be heaps. If I eat pig I'll turn into a pig, a great big swollen-bellied porker. I imagine myself a vast sow wallowing in muck – and I put the sandwich back on the plate.

'Here, Eggs, you have it if it means so much to you.'

'*Really*?' says Eggs, astonished. He takes a big bite immediately in case I change my mind.

'Well, you have this one, Ellie,' says Dad.

'I'm not really hungry, actually,' I say. 'In fact I feel a bit sick. Maybe it's the smell of the bacon. I think I'll go up to my room.'

'Ellie? I *thought* you looked a bit odd. I hope you haven't got some dreaded bug,' says Dad.

I go upstairs, my tummy feeling like a huge cavern, my mouth slavering like a waterfall with that glorious smell.

I want a bacon sandwich so *much*. Just *one* won't hurt.

No. Think pig. Big big big pig.

I draw an Ellie pig upstairs. I start on an entire menagerie of Outsize Ellie Animals. Ellie warty warthog. Ellie snaggle-tooth rhino. Ellie blubbery seal. Ellie humpback whale.

I hear the phone downstairs and then Dad calling. It's Nadine.

I don't want to talk to Nadine just now.

'Tell her I'm not feeling very well. I'll call her back.'

I hear Dad muttering. Then he calls again. 'She wants to come round to see you, OK?'

'*No!*'

I jump up, hurtle downstairs, and snatch the phone from Dad as he's about to put it down.

'Nadine?'

'Oh, Ellie. What *is* it? You just ran off!' There's a buzz behind her. She's obviously still out.

'Yeah. I'm sorry. I've just got this bug or something. I feel sick.'

'You're sure that's what it is? It's not that

we've done something to upset you?'

'No, of course not.'

'Magda thought it might be the modelling thing. She said you seemed fine before that.'

'Well, Magda's talking rubbish,' I snap. 'Let me speak to her.'

'No, she's gone off too,' says Nadine. 'We went to the Soda Fountain, right, and there were these boys and they were all going on somewhere else and they asked us too and I didn't want to go but Magda did.'

'I get the picture.'

'So can I come round to your place, Ellie? I know you don't feel very well but you can just loll on your bed and take it easy if you want.'

'Well,' I say, weakening.

'And I need your advice. You see this photographer guy, you know, the *Spicy* one, he told me he reckoned I was really in with a chance, and he said they'd be getting in touch with all the possibles quite soon and we'd have to go to this new photo session in a proper studio, and I don't know what clothes to wear, whether to go dead casual in jeans or whether they expect you to dress up in all sorts of fashion stuff. And then there's make-up. Do you think Magda would do it for me because she's much better at that sort of thing? And what about my hair? Do you think the ends need cutting, Ellie? *Ellie?* Are you still there?'

'Mmm. Nadine, I really do feel sick. Don't come round, eh? I'll phone you tomorrow. Bye.'

I can't stand to listen to Nadine another second. She's obviously getting in a twitch about nothing.

This photographer probably says that to all the girls. And there were so many pretty ones there today. Lots of them were heaps prettier than Nadine. She won't get chosen. She won't get to be a *Spicy* cover girl.

Oh, God, what's the matter with me? Nadine's my best friend. I *want* her to get chosen.

No, I don't.

I do. And I don't.

I can't stand feeling like this. Jade-green with jealousy.

I creep back to my room, feeling like I'm covered in shameful green slime. I don't feel like drawing any more. I try to find something to read. Mrs Madley, our English teacher, said we've all got to read *Jane Eyre* over the Christmas holidays. Everyone's outraged and says how can they possibly plough through such a huge long boring book. I moaned too, of course. Catch me letting on that I've already read it for fun. I liked the video of it so I thought I'd see what the book was like. Anna's got an old Penguin copy.

Maybe I'll get stuck into *Jane Eyre* again. Perhaps I'd better try to be as highbrow as possible seeing as I'm so hideous. And it's a good story. Jane's OK. At least she's not pretty.

I read and read and read. It's fine at first. I like all the little-girl-Jane bits because she's so fierce and then when she's sent away to school and starving all the time I identify totally. My tummy's rumbling so crazily I'd wolf down Jane's bowl of burnt porridge, no problem. Though porridge is ever so fattening, isn't it?

190

That's the trouble. Jane might be plain but she's this skinny little thing. People go on about it all the time. I start to get irritated. What's she got to grouch about if she's tiny? And Mr Rochester loves her. Why can't they both shut up about the first mad wife up in the attic? I skip forward to find the bit where mad Bertha growls and bites. My heart starts thumping as I read the description. She's not just hairy and purple. She's got bloated features. It says she's *corpulent*, as big as her husband. Rochester says is it any wonder that he wants Jane. He asks them to compare Jane's form with Bertha's *bulk*.

He doesn't want Bertha because she's fat. And mad. But maybe she only went mad because Rochester didn't fancy her any more when she started getting fat.

Maybe Dan won't fancy me.

Well, I don't fancy him. I mean, he's OK, he's funny, he's my friend, we sometimes fool around together – but he's just too odd and geeky and imma-ture to be a real *boyfriend*.

He's never seen things that way. He's been nuts on me ever since we met in the summer. He's travelled down from Manchester to stay with me and he writes heaps of letters and he phones every now and then just to say hello.

I suddenly run downstairs and start dialling.

'You OK now, Ellie?' Dad calls. He's sprawling on the sofa with a can of beer. Eggs is sitting on Dad's stomach, sipping Coke. They're both dipping into a big bowl of crisps, watching football on the telly.

I think of a salty golden crisp cracking inside my mouth. Water oozes over my tongue. I'm so *hungry*.

'You ready for something to eat yet?' Dad says, proffering the crisp bowl.

'No, thanks,' I say, turning my back.

One crisp would be fatal. Then there'd be another and another until I'd munched the lot *and* licked round the bowl for the crumbs.

The phone rings for ages at Dan's house. Then one of his even geekier brothers answers. He starts waffling some nonsense about Dan being otherwise engaged. At last Dan comes to the phone himself.

'Hi! It's me.'

'Hi,' says Dan.

There is a little silence. I thought he'd act more thrilled. I've never phoned him up before, it's always him phoning me.

'What was your brother wittering on about?'

'Oh, nothing. You know what he's like.' Dan sounds awkward. 'What are you phoning for, Ellie?'

'Just to say hello.'

'Right. Well. Hello.'

I wait. There's a long pause.

'Well, can't you say something else?' I say.

'You're not saying anything either.'

I don't usually have to. He's the one who burbles nineteen to the dozen. I can't normally get a word in edgeways. But the edges are wide open now.

'What have you been up to?' I say limply.

'Well, right now I'm watching the match on television.'

'What, football? Are Man U playing?'

'*Rugby.*'

'*What?* Rugby? You hate rugby. *Everyone* hates rugby.'

'I've got quite interested recently. It's a great game actually.'

There's a distant roar his end of the phone.

'Oh nuts. I've missed a try,' says Dan.

'Don't let me keep you then,' I say sharply, and I slam down the phone.

# Chapter Three

I can't sleep. I lie on my back and think f-o-o-d. If I breathe in deeply I can still smell the takeaway pizza they had for supper. Dad ate a good half of it. Eggs nibbled the topping and the crusty bits. Anna went without, saying she'd eaten a lot with her friend. And I said I still felt sick.

I feel sick now. Sick with hunger. My tummy is like a geyser, gurgling endlessly. I'm so hungry it hurts. I groan as I toss and turn. I feel like a baby bird with its beak gaping, cheeping non-stop. Think cuckoo. Great big blobby baby cuckoo, twice as big as the other birds, far fatter than the frantic step-parent feeding it. That's me, that's Anna.

I'm sick of her being so much skinnier than me. I'm sick of being Nadine and Magda's fat dumpy friend. I'm sick of being fat. I'm sick. *Think* sick to stop yourself eating. I've got to lose so much weight, I've got to get thin, I've got to, *I've got to* . . .

I'm out of bed, running barefoot down the stairs, into the kitchen, where's the pizza box? I thought there was a huge great slice left. Oh, God, did Anna dump it straight in the dustbin, no, here it is, oh, food, food, food!

The pizza is cold and congealed but I don't care. I bolt it down, barely stopping to chew, tearing off great chunks. I even eat the bits that Eggs has licked. I run my finger round the box. I get a carton of milk from the fridge and wash it all down so quickly that milk dribbles down my nightie but I'm still not satisfied. I feel hungrier than ever.

I go to the bread bin and make myself a jam sandwich, then another, then another, then a spoonful of jam by itself, more, more . . . Now, what else is there? Frosties! I eat them straight out of the packet, scooping them up in my hand, and there's sultanas too, I'm cramming so many into my mouth I nearly choke. I cough and a disgusting slurp of sultanas dribbles down my chin. I catch sight of myself in the shiny kettle and I can't believe what I look like. Total crazy woman. Oh, God, what am I doing? What have I eaten? I can *feel* the food going down into my stomach. It's starting to hurt. What am I going to do?

I run to the downstairs loo by the back door. I crouch over the toilet. I try to make myself sick. I heave and heave but I can't do it. I shove a finger in my mouth. It's horrible, oh, my stomach, two fingers,

197

I've got to, I've got to . . . oh . . . oooooh . . .

I am so sick. So horribly revoltingly disgustingly sick, *slowly* – again and again and again. I have to hang on to the edge of the toilet to stop myself falling. Tears stream down my face, sweat runs down my back. I pull the chain and then try to get up, the room spinning round me. My throat burns and my mouth stays sour no matter how many times I swill it with water.

'Ellie?' It's Anna in her blue pyjamas, her pageboy hair ruffled, so she only looks about my age. 'Oh you poor thing. Have you been very sick?'

'Mmm.'

'Come here, let's get you sorted out.' She puts the lid down on the loo and makes me sit on it. Then she runs the towel under the tap and gently mops my face and hair as if I were Eggs. I lean against her weakly and she puts her arm around me.

This is weird. Anna and I are acting like a regular mother and daughter. We never ever act like this. I made it quite plain right from the start when she came to live with us that I didn't want another mum. I *had* a mum, even if she was dead. For years I wouldn't let Anna near me. We didn't exactly *fight* – we were just like two strangers forced to live under the same roof. Just recently we've started to get a bit closer. We go shopping together or we watch a video or we flick through a glossy magazine but it's just like sisters. Big sister, little sister. Well. I'm bigger than Anna. Not taller. *Fatter.* It's so unfair. Why do I have to be fatter than everyone?

Tears are still running down my cheeks.

'Hey,' says Anna gently, wiping my eyes. 'Do you feel really terrible, Ellie?'

'Yes,' I say mournfully.

'Have you got a bad tummy-ache? Headache?' Anna puts her hand on my forehead. 'I wonder if you've got a temperature? Maybe I should call the doctor?'

'No! No, I'm OK. I was just sick, that's all. Probably just something I ate!'

'You're still ever so white. And you're shivering.' Anna leads me into the kitchen and gets her old denim jacket that's hanging on the back door. 'Here.' She wraps it round me and sits me down at the kitchen table. 'Do you want a drink of water?'

I sip it delicately.

'Your dad said you've been feeling lousy all day, not eating anything.' Anna sighs. 'I wish I could say the same for him. Look at the state of the kitchen! He must have had a secret midnight feast – and then he moans because his jeans won't do up!'

'Why does he still try to squeeze himself into those jeans anyway,' I say, feeling guilty that Dad's getting the blame.

'He just won't admit that he's too fat,' says Anna, sticking everything back in the food cupboard.

'I'm even fatter,' I say, the glass clinking against my teeth.

'What? Don't be silly,' says Anna.

'I *am*. And I didn't even realize. I mean, I knew it, but it didn't really bug me. But now . . .'

'Oh Ellie. You're *not* fat. You're just . . . rounded.

It suits you. It's the way you're supposed to be.'

'I don't want to be fat, I want to be thin. As thin as you.'

'*I'm* not thin,' says Anna, though she looks like a little pin person in her schoolboy pyjamas. 'I wore my old black leather trousers today because they're about the only sexy garment I've got nowadays and I was so desperate not to look dull and mumsy and suburban, but the zip's so tight now I could barely *breathe*. It was cutting into my stomach all through lunch. Which was *not* a success. Oh God, Ellie, this friend of mine, Sara, she looks incredible. She's got this fantastic new hairstyle, all blond highlights, and the *shoes* she was wearing, really high, and the way she walked in them! Every man in the restaurant was staring at her.'

'Yes, but you don't want to look like some blond bimbo,' I say.

'But she's *not* a bimbo, she's the top designer for this new fashion chain. They're even going to be bringing out her own label, Sara Star. She showed me the logo, two big Ss in shocking pink. Oh, Ellie, she's really made it big now. She kept politely asking me what I'm doing and I had to say I haven't even got a job at the moment.'

'You've got Eggs to look after.'

'Yes, but it's not like he's a baby.'

'And Dad.'

'OK, he *is* a baby,' says Anna, smiling at last. 'But even so . . . I just feel . . . Anyway, I'm going to try even harder to find some work, even if it's just part-time. And I'm going to do something with my stupid hair. *And* I'm going to go on a diet.'

'I'm going on a diet too,' I say.

'Oh, Ellie. Look, you're still a growing girl.'

'Exactly. Growing fatter and fatter.'

'Well, we'll see when you're better. I do hope you haven't got gastric flu. It sounded as if you were being so terribly sick.'

'I'm fine now. Really. I'm going back to bed.'

'Ellie? You're acting sort of funny.' Anna looks at me worriedly. 'You would tell me if . . . if there was anything really wrong, wouldn't you?'

'*Yes.*'

Well, no. I can't tell Anna my throat is raw and my stomach still heaving because I've eaten half the food in the cupboard and then practically clawed it out of my insides with my own hand. What sort of mad revolting loony would she take me for?

I go back to bed and pull the covers right over my head. I remember this game I played when I was little, after my mum died. I'd kid myself that when it was morning I'd wake up in a different parallel life and Mum would be sitting on the end of the bed smiling at me. It was years before I gave up on that game. But now I catch myself playing a new version. No Mum. No Ellie either. Not the old one. I'll wake up and I'll get out of bed and pull off my nightie and then I'll peel off all my extra pounds too and there I'll be, new little skinny Ellie.

The old huge fat Ellie sleeps late and slouches to the bathroom in the morning. I can smell faint eggy toasty smells. Oh, God. I hope they've all finished eating when I come down.

Dad is on his third coffee and delve-into-the biscuit-tin stage. Eggs is busy making some kind of collage with macaroni and what's left of the sultanas. I can't look at them without feeling sick.

'Toast, Ellie?' says Anna.

'No thanks. Just coffee. Black,' I say quickly.

'Look at my lovely picture, Ellie, *look*,' says Eggs.

'You *still* not well, chum? Anna said you were horribly sick in the night,' says Dad.

'I'm OK. I just don't fancy anything to eat yet.'

'Are you sure?'

'Mmm. Maybe I'll go back to bed in a bit, OK?' It'll be easier avoiding food upstairs. And if I can sleep I won't be feeling so starving hungry all the time.

'Well, we were planning on eating out at lunch-time and then maybe having a little jaunt somewhere,' says Dad.

'To see some pictures, Dad says,' says Eggs. 'Look at *my* picture, Ellie. See what it is?'

'Yes, macaroni and sultanas, very fetching,' I say. 'You lot go out. That's fine with me. I'll just flop around.'

'But I haven't got any food in for your lunch, Ellie,' says Anna. 'I missed out on the big Saturday shop because I was seeing Sara.'

'I'll cook myself some eggs or something. It's OK,' I say.

'It's a *lady*, Ellie, can't you see? The macaroni is all

202

her *curls*, and the sultanas are her eyes and her nose and her smiley mouth, see.'

'Well, she's got a dirty nose and very black teeth and she's having a seriously bad hair day,' I say.

'Don't be mean to him,' says Dad, giving me a little nudge. 'Come out with us, eh? You'll feel better for a bit of fresh air.'

'No, thanks.'

Nadine rings around twelve, pained that I haven't phoned her back. She wants to come round this afternoon and she's still burbling about her hair and her make-up and her clothes in case she gets selected as a *Spicy* cover girl.

'Nadine! Look, wait till they get in touch with you, right?' I'm not quite bitchy enough to add 'Maybe they won't' but I imply it.

'I want to be *prepared*, Ellie. *Please* can I come round?' Nadine lowers her voice. 'My gran and grandad are here and this Happy Families lark is getting way too heavy for me. They're all gathered round Natasha just *watching* her, as if she's a little television set or something, and my God, is she performing with her volume turned right up.'

'Oh, Nad,' I say, weakening. 'Look, I don't know what help *I* can be. I'm no expert when it comes to make-up and stuff. Why don't you go and see Magda?'

I expect Nadine to say that she and I are best friends from way back and that she wants to plan it all with me. Then I'll swallow the last sour jealousy pill and ask her over and fuss round her like a real friend. I'll try terribly hard not to mind that she's got serious model girl potential, and I'm just her fat freaky friend.

'Oh, I've tried Magda. She's so great with make-up. I thought she'd maybe trim my hair for me too. But she's going out with this guy she met at the Soda Fountain. Not the one she really fancied, this is his friend – but life's like that. Anyway, I can come over, Ellie, can't I? Straight after lunch?'

I take a deep breath.

'Sorry, Nadine. We're going out for lunch, and then on up to town somewhere,' I say. 'See you tomorrow at school. Bye.'

'You're coming,' Dad calls from the kitchen. 'Great.'

'I wish you wouldn't listen to my phone calls. They're *private*,' I say. 'And I'm not really coming. I just said that to get out of seeing Nadine.'

'Of course you're coming,' says Dad. 'And what's up with you and Nadine? I thought you two girls were practically joined at the hip? Have you broken friends?'

'Of course not. You make us sound like little kids,' I say haughtily.

'Just don't break friends with Magda too. She's a really cracking little girl,' says Dad, with a touch too much enthusiasm.

'Stop bugging Ellie,' says Anna sharply. 'And Magda's young enough to be your daughter.'

So I end up going out with Anna and Dad and Eggs to this teashop in Clapham. It's a great place, actually, with lovely deep blue and pink decor and Lloyd Loom cushioned chairs and round glass-topped tables, and all sorts of interesting people hang out there, students, actors, huge crowds of friends or romantic couples . . . but it's not the place to go with your *parents*. I feel a total idiot, convinced everyone is staring at this sad fat girl who has no social life of her own. And the menu is agony. I read my way through all the delicious choices twice over: bacon lettuce and tomato sandwich, smoked salmon and scrambled eggs, bagels, scones with jam and cream, cheesecake, banoffee pie, sticky toffee pudding . . .

'Just a black coffee, please.'

'Isn't there *anything* you fancy, Ellie?' Dad says worriedly. 'What about chocolate fudge cake? I thought that was your favourite?'

Oh, Dad, they're all my favourites. I could easily eat my way through the entire menu. I'm almost crying with hunger as I look at everyone's piled plates.

'She's still feeling a bit queasy,' says Anna. 'But you'll have to eat something, Ellie, or you'll pass out.'

I end up agreeing to a plate of scrambled eggs. Eggs aren't too fattening, are they? Though they come with two rounds of golden toast glistening with butter. I tell myself I'll just toy with a forkful of egg – but within five minutes my plate looks as if it's licked clean.

'There! Great, you've obviously got your appetite back,' Dad says happily. 'So how about a wicked cake too?'

'Yes, I want cake, Dad,' says Eggs, although he has only nibbled his prawn sandwich. He pulls out every prawn and puts them in a circle on his plate.

'Eat them *up*, Eggs,' says Anna.

'They don't want to be eaten! They want to have a swim round my plate, don't you, little pink prawnies?' says Eggs. He's playing up to his audience in sickening fashion.

'All those little prawns want to swim in your tummy, Eggs,' says Dad. 'Open your mouth and I'll make them dive in.'

'Oh please. He's not a *baby*,' I hiss.

I have to sit through this entire performance and then watch while Eggs is rewarded with a strawberry mountain cake. He eats the strawberries and leaves the mountain of cream after one or two token licks. I want to snatch it up and gobble it down. I have to clench my fist to stop my hand reaching out. I think of myself as a mountain with little strawberry blobs in appropriate places and manage to resist.

Anna sips her coffee without obvious envy. Dad wolfs down a whacking great slice of banana cake with no inhibition whatsoever. His shirt buttons are straining, his belly bulging over the top of his jeans. He doesn't seem to care. And it's so unfair, it's different for men – women *still* seem to fancy my fat old dad. The pretty waitress in her tiny skirt has a happy little chat with him as he pays the bill. She's so skinny. Her skimpy top only just reaches her waist and as she moves you can see her beautiful flat tummy. How does she work here surrounded by all this super food and not eat?

Oh God, I'm so hungry. The scrambled eggs and toast have made me even *hungrier*. And it gets worse when we park the car near Trafalgar Square and go in the National Gallery. I don't mind art galleries but they *always* make me starving hungry, especially after the first fifteen minutes when I'm starting to get bored.

I get bored very quickly today. Eggs is being ultra-exasperating, asking endless idiotic questions.

'Who is that funny little baby?'

'Why does that pretty lady in blue have that gold plate round her head?'

'I can see the donkey and the cow but why don't they have any pigs and chickens on their farm?'

All the people in the gallery smile at him. Dad explains, going into great long rigmaroles although Eggs isn't really listening. Anna pats him on the head and picks him up to show him special things.

I pretend I'm going round the gallery by myself. The paintings start to soothe me. I stand for ages in front of a serious pale woman in a sumptuous green velvet dress sitting on the floor engrossed in a book. I feel as if I'm being sucked right into the painting . . . but then I'm dragged off to another part of the gallery and Eggs starts his little act again.

He clasps his hands and pops his eyes at a painting called *The Origin of the Milky Way*.

'Ooooh! Look at that lady! Isn't she *rude*?' he pipes.

I sigh. Anna shushes. Dad tells Eggs that it isn't rude at all, not when it's a great painter illustrating an extraordinary myth.

'*I* think she's rude,' says Eggs. 'She is rude, isn't she, Ellie?'

I find the painting a bit embarrassing myself but I affect a lofty air.

'You're just too young to appreciate great art, Eggs,' I say.

'No, I'm not. I *like* the art. I just think it's rude. That lady's got wobbly bits just like *you*.'

I know he just means breasts, any shape or size. But the word wobbly still makes me want to burst into tears. I feel myself going hot. A bright pink wobbly blancmange.

'I'll meet you lot at the entrance in half an hour, right?' I say, and I shove off quickly by myself.

The word wobbly wiggles around my brain like a great worm. I try to absorb myself in the art now I'm on my own but it doesn't work. I find I'm just staring desperately at every painted woman to see how fat she is. It's hard to tell with all the virgins because their blue robes are voluminous.

I concentrate on the nudes. The thinnest is a languid pin-up Venus wearing a huge fancy hat, two strings of beads and nothing else. She poses suggestively, one arm up, one leg bent. Her beautiful long lean body makes me think of Nadine.

There's another rounder Venus kissing a very young Cupid while all sorts of strange creatures cavort in the background. She's disturbingly sexy, very aware of all her charms, not really *thin* but well-toned and taut, as if she worked out in the gym every day. She's the spitting image of Magda.

I look for myself. I don't get any further than Rubens. I look at double chins, padded arms, flabby thighs, domed stomachs, enormous dimpled bottoms. Three huge hefty women are being offered a golden apple. They look as if they eat an entire orchard of apples every day.

I am never going to eat again.

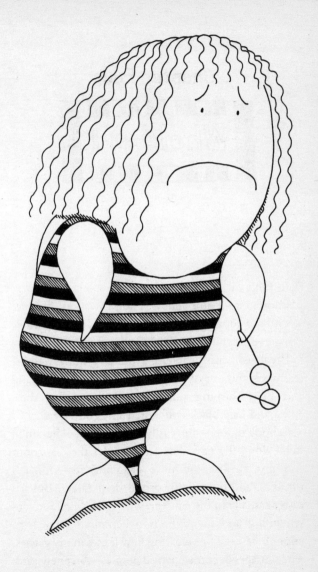

# Chapter Four

So I don't eat.

I don't bite. I don't chew. I don't swallow. Simple.

Only of course it's not simple at all. It's the hardest thing ever. I think of nothing else all day long.

Breakfast is no problem. I wake so hungry that I feel weak and queasy and the sight of Dad chomping and Eggs slurping puts me off food altogether. Anna and I sip black coffee in a smug sisterly way.

School dinners are easily solved too. The smell steals along the corridors and invades the classroom and just at first my nose twitches, my stomach rumbles, and my mouth drools desperately. But it's easier actually in the canteen where the smell is over-whelming and the sight is sickening if I try hard enough. It's as if I'm wearing new lenses in my glasses. The sausages become charred penises, obscenely pink where the skins are split. The pizza looks diseased, oozing bloody tomato and pus-yellow cheese. The baked potatoes steam like horse droppings. It's easy to back away.

It's far harder when Magda and Nadine offer me food. Magda presses a whole slice of her mother's home-made pecan pie on me at break and before I can contaminate it with my thoughts I have eaten it all, the sweet moistness sliding straight down my throat in seconds. It's so good I feel tears in my eyes. I've been near-starving for days and it's so wonderful easing that gnawing need inside me – and yet as soon as it's all gone and I'm left with sticky lips and crumbs on my fingers I'm horrified.

How many calories? 300? 400? Maybe 500? All that syrup, all that butter, all those wickedly fattening pecans.

I say I have to go to the cloakroom but Magda and Nadine come too, and I can't thrust my fingers down my throat and throw up because they'd hear me.

Nadine is forever nibbling at Kit Kats and Twixes. It's so unfair. *How* can she stay so skinny? And her white skin is flawless, she doesn't even get spots. She eats her chocolate bars absent-mindedly, snapping off a couple of pieces every so often and offering them to Magda and me.

'Nadine. I'm on a *diet*,' I say, brushing her hand away.

'Yeah, yeah, you and your diets, Ellie,' says Nadine.

So OK, in the past I've tried dieting, but never *seriously*. This time it's different. It has to be.

It's even harder when I get home. I'm so used to eating tea the minute I get in from school, bread and honey, oatcakes and cheese, bunches of grapes, hot chocolate, home-made shortbread – good wholesome wonderful food. No, *bad* food that bloats me into a great big wobbly blob. I can't eat it. I won't eat it.

Anna doesn't argue. She makes Eggs his own tea and we have ours: celery and carrot sticks and apple wedges. We snap and crunch briskly. Eggs wonders if he is missing out on anything. He demands a stick of celery too.

'It doesn't taste of anything,' he says, astonished. 'I don't like it.'

'We don't like it either.'

'Then you're silly to eat it,' says Eggs.

Dad thinks we're even sillier. He watches Anna and me cut our one slice of ham and quarter our one tomato and eat our way through endless lettuce leaves for supper.

'You're both nuts,' he says. 'What are you *doing*, going on this crazy diet? You're still matchstick thin, Anna – and I don't know what's got into *you*, Ellie. You've always been a girl who loves her food.'

'Meaning I've always been a fat pig so why don't I stay one?' I say, choking on my forkful of lettuce. It stays in my throat, rank moist vegetation. What am I doing trying to eat it? I spit it out into a paper hankie, shuddering.

'Yuck! Ellie spat! *I'm* not allowed to spit, am I, Mum?'

'Just be quiet, Eggs.'

'Don't do that, Ellie! I didn't *say* you were fat, for God's sake.'

'That's what you meant.'

'No, I didn't. You're *not* fat, you're . . .'

'Yes? What am I?'

'You're just . . . ordinary nice girl-size,' Dad says desperately.

'Nadine and Magda are ordinary nice girls but I'm much fatter than them, aren't I?'

'*I* don't know.'

'Of course you know! Magda's got a lovely figure. You certainly should know that, Dad, you can't keep your eyes off her when she calls round.'

'Ellie!' says Anna sharply.

'And Nadine is so thin and gorgeous she's going to be a model for *Spicy* magazine,' I shout, leaving the table.

I charge up to my room, crying. I stare at myself in my mirror, hoping I might look tragic with tears coursing down my face, but I just look blotchy. My nose is running. I have slimy green lettuce stuck to my teeth. And I'm still fat. Fat fat fat. I've hardly eaten for days and I've only lost four pounds. I stand on the scales stark naked every morning – and I strip off when I come home from school, *and* try again last thing at night. Four pounds sounds a lot when you look at two bags of sugar, but I don't know where it's come off *me*. My cheeks are still puffed out like a frog,

215

my body still bulges, my bum wobbles, my hips spread. I feel myself swelling up all over so that the mirror can barely contain me.

It turns out it's true about Nadine. She comes waltzing into school waving a letter.

'Ellie! Magda! You'll never ever guess what!'

I guess. We guess. The whole class guesses, circling Nadine in awe.

'Are you *really* going to be a model, Nadine?'

'Well, it's just the first heat, on the nineteenth of December up in London, but they say there were heaps of girls, *thousands*, who didn't make it through to this stage.'

'Thanks, Nadine! I know my place. Bottom of the heap,' says Magda. 'Here, maybe I left home before the post came. Maybe *I'm* through to the first heat too.'

'What's going on, girls?' says Mrs Henderson, coming into the classroom. 'You're all buzzing like a hive of bees.'

'Well, we're just the drones. Nadine's the Queen Bee,' I say.

It comes out a little too sharply. I smile at Nadine to show her I'm just joking. She's so out of her head with excitement she doesn't even notice. Oh, God, she looks so beautiful. Of course she'll end up the winner.

'A cover girl on *Spicy* magazine?' says Mrs Henderson, eyebrows raised.

'Isn't Nadine *lucky*?' the class chorus.

'I'm only in the first heat,' Nadine says modestly.

'I don't think I'll ever make it. I'll be so *nervous* on the nineteenth.'

'What's happening then?' says Mrs Henderson, her hands on her hips.

'That's when I have to go to this studio in London. We all have to wear these special clothes and pose.'

'Oh Nadine! You'll actually be *modelling*.'

'Modelling,' Mrs Henderson repeats, but she puts an entirely different spin on the word. She makes it sound as if it's the last thing in the world she'd want to do. I feel a shameful stab of relief. Then I look at Mrs Henderson properly. Fat chance *she'd* ever have of being a model. Fat being the operative word. Well, she's not *fat* fat, but she's stockily built, with big muscles, and her grey sweatsuit fits a little too snugly.

'When are you intending to go to this studio, Nadine? In the evening? You will make sure this is a properly supervised modelling session, won't you? Take your mother with you,' says Mrs Henderson.

'I'm not going with my mum!' says Nadine. 'But it's OK, Mrs Henderson, it's totally respectable. There'll be heaps of other girls there – and it's in the daytime.'

'The daytime,' says Mrs Henderson. She pauses. 'Then you'll be at school.'

'It's on *Saturday*, Mrs Henderson.'

'Ah! Just as well.'

'But you'd have let me have a day off school anyway, wouldn't you, Mrs Henderson?'

'Dream on, Nadine,' says Mrs Henderson briskly. 'I shall expect you to volunteer for extra PE lessons to keep you in beautifully toned condition.'

'Dream on, Mrs Henderson,' says Nadine, a little too cheekily.

Nadine ends up tidying the sports equipment cupboard in her lunch hour. Magda and I help her out. They eat crisps and swig Coke as we coil ropes and assemble hoops and herd netballs into neat piles. I sip mineral water, first one can, then another.

'Have you turned into a camel, Ellie?' says Magda.

'What do you mean?' I say defensively, looking down at my bulging body. 'Are you saying I look like I've got humps?'

'No! I'm saying you've got a *thirst* like a camel. That's your second can, isn't it?'

'So?'

'So sorry I asked,' says Magda, pulling a face at Nadine.

'You're drinking and drinking and yet you're not eating anything,' says Nadine, thrusting her bag of crisps under my nose. '*Eat*, Ellie. A few measly little crisps aren't going to make you fat. I scoff them all the time.'

'Meaning you're the one with the thin-as-a-pin model looks and yet you can still eat crisps,' I say.

'Meaning *nothing*. What's the matter with you, Ellie? Don't be such a grump.'

'Sorry, sorry.'

I *am* sorry too. I know I'm being paranoid. I know Magda and Nadine aren't getting at me. *I'm* the one who keeps griping at them.

I grit my teeth and try hard to act normally but it's

so hard when I want to snatch handfuls of their salty golden crisps and cram them into my mouth, bagful after bagful . . . I raise my second can to my lips and drain it.

I hiccup. I feel totally water-logged, a great bloated balloon – but I still don't feel *full*. I haven't eaten since yesterday's supper, and that was only salad.

I've decided now that I'm going to stick to one meal a day until I've lost at least a stone. Six more hours to go.

I start stacking quoits energetically to divert myself. I bend and stretch . . . and then the store cupboard lurches sideways and I grab at Nadine.

'Ellie?'

'She's fainting,' says Magda.

'No, I'm not,' I mumble.

The cupboard whirls round and round, the walls closing in on me.

'Put her head between her legs,' says Magda.

'You what?' says Nadine.

'It's a recovery position, nutcase. Here, Ellie, sit down. Put your head right down too. You'll be better in a minute.'

'I'm better now,' I say.

The cupboard is still spinning, but slowly.

'Shall I go and get Mrs Henderson?' asks Nadine.

'No!'

'You're still ever so pale, Ellie.'

'I'm always pale. I just went dizzy for a minute, that's all. No big deal.'

'Well, no wonder you're going dizzy if you won't

eat,' says Nadine. 'You and this stupid diet.'

'Don't start that again.'

'You know the best way to lose weight?' says Magda, taking a discus in either hand and trying to flex her muscles. 'Exercise. That's what you should do, Ellie.'

'Ellie, exercise?' Nadine laughs.

We are famous for being the least sporty girls ever. But I've been privately experimenting recently. I tried doing sit-ups in my bedroom to firm up my horrible wobbly tummy, but I'm so useless at it I can only sit up at all if I wedge my toes under the chest of drawers handle. I practically pulled my toes right off – they've still got painful mauve grooves across them now.

I've also tried jogging to school, though I felt ultra stupid and hoped everyone would think I was running for a bus. I only managed to go the length of two streets before collapsing. I was so sweaty I was terrified I'd overwhelmed the efficiency of my Mum rollette and I had to keep my distance from everyone all day long.

'I know exercise is a good idea,' I say. 'It's not that I don't want to do it. I can't. You know how useless I am, Magda.'

'It's only because you're not fit,' Magda persists. 'How about going to a gym?'

'Please!' says Nadine, shaking her long locks in horror.

'Go on, Ellie, you might find it fun. There's a

special early gym session down the leisure centre. We could meet up before school,' says Magda.

'What?'

'Stop it!' says Nadine. 'You two are going completely bananas. It's like something out of *The X-Files*. My two best friends have been taken over by crazed zombies. First Ellie gets this thing about being fat and gives up eating altogether – *Ellie*, the girl who once ate three Mars Bars on the trot! – and now Magda's saying she wants to get up at the crack of dawn and go and work out in a gym. *Why?*'

I wonder if Magda's desperately envious about Nadine's modelling chance too. Then my brain starts working *properly*.

'This guy you met in the Soda Fountain – *he* doesn't happen to have an early morning gym session, does he?' I say.

'Aah!' says Nadine.

'No, Jamie doesn't,' says Magda. 'He's not into anything physical. Apart from sex. He can't keep his hands to himself. He's like an octopus. I'm not going out with *him* again.'

'No, but Jamie wasn't the one you really fancied. It was the dark dishy one. Mike?'

'*Mick*. Oooh, he is so gorgeous! He was round at Jamie's place the other day. He sat next to me on the sofa and OK, we weren't even touching, but it was like these electrical currents were going sizzle sizzle sizzle between him and me. I felt my hair was practically standing on end. I tried so hard with him and

221

I just know he's interested, but he's Jamie's best friend and he obviously doesn't want to cause trouble. He and Jamie are ever so close.'

'Maybe they're too close,' I say. 'Are you sure Mick isn't gay, Magda?'

'No, of course he's not gay! Look, OK, he did just happen to let slip that he works out at the Sun-risers club down the leisure centre—'

'Then I should think he *is* gay. Straight guys don't bother about their bodies half so much,' says Nadine, flexing her own arms. 'Hey, what do you think of my muscle definition? Do you think I ought to try to develop it?'

'Try developing your bust, darling,' says Magda, sticking out her own Wonderbra bosom.

'It's OK to be small. Lots of models are. And anyway, I could always go for a breast enhancement later,' says Nadine.

'Sounds like you're more in need of a *brain* enhancement,' I say sourly. 'And you, Magda. I'm not going to a sweaty old gym just so you can make out with this Mick.'

'OK OK, not the gym. Maybe it would be almost too obvious. Anyway, it costs a fortune. No, I thought we could go swimming? The pool opens at seven same as the gym. How about going just *once*? Ellie? Nadine? Then we could fetch up in the cafeteria for breakfast afterwards and surprise surprise, there's Mick. Hopefully. *Please!* I don't want to go on my own. I'll stand you both breakfast afterwards. They do super raspberry Danish pastries.'

222

'I'm on a diet,' I snap.

'Looks like your little ploy's not working, Magda. You can certainly count me out. I need my beauty sleep,' says Nadine.

'Ellie? Listen, I was reading this article about swimming, how it's the best exercise you can take because you're using every single muscle in your body, right – and if you go early in the morning, before you've eaten anything, it speeds up your metabolism so that whatever you eat after gets burnt up in double quick time. So you could eat up that raspberry Danish and not put on an ounce in weight.'

I know she's just shooting me a line. Yet maybe there's some truth in what she's saying. It sounds logical. Well, not the raspberry Danish bit, sadly. But if I could *really* kick-start my metabolism into superdrive every morning it might make a real difference.

'Yes, Ellie!' says Magda, seeing my face. 'I'll meet you outside the leisure centre at seven tomorrow morning, right?'

'Wrong,' I say. How can I go swimming and show off my great white whale body to everyone? And yet . . . half an hour's strong swimming would burn up so many calories . . .

'Just *once*, Ellie. Please. Pretty please.'

So I say I will. Just once.

I spend most of the evening peering at myself in my awful old swimming costume, convinced I cannot possibly expose myself in all my horrible wobbliness. Plus what should I do about all my hairy bits? I try shaving under my arms, snaffling Anna's razor, and cut myself, which smarts terribly.

I phone Magda to call the whole thing off. She tells me that swimming tautens all your muscles, and points out that even the biggest beefiest serious swimmer has a washboard stomach, tight bum and taut thighs. I miserably feel my flabby flesh as she speaks. I agree to go after all.

I feel like death getting up at quarter past six but the cold air revives me a little. I jog-shuffle most of the way to the leisure centre, deciding I might as well get in a little extra exercise on the way. I make good progress and get there at three minutes to seven, before the doors are even open. There's a little group of fitness freaks waiting, huddled into the hoods of their tracktops. Magda isn't here yet. There's no dark dishy hunk that could be Mick either. I stand in my school uniform, clutching my duffle bag, feeling horribly out of place. People will be wondering what on earth this squat blobby schoolgirl is doing at a fitness centre – *fat*ness centre, more like. There's an enviably thin girl in a green tracksuit staring at me right at this minute.

'Ellie?'

I stare back, startled. The thin girl is smiling. It's Zoë Patterson!

Zoë is famous at our school. She's a real brainbox. She should be in Year Ten but she's been put up a year to take all her GCSEs a year early. God knows how many she's doing – ten, eleven, maybe even twelve. I bet she gets As in all of them. Zoë wins her form prize every year. And the Art prize too.

That's how I know her. We both spend a lot of time in the art room doing all sorts of stuff, and when Mrs Lilley, the Art teacher, wanted a special mural to brighten the room up she asked Zoë and me to work on it together during our lunch hour.

We hardly spoke to each other at first. I thought it was because Zoë was older than me and might be a bit snobby, but then I realized she's actually even shyer than I am. So I got up the nerve to start talking to her and she soon got ever so friendly and funny. By the time we'd finished our mural (a crazy summer camp scene of all different creative women through time: we had Virginia Woolf with her skirts tucked in her drawers paddling in the stream, Jane Austen in an apron peeling potatoes, all the Brontë sisters with their sleeves rolled up sizzling sausages on the barbeque, Florence Nightingale pitching a tent, Billie Holliday picking flowers, Marilyn Monroe hanging out the washing, Frida Kahlo painting pictures on her welly boots) it seemed like we were firm friends.

But this school year Zoë hasn't been coming to the art room and whenever I've bumped into her in the corridors or the cloakroom we've just said hi and hurried on. I wondered if she'd gone off me or thought me too babyish or was maybe just too busy to be friendly when she was swotting for all those scary exams.

'Hi, Zoë. I never expected to see you here,' I say.

I assumed Zoë thought along the same lines as me when it came to sport.

225

'I come here every day,' says Zoë. 'Are you here to swim too?'

'Yes. I said I'd come with Magda. You know, my friend. The blond one. Though goodness knows when she's going to get here. I bet she's slept in.'

The doors open. I say I'd better wait for Magda so Zoë goes hurrying down to the changing room. She didn't used to be anywhere near as thin. She's got amazing cheekbones now. Her tracksuit bottom is all baggy. Zoë was never fat – not like me – but she used to be a bit pear-shaped with a biggish bum. Hey, maybe swimming really works!

I think I might start going every day too. Though not with Magda. She doesn't arrive until *twenty past*.

'Hi, Ellie. God, isn't it awful getting up this early,' she mumbles.

'You're not early, Magda, you're *late*.'

She's not taking any notice, peering all over the place as we go into the centre and pay for our swim.

'Have you seen anyone that looks like Mick, Ellie? You know, dark and truly dishy.'

'I don't know. Heaps of people have gone in. I didn't see anyone *that* fantastic – but we've got different taste when it comes to boys.'

'You're telling me,' says Magda. 'You've got Dan for a boyfriend.'

'He's not my *boy*friend,' I say.

'Well, what is he then?' says Magda.

'I don't know,' I say.

Dan was so keen on me it was embarrassing. We've fooled around a bit together in a totally chaste sort of

226

way, but it's not been the Love Match of the Century. Or the year, month, week, day, minute. Scarcely Love Match of the *Second*. Though Dan's always insisted he loves me. I've never worked out whether he was totally serious. I'm even less sure now. He hasn't written to me recently. And he hasn't phoned me back since that time I phoned him and he was watching some stupid rugby match.

Maybe I need a new boyfriend.

Ha. Who would ever want to go out with me?

Plenty of boys want to go out with Magda. I can see why she was so late getting here. She's fully made up and her hair's freshly washed and styled. She wriggles into a new slinky scarlet lycra costume. It's so tight it must feel like wearing a full-size elastic band – but she looks incredible.

I turn my back to take off my clothes, embarrassed to strip off even in front of Magda. My hair sticks up in a giant bush, my face is all blotchy from the cold and yet in the sudden heat inside my glasses steam up so I can't see. It feels better when I take them off and shove them in my locker. If I can't see anyone clearly I can kid myself that maybe they can't see me.

I grope my way to the poolside and slide in as quickly as possible so that I'm hidden, up to my neck in sparkling turquoise water. It's beautifully warm, but Magda takes for ever to get in, standing on the side of the pool, dipping her toes in and squealing. It's obviously just to show herself off. It works. I swim two fast and furious laps and when I get back to the shallow end there are *five* boys surrounding Magda, laughing and jostling and offering her advice.

I swim off again. I'm trying not to mind. I'm not here to get off with boys anyway. I'm here to lose weight.

So I plough backwards and forwards, ten lengths breaststroke, ten lengths freestyle, ten lengths backstroke. Then repeat. Thank goodness I'm quite good at swimming so I don't look too stupid. Some of the boys are faster than me but I'm quicker than all the women – apart from Zoë.

We're about even-steven and find we can't help racing each other. First she steams ahead so I concentrate fiercely and push myself that little bit harder so that I'm gasping every time I take a breath. I draw closer, closer – and then I'm suddenly in front, and I whizz off even faster, but it's hard to keep it up. I'm slower the next lap, floating a little, and Zoë suddenly flashes past.

We carry on this mad competition and end up neck and neck, laughing at each other.

'We'd better get out now or we'll be late for school,' says Zoë.

'Right,' I say, scarcely able to draw breath.

Magda got out ages ago. She was barely *in*. She swam about ten measly lengths, keeping her head artificially high out of the water so that her hair wouldn't get messed up and then she was off back to the changing room to replenish her make-up.

She's hogging the mirror now, applying the finishing touches.

'Right, Ellie. See you in the café, OK?' she says. 'I don't want to miss Mick – *if* he's actually here.'

Zoë and I take a shower. We're very modest, looking away from each other as we soap ourselves under the streaming water but once we're towelling dry and stuffing damp bodies into underwear I take a quick glance at her when I've put my glasses on. I stare.

Zoë is thin. Not just slender. Not even skinny. Her ribs are sticking out of her skin, her pelvis juts alarmingly, her arms and legs look as if they're about to snap.

'Zoë!' I wonder if she's ill. I've never seen anyone this thin before. She looks *awful*.

'What?' she says, looking anxious.

'You've lost so much weight!'

'Not really. Not enough. Not yet,' says Zoë.

# Chapter Five

Turkeygirl

I'm not stupid. I know Zoë's sick. She's obviously anorexic. She's not thin and beautiful. She's thin and sad. Thin and mad. She's starving herself. She looks like a living skeleton. There's nothing desirable about her gaunt body, her jutting bones, her beaky features.

I don't want to end up like Zoë.

I eat chicken and broccoli and baked potatoes for supper. I even put butter inside my potatoes and follow my first course with chocolate ice-cream and extra chocolate sauce.

'Thank God,' says Dad. 'I was so sick of that stupid diet. Have you seriously seen sense at last, Ellie?'

'You bet,' I say, running to the fridge and getting out a second carton of chocolate ice-cream.

'Me too,' says Anna, getting her own bowl.

It feels so wonderful to eat my meal slowly,

savouring every mouthful. I feel full and warm and peaceful. I chat to Anna, I chat to Dad, I even chat to Eggs. I don't shut myself away in my bedroom after supper. I curl up on the sofa in the living room. Dad brings out his all-time favourite video, the one he loves us all to watch together when we're playing happy families. *The Wizard of Oz*.

I get a little tense watching Judy Garland at first. Is she too fat or is she just fine? She's thin compared to me. But when she steps out of her little grey house into the colour of Oz I step with her and stop worrying. I just sit back and enjoy the movie.

I take Eggs up to bed singing, 'Follow, follow, follow, follow, *follow* the purple stair cord', and we do a little Munchkin dance on the landing. His arms wind tight round my neck as I tuck him up in bed.

'I love you, Ellie,' he whispers.

'I love you too, Eggs,' I whisper back.

I wonder why I'm usually so mean to him. I don't feel like being mean to anyone now. I even give myself a grin in the mirror when I go into my bedroom. I have a tiny panic when I get undressed. My full tummy looks so big. I stand sideways and peer in the mirror to see just how much it's sticking out. But then I pull my nightie on quick and jump into bed. I think about the film. I click my bare heels in their invisible ruby slippers over and over again.

I try to cling to this new common sense next day at school. It's not easy. I feel so dumpy in my tight uniform. Nadine's skirt hangs so gracefully on her, in real folds. Mine is so taut it feels like my knees are tied

233

together. Nadine's sweater is so loose. Mine is strained over the jutting shelf of my chest. I stare at everyone. They all look much thinner than me. I can't seem to help myself. I even start staring at poor huge Alison Smith and wonder if we're of similar size.

I try to calm down in Art. Mrs Lilley says we can paint any kind of Christmas scene we fancy – and offers us a chocolate Father Christmas as a prize for the most amusing and original effort.

Magda does a glamorous male stripper wearing a few sprigs of holly in strategic places and a silly Santa beard. Nadine paints a fashion model fairy on top of a Christmas tree. I do an extremely anxious turkey, eyes bulging, wattle quivering, beak wedged open while a farmer shovels great scoopfuls of food down its throat. It's already so fat it can barely waddle. The turkey's tail is a great fuzz of feathers. It's starting to look uncomfortably like a self-portrait. Lithe little sparrows fly happily about the turkey's head, free as the wind. I can't seem to make it funny. It's sad.

'Oh dear, Ellie,' says Mrs Lilley. 'Have you joined an animal rights group?'

I don't win the chocolate Father Christmas. I don't know why I mind so much. It's not as if I'd necessarily eat the chocolate anyway, not at 529 terrible calories per 100 grammes. I have gloomily inspected every kind of chocolate bar for their calorific value and then shoved them back on the shelf quickly, as if even handling them could make you fat.

Mrs Lilley is looking a little tubby lately, come to think of it. She's always been quite skinny but now she's getting a bit of a tummy and her waist is thicker too. Yet she looks OK in her denim shirt and waist-coat and long black skirt. She's wearing a big chunk of dark amber on a long black cord round her neck. Her eyes glow the same colour. She's looking great even though she's definitely put on a good half stone, maybe more, during this term. She doesn't seem to care. She looks really happy.

I think of pale sick skinny Zoë. I don't really wish I looked like her, do I? Maybe I could go in for the Mrs Lilley look, plumpish but still pretty in lovely loose clothes. Artistic.

I *wish* I'd won the chocolate Father Christmas.

Mrs Lilley calls me over to her desk at the end of the lesson.

'I'm sorry you didn't get the prize, Ellie,' she says.

'That's OK.'

'You know I think you're really gifted at Art, don't you?'

'Thank you.' I know I'm going red.

'I do hope I can come back long before you do your Art GCSE.'

'Come back?'

'I'm leaving at the end of this term.'

'Oh Mrs Lilley, *why*?'

She smiles at me.

'I thought you'd guessed! I saw you staring at my tummy today.' She pats it gently. 'I'm going to have a baby.'

'Ooh!'

'Yes, I didn't show for a while, but now I'm fast

approaching the waddling stage. I feel like your poor Christmas turkey.'

I feel like bursting into tears.

'Cheer up, Ellie. Maybe you can come and see me sometime after I've had the baby.'

'Mm, maybe. Well. Congratulations.'

I have to rush away. Mrs Lilley isn't fat. She is pregnant. My role model for a reasonable figure – *still* thinner than me – is probably six months pregnant.

Oh, God.

Anna is preparing a huge spag bol when I get home from school.

'I can't eat *that*!' I say, appalled.

I eat half a small tub of cottage cheese garnished with chopped cucumber and carrots. It looks and tastes disgusting, as if someone else has already eaten it and thrown it up. The smell of spaghetti bolognese makes me feel faint but I manage to hold out. Somehow. If only I could seal my lips with Superglue, then I'd feel really safe.

I even dream about it at night and wake up sucking my own hand. I curl up tight and clasp myself. I mustn't creep down to the kitchen and raid the fridge. I daren't have another stuff-my-face session because Anna might hear if I make myself sick.

I'm scared of getting really bulimic. I read an article in Nadine's *Spicy* magazine (she's its most avid reader now) and it says if you keep throwing up the acid rots your teeth. This famous model went through a six-month spell of being sick to keep in trim for her fashion work and now she's had to have a full set of false teeth fitted.

'Thank goodness I'm naturally slim,' Nadine says smugly, reading over my shoulder.

I make sick noises myself. Nadine isn't half getting on my nerves at the moment. I ask her privately what she thinks of Zoë, pointing her out in Assembly.

'How do you mean?'

'Well, don't you think she's sort of weird now?' I don't want to prompt Nadine in any way, I want her honest opinion.

'Zoë's *always* been weird. She's such a swot. All those prizes every year. Why doesn't she get a life?' Nadine says heartlessly.

'Yes, but don't you think she *looks* weird now,' I say. 'Haven't you noticed she's got a lot thinner?'

Nadine glances at Zoë again. She's bunched up in her baggy school uniform. Her skirt's much longer than anyone else's and she's wearing very thick woolly tights. There isn't really much of her on show.

'I suppose she's got a bit skinny, yeah,' says Nadine, as if it's no big deal.

Maybe it isn't. Maybe Zoë is a perfect size now. After all, she really did have a biggish bum before. But now she's worked as hard as always and she's won the slimming stakes too.

I struggle to remember exactly what she looks like without her clothes. Different sized Zoës dance in my head like reflections in a crazy mirror show. I can't work out which is the right one. I need to know.

'Coming swimming tomorrow, Magda?' I say.

'There's not much point. Mick wasn't there, was he?' says Magda.

'Still, look at all those other boys who started chatting you up.'

'They were OK, I suppose. Larry, the fair one, asked me out, as a matter of fact. I said I might meet up with him this weekend.'

'*When*?' says Nadine. 'Oh, Mags, you've got to help me with my hair and my make-up and everything. It's the *Spicy* heat!'

'You still like Mick best, don't you?' I persist. 'Come swimming tomorrow. You come too, Nadine – you want to be in good shape for Saturday.'

'Yes, but I don't want my hair all mucked up with chlorine,' says Nadine. 'And I'm trying to get eight hours sleep every night this week. I don't want bags under my eyes. I can't get up ultra-early.'

Magda can't get up ultra-early either. She keeps me hanging around outside the pool for ages. Zoë arrives when I do, jogging along the path, her face screwed up with concentration. She carries on jogging on the spot while she's in the queue, as if her trainers are fitted with springs.

'How can you be so energetic so early in the morning, Zoë?' I say.

'I've been up since five,' says Zoë, panting a little.

'*What?*'

'I have to, to get everything done. I do some stretching and some sit-ups, and then an hour's studying. I'm desperate to get my own exercise bike at home and then I could set up my books so I could

238

read *and* work out. It's mad, my mum and dad are forking out a fortune to spend Christmas in this posh hotel in Portugal and I've begged them to let me stay at home and with the money they save on my fare they could buy me the bike, but they won't *listen*.' Zoë talks faster than she used to, as if her thoughts have speeded up. 'My dad's just doing this to spite me. He's admitted it. He wants to fatten me up. He's *sick*.'

I wish I had the courage to contradict her. *She's* the one who's sick, only she can't see it. Or *is* she? She's extremely fit so she must be healthy. She's top of her class. Best at everything. Especially Art.

'Do you still paint, Zoë?'

'Well, just my GCSE work.'

'You don't do any art just for fun? You know, like when we did that mural together in the art room?'

Zoë shakes her head, looking pitying.

'I don't really have time for that sort of stuff nowadays,' she says, as if I'm a toddler wondering why she won't do finger-painting with me.

She disappears inside the pool. I hang around waiting for Magda. I see a tall dark hunky guy in a very stylish black sweatsuit go through to the Gym. I wonder if he's Mick? I can't really *ask*. The bunch of boys who were all over Magda the other day are here too. The fair one asks me where my friend is.

'She's coming,' I say.

One of them mutters and they all snigger.

I blush, hating them. I'm not going to stand about

any longer. Why should I always wait hours for Magda? And I *must* see Zoë.

I push past the boys and go through to the changing rooms. Zoë is already undressed, bending over her bag looking for her goggles. Her back is alarmingly ridged with her vertebrae. It looks as if her spine could snap straight through her skin. She hasn't got any flesh anywhere. I can see all the cords and tendons in her legs as she stretches. She straightens up and I see there's a gap between her thighs now so that she looks bow-legged. When she reaches up to put on her goggles her breasts are two little puckers on her rib cage, nothing more. There are great ugly grooves around her throat and collarbone. Her face is so shrunken in on itself you can see the shape of her skull. She is seriously starving herself to death.

But when she shivers through the shower, raising her fragile arms, her tummy totally flat in her skintight lycra costume, I still feel a stab of envy. I *must* lose weight. I want to be thin. All right, not as thin as Zoë. Not sick. But she's shown me you *can* change yourself. Last year Zoë might have been nearly my size. Now she's much thinner than Magda, thinner than Nadine, thinner than anyone I've ever seen, apart from those poor starving children you see on the news on television.

I'm going to be thin too. It's simple. I just won't eat. And yet all the time I'm thrashing up and down the pool I think Danish Pastry – golden, succulent, oozing jam. Magda turns up at last, in her strawberry swimsuit and matching red waterproof lipstick. She

240

smiles her oh-so-jammy smile and all the boys hurtle down to her end of the pool and surround her.

When I can get her on her own for half a second I tell her that a guy exactly her description of Mick is busy pumping iron in the gym. Magda's own muscles clench excitedly.

'Great! Well, we'll get out soon, right, and go for breakfast.'

'There's no point coming here and swimming like crazy, just to make myself even fatter,' I say.

'You're not fat,' Magda says automatically. Then she glances down at me as I hunch under the turquoise water. 'And you're getting thinner now anyway.'

'What? Really? How much thinner? Or are you just saying it to get round me?'

'Ellie, you're paranoid. *Yes*, you're thinner. How much weight have you lost?'

'Only about five pounds so far.'

'Well, there you go. You look five pounds thinner. That's heaps. So you can come and have a yummy Danish pastry with me and help me go Mickspotting.'

'There! I *knew* you were just saying it.'

'It's true. Look, you're going to go seriously anorexic if you're not careful. You'll end up a bag of bones like that poor sad Zoë.'

'You think Zoë's almost too thin then?' I ask eagerly.

Magda stares at me.

'Wake *up*, Ellie. She looks terrible. I'm amazed they don't cart her straight off to hospital. I don't know how her parents can let her get like that.'

'Her dad's taking her away at Christmas to feed her up.'

'He'll have to give her twenty meals a day then – she's like a skeleton.' Magda drops her voice as Zoë zips to our end of the pool and hauls herself up the steps.

I stare at her stick limbs. She's shivering, her hands pale purple with the cold. I watch the papery skin across her ribs as she gasps for breath. I know Magda is right – and yet I jog to school with Zoë rather than have breakfast in the café with Magda.

Zoë might be seriously ill but she's far fitter than me. I'm staggering in agony by the time I get to school. Mrs Henderson finds me in a state of collapse on the cloakroom floor.

'Ellie? What is it?'

'I'm . . . just . . . out of . . . breath.'

'I thought you were having an asthma attack. Have you been *running*? And you're not even late for school!'

'I've run all the way from the leisure centre,' I gasp.

'My goodness. I think *I* need to sit down. Eleanor Allard on a fitness kick!'

'I've actually never felt *less* fit in my life,' I say, clutching my chest. 'I think I'm having a heart attack.'

'Maybe you need to come to my lunchtime aerobic session,' says Mrs Henderson.

'OK, maybe I will,' I say.

It'll burn off two or three hundred calories – *and* stop me craving lunch. It's a special lunch today, the cook's traditional Christmas dinner treat for the end of term. Turkey, one chipolata sausage, two roast potatoes, a dollop of mash and garden peas, and then mincemeat tart with a blob of artificial cream. We're talking mega-calories per trayful.

I can't risk setting foot inside the canteen. I go to the aerobic session. It's hell. Total burning hellfire.

I feel such a fool amongst all the seriously-fit muscle-girls leaping about in their luminous lycra. I stand behind Zoë, who is bunched up in a huge T-shirt and tracksuit bottoms. She looks hopelessly weak and weedy, but she's fighting fit. She never misses a beat, her lips a tight line of effort.

I get so hot I can't see out my glasses and the spring goes out of my hair. I've got such a stitch I have to fight not to double up. I still try to swing my arms and stamp my legs but they've turned to jelly.

'Take two minutes' break, Ellie,' Mrs Henderson calls.

I crash to the floor. Gasp gasp gasp. But I'm not going to lose any weight lying here going wibble-wobble. I drag myself up and get going again. I last to the end of the session . . . just.

I've got to take a shower, obviously, but I seriously hate the school showers because there aren't any curtains at all. I hunch in a corner, trying to keep my back to everyone, taking envious peeks at all the taut thighs and flat tummies surrounding me.

Zoë avoids this ordeal. She runs off in her sweaty T-shirt clutching a sponge bag, obviously going to have a little wash in the toilets.

I shove my school uniform over my sticky pink blancmange body as quickly as possible. Mrs Henderson catches hold of me.

'Can I have a word, Ellie? Come in my changing room.'

Oh, God. The only times I've been invited into her inner sanctum it's to get severely told off for pretending to have a permanent heavy period to get me out of games. She's surely not going to tell me off for volunteering for *extra* games?

'So, Ellie, what's going on? First it's swimming, then running, now aerobics. Why?'

'You told me to come along this lunchtime.'

'I was joking – though it was certainly a pleasant surprise when you turned up. But I just wonder what you're playing at, Ellie.'

'I told you. I'm trying to get fit. I thought you'd be thrilled to bits, Mrs Henderson. You're always nagging at me to take more exercise. So I am.'

'Do you want to get fit, Ellie – or thin?'

'What?'

'I'm not stupid. I know why poor Zoë comes to aerobics. I'm very worried about her. I've tried talking to her umpteen times – and her parents. She's obviously severely anorexic. But I want to talk about you, Ellie, not Zoë.'

'You can hardly call me anorexic, Mrs Henderson,' I say, looking down at my body with loathing. 'I'm fat.'

'You've lost weight recently.'

'Only a few pounds, hardly anything.'

'You've done very well. But you mustn't lose weight too rapidly. You girls go on all these crazy diets but all you really have to do is cut down on all the sweets and chocolate and crisps and eat *sensibly*. Lots of fresh fruit, vegetables, fish, chicken, pasta. You *are* eating a reasonably balanced diet, aren't you, Ellie?'

'*Yes*, Mrs Henderson.'

One apple. Two sticks of celery. Half a tub of cottage cheese. One Ryvita. Fruit, veg, protein, carbohydrate. Brilliantly balanced.

'Because you're a perfectly healthy normal ordinary size, Ellie.'

'Ordinary – for an elephant.'

'I *mean* it. What's brought all this on, hmm?' Mrs Henderson looks at me. 'It wouldn't have anything to do with Nadine suddenly acting as if she's the second Kate Moss?'

'*No!*' I say, perhaps a little too fiercely.

'Do *you* want to be a fashion model, Ellie?' says Mrs Henderson.

'Me?' I say, snorting at the idea.

How could I ever get to be a model? OK, I could staple my lips together for good and starve myself slim. But what could I do with my mane of frizzy hair, my little owl glasses, my dumpy five foot two physique?

Mrs Henderson misunderstands the true meaning of my snort.

'Ah! At least you haven't dieted away your basic common sense, Ellie. You seem to share my feelings about fashion models and their ludicrous strutting and vacant posing. Why can't girls ache to be scientists or surgeons?'

'Count me out, Mrs Henderson. I come nearly bottom in Science – and I can't stand the sight of blood so I doubt I'd make a very good surgeon either.'

'*You're* going to be an artist,' says Mrs Henderson.

I blink at her, going red.

'What do you mean?' I stammer. I didn't have a clue Mrs Henderson knew I even *like* Art.

'We teachers do talk amongst ourselves, you know. It sounds as if you're Mrs Lilley's pet pupil.'

'Yes, but she's leaving.'

'Then you'll doubtless be the new art teacher's pet pupil too,' says Mrs Henderson.

'She'll probably think I can't draw for toffee,' I say.

Stupid word. I think of soft gooey buttery brown toffee and my mouth drips with saliva. Do I like toffee best – or fudge? No, nougat, the sort with the cherries. I open my lips and imagine chewing a huge sticky slab of nougat . . .

'Ellie? Are you listening to me?' says Mrs Henderson.

'Yes, of course,' I say, swallowing my imaginary sweets. 'Don't worry, Mrs Henderson. I swear I don't want to be a model. I couldn't care less about Nadine and her big chance. Honestly.'

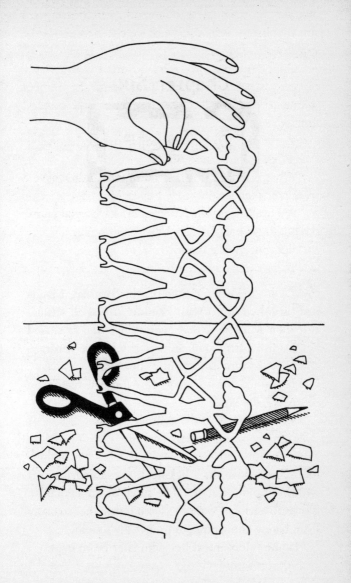

## Chapter Six

I was going to keep right out of it on Saturday. Magda had promised to go with Nadine. It was all settled. But then Mick *un*settled everything. Magda shared her Danish pastry with him at the leisure centre – and now has him eating out of her hand.

'He's asked me to go to this football match on Saturday,' she says.

'Oh wow! Date of the century,' I say.

Magda is eating a Mars bar. She's been nibbling along the top with her little white teeth like a chipmunk, and now she's licking the exposed caramel with her pointy tongue. The smell of the chocolate is overpowering. I want to snatch it from her so badly I can barely concentrate on what she's saying.

Nadine is looking at her with laser beam eyes.

'Not *this* Saturday?'

'Mm.'

'But you can't. You're going to make me up.'

'Yes, yes, well, I can still do that, can't I? The match is in the afternoon, *right*?'

'But you're coming *with* me.'

'Well . . . you don't really need me there, do you?'

'We're supposed to go with someone. It *says*. Relative or friend.'

'They probably mean an adult friend, as a chaperone. So you'd really better go with your mum.'

'I'm not going with my *mother*. Are you crazy? What sort of an idiot would I look, trotting along with her. I haven't even told her about it. You know what she's like. Dear goodness, she'd get me to perm my hair in ringlets and put me in a frilly frock!'

'OK, OK, point made. Go with Ellie.'

'What?' I say, snapping to attention. 'No!'

'But I can't go on my own! Magda, you can't stand me up to watch a lousy football match!'

'Mick's *playing*, Nadine. He said I'd bring him luck. I *can't* stand him up. We're going out after too. It's my big chance with him, I just know it is.'

'It's *my* big chance on Saturday. I can't believe you could be so selfish,' says Nadine, nearly in tears. 'You're letting me down just for some stupid boy. That's just typical of you, Magda.' She turns to me. 'Ellie?'

'No! I'm not going with you, Nadine. I can't. I won't.'

But she keeps going on and on at me. So on Saturday morning I go with her to Magda's. Magda is already carefully got up in her version of football watching gear: scarlet sweater that clings to every curve, label-to-die-for jeans and high-heeled boots, with her beautiful fur jacket to keep her cosy.

'OK, Nadine, let's get cracking,' she says, rolling up the sleeves of her sweater.

'I don't want anything too bright,' Nadine says anxiously.

'Just leave it to me, OK?'

'I mean, I can see that my usual look isn't quite right—'

'Your chalk-white just-stepped-out-your-coffin look? Yeah, you'd frighten them to death.'

'But I can't be too colourful. Look at the way all these girls look in the magazine.' Nadine stabs her finger at various models in *Spicy* magazine. 'They look . . . natural.'

'Right. Natural,' says Magda, scraping Nadine's hair back.

'You can *do* natural, can't you, Magda?' says Nadine.

'I won't do anything at all if you carry on. Now lie back and shut up.'

It takes Magda nearly an hour to get Nadine looking natural enough. I can't help being riveted. It's so weird seeing her blossom beneath Magda's deft fingers.

'There!' she says at last, holding the mirror up for Nadine. 'You like?'

'Well . . . I don't know. I look ever so pink and girly. Can't we rub off some of the blusher?'

'Don't you dare touch it! It's perfect. Now, your hair.'

'Yes. What am I going to *do* about it?' says Nadine, running her fingers through it despairingly.

'What's the matter with it?' I say. It looks lovely. It always does. It's a long black shiny waterfall, glinting almost blue when it catches the light.

I've always loved Nadine's hair and wished that my own hair could somehow be shocked out of its corkscrew curls. When we were little girls I'd brush Nadine's glossy long hair until it crackled. When we slept at each other's houses I'd cuddle up close to Nadine and pretend that the shiny dark hair on the pillow touching my shoulder really belonged to me.

I remember *that* – and yet I *don't* remember longing for Nadine's body to set off her long glossy hair. I knew that I was quite a fat little girl and Nadine a thin one – but it didn't really bother me then.

It's really weird – the me *then* won't match up with the me *now*. I wish I could still be the old Ellie. It's so hard being this new one. It's such a battle all the time. I feel so sick now because I didn't dare have anything for breakfast and I don't know what I'm going to do about tea this evening because we always have takeaways on Saturdays and they always smell so good and yet they're all hundreds and hundreds and hundreds of calories, flakey white fish in golden crunchy batter with mounds of salty savoury chips, or a great Catherine wheel of pizza sizzling with cheese, or tangy tandoori chicken, ruby red and hot, with pearly rice to fill my empty aching stomach . . .

'Ellie!' says Magda, busy parting Nadine's hair. 'Is that your stomach rumbling?'

'I can't help it,' I say, going red.

'What about a little plaity bit on top?' says Magda.

'I was wondering about lots of little plaits,' says Nadine, holding her head on one side and fiddling with wisps of her hair.

'Plaits!' I say. 'Come on. How childish can you get.'

'Not childish. Cute,' says Magda, starting to plait.

'Look at this girl – *she's* got little plaits,' says Nadine, stabbing her finger at *Spicy* magazine. 'Yeah, plaits, please, Mags.'

The plaiting process takes for ever. I yawn and sigh and fiddle and clench my stomach to shut it up.

'This is s-o-o-o-o boring,' I moan. 'What are you going to wear anyway, Nadine?'

'What I've got on!' says Nadine.

I stare at her. I thought she was wearing dreary old things to save her posh outfit getting mucked up. Nadine usually wears amazing clothes, black velvet, black lace, black leather. Now today of all days she's got on just an ordinary pair of blue jeans and a skimpy little pink T-shirt.

'Why aren't you wearing anything black? You don't look like you,' I say.

'That's the whole point. I want to look like a model,' says Nadine.

'But shouldn't you dress up a bit?' I ask.

'Take no notice of Ellie, she hasn't got a clue,' says Magda, sighing.

'This is the sort of stuff models wear when they go on shoots,' says Nadine. 'You dress down, see. Though these jeans are French and cost a fortune. My mum's going to do her nut when she finds out I've drawn out some of my building society money.'

'Yeah, but think of the fortune you might be earning soon, Nadine,' says Magda. 'And the minute you've made it, you're to start introducing me to all the right people, OK? The rounded voluptuous look is very in too. They don't just want stringbeans like you.'

'Dream on,' I say sourly.

What if Nadine *does* make it as a model? She looks so different now. I stare at her and it suddenly all seems real. She looks just like all the models in *Spicy* magazine. She'll win this heat. She'll go through to the final. She'll get to be the *Spicy* cover girl. She'll be photographed with a pretty little pout for all the magazines, she'll prance up and down the catwalks, she'll jet across the world on special fashion shoots . . . and I'll stay put, still at school, Nadine's sad fat friend.

I feel as if this title is tattooed to my forehead as I go up to London with Nadine. I have to go with her because she *is* my friend. I've put almost as much thought into my appearance as Nadine has with hers. I've left my hair an untamed tangle, my face is belligerently bare, I'm wearing a huge checked shirt and black trousers and boots, and I'm carrying my sketch book to try to show every single person at the *Spicy* place that *I* don't want to be a model, *I* couldn't care less about my appearance, I'm serious-minded,

I'm *creative* . . . OK, OK, I'm talking crap, I know. And *they* know when we get to the special studio *Spicy* magazine has taken over for the day.

It is crowded out with a galaxy of gorgeous girls, thin as pins.

'Oh, God, look at them,' Nadine says. She shivers. 'They all look like real fashion models already.'

'Well, so do you,' I say.

'Oh Ellie,' says Nadine, and she squeezes my hand.

She's clammy-cold, clinging tight like we're little kids in Primary One on our first day at school.

'I wonder what we're going to have to do?' she says. 'If I have to stand up in front of all these girls I'm going to die. They all look so cool, as if they do this kind of thing every day.'

They do too. They're all standing around in little groups, some chatting, some smiling, some staring, looking everyone up and down, looking at Nadine, looking at me, raising their perfectly plucked eyebrows as if to say: Dear God, what is that squat ugly fat girl doing here?

I try to stare back. My face is burning.

'I'm desperate for a wee, Ellie. Where's the Ladies?' Nadine asks.

It's even worse inside the crowded Ladies room. Girls crowd the mirror, applying glimmer eyeshadow and sparkle blusher and lip gloss so that their perfect oval faces are positively luminous in the strobe lighting. They tease their hair and hitch up their tiny jeans and smooth their weeny T-shirts with long manicured nails.

'Help, look at *my* nails,' Nadine wails. She clenches her fists to hide her little bitten stubs. 'Oh God, this is a waste of time, Ellie. Why did I ever open my big mouth to everyone at school? I don't stand a chance. I must be mad.'

'Well, we don't have to stay. We can just push off home again.'

Nadine looks at me like *I'm* mad. 'I can't give up now!'

'OK. Well. The very best of luck, Naddie,' I say, and I give her a quick hug.

'I'm so scared,' she whispers in my ear, hugging me back.

But she's fine when it comes to the crunch. All us friends and relatives are told to sit at the back, minding the coats and bags, knowing our place in the dark. All the model girl contenders are invited to come forward into the spotlit area. A bright bossy woman in black tells everyone what to do. She says she thinks everyone looks great and that they could *all* be a super *Spicy* cover girl. She wishes everyone luck. Then she gets them to do these funny warm-up exercises. Some of the girls blush and bump into each other first, losing their cool – but others leap into action, teeth gleaming, determined to show themselves off to their best advantage.

I'd planned to make sketches but instead I just gawp. Enviously. I stare at their long lithe limbs and their beautiful willowy bodies until my eyes water.

The bossy lady shows them how to walk like a model now. They all have to prance forwards, hips swinging, heads held high. Nadine catches my eye and goes a bit giggly, but then she puts her chin up and strides out, her mouth parted in a perfect little smile. I put my thumbs up, trying to spur her on. She's doing well. Maybe she's not quite as swishy and sophisticated as some of the others but perhaps that's good. They want someone with potential, not someone already polished. Nadine looks fresh and sweet. The bossy lady is looking in her direction.

Now it's standing still and posing time. They take group shots of all the girls smiling at the camera, then looking up, sideways on, head tilted. They keep calling out to the girls. Look sassy, look sad, look happy – call that happy, come *on*, it's happy–happy–happy time. My own mouth puckers in a silly little grin as all the girls bare their teeth. Some of the friends and relations really let rip. One terrible mum keeps shouting 'Go for it, Hayley! Big smile now. Look like you're enjoying it. You look a million dollars, darling!'

It's easy working out which one is Hayley. She's the girl who's purple with embarrassment, looking like she wants to kill her mother.

There's a coffee break and then suddenly it's the real thing. The girls are called out one by one in alphabetical order. They are videoed as they walk right round in a big circle and then stand in the spotlight in the centre and pose while a stills photographer flashes away. Then each girl has to go to the mike and say who she is and add a sentence or two about herself.

Hayley's surname is Acton, so she gets to go first. She makes a muck-up of it, tripping over her own feet as she walks in a circle, blinking like a trapped rabbit while she's photographed. She stammers her name into the mike and then there's a long silence while everyone closes their eyes and prays. Eventually she whispers 'I don't know what to say.'

My shirt is sticking to me with embarrassment. The poor girl. Oh God, I'm not going to be able to stand it if Nadine makes a fool of herself too. Hayley's mother can't stand it either. She's rushed up to the bossy woman, insisting that it's not fair her Hayley had to go first, she didn't know what she was doing, all the others would have someone to copy (though who would wish to copy poor Hayley?). The bossy woman is kind and says Hayley can wait if she wants and have one more go right at the end. Hayley's mother is thrilled. Hayley isn't. She's walking right out of the studio.

'Hayley! Hayley, come back! Don't go, sweetheart! You can have another go, darling,' Mum yells, rushing after her.

I am glad I'm not Hayley, even though she's much thinner than me. The girl who gets to go next is almost as nervous, practically running round the circle. She forgets about posing for her photos and is in the middle of announcing herself when the photographer starts flashing so she stops and blinks and gawps. This is awful, total public torture. I'm starting to feel almost sorry for them.

Almost. The next girl is blond and tall, very

pretty, very skinny. She doesn't lose it like the other two. She walks proudly all around, swinging her tiny hips, and then she stands and smiles, head back a little, eyes shining, turning this way and that as the photographer clicks. She says softly and sexily into the mike 'Hi, I'm Annabel. I'm fifteen and I like acting and singing and skiing – and reading *Spicy* magazine.' She smiles cheekily and then saunters off. Little Ms Perfect.

I catch Nadine's eye from across the room and mime being sick. I *feel* sick when it's Nadine's turn. My own legs wobble as she strides out. My own mouth aches as she smiles bravely.

Nadine walks in a perfect circle, slowly, gracefully, with a little bouncy twirl as she steps into the spotlight. She smiles at the guy with the camera and he waves his fingers at her. She poses brilliantly, turning this way and that. All those hours staring at herself in her bedroom mirror have paid off at last. She seems entirely at her ease. She doesn't blink when the camera flashes right in her face. She smiles at the lens. Then she reaches for the mike.

'Hello, I'm Nadine,' she says. 'I'm nearly fourteen. It feels weird to be standing here looking so girly. I usually have a white face and black clothes. My best friend Ellie calls me a vampire. But it's OK, I actually feel faint at the sight of blood.' She bares her teeth in a jokey way and everyone laughs and claps.

Fancy Nadine mentioning me! She's so clever to say all that stuff so that people like her and remember her.

'Great, Nadine. Well done,' I whisper as she comes

over to join me. I give her a hug. 'Hey, you're *shaking*.'

'It was so scary standing there with everyone staring,' she whispers. 'I didn't make a complete idiot of myself, did I?'

'No, you were great. Honestly. Heaps and heaps better than the others – even that awful Annabel.'

'Do you think I should have said I read *Spicy* magazine too?'

'No, it sounded far too sucky. What you said was brilliant. I can't believe you could do it all so well. I couldn't have acted like that in a million years.'

I couldn't – even if I was as thin and striking as Nadine. She's sitting cross-legged like a little girl, her neck bent so that her hair falls forward, the weeny plaits looking cute. Her jeans are almost baggy on her she's so skinny. Her tiny T-shirt is taut against her body. She doesn't have even one little roll of fat sitting hunched up like that. Her elbows stick out, delicately pointed, emphasizing the skinniness of her arms.

It's so *unfair*. Nadine eats like a horse. On cue she fumbles in her jacket pocket and finds a Twix bar. She offers me a chocolate stick.

'I'm on a *diet*.'

'Oh. Right. Sorry,' she says, munching. 'Yum. I'm starving – I was too het up to eat any breakfast.'

I didn't have breakfast either. Or any supper last night. It's easier to skip a meal altogether rather than discipline myself to nibble just a tiny amount. Once my mouth starts chomping I can't stop it. I breathe in the rich chocolatey smell wistfully.

'Don't look at me like that, Ellie. You make me feel bad,' says Nadine, gobbling the last little bit. 'Still, you've done ever so well. I never thought you'd keep it up like this. You've lost quite a bit of weight now.'

'No, I haven't.'

'You *have*. Look at your tum!' Nadine reaches across and pats my tummy.

I try to suck it in, hating even Nadine to feel how huge it is.

'It's all gone. Practically flat,' says Nadine.

'I wish,' I say sourly.

We sit through endless hours while each girl has her go. I stare at their stomachs, all much much flatter than mine. I cuddle into my check shirt and under cover of its enveloping material I pinch my waist viciously, wishing I could tear pieces off with my fingertips.

Some of the girls are so nervous they muck it up like Hayley. Some of the girls are so gorgeous they prance professionally like Annabel.

'Only three girls get chosen from each area,' Nadine whispers. 'I haven't got a chance.'

'Yes you have! Wait and see. You'll walk it. You're heaps more attractive than any of the others.'

'Not that Annabel.'

'*Especially* that Annabel.'

But when they announce the winners Annabel is the first to be chosen. Then another blonde, an Annabel clone.

Nadine tenses beside me, praying so hard I can

almost see a please-please-please speech bubble above her head. I squeeze her hand. The third girl is announced. There's one squeal of triumph — and dozens of sighs all round the room. It isn't Nadine. It's a redhead with long white limbs and big green eyes, a striking girl, but she can't hold a candle to Nadine.

'It's not *fair*!' I wail.

Nadine says nothing. She looks totally stunned.

'So — is that it?' she says. She swallows hard. She's trying not to burst into tears.

Some girls are already crying, and another mother from hell is remonstrating with the bossy lady, demanding to know why her daughter wasn't picked.

'All you girls did splendidly. You look model-girl marvellous,' says the bossy lady into the mike. 'I just wish it were possible to pick you all. Thanks so much for taking part. Have a safe journey home — and please pick up a complimentary copy of *Spicy* magazine on your way out.'

It's the last thing most of the girls want to look at now.

'Never mind, Nad. It's obviously a total lottery. You still look terrific.'

Nadine shakes her head, her face contorted.

'I look idiotic,' she says, unravelling her cute plaits, tugging so hard it's a wonder her hair doesn't come out in handfuls. 'Come on, let's get out of here, Ellie.' She starts pushing her way through the crowd, her lips pressed tight together, a vein standing out on her pale forehead.

'Hey, hang on! You! The dark girl!'

Nadine whips round, sudden hope flashing across her face – but it's just the photographer.

'Bad luck. I really thought you were in with a chance when I spotted you at that shopping centre.'

Nadine shrugs bravely. 'I just came along for a laugh,' she lies.

'I still think you've got a hell of a lot of potential. I don't know what you've done with yourself today though. You don't stand out from the others. I didn't even recognize you at first. You should have stayed with the white face and the dramatic sweep of hair.'

'Oh!' says Nadine, stricken.

'Never mind. You could really make it as a model, you know. You should get yourself a decent port-folio. Look, here's my card. Give me a buzz and I'll take the photos for you at my studio. I'll have to charge, of course, but as you're a half-pint I'll do you for half price.'

'Oh, right! Great!' Nadine burbles.

I seize her wrist and drag her away.

'Hang on, Ellie! Oh wow! Look, he gave me his card. And he says he'll photograph me half-price.'

'And probably half-*clothed*. For God's sake, Nadine, get real. It's the oldest con trick in the world. That's just such a seriously sleazy offer, can't you see that?'

'No, it's not. He's *nice*. He says I've got real poten-tial. He's a professional photographer so he ought to know.'

'Yes, I bet he gave his card to half the girls here today.'

'Well, maybe you're just being bitchy because he didn't give his card to *you*,' Nadine snaps. 'Fat chance of that!'

She stops. I stop. We both stand still in the street outside the studio. Nadine's words buzz in the air, sharp as stings.

'Thanks,' I say weakly.

'Oh Ellie. I didn't mean it to sound like that.'

'Yes, you did,' I say. 'Look, I came today when I didn't want to, I tried to be ever so helpful and supportive, I've sat for hours and hours and *hours* watching all you lot, I've tried to stop you minding too much when you didn't get chosen – and when that cheesy photographer hits on you I try to make you see this is a seriously dodgy proposition – because I'm your *friend*, Nadine. Not because I'm a fat jealous bitch. I'm sorry you feel that way.' I turn on my heel and march off. Nadine follows me, tucking her hand in my arm, telling me she's really sorry.

'Of course you're not a bitch, Ellie. *I'm* a bitch for saying it. Oh come on, don't go all moody on me. I'm the one who should be cast down with gloom because I didn't get chosen.'

I let her carry on as long as possible, rather enjoying it. We pass lots of would-be model girls, all of them letting off steam. Several are quarrelling just like us. One girl is being dragged along towards us by her mother.

'It's not just that you've let *me* down so badly. You've let yourself down too,' the mother shrieks. 'Now we're going back to the studio and you're going to ask them to give you another chance.'

Oh God. It's Hayley. Her mum's managed to drag her all the way back – though it's too late now.

'Never mind poor you and poor me. Poor Hayley,' I say.

'Poor poor Hayley,' says Nadine. 'Ellie – are you still in a huff?'

'Sure, I'm as huffy as hell,' I say, putting my arm round her.

It's a pain maintaining my self-righteous pose. I'm ready to make friends too. On the train going home we see a whole load of boys playing footie and we wonder if Magda's Mick is one of them. We strain our eyes but don't spot her blond head and fur jacket on the sidelines.

'I wonder where they'll go after? Do you think he'll take her out clubbing?' I ask.

'No, he'll be too knackered after playing football. A meal, is my bet. Hey, shall *we* go out for a meal, Ellie? My treat, because you've been a real pal today.'

'Not a meal. My diet.'

'Oh, Ellie. Look, we could go for a pizza and you could just have a weeny slice and some salad.'

'*No*, Nadine.'

'You're still mad at me.'

'No, I'm not. Though I don't exactly relish being called a fat bitch.'

'I didn't! *You* said that.'

264

'But you implied it.'

'No I didn't. Listen, if you don't mind my saying so, Ellie, you're getting positively paranoid.'

'So now I'm a paranoid fat bitch?' I say – but I'm laughing now, because even I can see I'm getting ridiculous.

I still bow out of the meal idea even so. When I get home I tell Dad and Anna that I've eaten with Nadine. I don't hang about downstairs. I go up to my bedroom and play music and do a huge crayon drawing – a mad landscape where the sun is a giant pizza, the mountain peaks are vast cherry-tipped iced buns, the forests are fairy cakes, the rivers are bubbly strawberry milkshakes, and the grass is studded with Smarties flowers.

I go to bed early and try to sleep late because it's one way of avoiding eating times.

Anna comes into my room at ten o'clock.

'Magda's on the phone for you, Ellie.'

Oh God, what does she want at this time? I remember her big date with Mick. She probably wants to boast and give me a blow-by-blow account. I groan and get out of bed. The room suddenly spins.

'Ellie?' Anna's by my side looking worried. 'Are you all right?'

'Mmm. I just went a bit dizzy, that's all. I'm OK now.'

'You don't look OK. Are you feeling sick again?'

'A bit.'

Sick with hunger, hunger, hunger.

'Ellie . . .' Anna is staring at me, biting her lip.

265

'Look, I can't keep Magda waiting,' I say, pushing past her.

I don't want Anna fussing and finding out how little I've been eating. Just because she's given up on her diet it doesn't mean I've got to. And besides, Anna is skinny as anything anyway.

'Hi, Magda,' I say into the phone. 'It's a bit early, isn't it? I was trying to have a lie-in.'

'Oh. Sorry. I didn't think. I just wanted to talk to you,' says Magda. She sounds unusually subdued.

'Mags? What's up?'

'I don't want to go into details just now,' says Magda. I can hear music in the background and family noises. 'It's pandemonium here. Can I come round to your place, Ellie?'

'Yeah, OK.'

'Like . . . now?'

'Fine.'

I have a quick shower and shove on some clothes. Anna's made me tea and toast. She means to be helpful, but I'd much sooner coffee and then I can have it black and not waste calories on milk. And she's buttered my toast for me, making big yellow puddles, absolutely oozing.

'Thanks, but I seem to have gone off tea,' I say, trying to be tactful. I gnaw delicately at the crust of my toast, and then leap up thankfully when Magda rings the doorbell.

She looks awful. Her hair's brushed straight back, she's got no make-up on at all, and she's wearing an old grey fleecey thing instead of her beautiful fur coat.

'Magda? Hey, come in.' I bundle her quickly upstairs to my room so she doesn't get waylaid by Anna or Dad or Eggs. She doesn't look in the mood for socializing.

She sits on the end of my unmade bed. My Patch hot-water bottle tumbles out of my duvet. Magda sits it on her lap and strokes it absent-mindedly, as if it were a real dog. She looks like a little girl again.

'Magda?'

She starts to say something, clears her throat, tries again, fails. She shakes her head impatiently.

'What's the matter with me? I'm so desperate to tell you I get you out of bed specially – and yet now I'm here I can't get started.' She seizes Patch by the ears. 'It's Mick.'

'Yes. I sort of gathered that.'

I wait. Magda waits too. If Patch were real he'd be squealing.

'Didn't he turn up?' I prompt.

'Oh yes. Well, I watched him play his football, didn't I? Hours I stood there. It's so cold and it's so boring and I was dying for a wee but I hung on with my legs crossed and every time he came near the ball I shouted encouragement like a loony.'

'So? After?'

'He was ages getting changed, with all his mates. I just hung about. I nearly lost my temper and went home. I mean, I don't *usually* lurk outside sweaty dressing rooms for hours. And they were singing utterly infantile songs, you know the sort. But anyway, I hung on in there, and at long last out he comes, still with all the mates. And he did look pretty fabulous, in this black leather jacket, and his hair all floppy and shining because he'd just washed it. It's so unfair, how can such a creep look so drop-dead gorgeous?'

'He's a creep?'

'The lowest of the low. Because . . . well, we wandered off to the park.'

'You and Mick?'

'And all the mates. I mean, I know most of them, Jamie's OK, and I went out with Larry that time. They all seemed in a good mood, larking about, making a bit of a fuss of me, you know.'

'Well, I don't know. Not personally. But I've seen the way all the boys act when they're around you. Flies. Honeypot.'

'I certainly started to feel sticky. They had all these cans of lager – and after a while they got a bit silly. One or two of these guys started kind of mauling me about. But I thought it was all just a bit of fun. Nothing heavy. And anyway, I was sure we'd be shot of them all soon enough. I suggested to Mick that we go off for a meal. He said, "Come on, guys, Magda's hungry, let's all go to McDonald's." I didn't think this sounded very romantic and I wanted to get rid of all the mates, so I asked if we could go to a proper restaurant, just him and me. He says, "Oooh, Magda can't wait to get me on her own," in this stupid nudge-nudge wink-wink way. Larry and all the rest fall about laughing and I'm starting to get seriously pissed off by all this and so I start walking off by myself. Mick can see I'm serious and he puts his arm round me and suddenly starts to be so sweet. He apologizes and asks me where I want to go, saying we'll eat anywhere, so I suggest going to the Ruby – you know that lovely Indian restaurant with the marble elephants? I always thought it would be dead romantic to eat there on a proper date. He goes OK, for you, Magda, anything, but let's hope you're worth it . . . and I *still* didn't twig what this was all about. Oh, God.' Magda bends her head over Patch, trying not to cry.

I sit on the bed beside her and put my arm round her. I can feel her quivering.

'What *happened*, Mags?'

'I – they—'

'They didn't *rape* you?'

'No! No, I'm just making this stupid fuss over nothing. *They're* nothing. I don't know what's the matter with me. I should have just laughed in their faces. Anyway. We went to the Ruby, Mick and me. The others were still hanging around the park so I thought everything was fine. Mick was . . . he was really sweet, he said all this stuff . . . It makes me feel sick now, but I liked it at the time, I liked *him*, I thought – I thought this was really it. True Love. Oh, God. *So*, we had a couple of beers, Mick told the waiter we were eighteen, and we had a curry. Well, we shared one. It was a bit embarrassing, the waiter wasn't happy about it, but I thought maybe Mick doesn't have much cash. I started to feel mean for suggesting the Ruby. I decided I'd offer to pay myself, doing it ever so discreetly so he wouldn't be embarrassed.

'It was getting hard to think straight. I'm not really used to beer. I slipped out to the Ladies and splashed my face with cold water, and I started making all these stupid kissy-kissy faces in the mirror, thinking of Mick – and then when I came out the Ladies there he was, right in front of me, waiting for me. He kissed me and it was just amazing to start with, the way I'd imagined it would be, *better*, and he said he'd paid and said "Come on, let's get out of here," and he took me round the back to the place where people park their cars and I thought this was a bit crazy because Mick doesn't have a car and I started to tell him this but he wasn't listening, he just had hold of me practically under the arm so he could shove me along, and he got me to these trees right at the back and then – well, at first I didn't mind, he was just kissing me, I *liked* it, though I was a bit worried about my shoes because we were standing in all this leaf mould and mud, so I said couldn't we get out of the mud and he didn't understand, he took off his jacket and said I could lie on that. I said, "What do you mean, I'm not lying down," and he said, "OK, OK, standing up, fine by me," and then he pressed me back against this tree and . . . Well I just thought he was trying it on at first, and I told him to stop it, but he didn't, and his hands started going all over the place, and then he got to my jeans and I started to get mad and told him to cut it out, what sort of girl did he think I was and he said . . . he said, "Everyone knows what sort of girl you are, Magda, so stop acting hard to get, right?" and he started getting really rough then, and I got scared he really *might* rape me. I slapped his face but it just seemed to make him madder so I sort of twisted round and suddenly jammed my knee up hard and he practically fell over, grunting and groaning.'

'Good for you, Magda!'

'But then when I started running away from him and got back to the cars there were all these cheers and his mates all bobbed up and one of them said, "It's our turn now, Magda," and then Mick staggered out of the trees and he was calling me these awful names, and then they all started, and this couple came out into the car park. They'd been in the Ruby and they looked at all these boys and they looked at me, and the woman came over to me and asked me if I'd like a lift home and so I said yes. They were very nice to me, but I felt so dreadful, I knew they must be thinking I was a real little slag, just me and all those horrible drunken boys. I had my lipstick smeared all over the place and mud all up my jeans. I looked like a slag and . . . maybe I *am* a slag. That's what they kept calling me, that's what they think I am.'

'You're *not* a slag, Magda. Don't be so crazy. You're a lovely gorgeous-looking girl who went out with a total perve who got entirely the wrong idea,' I say fiercely, hugging her. 'I hope you kicked him so hard he still feels sick. How *dare* he treat you like that!'

'He said I was asking for it. He said why did I dress like a tart if I wasn't willing to act like one,' Magda sobs.

'Well, he acts like a sick creep and he talks like a sick creep and he *is* a sick creep,' I say. 'Forget him, Magda. Forget all about him.'

## Chapter Seven

I go swimming on Monday morning. Zoë is there too. I hear two girls gasp as she takes off her tracksuit in the changing rooms. Zoë turns her back on them and ties her hair up in a ponytail. It hangs lankly, much thinner than it used to be.

'Zoë?' I say uncertainly. 'Zoë, you're getting *so* thin.'

'No I'm not,' she says, but she looks pleased.

'How much do you weigh?'

'I'm not sure,' says Zoë. 'Anyway I need to lose a lot more because my dad's still insisting we go away for Christmas and he'll practically *choke* me with food so I've got to be a bit on the skinny side to start with.'

'Zoë, you're not skinny, you're skeletal,' I say, but I can't persist.

Maybe she'll only think I'm jealous. Maybe I *am*.

'Is your friend Magda coming today?' Zoë asks.

'No,' I say, and my heart aches thinking about her.

I forget Zoë. I forget me. I just think of Magda as I swim up and down, up and down, up and down. I can feel the adrenalin pumping in my veins. I swim faster than usual, faster than Zoë, faster than all the girls, faster than some of the boys.

There's a little crowd larking about at the shallow end. I can't see them clearly without my glasses. I'm not sure if they're any of the ones who know Mick, ones who might have been there on Saturday night.

But there's no mistaking Mick himself in the café. I go in there, hair still wet, glasses steaming up, legs bright pink from swimming, but I don't care if I look awful. I march straight up to him, sitting there with his mates. He's smirking all over his face.

'Who's this then?'

'What do you want, girlie?'

'It's Magda's mate.'

'Where's Magda then?'

'Where's Slaggie Maggie?' says Mick, and they all laugh.

My hand reaches out and I slap him really hard across the face. His head rocks in shock, his eyes popping like they're going to roll right down his cheeks.

'You shut up, you creep,' I say. 'Magda's not a slag. She's a very picky choosy girl and she'd never have a one-night stand with you or anyone else for that matter. If you dare call her names or spread rumours about her I'll tell her brothers and their mates and they'll chop you stupid schoolboys into little pieces. So shut *up* about her, see?'

I storm off, the whole café staring. Some of the boys jeer, some laugh. Then they start shouting after me. They call *me* a slag. They call me Frizzy Face and Four Eyes. They call me Fat Bum. And yet I don't care. I truly don't care. I'm pleased I struck a blow for Magda. That's all that matters.

She's still very quiet and droopy at school. Nadine is also totally hang-dog because everyone naturally asks her how she got on at the *Spicy* heat and she has to say she wasn't chosen. So at lunchtime we go off by ourselves. We huddle on our favourite steps by the portakabins and we have a good long self-indulgent moan. Magda goes on about boys and what pigs they are and so why does she still fancy them? Nadine goes on about *Spicy* magazine and what a tacky tedious bore it was on Saturday so why is she still desperate to model for them? I go on about being fat and how I know it's what you are that matters, not how you look, so why am I still desperately dieting?

'But you're *not* fat, Ellie,' says Magda.

'And your diet's driving *me* bonkers the way you drool whenever I eat a bar of chocolate, so God knows what it's doing to you,' says Nadine.

'Hey! Thanks for your overwhelming sympathy and understanding,' I say. I'm sitting in the middle so I can elbow them both in the ribs. 'Look, I've been Ms Incredibly Supportive Friend to both of you. You could try being a bit sympathetic about *my* problem.'

'You haven't *got* any problems, you nutcase,' says Magda, snapping back to life.

'That's right, you're just being completely and utterly loopy,' says Nadine. 'You'll end up like Zoë if you're not careful.'

'All right, I can see Zoë's really gone a bit too far. But . . . if I could just get to be *normal* size—'

'You *are* normal! For God's sake, you keep acting like you're a freak or something, total fat-lady-in-the-circus time,' says Magda. She grabs a hank of my frizzy hair and holds it against my chin. 'You could be the Bearded Lady, easy-peasy. But fat? Forget it.'

'I *am* fat. I'm much much fatter than you two.'

'I bet we're about the same weight,' says Magda. She says how much she weighs.

It's only a few pounds less than me.

'Rubbish. You're fibbing. You can't weigh as much as that,' I say. 'Or if you really do then it's because your body's different. Heavy bones. And big muscles from all your dancing.'

'You're making me feel like a Russian shot-putter,' says Magda. 'How much do you weigh, Nadine?'

Nadine says. It's a *lot* less.

'See! Nadine's much taller too,' I say. 'I'm the squat tubby one.'

'You're the deluded nutty one,' says Magda. 'But we still love her to bits, don't we, Nadine?'

'Our old Ellie-Belly,' says Nadine, and she starts tickling my tummy.

'Don't! Get off! Stop it!' I shriek, as they both tickle me mercilessly.

I try to tickle them back and we roll down the steps, writhing and squealing.

Two Year Sevens scuttle past, looking as if they've stumbled on an orgy. That makes us laugh even harder. I feel so good that when Nadine produces a Twix bar I accept a bite happily. Two bites. Half the bar.

Maybe I'm going to stop dieting now. Maybe it's mad to fuss about the way I look. It's all so stupid anyway. Magda looks like a movie star and yet it just gives all those slimy sluggy schoolboys the wrong idea about her. Nadine looks like a fashion model and yet she was just one of a huge crowd of thin pretty girls on Saturday.

Maybe it's OK being me. Magda and Nadine like me. And Dan likes me too.

Dan.

What's *happened* to Dan? He sent me a funny post-card last week – but no letter. He used to write practically every day. And phone. He came down to stay one weekend. But he hasn't been back since.

I *did* tell him that he shouldn't keep bobbing up like a jack-in-the-box and we'd have to wait to see each other at Christmas. He seems to have taken me at my word.

I ask Anna when we're going to the cottage for Christmas.

'A couple of days before, I thought – just to get that awful cooking range prodded into action,' says Anna, sighing. 'Oh, God, the thought of all those lists, and all the shopping, and the packing, and the *un*packing, and then all of us shut up in that damp cottage for days—'

'I thought you *liked* going to Wales for the holidays.'

'Well. Yes. Of course I do. It's just . . . I saw Sara again today, you know, my designer friend, and *she's* spending Christmas in New York.' Anna sighs enviously. 'I mean, I wouldn't really want to swap with her, not seriously, but imagine wandering round great big luxurious shops like Bloomingdales and going up the Empire State building on Christmas Eve.'

'Imagine looking at all the Nativity paintings in the Metropolitan Museum and then going skating outdoors at the Rockefeller Centre,' I say, because I've seen them doing it in films.

We both imagine endlessly . . . and sigh.

'Tell you what,' says Anna, 'if I ever get a decent job when Eggs is a bit older – Sara says *she* can maybe fix me up with something – I'll save up and *we'll* go to New York one Christmas.'

'Dad hates flying. And Eggs would be a right pain in the shops.'

'Not them. Us. Well, we'll maybe come back for Christmas itself, I wouldn't want to be away from them then, but we could easily whizz away for a few days, just you and me.'

I feel an odd squeezing feeling inside me. I know Anna's only playing games, it's not like it'll really happen – but even so, it's weird us playing games together. We've always been on separate sides of the family. Yet now it's almost like we're best friends.

I don't mind. I *like* Anna. And yet, I think of my own mum and I feel so horribly mean to her.

'Ellie? What is it?' Anna says.

'Nothing,' I say, and I rush away quickly before I burst into tears.

I seem to be in an ultra-weepy watery mode at the moment. The last day at school is a serious strain. Oh, it's fun too, because the Sixth Form put on this special entertainment and it's seriously rude and we all fall about laughing. But when we have our last form lesson with Mrs Henderson she suddenly produces this big carrier bag and she's bought every girl in the class a little chocolate Santa. Not as big as the one Mrs Lilley offered as a prize but this is a Santa for every single girl. Sometimes the teachers give you cards but I've never had one give you presents before, especially a really strict old-fashioned teacher like Mrs Henderson.

Most of the others chomp up their chocolate straight away, a gulp of bearded head, a gollup of tummy, a crunch of boots and he's gone. I wrap mine up carefully in a hankie and put him in my schoolbag.

'For God's sake, Ellie, one little chockie isn't going to make you fat,' says Magda.

'I'm saving him for sentimental reasons, not because I'm trying to get slim.'

'Don't you overdo things, Ellie,' says Mrs Henderson, overhearing as always. 'Tuck into a few mince pies and the Christmas pud and really let rip this holiday. You can always work it off in my aerobics class in January.'

She's being so nice I almost wish I'd got *her* a present.

I *have* got a present for Mrs Lilley. Well, for little baby Lilley. I find her in the art room at lunchtime and hand it over, feeling stupidly shy as I thrust the little red crepe parcel into her hand.

'Can I peep at it now?' Mrs Lilley asks.

'OK. If you want,' I say awkwardly, wishing it was more special.

I made it in a rush in a couple of hours last night. It's a little yellow cloth teddy bear wearing a red jumper and purple trousers.

'I had buttons for his eyes at first but then I thought the baby might choke, so I sewed eyes on instead. They look a bit crossed, actually.'

'No, they don't, he just looks a bit anxious. Oh Ellie, he's *lovely*.' Mrs Lilley makes him pad about on his soft paws, acting like a little kid herself.

I'm so pleased she likes the teddy and so sad that she's going that I have to swallow hard and sniff.

'It's going to be horrible without you for Art,' I mumble.

'Ah! I think you might enjoy Art even more,' she says. 'I met your new art teacher the other day. I think you're in for a surprise.'

'Is she really nice then? Is she young? What does she look like?'

'I'm not going to say another word,' says Mrs Lilley, laughing. 'But I think your art lessons are going to be fun. You could do with a bit of fun, Ellie. You've seemed a bit down the last few weeks. There's nothing really serious troubling you, is there?'

'No. Not really. I just wish I could change myself sometimes,' I say.

'In what way?'

'Oh. You know,' I say, blushing. I wish I hadn't started this now.

I wish I could tell her how much I want to be thin. But what's the point? She'll just say something comforting about my looking fine the way I am. And I know it's stupid to be so utterly self-obsessed. I know I should start caring about heaps of other things. I *do* care about the awfulness of war and starving babies and tortured animals and destroying the countryside. It's just that if I'm totally one hundred and one percent honest I care about being fat just a weeny bit *more*.

As the teddy seems such a success I decide to revert to my old home-made habits and make everyone an appropriate soft toy for Christmas. I quite enjoy the first few days we break up from school because I go shopping for material in the market and then cut and pin and stitch for hours on end.

Eggs is a bit of a pest because he keeps wanting me to play with him, so I get him some card from a corn-flakes packet and show him how to do cross-stitch. He quite likes stabbing away at it, doing these great big wobbly crosses.

I find it helps me stop wanting to nibble all the time as you can't really eat and sew. It's annoying that it's such a sedentary occupation. I haven't been swimming for a bit. I'm a bit scared Mick's mates might drag me right under and drown me if I dared show up. I wonder if Zoë's still going, or if she's already been hauled off for her holiday abroad? I bet she'll do aerobics up and down the aisle and refuse to eat so much as one free peanut on the plane. I don't know Zoë well enough to make her a present but if I did, her soft toy would definitely be a stick insect.

I make Magda a fluffy white cat with big blue eyes, very proud and purry looking. I tie a red satin ribbon round its neck. I make Nadine a lemur with huge black-ringed eyes, black claws and a long stripy tail.

We have a special Girls Day Out on the 22nd so we can give each other our Christmas presents. Magda and Nadine want to meet at Pizza Hut. I argue. I don't win. So I go through agonies before I order. I so badly want a pizza, a huge great deep pan four cheese pizza with garlic bread and a giant glass of Coke – and yet I add up the calories in my head and the numbers flash like pinball machines, 100, 200, 500, *1000* – and so I dither desperately.

Magda orders. Nadine orders.

'Shall I come back in a few minutes?' says the waitress, raising her eyebrows.

'No, she'll have a pizza too, with all the trimmings you've got, pineapple, pepperoni, you name it,' says Magda.

'No I won't!' I say.

'Go on, have it on me. You've got to start eating properly sometime, Ellie, it's getting to be such a *pain.*'

'You've lost heaps of weight, look,' says Nadine,

fiddling with my skirt waistband. 'Positively fading away. Have the pizza special, eh?'

'Get *off*, Nad. No. I'll have a mozzarella and tomato salad and a mineral water,' I say, although the only time I ate mozzarella cheese it was like someone had filled my mouth with soap.

I leave the cheese. I eat the tomato and the little leaves of basil and I drink my fizzy water and I'm so hungry watching Magda and Nadine I even fish out the lemon from my glass and chew up every little bit.

'Yuck, don't *do* that,' says Magda, stuffing her face with pizza.

'Honestly, Ellie, you are a prize nutter,' says Nadine, biting on a huge piece of garlic bread.

'Quit nagging me, both of you.'

'But we're *worried* about you.'

'You've got obsessed with this *stupid* diet.'

'Look, I'm fine. I'm just not very hungry, actually. Don't keep *getting* at me, both of you.'

I can't help feeling hurt. I was so supportive to Nadine. I was so supportive to Magda. Why can't they give me a bit of support for a change?

I feel so upset my tummy ties itself into a knot and I truly do lose my appetite. I put down my knife and fork and wait for Magda and Nadine to finish. They take a long time. They talk with their mouths full, their lips greasy, cheeks distorted, throats convulsing as they swallow.

'Ellie! Pack it in,' says Nadine.

'What? I'm not doing anything.'

'You're staring at me like I'm a boa constrictor and I'm eating a little bunny alive.'

'Well, come *on*. Let's do the presents.'

'When we've finished eating.'

'You have, almost.'

'Pudding!' says Magda. 'I want an ice-cream, don't you, Nadine?'

It is exquisite torture. I have always *adored* ice-cream. Maybe they're just doing this to be mean to me. The waitress brings *three* bowls of strawberry ice-cream.

'Not for me, thanks. It was only two,' I say quickly, not daring to breathe in the sweet strawberry smell.

'I signalled to her to bring three. Eat it, Ellie. Don't be such a spoilsport. You're stopping us having fun, sitting there all po-faced and plaintive,' says Magda.

'Well, if my presence bothers you that much then it's easy, I'll make myself scarce,' I say, getting up.

'Sit *down*, Ellie-phant,' says Magda.

'Don't go all snotty on us, Ellie-Belly,' says Nadine.

'No *wonder* I have a complex about my weight,' I say.

But I sit down again – and I have just one lick of the strawberry ice-cream.

It's as if a strawberry firework has exploded in my head. Another lick, another, another . . . and in less than a minute it's gone. It's so good. I can still taste it all over my tongue. But my heart is hammering. Four hundred calories? Five hundred? Plus the sauce and the whipped cream?

'Relax!' says Magda. 'Here, have your Christmas pressie. Open it now.'

She gives me this pink parcel tied with purple ribbon. It's soft and flat. I open it up – and it's a T-shirt with a picture of the famous statue Venus de Milo gorging chocolates. She's armless, so she's being fed by little fat flying cherubs. She's got a speech bubble above her head saying 'I'm the most beautiful woman in the world and I'm size sixteen – so eat up, babe!'

I laugh and give Magda a hug.

'Have mine too, Ellie,' says Nadine.

Her present is wrapped in black crepe paper tied with silver ribbon. It's very little. When I open it up I find a tiny silver elephant charm on a thin black velvet ribbon.

'It's beautiful,' I say, and I give Nadine a hug too. 'You're the two best friends in all the world. Oh, God, you've both given me such super things and I've reverted to type and done you my stupid hand-made junk again.'

'Christmas wouldn't be Christmas without Ellie's amazing hand-made junk,' says Magda. 'Come on, gimme, gimme.'

'Me too,' says Nadine.

I hand over their presents with immense trepidation but, thank goodness, they actually seem to *like* their toy animals. Magda gives her cat a big cuddle and Nadine makes her lemur climb all over the table and chairs.

Magda and Nadine swop presents too – one has an ultra posh Chanel lipstick and the other has Wolford black glossy tights – a perfect choice for each.

We all end up having a big big big hug when we say goodbye. I wish more than ever we weren't going to the boring old cottage for Christmas.

It takes for ever to load the car up the next morning. It's not just our clothes – there's all sorts of boxes and baskets full of food and drink – and *then* there's the special big box of presents. I have a little peer and prod to see what my presents might be. Looks like books, though there's a little soft parcel too, and a bigger one that rattles.

'Hey, leave that alone, Ellie!' says Dad. 'You're worse than Eggs.' He gives me a quick kiss on the cheek.

He's so happy to be off to the cottage. It's annoying but it's also kind of endearing too. He gets us singing all the crazy old Christmas songs on the journey, awful ancient things like *I Saw Mummy Kissing Santa Claus* and *Jingle Bells* and *Rudolph* and we bellow our way through all those corny Christmas hits of the Seventies and Eighties too. Eggs interrupts every five minutes to ask if we're nearly there but by the time we *are* there he's sound asleep. He doesn't even wake up when Anna lifts him out the car and staggers along the path with him to the front door.

It's raining of course, and blowing a gale too. Wonderful Welsh weather. The cottage looks exactly the same. Worse. When Dad unlocks it this damp smell oozes out as if our faces are being rubbed with an old wet flannel. Dad breathes in deeply, a great smile on his face.

'Home sweet home,' he declares, without a trace of irony.

It's not home and the smell certainly isn't sweet. Even Dad recoils from the kitchen. We forgot to throw out a bag of potatoes from last time and now they've grown so many tentacles they're like something out of *Alien*. Dad has to hold the bag of rotting spuds at arm's length as he throws it out.

Anna tries to get the stove going, hampered by Eggs, who whimpers and clings like a limpet every time she tries to put him down. We have to work hard for *hours* to restore all the ordinary necessities of life to our holiday hovel – heating, hot water, warm food and drink, aired beds – and then when we've got rid of Eggs at last and Anna and Dad and I settle down in the dreary living room with cups of stale instant coffee we find the telly's completely on the blink. There's just a roaring noise like a waterfall and a surge of little starry dots.

'Great,' I say, sighing heavily. 'And I bet there isn't a TV repair place for a hundred miles or more or if there *is* then it'll be closed for Christmas.'

'Old gloomy-guts,' says Dad, refusing to be phased. 'I'll soon fix it.'

The set remains seriously unfixed.

'Oh well, who needs boring old television any-way. We'll play games and chat and make our own amusement. We'll have a really old-fashioned family Christmas—'

'I'll look in Yellow Pages in the morning,' Anna mutters to me.

'Of course it might not be the set at all,' says Dad. 'It could be the transmitter. The line might have gone down in the heavy wind.'

'So we might be in for a total power failure,' I say. 'No telly. No heat. No light. No food.'

'Well, no food will suit you. You've hardly eaten anything for weeks,' says Dad.

He suddenly sounds serious. Anna's looking at me too. Oh, God, I can't face a Spanish Inquisition on my Eating Habits, especially not now. It's an immense relief when the phone starts ringing. I rush to answer it. It'll be Dan. I wonder when he arrived with all his family? I can't wait to catch up with all his news. It's really been ages. I wonder if his ridiculous haircut has improved any. It couldn't look *worse*.

But it isn't Dan at all. It's some sad person trying to sell double-glazing over the phone. They rabbit on before I can stop them, though it's pointless, because the cottage windows could be *triple*-glazed and it wouldn't be near lukewarm and there's no point them banging on about less noise from traffic because there's only the odd passing tractor that manages to make it halfway up this mouldy muddy mountain.

'Sorry, you're wasting your time,' I say, and I put the phone down.

'Playing hard to get with Dan?' says Dad, looking surprised. 'I thought you were getting kind of keen on him. I thought that was maybe why you'd gone into this dire droopy decline. I thought you'd chirp up as soon as he called.'

'Well, you thought wrong, didn't you,' I say. 'And as a matter of fact that *wasn't* Dan. It was someone selling double-glazing, OK? Right, as there's no telly I think I'll have an early night.'

I stomp out the room. I hear Anna groan and say, 'Why do you have to be so tactless?' and Dad moan, 'How was I to know it wasn't Dan? Why hasn't he phoned Ellie anyway?'

I don't *know* why he hasn't phoned. I thought he might try first thing Christmas Eve – but no. When Dad and Anna and Eggs are upstairs I quickly lift the receiver just to make sure the phone hasn't packed up as well as the telly. No, it's still working, and Anna does her best later on, phoning all over the place to find someone to come out and repair the television. With no luck.

'Do not despair. I'll call on Father Christmas,' says Dad, and he jumps in the car.

'*I* want to see Father Christmas, too,' Eggs clamours, but Dad makes him stay with us.

Dad is gone *ages*. Practically long enough to get to Iceland and back.

'Your dad is supposed to cook when we're at the cottage,' says Anna crossly, whipping up omelettes.

It's way past lunchtime and Eggs is driving us mad wailing that he's starving to death.

I feel I'm starving to death too. I managed to go without breakfast altogether, simply slipping my toast

290

in my pocket when no-one was looking and then secretly chucking it in the wastebin. But Anna's omelettes are runny. If I try pocketing mine it'll seep right down my leg and into my sock. Anna makes superb omelettes – and eggs aren't *too* fattening. Though there's the milk and the butter and the cheese – and the crusty bread to go with them. Two slices.

Dad comes back at last, red in the face and ho-ho-hoing like a real Father Christmas. He's bought a brand new portable television. And four portions of fish and chips.

'But we've already eaten lunch, you silly darling,' says Anna, giving him a hug.

'I've had lunch too – a pint and a meat pie down at the pub. But it's Christmas. Let's eat two lunches,' says Dad.

Anna sees my face.

'It's all right. You don't have to, Ellie,' she says quickly.

But takeaway fish and chips have this amazingly pungent smell. My mouth waters as Dad opens up the steaming parcels. Fish and chips from the shop back in London are frequently a disappointment, limp and greasy, but the chippy down the valley is marvellous. The fish is snow-white with wonderful crispy batter and the chips are golden and salty. I try just one – and it's fatal. I end up eating my entire portion of fish and chips, and half of Eggs's too when he tires. Two and a half lunches.

As soon as I've finished I feel terrible. Utterly disgusted at my own greed and weakness. The waistband of my jeans cuts into my full-to-bursting stomach. I wish I could slice it right open so I could scrape all the food out. Well . . . I *could* get rid of it. As long as I don't hang about too long.

I can't risk the bathroom upstairs. The cottage is so small everyone's bound to hear. But there's an ancient outdoor privy we used while Dad was still organizing an indoor bathroom when we first bought the cottage. I've always been frightened of the outside toilet. There isn't a light so you have no idea if there are spiders about to scuttle all over you and you can't properly see the horrible wooden seat and its disgusting smelly hole. I've never dared sit on it properly in case any stray rats splashing around down there might suddenly want to come up for air and bite my bottom.

There's one advantage of such primitive plumbing. When I fight my way through the weeds and get in there the smell is so foul it's easy enough making myself sick. I'm heaving even before I stick a finger down my throat.

It's horrible horrible horrible while it's happening. My heart is hammering and the tears are pouring down my face. Even after it's all over I don't feel much better. I stagger weakly out into the open air and splash dubious water on my face from the old rain butt. It's not raining at the moment but the vicious wind is hopefully bringing some colour back to my cheeks.

I go indoors again, though the smell from the fish and chip papers Anna's bundling up makes me want to puke again.

'Ellie? Are you all right?'

'Mm? Yeah. Fine.'

'Where have you been?'

'I just went to use that horrid outside loo. Eggs was in the proper toilet and I was desperate,' I say. 'Has Dad got the new telly working then?'

I try to edge past her and go into the living room but Anna takes me by the arm.

'Ellie, you look awful.'

'Gee, thanks.'

'You're as white as a sheet. Have you been sick?'

'No.'

'Are you sure? You smell a bit sicky.'

'Oh, this is really Let's Flatter Ellie time. First you say I look awful and then you say I smell. Terrific.' I'm trying to joke but I feel ridiculously tearful and my mouth is starting to burble of its own accord. 'I *know* I look awful, you don't have to rub it in. I'm just a flabby fat fright, I know. No wonder Dan's gone off me, can't even be bothered to come and see me when he's just the other side of this stupid mountain, he was the one meant to be mad about me but that didn't last five minutes, did it, and now . . .'

'Now?' Anna repeats urgently.

There's a burst of cartoon music from the living room and Eggs yells triumphantly.

'Wallace and Gromit!'

'Hey, come on, you girls, come and watch the telly!'

'Come on,' I say, sniffing. 'Seeing as he's gone to such trouble to get it.'

'No. In a minute. Let's have this out now,' says Anna, hanging on to me. 'Ellie.' She takes a deep breath.

'*What?*'

'Are you going to have a baby?'

'WHAT???'

I stare at her in total astonishment.

'I've been trying to psych myself up to asking you for ages. I kept telling myself I was jumping to mad conclusions. I haven't said anything to Dad. I promise I won't breathe a word till you say it's OK. And it *is* OK. I mean, obviously it's not what anyone planned, and we'll have to consider all the options but the world isn't going to come to an end. We'll manage no matter what you decide. And it's *your* decision, Ellie, because it's *your* baby.'

'Anna. Listen. I'm not going to have a baby.'

'Well, if that's what you've decided—'

'I'm not pregnant! Anna, are you crackers or something? Baby? Me?' Then I suddenly gasp. 'Oh, God, is it because I've got so fat?'

'No! You've got *thin* over the past few weeks, but I thought that was because you were worrying – and unhappy because Dan hadn't got in touch.'

'Dan? Oh Anna, you didn't think *Dan* was the father!' The idea is so ludicrous I burst out laughing.

Anna can't help giggling too.

'Look, Dan and I haven't done anything at all. Just a few kisses, that's all. How could you think . . . ?'

'I know, it did all seem so unlikely. But you must admit, you've been a bit withdrawn and moody lately, completely off your food, being sick, suddenly terrified of looking fat – and then I couldn't help noticing you haven't touched your Tampax box this month. I know you're not really regular just yet but it all started to add up. Oh Ellie, you've no idea how great it feels that I've got my sums wrong!'

She gives me a hug, but then she tenses.

'You *do* smell of sick.'

'Stop it! Don't start *again*!'

Anna holds me at arms' length and looks me straight in the eyes.

'What *is* wrong, Ellie?'

'Nothing.'

'Come on. You haven't been yourself for ages.'

'Well, good. I don't like myself. I want to be a *new* self.'

'I liked the old Ellie,' says Anna. 'You've lost some of your sparkle. You're so pale and drawn looking. I was mad to encourage you with that stupid diet. You've lost too much weight.'

'No, I haven't. I've hardly started. I'm still horribly fat, look.' I pluck at my clothes with disgust.

'*You* look,' says Anna, lifting my thick jumper.

'Get *off*, Anna,' I say, trying to pull away. 'Stop staring at me.'

'You've lost *lots* of weight. I didn't realize just how much. Oh God. Ellie, you're not anorexic, are you?'

'Of course not. Look, I eat heaps. Like two dinners today, right?'

'Yes, I suppose so. Unless . . . Ellie, you didn't deliberately make yourself sick, did you?'

My heart is thumping but I manage to meet her eyes.

'Honestly, Anna, give it a rest. First I'm pregnant, then I'm anorexic, then bulimic!'

'Sorry, sorry. I'm making a complete mess of all this. Look, the Dan situation. You say you're not friends any more?'

'I don't know. I don't know what the situation *is* because I haven't seen Dan for ages.'

'Are you two women going to stay gassing in this kitchen all day long?' says Dad, putting his head round the door. 'Come and watch the new telly now I've got it.'

'OK, OK, we're coming.'

'And you'll be seeing Dan soon enough,' says Dad. 'I bumped into his dad in the pub. I invited the whole family over for a Christmas drink this evening!'

# Chapter Eight

'You've done *what*?' I say to Dad.

'I thought you'd be pleased,' says Dad, bewildered. 'You've been dying to see young Dan, haven't you?'

'No! Well . . . the point is, I wanted *him* to get in touch with *me*. Now he'll think this is all my idea. Oh Dad, how could you?'

'Yes, how *could* you?' says Anna. 'You idiot! Christmas drinks? What drinks? We've only got wine for the meal tomorrow and a few cans of beer. And then there's all their kids. How many are there, five, six? And what about *food*? We'll have to give them snacks of some sort. I've got one jumbo bag of crisps and one tin of peanuts. They'll wolf them down in one gulp.'

'Is Dan coming, Dad? I like Dan. He plays good games and makes me laugh,' says Eggs.

'Yes, pal. Dan is coming. I'm glad *someone's* pleased.' He hoists Eggs onto his shoulder and they go back to the television.

'I'm not going to be here when they come,' I insist. 'I'll go out.'

'Don't be daft, Ellie. Where can you go? You can't tramp up and down the mountain in the dark.'

'But it'll look so gross. Oh God, if I stay *I'll* look gross. I haven't brought any of my decent clothes with me.'

'Neither have I. Still, Dan's family aren't exactly stylish dressers.'

We both have a catty giggle. They are dedicated anorak wearers.

'So what *are* we going to give them to eat?' Anna says, looking through the cardboard boxes in the kitchen. 'I'll have to drive down to the village and raid the Spar shelves. Honestly. As if I haven't got enough to do. I was going to get all the veg prepared and stuff the turkey ready for tomorrow.'

'I'll get started on all that,' I say.

I scrub potatoes and peel sprouts and stuff turkey until my hands are sore. Then I dab at my face in the freezing bathroom and try to pull my hair into place. I pull on my black jeans and my black and silver shirt. My stomach still seems bloated and I'm scared they won't fit – but I can button the jeans easily and the shirt doesn't pull across my chest the way it used to. So I must have lost weight. Quite a lot . . .

Anna is really grateful when she gets back from her trip to Spar, and even more so when I grill little sausages and fill vol-au-vent cases and wrap brown bread around tinned asparagus spears. I arrange them ultra-decoratively, making little faces with wedges of cheese and pineapple and olives on crackers for the children. I don't have as much as one nibble although I'm feeling a bit faint – but I get a weird little thrill out of this. I'm in control now. I'm getting thinner.

I'M GETTING THINNER!

But I feel fatter-fatter-fatter when I hear the car draw up outside the cottage and the slam of doors and lots of voices.

Anna, Dad and Eggs go to the front door. I hang back, trying to look cool.

Dan's brothers and sisters pour in, wearing hand-knitted old jumpers and baggy dungarees. There are far more than I remembered – some have got friends with them. It's a good job Anna did her Spar trek. Then Dan's mum and dad come in and they're wearing matching sheep sweaters and jeans that go in and out in all the wrong places. They've got friends too – a man with yet another jolly jumper (manic woolly frogs) and smelly old cords, and a droopy woman in a patchwork waistcoat and an Indian skirt with an uneven hem.

Then another stranger comes in. A girl about my age. Another refugee from the Style Police. She's wearing a man's rugby shirt and saggy tracksuit bottoms. There's a lot of bottom in the bottoms. She's not exactly fat – just big all over, and brawny with it. There are serious muscles under those stripes. She's got long hair that looks even frizzier than mine but it's scraped back in a schoolgirly plait so tight it's making her forehead pulse. She smiles.

'Hi there, folks.'

Oh, God. She's even heartier than I thought. Who is she?

'I'm Gail,' she says, waggling her fat fingers. 'I'm Dan's friend.'

I stare at her. The whole room goes suddenly quiet. Waiting. Dan himself makes his entrance. He trips over the doormat, staggers dramatically, and is about to go headlong but Gail catches his arm and yanks him upright.

'Whoops!' she says.

'Whoops indeed,' Dad mutters, suddenly by my side. 'Hey Ellie, what are you drinking, sweetheart? Coke? Orange juice? Tiny drop of wine?'

He is being sweetly supportive, even offering me a chance to drown my sorrows.

'Ellie, can you pass round some of the plates? Ellie did all the food. Hasn't she done it artistically?' says Anna, forcing everyone in the room to nod admiringly.

Dan is standing still, red in the face, but his eyes are gleaming behind his steamed-up glasses. His severe crewcut has grown into a strange scrubbing brush that defies gravity. Gail grins and ruffles his bristles affectionately.

'Honestly, Danny, you are a fool.'

Dan certainly looks a fool. He's wearing a man's rugby shirt too. The shoulders droop at his elbows, the hem flaps round his knees. It is sadly obvious that this is a virgin rugby shirt that has never seen action on a muddy field. Perhaps Gail has another kind of action in mind. She can hardly keep her hands off him.

Eggs does his best to elbow her out of the way.

'Hi, Dan, hi! It's me! Eggs!'

'Hi, Eggs,' Dan says, and he picks him up and turns him upside down and tickles him.

Eggs squeals and wriggles and kicks. One of his feet catches Gail right in the stomach. Anyone else would double up, but she seems to be made of india rubber.

'Hey, little sprog! Watch those Kickers!' she says, and she takes him from Dan and shakes him.

It's good-humoured and if it was Dan Eggs would adore it – but he stiffens instead.

'Stop it! Put me down! You'll make me sick!' he screams.

Gail puts him back on his feet, her eyebrows raised.

'Hey, calm down! You're fine,' she says.

Eggs ignores her. He looks straight at Dan.

'Who *is* that girl?'

'That's Gail. She's my friend,' says Dan.

'Do you mean your *girlfriend*?'

'Hey, hey, Eggs, that's enough,' says Anna. 'Come over here.' She can't remove him physically because she's balancing three platefuls of food and her hands are working overtime as it is.

Dan shuffles in his plimsolls. Gail is nowhere near as reticent.

'Sure, I'm Dan's girlfriend,' she announces.

'No you're not,' Eggs says, outraged. '*Ellie's* Dan's girlfriend, not you.'

'Shut *up*, Eggs,' I say, backing against the wall.

Eggs won't shut up.

'Why can't Ellie still be your girlfriend? She's much nicer,' Eggs insists.

'Button it, Eggs,' says Dad, and he whisks him up and takes him upstairs.

Eggs remains unbuttoned, shrieking as he goes. There's a terrible silence downstairs.

Oh God. Everyone's trying very hard indeed to pretend I'm not here.

'Who'd like a vol-au-vent?' Anna says desperately.

'I'll fetch some more,' I gabble and rush out to the kitchen.

I lean against the sink and pour myself a glass of water. I gulp it, trying to calm down.

'Ellie?'

I splutter. Dan has followed me into the kitchen.

'Are you OK?'

I've got water dribbling out of my nose and he asks me if I'm OK! Dan thumps me hard on the back.

'Hey! Don't!'

'Sorry, sorry, I just thought you might be choking.'

'Well I'm not. And it should be me thumping you, not the other way round.'

'Oh I'm sorry, Ellie. I didn't know what to *do*. I thought I'd just sort of fade out of the picture. It would be easier for everyone, right? I thought you'd maybe sussed things out already, and anyway, it was always me crazy about you, not the other way round.

303

I thought we'd maybe not even meet up – but then your dad invited us all, and *my* dad said it would look ever so rude if Gail and I didn't come too. I felt awful. I mean, it wasn't like I was trying to flaunt Gail in front of you. Even though I'm so crackers about her now you're still my *first* girlfriend and – and – and I know I should have told you about her but I kept putting it off and—'

'Dan. Stop burbling. It's not like we were ever a real *item*. It's no big deal. Honestly.'

Am I just saying this or do I really mean it? Dan is a good mate but I was mad to think I could ever nurse a grand passion for him. Or a weeny passion. Or any passion at all.

If Gail was a slender stylish sort of girl then I'd feel horrible. But she's like a cartoon version of me – only even fatter. Built like a tank, in fact. With the same knack of squashing people flat. She comes bounding into the kitchen even though it's obvious Dan and I need five minutes together to sort things out in private.

'No hard feelings, eh, Ellie?' she says, clapping me on the shoulder.

I'll have a large bruise there tomorrow.

She insists on telling me this long and totally dreary tale of how they met. She was part of a girls' rugby team playing a match at Dan's school and he provided the oranges at half time. Oh please, is this *romance*? Then they saw each other on a bus and Dan was just bowled over. Apparently. Anyway, what do I care?

I really *don't* care. And yet . . . even though Dan is

such a totally sad case it feels a bit weird not to have anyone at all now. I originally invented a relationship between us just to kid on to Magda and Nadine that I had a proper boyfriend at long last. After they found out I went through a stage of thinking maybe Dan could still be a boyfriend. He looks a complete idiot and acts like it too but he *can* be bright and funny and inventive. Occasionally. And he always had this one redeeming feature. He treated me like I was Juliet and he was Romeo.

Only now it turns out I was just his Rosaline. *Gail* is Juliet. They're acting out their major love scene right in front of my eyes. They're hardly Leonardo di Caprio and Claire Danes, granted. But when they look into each other's eyes and laugh it's as if they're in a little world of their own. And everyone crammed into our mouldy cottage belongs to someone else and I suddenly feel so lonely, because I'm on my own and I haven't got anyone – not even Dan.

There's one good thing. I feel so out of it that I don't even feel hungry. I pass plates of food round and round the room and I hand out glass after glass of drinks but the only thing I have all evening is water from the tap. No calories at all.

Anna dodges out to the kitchen and comes up to me.

'I think you're being marvellous, Ellie.'

'It's just as well you don't still think I'm pregnant,' I say. 'Oh Anna, imagine Dan being a dad. He'd wrap a nappy round its head and tie a bib on its bottom.'

Anna and I laugh, all girls together. Half an hour

later I see Dad hold up this corny bunch of mistletoe and they kiss like love's young dream. I feel so lonely again. So totally out of it that the social smile stiffens on my face and tears prick my eyes.

I know what I want to do. I want to phone my girlfriends. But the phone is in the living room and all these people are milling about talking and kids are dashing around all over the place and it's simply not possible.

'Ellie?' Dad leaves Anna and comes over to me. 'Ellie, are you all right?'

'No. I'm all wrong.'

Dad drops the mistletoe onto the carpet.

'I'm sorry. This is all my fault. I'm an idiot. What can I do to make it up to you?'

'Make them all vanish so I can phone Nadine and Magda.'

'Mmm. I'll try,' he says. He wiggles his nose, shuts his eyes, and mumbles, 'Hocus pocus, Gobbledegook, Please disappear when I next have a look.'

'Er . . . it hasn't worked, Dad.'

'True. Do you really badly want to phone Magda and Nadine?'

'Yes. But I can't. Not in front of everyone.'

'Well, I'm Father Christmas, right? So shove a coat on and come and have a ride on my sleigh.'

Dad takes my hand and we slip out of the house. He drives me down to the village, parks outside the public phone box, and presents me with his own phone card.

'Oh, Dad! Hey, you're *my* Father Christmas.

Thanks ever so,' I say, giving him a hug.

I phone Nadine first.

'Oh Ellie, I'm going completely off my head,' Nadine whispers. 'My aunty and uncle and my gran are all here and the curly-haired lisping infant is showing off till it makes me sick and everyone keeps nagging me to cheer up because it's Christmas. It's the total pits.'

I soothe in sisterly fashion, and reassure her that I'm actually having a *worse* time, with my ex-boyfriend parading his new girlfriend at my party.

Then I phone Magda and she's got a party going on at her house too.

'But I just can't get into the party mood somehow,' Magda says. 'There's several really tasty-looking boys, my brothers' mates, and normally I'd be bouncing about in my element but since that awful night with Mick I'm kind of scared. I don't want anyone else to get the wrong impression, so I've just been really quiet and hardly talking to them and my entire family keep telling me to cheer up because it's Christmas and I'm, like, *so*?'

'I've just phoned Nadine and she feels exactly the same way.'

'Well, at least you're OK, Ellie. You've got Dan and *he's* hardly likely to leap on top of you and then spread filthy stories about you. He's a total sweetie even if he's a bit of a berk. Oh sorry, I didn't mean that the way it sounds.'

'Feel free to insult him all you like, Magda,' I say, and I tell her about Dan and his new love.

We end up having a really good laugh about it until Dad's phone card runs out.

'That was a *great* Christmas present,' I say.

I get some great real presents the next day too – a book on Frida Kahlo, *The Bell Jar* by Sylvia Plath, *The Color Purple* by Alice Walker, a stylish black designer swimming costume and a big box of very expensive artists' chalks – all from Dad and Anna. Eggs gives me a new sketch book. I spend most of Christmas morning doing a portrait of each of them.

We're playing Happy Families.

But then it all goes wrong.

We sit down to Christmas dinner around two o'clock. I've told Anna I want a really small portion but all the plates are piled high. She sees me looking anxious.

'Just leave what you don't want, Ellie,' she says, trying to keep the peace.

It's not that easy. Once my teeth get started they won't stop. It's truly delicious: large glistening golden turkey with chestnut stuffing and cranberry sauce, little chipolatas and bacon rolls, roast potatoes, sprouts, parsnips, beans. I eat and eat and eat, and it tastes so good I can't put my knife and fork down, I cut and spear and munch until every morsel is gone. I even wipe my finger round my plate to savour up the last smear of gravy.

'Ellie! You'll be licking your plate next,' says Dad, but he's smiling. 'It's great to see you've got your appetite back.'

I don't stop there. The mince pies were all eaten at

the party last night but there's still Christmas pudding with brandy butter, and then I have a tangerine, and then three chocolates with my coffee.

'Glug glug,' says Eggs, downing a cherry brandy liqueur chocolate.

'Oh God!' says Anna. 'Spit it out at once, Eggs!'

Eggs swallows, his eyes sparkling.

'Am I drunk now? Ooh, goodee! Am I going to sing silly stuff like Dan's dad did last night?'

'You sing silly stuff without being drunk,' says Anna. 'Don't you dare touch any more of those liqueur chocolates.'

'That's not fair. You let Ellie.'

'Well, Ellie's nearly grown up.'

I'm not so sure. I don't know whether it's the half glass of champagne at the start of the meal or the three chocs at the end, but I'm starting to feel seriously woozy. My stomach hurts I've stretched it so much. I put my hands on it gingerly. It's huge, like I'm suddenly six months pregnant.

I suddenly panic. What am I *playing* at, stuffing myself with all this food? I must have put on pounds and pounds. I've messed up all the past weeks of careful dieting.

I've got to do something about it. Quick.

'I feel like a bit of fresh air,' I say, getting up from the table.

'Hang on. We'll just tackle the dishes and then we'll all go for a walk,' says Dad.

'No, I feel all funny. I'm just going outside for a bit. Leave the dishes. I'll help with them later,' I say.

I rush out without even stopping to grab a coat.

'Ellie?' says Dad.

'She's drunk!' Eggs declares. 'Um! Ellie's drunk.'

I do feel drunk as the icy air hits me. The mountain moves, the woods waver, the little brick privy fades in and out of vision. I feel sick. Thank God, it's going to be easy.

I breathe in deeply inside the loo. I retch at the smell. I get ready, tuck my hair back behind my ears, shove two fingers down my throat.

It all happens in a rush and a roar. My eyes are tightly shut, tears seeping down my cheeks. Then I hear someone gasp. I open my eyes and see Anna peering round the door at me.

'Anna! Leave . . . me . . . alone!' I gasp.

She's waiting outside when I stagger out.

'What the hell are you doing to yourself, Ellie?'

My heart pounds. I hold my neck. My throat's so sore now. I'm trembling.

'I was being sick, that's all. Don't look at me like that. I couldn't help it. It's because I ate so much. The chocolates must have been the last straw.'

'Don't lie, Ellie. I followed you. I saw what you were doing.'

'You followed me into the lavatory? What sort of weird snoopy act is that?'

'I care about you, Ellie. I've let you pull the wool over my eyes these past weeks but now we've got to sort this out. We're going to talk it over with your father.'

'Now? For God's sake, Anna, it's Christmas Day.'

'Yes, and it was the Christmas dinner I spent all morning cooking on that awful stove, and it all turned out OK in the end, and I was so thrilled when you ate it all up so appreciatively, and we were having such a lovely time and then, *then* you go and spoil everything.'

'I was sick. That's not my fault.'

'You liar! I saw you put your fingers down your throat.'

'OK, OK, I felt sick and I just needed to help myself—'

'You're bulimic, Ellie. You did it yesterday too. I knew you had, but you kept lying to me. *Why* are you doing this? It's so mad. I can't understand how anyone could want to make themselves sick.'

'I don't enjoy it! It's awful. But what else can I do when I'm so weak-willed and eat myself silly. I've *got* to get rid of all that extra food before it makes me even fatter.'

'But you're *not* fat.'

'I *am*. Horribly fat.'

'You're not, you're not!'

'What on earth are you two doing out there?' Dad calls from the open kitchen door. 'Why are you shouting at each other? Come indoors, you're both shivering. What is it? What's happened?'

We go in. Anna starts. I tell her to leave it for another time. Dad tries to lighten things up, but Anna insists he listen to her. She says all this stupid stuff about me, exaggerating heaps. I'm *not* bulimic. I've made myself sick three times, that's all. No big deal.

And I'm not anorexic either, though Anna insists I'm that too.

'Ellie can't have that slimming disease thingy,' says Eggs. 'She isn't thin, she's fat.'

'See!' I say, and I burst into tears.

Anna says Eggs doesn't really mean fat. Eggs says he does. Anna tells Eggs to be quiet. Eggs says it's not fair. *He* bursts into tears. Dad says this is ridiculous, it's Christmas, and he's bought this brand new television and now nobody's watching it and why did Anna have to start this stupid row. Anna says she's desperately concerned about me and Dad ought to be a better father and she's sick to death of worrying about me and *she* bursts into tears. Dad says we're all getting upset about nothing and of course Ellie isn't really anorexic or bulimic and neither is she fat and there's nothing to worry about and let's stop all this nonsense and make the most of Christmas.

So we try.

Thank God for the television. There's a good film on and after a few snuffles and sighs and wounded glances we all get absorbed. We're almost playing Happy Families again – but then it's teatime.

I daren't risk starting eating again in case I can't stop. So I just sit there quietly, sipping a cup of Earl Grey tea with lemon, doing nobody any harm.

'Ellie! You're not eating,' says Anna.

'I still feel a bit sick.'

'Don't start now.'

'I *do*.'

'Have some of this yummy Christmas cake. Look,

312

this bit's got extra icing,' Dad says heartily, as if I'm Eggs's age.

'I don't want any cake, thank you,' I say, though the rich moist fruity smell is making my mouth water. I especially like the icing, that lovely crisp bite in and then the sweetness spreading over the tongue blended with the odd almondy tang of marzipan.

'How about just a tiny slice if you've really not got any appetite?' says Dad.

I could eat a huge slice. Two. I could eat the entire cake in one go, for goodness' sake.

'I'm really not hungry.'

Anna sighs. 'OK. No cake. But your stomach is completely empty now. You must eat something. A slice of bread and butter – and some fresh fruit – and a slither of cheese.'

She cleverly arranges a dainty slice of bread on a plate and puts a Cox's apple and a few green grapes and a slice of brie beside it.

'Hardly any calories, and it's all good wholesome nourishing food,' she says.

It's so tempting – but my total splurge at lunchtime has scared me. Once I start I won't stop. It'll be another slice of bread and then another, more fruit, all the brie, then I'll get started on the stilton . . .

'No thank you,' I say primly, pushing the plate away.

'Oh for God's sake, Ellie,' says Dad. 'Eat the damn food.'

'No.'

'Look, you're acting so childishly. Just eat it.'

'I don't want to.'

'Then get down from the table and stop spoiling Christmas tea for everybody else,' says Dad.

'Certainly,' I say, and I march out of the room.

Anna is crying again. I feel guilty. She was trying to be kind. But I can't help it. I'm not being difficult on purpose. I've been a positive saint this Christmas helping with all the cooking and not throwing a tantrum when Dan paraded his girlfriend before me. I'm not demanding special treatment or my own diet. I tried to be as discreet as possible when I was sick. It's not my fault Anna came snooping after me. Why can't they all just leave me alone?

Dad comes to talk to me.

'Leave me alone.'

Anna comes to talk to me.

'Leave me alone.'

So I am left alone for the entire evening. I can hear them downstairs laughing at something on the television. I take my new chalks and my new sketch book and draw a table groaning with Christmas fare. But it's all been spoilt – there's furry mould growing on the sandwiches, the fruit is rotting in the bowl, little mice are nibbling the cheese, and flies crawl all over the white icing on the cake.

# Chapter Nine

A pattern sets in. I don't eat. Anna cries. Dad shouts. I go to my room and draw. I don't eat. Anna cries. Dad shouts.

I go to my room and draw . . .

Eggs stays on the sidelines.

'You're mad, Ellie,' he says, slurping chocolate in front of me.

'She's driving us all mad,' says Dad. 'For God's sake, Ellie, how can you be so selfish and self-obsessed? You're just playing for attention.'

'I don't want attention. I want to be left alone.'

'It's all my fault,' says Anna.

'What?'

'I was the one who suggested a diet in the first place. It was crazy of me. And then it's been hard for Ellie, losing her mother and having to get used to a stepmother. I think it's partly symbolic. Ellie and I have got closer recently and this is worrying for her. She must feel she's being disloyal to her mother's memory. So she rejects my food. It's a way of rejecting all my nurturing and care.'

'I've never heard such silly rubbish,' says Dad. 'I can't stomach that psychological claptrap. Don't you start blaming yourself, Anna! You've been great with Ellie. Look, she's just gone on a diet and got obsessed with it, that's all. She's got nothing else to think about while she's here. And she's probably brooding about the Dan situation – which I didn't help, I know.'

They're both so *wrong*. It's certainly nothing to do with Dan. We saw them when we were out for a very wet walk. Dan and Gail were wearing matching orange cagoules, hoods pulled low over the forehead. They were clasping woolly gloves and striding out in step, left, right, left, right. They might have been made for each other. I must have been mad ever to think Dan might have been made for *me*.

It's not anything to do with Anna either, although that gets to me more. I feel guilty about Anna. I don't want to make her so worried about me. I didn't realize I could bother her so much. And fancy her saying that about my real mum! I never talk about Mum to anyone. Dad thinks I've forgotten all about her.

I'll never forget. I still talk to her sometimes in my head. I've got her photo on my bedside table at home but I didn't bring it to the cottage. I suddenly long to see it. I try drawing Mum from memory but it doesn't work out too well. The line falters as I try to sketch her chest, her waist, her hips. I've always thought my mum looked beautiful — long dark properly curly hair, not frizzy like mine. Big dark eyes, heart-shaped face, soft cheeks, soft white arms, soft cushiony breasts — I can still just about remember the way she used to cuddle me when she put me to bed. But now I think of her soft curvy body and I wonder. Was my mum a little bit fat? Not as fat as me, of course, but still pretty chubby.

I try to remember what she looked like without any clothes. I must have seen her in her bath, or pottering around the bedroom in her bra and knickers? I feel bad, as if I'm snooping through a keyhole at her. What does it matter if she was fat or thin? This is my dead mother, for heaven's sake.

I don't believe in heaven but I draw a child's version of it, all snowy clouds and golden gateways and I seat my mum on a special starry throne, decked out in a spangly robe and designer wings in sunset shades. Just for a moment her sweet chalk face softens in a smile and she says 'What does it matter if *you're* fat or thin, Ellie?'

I know she's right and I try to hang on to this. Maybe if she and I were by ourselves in the cottage we'd have a meal together and we'd laugh and talk and eat, no trouble at all. But when Dad insists I come down for dinner he's all bossy and blustering.

'Now stop this silly nonsense right now, Ellie. You're going to clear your plate, do you hear me?'

Anna is all tense and tearful.

'I've fixed you a special salad, Ellie, and there's cottage cheese, no calories at all. You can just have a tangerine for pudding – just so long as you eat *something*.'

Eggs is ultra-irritating.

'I'm eating all my turkey pie and all my mashed potatoes and all my sweetcorn and *then* I'm eating all my ice-cream because it's yummy and I want it in my tummy. I'm good, aren't I, not like silly smelly Ellie belly who's still f-a-t even if she *is* on this stupid diet.'

How can I relax and say, 'OK, folks, drama over, I'll eat normally now?'

So I don't eat (apart from a few mouthfuls that I chew for ages and sometimes manage to spit into my paper hankie) and Anna cries and Dad shouts and I go to my room and draw.

'Thank you for spoiling Christmas for everyone, Ellie,' says Dad as we drive home. He's gripping the steering wheel so fiercely he'll rip it right out of the dashboard in a minute.

'I didn't do anything. I don't know why you're being so horrible to me.'

'Now listen to me, young lady. I'm making a doctor's appointment for you the minute we get home, do you hear me?'

'You're shouting so hard the whole *motorway* can hear you.'

'I've just about had *enough* of you and your wise-crack answers and your pained face and pursed lips at the dinner table and your sheer bloody obstinacy. You've not eaten properly for days. *Weeks*. You're making yourself ill. It's dangerous to lose so much weight so quickly. You look a complete wreck, all gaunt and pale and ghostly, like some poor soul with a terminal illness.'

Do I *really* look gaunt? I try to see myself in Dad's driving mirror. I suck in my cheeks hopefully but it's useless, I look as round and roly-poly as always, baby cheeks and chubby chin.

'I suppose you think you look soulful and interesting,' says Dad, catching my eye in the mirror. 'Well, you don't, you look dreadful. And you're so undernourished you're coming out in spots.'

'Thanks a bunch, Dad,' I say, feeling a hundred suppurating boils erupt all over my face.

I *had* been feeling a bit mean because I know how much Christmas at the cottage means to Dad, and he'd tried to be really sweet, buying the little telly and taking me down to the phone box so I could chat to Nadine and Magda but now he's being so horrid I don't care at all if he feels I mucked up his Christmas. *Good*. I can't stick him. He can't force me to go to the doctor. It's *my* body and I can do what I want with it.

I can't be bothered unpacking and doing any of the boring stuff when we get home. Why should I help Dad and Anna when they just nag at me all the time? I rush to the bathroom, take off my shoes and my jeans and my heavy bangle and weigh myself. Wow. I really have lost weight. Of course I'm still *fat*. I stare at myself sideways on in the bathroom mirror, hiking up my shirt to get a proper peek at my tum and bum and OK, I'm maybe a *weeny* bit smaller but I'm still huge. But not *quite* as huge as I was. Still a lot fatter than Magda, and totally gross compared with Nadine. But improving. I wonder if Nadine and Magda will notice?

I phone them. Magda first.

'Let's meet up, right? *Not* my place, it's all doom and gloom with my family,' I hiss. 'What about the Soda Fountain?' I could just have a fizzy mineral water, no problem.

'No, not the Soda Fountain,' Magda says quickly. 'Let's go somewhere . . . quiet. How about upstairs in John Wiltshire's?'

'What?' John Wiltshire's is this dreary old department store where all these grannies meet for a cup of tea. 'Are you kidding, Mags?'

'No. They have luscious cakes. Or are you still dieting?'

'Well. Sort of,' I say casually. 'OK, John Wiltshire's will be fine with me if that's what you want. Four o'clock? I'll phone Nadine, right?'

Nadine sounds a bit odd too. Very subdued.

'Are you OK, Nad?'

'No,' says Nadine.

I can hear Natasha in the background, squealing and giggling, and Nadine's mother clapping and clucking at her.

'Family life getting you down?'

'Understatement of the century,' says Nadine. 'Oh Ellie, wait till you hear. I can't bear it!'

'*What?*'

'No. I can't tell you properly now, not with you-know-who around. I'll tell you when we meet up, right? Only don't say I told you so, *please*.'

'Promise. Four o'clock, John Wiltshire's. I can't wait!'

But when we meet up we're both so distracted by Magda we forget Nadine's revelations. My weight loss goes unremarked. We are just utterly *jawpunched* by Magda's appearance.

I don't even *recognize* her at first. I spot Nadine hunched at one of the twee pink-clothed tables with some mousey short-haired girl in a grey jacket. Then this same girl smiles wanly at me. I do a triple take.

'Magda! What have you *done*?'

Nadine signals to me frantically with her eyebrows.

'You look so different, but – but it looks . . . great,' I lie desperately.

'It looks totally crappy and so do I,' says Magda, and she bursts into tears.

'Oh Mags, don't,' I say, putting my arms round her.

I stare down at her poor shorn head. It isn't just the new brutal haircut. It's the colour. Magda's been a bright bottle-blonde right from our first day in Year Seven when she was eleven years old. I've never been able to picture her any other way. But now she's had it dyed back to what is presumably her natural pale brown. Only it doesn't look natural on Magda. She looks like she's taken off her own jaunty flowery sunhat and borrowed an old lady's 'Rainmate' by mistake.

Nadine orders us all pots of Earl Grey and toasted

teacakes. I am so distracted by Magda I munch teacake absent-mindedly. It's only when I'm licking the butter from my lips that I realize I've chomped my way through hundreds of unnecessary calories. Oh, God. I wonder about a quick dash to the Ladies but the cubicles will be in full earshot of everyone, and I don't want to miss out on anything when Magda and Nadine spill the beans.

'Sorry about the snivelling,' says Magda, wiping her eyes. She's not wearing any make-up either, so she looks oddly unfinished, as if someone has already wiped half her face away.

'Your hair really looks quite . . . cute when you get used to it,' I try again.

'That sort of gamine look is actually very hip now,' says Nadine.

'You liars,' says Magda. 'It looks awful. And the colour is the end too. Not even mouse, more like moulting hamster with terminal disease. I'm going to get it dyed again before school but how the hell can I grow it again in a week?' She tugs at the limp little locks in despair.

'So – *why*, Magda?' says Nadine. 'Did the dye go wrong so you had to cut it all off or what?'

'Or what indeed,' said Magda. 'No, it was just . . . Oh, it's so stupid. I thought I was over that night with Mick, you know, but I went into town last Saturday – remember I phoned you and asked you to come, Nadine, but you said you were busy?'

'Don't!' says Nadine. 'Oh, God, I wish I *had* come with you. Anyway. Go on.'

'And you were still stuck in Wales, Ellie, but I thought never mind, I'll go round the sales anyway, as I had lots of lovely Christmas lolly to spend. I went with my brother Steve because his girlfriend Lisa works at the Virgin record store so she's tied up on Saturdays and so Steve and I had a good look round the Flowerfields Shopping Centre and I got some new shoes and he did too and we went into *La Senza*, you know, that nice nightie place, and I bought this cute little nightshirt with teddies on and Steve bought this cream lacey negligee for Lisa because she'd said she liked it ages ago and now it was down to half price. Anyway, we were a bit tired by this time and I was wearing my new shoes and they were making my feet ache a bit so Steve suggested we go and have a milkshake in the Soda Fountain and . . .'

'Were Mick and his mates there?'

'Not Mick himself, but some of those guys he hangs out with, Larry and Jamie and several others. I sat right the other side with Steve and we were just clowning around. You know what fun our Steve can be. He took Lisa's negligee out of the carrier and held it up against himself, and I was laughing away at him when I suddenly looked up and all these boys were staring at me and then they all started mouthing *Slag* at me and I just about died.'

'Oh Magda, you mustn't take any notice of them. They're just pathetic scum,' I say fiercely.

'But I just couldn't stand the way they were looking at Steve and me. They'd obviously got completely the wrong end of the stick.'

'You should have told your Steve.'

'Yes, and he'd be banged up for grievous bodily harm right this minute. Anyway, I tried to work out *why* all these boys have got the wrong idea about me.'

'It's simple, you nutcase. You look a million dollars!'

Used to look a million dollars. Now it's down to thousands. Hundreds. Several dollars.

Magda reads my expression. 'Exactly. It was my blond hair and the make-up and the showy clothes. So I thought, right, I'll stop being blond, so I went to this hairdresser with the rest of my Christmas dosh and said I wanted it all cut off and dyed back to its original colour. They didn't think it a very good idea, but I insisted. Oh, God, why am I such a fool? Look at it!' She runs her hands through her hair.

'It'll grow,' says Nadine. 'Give it another month or so and it'll look great, you'll see. And maybe you can go back to being blonde again. I can't quite get used to you as a brunette, Magda.'

'And what's with this old grey jacket? You've got a red fur coat to die for,' I say. 'Honestly, Magda, I think you've had half your brain cut off as well as all your hair. How can you possibly let a sad little bunch of schoolboy prats affect the way you look?'

'Hello?' says Nadine. 'Do you hear what you're saying, Ellie? Just one kid calls you fat at that *Spicy* mag do and you go totally anorexic overnight.'

'That's nonsense,' I say, blushing hotly. I didn't realize Nadine actually *heard*. 'And I'm not anorexic. Look, I've just eaten a huge great buttery teacake. I bet that's 400 calories gone for a burton already.'

'You're *proving* my case,' says Nadine. 'And look at yourself, Ellie. You really are getting much thinner.' She flattens my sweater against my stomach. 'Look Mags. The incredible shrinking girl.'

'Oh, Ellie. *You're* mad too. It doesn't suit you going all skinny,' says Magda.

Skinny! Ow wow. SKINNY! I'm not, of course. I've still got a long long long way to go before I could possibly be called skinny. But still . . .

'You've no idea how scary this is,' says Nadine. 'It's like my two best friends have been taken over by aliens. *The X-Files* have got nothing on this.'

'*You* looked different the day you went to the *Spicy* girl heat.'

'Don't remind me,' says Nadine, and she flicks her last piece of teacake in my face.

'So anyway, what's with you, Nad? What was this seriously awful thing that happened to you?'

'Oh God,' said Nadine. 'Do I have to?'

'Yes!'

'Well, it's just . . . last Saturday, when I couldn't see you, Magda, it was because I went up to town to this place.'

'What place?'

'A studio.'

'Oh no! A photographer's studio? You went to see that creepy guy who gave you his card, didn't you? Oh Nadine, you nutcase. What did he try to do? Did he want to take sleazy glamour shots?'

'No, he didn't, Ms Clever Dick. He took entirely

respectable totally fully-clothed photos,' says Nadine. 'I've got a proper portfolio. And he did only charge me half price. Though I hadn't realized quite how much it would be. It used up all my Christmas present money.'

'So what's the big deal?' says Magda. 'That's good, isn't it?'

'That's the good part. The bad part – the truly infuriating awful part – was that my mum and my horrible little showy-offy sister came with me. Mum caught me sneaking off on Saturday morning, see, and wanted to know where I was going and asked why did I deliberately make myself look a sight wearing all the black and the goth make-up and stuff, I looked a total laughing stock. She was being really irritating, totally getting at me and trying to put me down, so I found myself telling her I'd been invited to this special fashion photo session. It was just to shut her up, which was crazy because as soon as I'd got her convinced she started insisting she had to come too. She jumped to just the same sort of conclusions as you two. She said she had to be like a chaperone and said I couldn't go at all if I didn't let her come along too. So I had to give in – but *that* meant Natasha tagging along as well because my dad had this boring old golf match—'

'So did Natasha show off and start her Shirley Temple stuff and embarrass you at the studio?'

'Worse. Far worse,' says Nadine. 'She was feeling sick from the bus journey when we first got there so she just lolled against Mum and said nothing at all,

327

like she was all sweet and shy. She kept staring at me with her beady little eyes. I felt so weird standing there under all the hot lights. And all my make-up started running too. I'd really gone a bit mad with it, you should have seen the eye make-up but that was a big mistake too. He said I'd maybe overdone the goth look.'

'But he *told* you to stick to your own style.'

'Yes, but he said I'd taken him a bit too literally and that anyway, fashions were changing. The little junkie weirdo look *had* been big in magazines but now the buzz word is wholesome. So, you can imagine how I felt, and, of course, I couldn't whip all the make up and clothes off and start all over again. He said it didn't matter, I still looked ever so striking, and he started taking my photo but it didn't really work. "Give me some oomph, babe," he kept saying.'

'What a berk.'

'No, I knew what he meant, that sort of special sparkly look like a light bulb has suddenly been switched on inside your head but mine seemed to have gone 'phut'. I mean, how can you slink about and smile sexily in front of your mother and your kid sister? You just feel stupid. Especially as I looked all wrong. I think these photos are going to be a total disaster.'

'Then that's his fault,' I insist.

'No. Wait. At the end, when he could see we really weren't getting anywhere, he said we might as well call it a day, and he said he had a few photos left at the end of the reel. He asked my mum if she'd like several family shots thrown in as a little extra or maybe a couple of the little girl, seeing as she'd been so good.'

'Oh-oh,' I said. 'I can guess what's coming next.'

'That's it. You've got it. Natasha stood up in front of the camera and it wasn't just a light bulb switching on. She blazed like a beacon with fireworks fizzing out of her ears. She smiled and she pouted and she wiggled and she giggled and the photographer suddenly went crazy. He forgot all about me. He started an entire new reel of film and he took *endless* photos of Natasha and burbled away at her and didn't once have to tell her to give him some oomph. She had so much of it she blasted me right out of the studio.'

'Oh Nad. I'm sure your photos will be just as good. Better.'

'Rubbish, Ellie. Of course Mum was over the moon at all this and happily forked out for Natasha's portfolio even though she isn't paying a penny of mine, which seems horribly mean to me. The photographer guy says he knows this woman who runs a kids' modelling agency and he's going to drop off some contact prints to her and he's pretty sure she'll be very interested in Natasha.'

'Oh *yuck*.'

'Double triple quadruple yuck,' says Nadine.

'Hey, don't be so mean to poor little Natasha, you guys,' says Magda.

We both elbow her indignantly. Magda has always had this annoying blind spot where Natasha and Eggs are concerned. She can't seem to see how irritating it is to have little pests for kid sisters and brothers. She thinks they're *cute*.

'You know what else he said? He said it was not only great to discover such a natural little beauty as Natasha — *natural*, Mum puts her hair up into little kinks each night just so she can flounce those awful ringlet curls around during the day — but he also said she was so unspoilt and ultra-well-behaved that he thought any modelling agency would welcome her on to their books.'

'And he didn't say anything about getting you into any agency, Nad?'

'Did he hell. So, my career seems to have fizzled out before I've even got started.'

'We haven't had a fun time this Christmas, any of us,' I say. 'Magda's had too much attention from boys and so now she's trying to look like one—'

'That's not true!' says Magda. 'Anyway, Ellie, you maybe haven't had *enough* attention so you're starving yourself to death to get everyone to take notice of you.'

'Oh, don't you start on the psychological tack. Anna's been bad enough coming up with all these weird and wonderful reasons why she thinks I'm doing it. She can't seem to understand that I just want to lose a bit of weight. That's all. Why does it have to be such a big deal?'

To my horror *Dad* suddenly goes all psychological on me too. He buys this paperback about teenage eating disorders and he sits with his nose buried in it, getting gloomier and gloomier as he turns the pages. Every now and then he gives a little groan.

I do my best to ignore him but he comes over to me, looking anguished.

'Ellie, can we have a little chat?'

'Oh, Dad, don't start again, please! Look, I ate a huge tea, a vast plate of scrambled eggs on toast, so quit nagging me.'

'You ate about three forkfuls. And you left both slices of toast on your plate.'

'Well, they went soggy and you know I can't stand soggy toast.'

'You've always got an answer for everything, haven't you? That's exactly what this book says.'

'Oh, *Dad*. Why do you have to take any notice of that stupid old book?'

'It's worrying me, Ellie. You really do have all the classic signs of an anorexic personality. You're clever, you're a perfectionist, you're very determined, you can lie like crazy, you've had a traumatic childhood . . . you know, losing your mother so young.' Dad's voice has gone wobbly. He'll never talk about my mum, even now.

There's something else bothering him too.

'Ellie, would you say we get on OK, you and me?' he asks gruffly.

'No! We're always arguing,' I say.

His face crumples. I suddenly feel awful.

'Oh, Dad. Don't look like that. I didn't really mean it. Look, *all* teenage girls argue with their dads. But we get on fine most of the time, I suppose.'

'Would you say I was very authoritarian? You couldn't possibly, could you? I mean, I'm usually quite a hip sort of Dad, right? I don't boss you around that much, do I? Ellie? Oh for goodness' sake, put those chalks down and look at me! I'm *not* authoritarian, am I?'

'Listen to yourself, Dad!'

'Oh, come on, give me a break,' says Dad. He's still not finished. He clears his throat. 'Ellie . . .'

'Mm?'

'Ellie . . . it says in this book that anorexia can also be a response to abuse.'

'What?'

'Some poor girls have horrible abusing fathers.'

'Oh *Dad*. *You're* not a horrible abusing father! Don't be so daft!'

'Remember that time when Eggs was just starting to toddle and I saw you push him over so that he bumped his head? I smacked your bottom then. You howled and howled, remember, and I felt terrible because I'd never laid a finger on you before.'

'Dad, that was years and years ago! Look, just because I'm on a diet it's got nothing at all to do with you – or anyone else for that matter.'

'But this isn't just a simple diet, Ellie. How much weight have you lost since you started to get obsessed?'

'I'm *not* obsessed. And anyway, it's only a few pounds.'

'I had a word with Dr Wentworth—'

'*Dad!* I *told* you, I'm not going to see her. There's nothing wrong with me.'

'She asked if you'd lost ten per cent of your body weight – and *I* don't know.'

'Well I do,' I say firmly. 'I haven't lost that much weight, Dad, honestly.'

I'm being anything but honest. I really seem to have got the knack of dieting now. I'm still starving hungry all the time and my tummy aches badly and I keep having to pee a lot and whenever I get up quickly or rush round I feel faint and most of the time I've got a headache and I feel a bit sick and I've got a filthy taste in my mouth and my hair's gone all floppy and I've got spots all over my face and on my back too – but it's worth it to lose weight. Isn't it? I'm not anorexic. Not like Zoë.

I wonder how she's getting on? I bet her dad's nagging her too!

I can't wait to see Zoë on the first day back at school. Will she have put on any weight or will she be even thinner?

Lots of the girls in my class notice that *I've* lost weight.

'Wow, Ellie! You're looking so different!'

'Look at the waistband of your skirt. It's hanging off you!'

'Have you been ill or something, Ellie?'

'What's the *matter* with you, Ellie?'

'*Nothing's* the matter. I've just been on this diet, that's all.'

'A *diet*? Over Christmas? You must be mad.'

'Catch me going on a diet! We went to my nan's and she does all this home baking. Oh, her Christmas cake! And her mince pies – I ate *five* in one day.'

They burble on about food and I find it so irritating I open up my desk and start rearranging all my school books, trying to ignore them.

There's a sudden shriek – a scream – an entire operatic *chorus*.

'Magda!'

'Look at *Magda*.'

'Magda, your *hair*!'

Oh, God, poor Magda. No wonder they're all going berserk. Maybe the newly shorn mousey Magda won't be able to shut them up. I bob up from my desk, ready to spring to Magda's defence.

I spot Magda.

*I* squeal.

She's not the old bouncy blonde. She's not the new subdued mouse. She's an utterly new sizzling scarlet Magda!

Her hair's a wonderful vibrant electric bright red, the exact shade of her beautiful fur jacket. It's been cut even shorter, but in brilliant elfin–punk layers like flaming feathers.

Magda looks totally *incredible*. And she knows it. She grins at me.

'I hated my new look so I decided to go for an even newer one,' she says. 'You were so right, Ellie. Why should I scuttle round like a colourless creep just because of those sad bastards. I want to be *me* again.'

'Well, well, Magda!' says Mrs Henderson, bustling

into the classroom. 'I think I'm going to need sunglasses to look at your new hairdo. That is *not* an appropriate colour for school. If I were in a bad mood I'd make you cover it up with a headscarf but mercifully for you I'm feeling *mellow*.' She smiles benignly. 'Did you have a good Christmas, girls?' She catches sight of me. 'Oh dear, Ellie. You did *not* have a good Christmas. You've obviously been starving yourself, you silly girl.'

'I'm just getting fit, Mrs Henderson. I thought you'd approve,' I say, secretly thrilled.

Mrs Henderson is frowning at me. 'You and I had better have a private chinwag later, Ellie.'

Then Nadine comes into the classroom – and Mrs Henderson is diverted. Her mouth actually drops open. The entire class stares, jaws gaping.

Nadine hasn't changed her hairstyle.

She hasn't changed her weight.

She's changed her *face*.

She stands nonchalantly in the doorway, the wintery sunlight full on her face. She has a tattoo! A long black snake starts at her temple and writhes right across her forehead and down one cheek, the tip of its tail ending in a wiggle at her chin.

'Dear goodness, girl, what have you *done* to yourself?' Mrs Henderson gasps.

'Nadine! That is so—'

'Amazing!'

'Gross!'

'Disgusting!'

'Incredible!'

'Super-cool!'

Nadine, the amazing gross disgusting incredible super-cool snake woman, grins at us all and then puts her hand to her forehead. She pulls – and the snake wriggles right off her face and hangs limply from her fingers.

'Father Christmas put a joke tattoo in my stocking,' she says, while we all scream at her.

'You bad bad girl,' says Mrs Henderson. 'My mellow mood is rapidly disappearing. I feel as if I need another holiday already!'

She's a good sport all the same but I'm going to do my best to keep out of her way the next few days. I don't like the sound of this private chinwag.

We have a morning assembly as it's the first day of term. I crane my neck looking for Zoë but I can't see her anywhere. Maybe she's still abroad with her family?

Magda gives me a nudge.

'Hey, who's the dishy dreamboat on the stage?' she whispers.

'He can't be a teacher!' says Nadine.

We have three male teachers already. Mr Prescott takes us for History. He looks as if he's stepped straight out of the Victorian age, and acts it too. He's stern, stiff, uptight and *ancient*. Mr Daleford is the IT teacher, with all the warmth and charisma of his own beloved computers. He even talks like a Dalek. And Mr Pargiter teaches French. He's quite sweet but very balding, very tubby and very middle-aged so he's not exactly dreamboat category.

The man on the stage is youngish, definitely still in his twenties. He's got tousled dark-blond hair which looks wonderful with his black clothes – black button-down shirt, thin black tie, black jeans, black boots.

'This is Mr Windsor, girls – our new Art teacher,' says the head.

Mr Windsor shyly nods his blond head. Every girl in the hall stares transfixed. *Wow!*

## Chapter Ten

We can't wait for our first Art lesson.

Mr Windsor talks for ages about Art, his eyes shining (dark brown, a beautiful contrast to his blond hair). He shows us these reproductions of his favourite paintings, whizzing through the centuries so he can tell us about the different techniques and styles. He also throws in a lot of interesting stuff about the painters themselves and their lifestyles.

'Yeah, it was fine for *them*, all these painter *guys*,' says Magda. 'But what about women artists? They didn't get a look-in, did they? I mean, you call all this lot Old Masters, don't you, so where are the Old Mistresses?'

'Ah! You're obviously a fierce feminist and you've got a jolly good point too,' he says, smiling at the newly-gorgeous scarlet Magda.

She's not a feminist at all. I don't think she cares tuppence about Art either. She just wants Mr Windsor to take notice of her, and it's certainly worked.

So then he goes on about the secondary role of women artists through the ages, starting off with nuns in convents poring over illuminated manuscripts. Then he tells us about a female artist called Artemisia Gentileschi who was raped and he shows us this amazing painting she did of Judith cutting off this guy's head, with blood spurting everywhere. Lots of the girls shudder and go 'yuck' but Nadine cranes forward to take a closer look as she's into anything seriously gory. She's applied her joke snake tattoo to her arm now, so that the forked-tongue snake's head wiggles out of her school blouse and down across her hand.

Mr Windsor spots this and admires it. He flicks through a big book on sixties pop art and holds up this picture of an astonishing model called Snake Woman. She's got snakes coiling round her head like living scarves, and her body is all over scales.

'And it's by a woman too,' he says, grinning at Magda.

I'm getting to feel horribly left out and let down. I'm the one who's mad keen on Art and yet I can't think of a single thing to say. He holds up a picture of Frida Kahlo and it's the very one I've got pinned up in my bedroom at home. I can't really put up my hand and announce this – I'll sound so wet. So I listen while he talks about Frida and her savage

341

South American art. I nod passionately at everything he says. Eventually he sees this and looks at me expectantly.

'Do you like Frida Kahlo's work?'

Here's my chance. I swallow, ready to say something, *anything* – and in the sudden silence my tummy suddenly rumbles. Everyone hears. All the girls around me snigger. My face flushes the colour of Magda's hair.

'It sounds as if you're ready for your lunch,' says Mr Windsor.

He waits for me to comment. I can't. So he starts talking about another artist called Paula Rego. I just about die. My stupid stomach goes *on* rumbling. There's nothing I can do about it. Why can't it shut up? He'll think I'm just this awful greedy girl who wants to stuff her face every five minutes. It's not fair. I've been so careful recently, totally in control. I've only eaten a few mouthfuls at every meal. I didn't even have breakfast this morning, *or* any supper last night.

Which is why my stomach is rumbling.

Why I feel so sick.

Why I feel so tired I can't think of a thing to say.

Why I keep missing out on what Mr Windsor is saying. It's really interesting too. I hadn't even heard of Paula Rego before. She's done all these extraordinary pictures in chalk. I can tell by the colours in his big book of reproductions that they're just like my new Christmas present pastels. She does pictures of women unlike anything I've ever seen before.

They are big women, ugly women, in odd contorted positions.

'Why does she paint women like that? They look awful,' says Magda.

'I don't think they look awful. I think they're incredible,' says Mr Windsor. 'Maybe they look awful to you because we've all become so conditioned to think women should only look a certain way. Think of all the well-known portraits of women. The women are all prettified in passive poses, the body extended so that all the bulges are smoothed out. The face is frequently a blank mask, no lines, no tension, no character at all. These are lively expressive real women, standing awkwardly, stretching, dancing, doing all sorts of things.'

'But they're *fat*,' I whisper.

Mr Windsor reads my lips.

'You girls! You're all brain-washed. They're big women, they're strong, they've got sturdy thighs, real muscles in their arms and legs. But they're soft too, they're vulnerable, they're valiant. They're not beautiful women. So what? Beauty is just fashion. Male artists have used beautiful women throughout the centuries but their sizes and proportions keep changing. If you were Giovanni Annolfini in the Middle Ages then your ideal pin-up girl had a high forehead and a tiny bosom and a great big tummy. A century later Titian liked large firm women with big bottoms. Rubens liked his women large too, but wobbly. Goya's women were white and slender, then Renoir liked them very big and salmon pink.'

343

'And Picasso liked his ladies with eyes in the side of their heads!' says Magda, and we all laugh, Mr Windsor too.

Why can't it be *me* making him laugh? I rack my brains for something to say . . . but I'm running out of time. The bell goes before I can come up with anything.

Mr Windsor sets us all Art homework.

'I want you all to do a self portrait. You can use any medium you like. Don't forget to bring it with you next time, right? When do we meet up for Art again?'

Next Friday. I can't wait. We spend the next lesson whispering about the wondrous Mr Windsor.

'Isn't he fantastic?' says Magda.

'He's got such a lovely sense of humour too,' says Nadine.

'It's OK for you two. You both made a big impression on him. I just made a right idiot of myself,' I wail.

'You should have spoken up for yourself,' says Magda.

'You should have told him that you and Zoë did all the mural. That would have impressed him,' says Nadine.

'I couldn't just announce the fact. It would look like I was showing off,' I say.

I wonder if Mr Windsor might like Zoë and me to do some special artwork like Mrs Lilley used to? I still haven't see Zoë. At lunchtime I go to Mrs Henderson's aerobics class to catch Zoë there.

Lots of girls in lycra shorts are bobbing up and

down but Zoë isn't one of them. I join in anyway though I find it horribly hard going. I have to stop several times to lean against the wall and gasp for breath. I don't seem to be getting any fitter. Is it because I'm still far too fat? Or is it because I've tried to get thin too quickly? My head spins. I can't think straight any more.

'Are you all right, Ellie?' Mrs Henderson asks at the end of the class.

'I'm . . . fine,' I gasp.

'Are you kidding yourself? Because you're certainly not kidding me,' says Mrs Henderson. 'Ellie, how am I going to make you see sense? I'm so worried about you. I think I'm going to get in touch with your parents.'

'No, don't, please! There's nothing wrong with me, Mrs Henderson, honestly.'

'You're obviously starving yourself.'

'No, I'm not. I eat heaps, honestly I do.'

'Oh, Ellie. This is a nightmare. It's the Zoë situation all over again. She wouldn't listen to reason either and now she's in hospital.'

'Why? What's the matter with her?'

'You know perfectly well she's anorexic.'

'But it's not an illness!'

'Of course it is. And now Zoë has made herself so dangerously ill she's had to be hospitalized. She collapsed over Christmas. She very nearly died of heart failure.'

It's so scary I can hardly take it in. I ask Mrs Henderson which hospital Zoë's in, and after school

I phone Anna and tell her I've got to go and visit a sick friend so I won't be home till late.

I hate the hospital. My heart starts pounding as soon as I get off the bus and see the big red building with its tower and chimney and endless odd extensions, like a perverted version of a fairy castle. People always go on about hospital smells but it's hospital *colour* that I can't stand. There are hideous orange plastic chairs in the waiting areas. I remember sitting hunched up on one for hours, sucking my way through an entire packet of fruit gums, whining for my mother. Who was somewhere I wasn't allowed to go. Dying.

Orange is supposed to be a cheerful colour but it always makes me want to cry. I feel tearful now, which is silly, because my mother died years and years ago. And Zoë isn't going to die – is she? I don't even know her that well, it's not like she's my best friend like Nadine and Magda. I suppose she's the girl I identify with most. So maybe I'm scared *I'm* going to die. Which is completely mad. I'm not too thin, I'm still really grossly fat.

It takes me ages to track Zoë down. I'm told she's in Skylark ward but when I get there and tiptoe past all these pale patients lying listlessly on their pillows I can't find her anywhere. There's one empty bed and I start to panic, thinking she really has died but when I eventually find a nurse she says that now Zoë's heart condition is stabilized she's been transferred to Nightingale ward in the annexe across the road.

I've heard of Nightingale. It's the psychiatric unit.

If one of the girls is acting extra loopy at school then people say she'll end up in Nightingale. The local nuthouse. Once we were in the car near the hospital and I saw a large wild-eyed woman running down the road in her nylon nightie and fur-trimmed slippers and Dad said she was obviously legging it out of Nightingale.

I remember her red sweaty face and the spittle drooling down her chin. What are they doing, shutting Zoë up with a lot of mad people? She's not *mad*.

I'm scared of going into the Nightingale building. I'm not even sure they'll let me in. Maybe they don't allow visitors.

But I force myself to go and see. There are people wandering round the grounds. No-one's wearing nightclothes. No-one looks particularly mad or distressed. Maybe they're not patients, maybe they're visitors or staff? Or maybe Nightingale isn't a psychiatric ward any more? There aren't any locked gates at the entrance to the ward. I can go right in.

An old man is leaning against the wall. He's saying something but when I look at him he hides his face, still mumbling into his fingers. A woman bustles past, walking too fast, biting the back of her hand agitatedly. Oh, God. It's the psychiatric ward all right.

I peer round, expecting mad-eyed maniacs to come hopping down the corridor in straitjackets but the people here seem sad rather than mad and they're not really frightening. I proceed up the corridor nervously until I get to the nursing station.

'Can I help?' says a woman in a T-shirt and jeans.

I can't work out if she's another patient or a nurse out of uniform. I mumble Zoë's name.

'Ah yes. She's upstairs, in the room at the end. I'm not sure how she feels about visitors at the moment. I think it might be family only.'

'That's OK, I'm her sister,' I lie smoothly, surprising myself.

'Oh. Well, I suppose that's all right,' she says doubtfully. 'You are over fourteen, aren't you?'

'Oh yes,' I say, and I make for the stairs before she can stop me.

I understand why Zoë's upstairs when I get to this new ward. It's as if it's a planet peopled by a strange new sisterhood. Painfully thin girls are sitting watching television, dancing jerkily to pop music, exercising in baggy tracksuits, flicking through magazines, huddling in high-necked sweaters, crying in corners. It's not just their skeletal state that makes them look alike. They've all got withdrawn absorbed expressions on their faces as if they're watching television screens inside their own heads. Even when they talk to each other they have a zombie look. It's like they're all under the same enchanted spell.

For one moment it works on me too. I look enviously at their high cheekbones and fragile wrists and colt-like knees, feeling grotesquely fat and lumbering in their ethereal presence. But then a nurse walks past carrying a tray – a lively looking young woman with shiny bobbed hair and a curvy waist and a spring to her step. She's not thin, she's not fat, she's just a normally nourished healthy person. I look at her and then I look at all the anorexic patients.

I see them clearly. I see their thin lank hair, their pale spotty skin, their sunken cheeks, their sad stick limbs, the skeletal inward curve of their hips, the ugly spikiness of their elbows, their hunched posture. I see the full haunted horror of their illness.

'Who are you looking for?' says the nurse.

'Zoë. Er – I'm her sister.'

'Pull the other one,' says the nurse, but she smiles. 'She's not feeling very co-operative so she's not supposed to have visitors at the moment but maybe you'll do her good. She's in the cubicle at the end.'

I approach the drawn curtains apprehensively. You can't knock on a curtain. I clear my throat instead, and then call out.

'Zoë?'

There's no answer.

'Zoë?' I say a little louder.

I peep round the curtain. Zoë is lying on her bed, curled up like a baby, her head tucked down on her chest. The bones at the top of her spine jut out alarmingly. She is even thinner, so small and sad and sick that I'm not shy any more.

'Hi, Zoë,' I say, and I sit on her bed.

She looks round, startled. She frowns when she sees it's me.

'What are you doing here?' she says fiercely.

'I – I just came to see how you are,' I say, taken aback by her aggression.

'How did you know they'd shoved me in here?'

'Mrs Henderson told me.'

'That nosy old busybody. So I suppose she's been telling everyone that I'm in the nuthouse.'

'No! Just me. Because – because we're friends.'

'No, we're not. Not really. Look, I don't want to see anyone, not like this. I look so awful. They're practically force-feeding me. I know I've put on pounds and pounds since I've been here. I'm getting so *fat*.' She clenches her fist and punches her own poor concave stomach.

'Zoë! Don't be crazy. You're thin – terribly thin.'

'But not as thin as I was.'

'Thinner. Much thinner. That's why you're here. Zoë, you nearly *died*. You had a heart attack or something.'

'It was just because I took too many laxatives, that's all. I'm fine now. Well, I would be if they'd only let me *out*. They've given me this absolutely ridiculous target weight. They want to blow me right up into an elephant.'

'They just want you to get better.'

'It's all right for you to talk. You're looking really thin yourself, Ellie. You're OK. You're not forced to eat huge mounds of mashed potato and drink great mugs of milk.'

'Come off it. I'm still huge compared to you. So's everyone. Zoë, you're not seeing things straight. *Look* at yourself.' I pick up her stick arm, terrified my fingers might poke right through her papery skin. 'You're literally skin and bone. You're starving yourself to *death*.'

'Good. I don't want to live. There's absolutely no

point, not like this, when everyone's against me and my parents keep yelling at me or they cry and they just won't understand, and all the nurses spy on me in case I can hide some of the food and they even ration my *water* now, just because I drink a lot before I get weighed. What sort of a life is it when I can't even go to the toilet without a nurse hanging round outside, listening?'

'So why can't you eat a bit? Then you can come out of hospital and get back to school. Zoë, listen, there's this fabulous new Art master, Mr Windsor, he's really young and good-looking, and he's great at telling you all sorts of things about Art. I made a bit of a fool of myself in our first Art lesson actually, it was dead embarrassing—'

But Zoë isn't listening. She's not interested in a new teacher, or Art, or me. She's not able to think of anything else in the whole world but starving herself.

She curls up in her ball again, her eyes shut.

'Do you want me to go, Zoë?'

She nods.

I reach out and touch the awful unpadded jut of her hip. She jumps at my touch.

'Goodbye Zoë. I'll come back again soon, if you don't mind,' I say, patting her gently.

A tear dribbles from under her closed eyelids.

I'm in tears myself as I walk down the ward. The nurse looks at me sympathetically.

'Did she give you a hard time? You mustn't take it personally. Poor Zoë thinks we're all conspiring against her at the moment.'

'Will she get better?'

The nurse sighs. 'I hope so. I don't know. We try to get the girls to a healthier weight and they have group therapy and individual counselling but so much depends on the girls themselves. Some of them get completely better. Some recover for a while but then go spiralling downwards. And others—'

'Do they . . . die?'

'It's inevitable after a certain stage. The body burns up all its fat and then starts on the muscle. The girls know what they're doing but they can't stop it.'

I can stop it. I can't stop Zoë. But I can stop myself getting to be like her.

I still feel fat, even though I've lost weight. I'd still like to be really thin. But I don't want to be sick. I don't want to starve.

I go home. Anna is full of questions but she can see I can't really bear to talk about it. She's prepared a salad for tea.

'Oh boring. I want chips,' says Eggs.

'You can have crisps with your salad,' says Anna.

She doesn't say so, but this is a carefully chosen special meal for me: fromage frais, strawberries, avocado, rocket and raddiccio. Anna is darting little apprehensive looks at me. I nibble my lip. My head is automatically calculating calories, panicking at the avocado. I put my hand up to my forehead to try to stop it. I look at the plate of lovingly prepared nourishing food, so carefully arranged in rings of red and green around the snowy fromage frais.

'This looks lovely, Anna,' I say. 'Thank you very much.'

I start to eat it. I bite. I chew. I swallow. Eggs is chattering but Anna and Dad are silent. Watching. Practically holding their breath.

'It's OK,' I say. 'I'm not going to hide bits in my lap. I'm not going to spit it into my hankie. I'm not going to make myself sick.'

'Thank God!' says Dad. 'Oh Ellie. I can't believe it. You're actually eating!'

'I'm eating too!' says Eggs. 'I *always* eat and yet no-one makes a fuss of me. We don't have to have special salads for Ellie every day, do we?'

'Of course we do,' I say, but I wink at Anna to show I'm joking.

Dad gets all fussed and suspicious when I make for the stairs straight after tea.

'Where are you off to, then?'

'I'm going to do my *homework*, Dad. Honestly.'

I'm telling the truth. Well, I'm not that fussed about my French homework. And I'm going to have to bribe Magda to do my Maths for me tomorrow morning. But I spend all evening on my Art homework, attempting a self portrait.

I don't just do one, I do half a dozen and they're all hopeless. I peer into the mirror and I still see this fat frizzy-haired girl staring back at me. When I draw her she gets even fatter and she's frowning, looking like she's about to burst into tears.

There's a knock on the door. Anna.

'OK, Ellie? I've just put Eggs to bed. Your dad

and I are having a coffee. Want one?'

'Yes, please.'

She comes in the room when she hears me sigh.

'What's up? Oh, Ellie, these are so *good*!'

'No, they're not. I look hideous.'

'You've made yourself look much fatter than you are – and you don't look very *happy*.'

'No wonder. I can't draw for toffee,' I say, and I crumple them all up.

'Oh don't! They were so good. Show your dad.'

'No. I'll have another go tomorrow.' I rub my eyes. 'I'm tired.'

'Me too.'

'Anna – thanks for being so nice.'

It's a silly inadequate little word. Our English teacher always has a fit if I put it in an essay. But Anna smiles as if I've declared an entire poem of praise.

She *is* nice. I'll never love her the way I love my own mother. But if I can't have my mum maybe Anna's the next best thing.

I go downstairs for my coffee. I have one of Anna's home-made cookies too, savouring every mouthful. I'm scared I'll want another and another, eating until I've emptied the tin.

No. I don't have to binge. I don't have to starve. I don't want to end up one of those sad sick girls in Zoë's ward. I'm going to eat what I want, when I want. I can do it. I *can*.

I sleep soundly for the first time in ages and wake up early, feeling full of energy. I feel like a swim but I can't, because of Mick and all his horrible friends.

I *can*. I'm not going to let those idiots stop me doing what I want.

I put my swimming costume on under my school uniform and grab a towel. Anna is in the kitchen buttering rolls.

'I don't want breakfast, Anna.'

'What?' She looks stricken.

'Only because I'm going swimming. I'll take a roll with me and eat if after, OK?'

'OK,' says Anna.

I don't know if she totally trusts me. I'm not even sure I trust myself. I stride out towards the swimming pool but as I get nearer I start to feel sick. There's every chance Mick and his mates will be there. I don't know what they're going to say to me, do to me. I slapped his face hard last time. There'll be a lifeguard on duty so they can't really drag me into the pool and drown me but they can still say stuff.

If they called Magda a slag they'll think up something far worse for me. I'm shivering now. I must be mad. I *can't* go swimming.

I can, I can, I can.

I pay, I go in the changing room, I take off my clothes. I fiddle desperately with my new swimming costume, pulling it down over my bottom, then haul it up to cover more of my chest, tugging it this way and that. I still feel so fat, even though I'm thinner than I've ever been before. I feel my figure in the dark of the changing cubicle. I think of poor Zoë and her desperate delusion that *she's* fat, even though she's a five-stone skeleton.

'I'm not fat,' I whisper. 'I think I am, but I'm not, and even if I *am*, it doesn't matter, it's not worth dying for. Now, I'm going to get out there in the pool. Who cares if anyone sneers at me in my swimming costume? Mick's mates can call me the fattest stupidest slag in the world and I shall take no notice whatsoever.'

I walk out determinedly, taking purposeful strides, my head held high. The effect is ruined when I trip over someone's flip-flop sandals and nearly fall flat on my face. I jump in the pool and start swimming so no-one gets a chance to stare at me. I can't see properly without my glasses. I have no idea whether Mick's mates are here or not. I gradually get into the rhythm of my swim and stop worrying so much. It feels so good to stretch and kick and glide.

There's a cluster of boys braying with laughter at the other end of the pool. I'm not sure whether it's *them* or not – or if *I'm* the butt of their joke. But I swim up to the end and back and no-one grabs me, ducks me, tears at my costume. They don't even come near me. It can't be the same boys. Thank goodness.

I don't want to try my luck too far. I get out the pool sharpish and go and shower, tingling all over, feeling so good. I whistle as I towel myself dry and pull my clothes over my damp skin. I feel Anna's roll in a bag in the pocket of my blazer. I take it out and munch it gratefully while I'm drying my hair.

I could do with a drink too. I've got money on me. I could go and have a quick hot chocolate in the café.

Those boys are still larking around in the pool. They won't be out for ages yet.

Oh God, hot chocolate! My mouth's watering.

I make for the café and order myself a hot chocolate with cream. The smell of it makes me feel weak. I spoon a little of the frothy cream into my mouth and savour the sweetness. Then I take a long swallow of the warm smooth chocolate. It is *so* good, the most beautiful drink in the world. I drain the last delicious drop and get up to go. I get to the door of the café – and collide with Mick.

Oh help! I'd better get away quick. I dart forward and he ducks.

Hey! He thinks I'm going to give him another slapping!

'You watch it,' he says gruffly, keeping well out of my reach.

'*You* watch it!' I say.

He glances round to see if any of his mates are about. No. It's just the two of us. And he's acting like he's really scared of me!

I grin triumphantly and march outside. I feel like singing and dancing and punching the air. I got the better of *him* all right. I didn't let him push me around. *I* did the pushing.

I feel so p–o–w–e–r–f–u–l.

That's the look I want for my self portrait. I use dark pastels and big bold strokes for this seventh attempt. I make my hair frizz with life, I stick my chest right out, I stand with my fists clenched and my legs spread out. I work and work at it, adding

357

highlights here, smudging and softening there. My eyes are aching and my hand has got cramp by the time I'm satisfied.

It's the best thing I've ever done.

I hope Mr Windsor likes it. Well, *I* like it, even if he doesn't. That's what really matters. That's what I tell myself anyway. But I feel stupidly anxious when it's Mr Windsor's Art lesson.

He draws his own self portrait to start things off, taking a black felt tip and squiggling it all over the page in a matter of seconds. We all laugh when we see the way he's done it. He's drawn a big cardboard cut-out super-cool man in black – but it's being held up like a shield in front of a nervous looking boy-man with a twitchy face and knocking knees.

Then he asks to see our portraits. Magda's first, waving her picture right in his face. She's copied a curvy black and white Betty Boop cartoon, adding her own face crowned with her new startling crop.

'I like it, Magda, especially the head,' he says. 'But you above all need the full technicolour treatment. Paints!'

He gets a pot of scarlet poster paint and dips in his brush.

'Do you mind, Magda?' he asks.

'Be my guest!'

He does several deft flicks with the tip of his brush so that the paper Magda sprouts fantastic flaming-red hair.

'Wow! How about nails and lipstick to match?' says Magda.

Mr Windsor colours her to perfection. He even does little scarlet hearts all over her dress. Then he dilutes the red to the palest pink and shows us how to get a good natural skin tone.

'Though someone's just complimented Magda on her hair so she's blushing a little,' he says, putting more colour in her cheeks.

Magda's own cheeks are pink with pleasure when he gives her back her portrait.

'Who's going next?' asks Mr Windsor.

There's a general clamour. Portraits flap in the air like flags. Mr Windsor picks at random.

Not me.

Not me.

Not me.

Nadine. Her turn. She's drawn herself very long, very lean, very Gothic Queen.

'Yes, Nadine, you've got a very elegant line – practically Aubrey Beardsley,' he says. 'I don't think we should colour you in. You're very much a black and white girl. Ah! You were the girl wearing the joke tattoo. Shall we indulge in a little skin art?'

'Yes, please!'

Mr Windsor takes his black felt tip and does the most wonderful swirly intricate tattoos up and down Nadine's drawing's arms and then he takes a special silvery pen and gives her a sparkly nose stud and earrings from the tip of one ear right down to the lobe.

'I wish!' says Nadine, who has been fighting a battle with her mum about body piercing for months and months.

We're running out of time. I'm not going to get picked.

I hold my picture up desperately – but he's looking the other side of the classroom, about to pick someone else.

'Pick Ellie!' says Magda.

'Yes, you must see Ellie's portrait,' says Nadine.

'Which one's Ellie?' says Mr Windsor.

'Me,' I mumble.

He looks at me and then he looks at my portrait. He looks at it a long long time while I wait, heart thudding.

'It's great,' he says. 'You really took in what I was saying last time, didn't you? This is fantastic.'

'What are you going to do to it, Mr Windsor?' asks Magda.

'I'm not going to do anything at all,' he says. 'It's perfect the way it is. It's such a powerful portrait. You're a true artist, Ellie.'

His words echo in my ears like heavenly bells. Then the real bell clangs and everyone grabs their stuff.

'Can I have a quick word, Ellie?' says Mr Windsor.

Magda and Nadine raise their eyebrows and nudge each other.

'Teacher's pet!' Nadine whispers.

'He could pet me all he wants,' Magda giggles.

'Behave yourselves, you two,' I say.

I go up to Mr Windsor while they clatter off.

'Can I hang on to your portrait, Ellie? I'd like to put it up on the wall if it's OK with you?'

'Sure.'

'Did you do the mural?'

'Some of it. With Zoë.'

'Which one was Zoë? Maybe you'd both like to come and do some extra Art at lunchtime?'

'She's not in my class. She's older. Only . . . she's in hospital.'

'Ah! Is she the girl with anorexia? They were talking about her in the staff room.'

'Yes.'

'What a shame. It sounds as if she had so much going for her too. I can't understand what makes girls starve themselves like that.'

'I don't think girls themselves understand either,' I say softly.

'Oh, well. Let's hope she gets better,' says Mr Windsor.

I nod, hoping and wishing and praying that poor Zoë really will get well.

'But anyway, you must feel free to come to the Art room any time, Ellie. With your two friends, if they want. Have you ever used oil paints? I think you'd love them. We'll give it a go sometime, right?'

'Right!' I say.

And with one bound the new powerful artistic talented me soars out of the classroom and down the corridor to join Magda and Nadine for lunch.

# girls

## out

## late

*To Meetal Malhi
and Harriet, Polina and Rebecca*

# Chapter One

## Girl Time

# Chapter One

We're going out tonight, Nadine and Magda and me.
It's not a Big Night Out. We're certainly not going
to stay out late. We're just going on this little after-
school shopping trip. No big deal at all. We'll meet
at half past six at the Flowerfields Centre. Wander
round the shops on their late night. We'll eat in
McDonald's, then home by nine like good girls.

I don't bother to dress up or anything. I change out
of my school uniform, obviously, but just into my
black baggy trousers. They've been in the washing-
machine one spin too many times so that they're
now technically not black at all, more a murky grey.
Still, they're just about the only trousers in the
whole world that are big without making me look
enormous. They almost give the illusion that there's
a weeny little bum and long lean legs hiding under all
that bunchy material.

I try my newest stripy pink top but I'm not too sure about it now. It's a little too bright to be becoming. It makes my own cheeks glow positively peony. I wish I looked deathly pale and ethereal like my best friend Nadine. I'm stuck with permanently rosy cheeks – and *dimples*.

I search the airing cupboard for something dark and plain and end up purloining a dark grey V-necked school sweater belonging to my little brother, Eggs. It fits a little too snugly. I peer long and hard in my mirror, worrying about the prominence of my chest. No matter how I hunch up it still sticks out alarmingly. I'm not like my other best friend, Magda, who deliberately tightens the straps of her Wonderbra until she can practically rest her chin on her chest. My own bras seem to be a bit too revealing. I try tucking a tissue in each cup so that I am not outlined too outrageously.

Then I attack my hair with a bristle brush, trying to tame it into submission. It's as if my entire body is trying to get out of control. My hair is the wildest of all. It's longish but so tightly curly it grows up and out as well as down. Nadine is so lucky. Her long liquorice-black hair falls straight past her shoulders, no kinks at all. Magda's hair looks incredible too, very short and stylish and bright red (dyed). It looks really great on her but if my hair was that short it would emphasize my chubby cheeks. Anyway, with my bright pink face I'd be mad to dye my hair scarlet. Not that my stepmum Anna would let me. She even gets a bit fussed when I use henna shampoo, for God's sake.

Anna eyes me now as I clatter into the kitchen to

beg for some spare cash. Eggs is sitting at the table playing with the hands of my old alarm clock, muttering, 'Four o'clock, telly time, fun. Five o'clock, more telly time, fun fun. Six o'clock, teatime, yum yum.'

'That's my alarm clock,' I say indignantly.

'But it's been broken for ages, Ellie. I thought it might help him learn the time. Do the big hand thing, Eggs,' says Anna.

'Honestly, it's embarrassing having such a moron for a brother. And he was the one who broke it, fiddling around with the hands.'

'Twelve o'clock, midnight, big sister turns into a pumpkin!' says Eggs and shrieks with laughter.

'Are you off out, Ellie?'

'I'm just meeting Nadine and Magda to go late-night shopping.'

'Seven o'clock, bathtime, splashy splashy. Eight o'clock, bedtime, yuck yuck.'

'What about your homework?'

'I did it when I came home from school.'

'No you didn't.'

'I did, honestly.'

'You were watching television.'

'I did it *while* I was watching television.'

I don't usually watch kids' TV but there's this new art programme that has some amazingly cool ideas. I'm going to be a graphic artist when I grow up. I'm definitely not going to the Art College where my dad lectures though. I'm certainly not cut out to be one of his adoring students. It's weird to think that Anna was once. And my mum. She died when I was little but I still miss her a lot. Eggs isn't my whole brother, he's just a half.

'Thief!' Eggs suddenly screams, pointing at me. 'That's my school jumper, take it *off*!'

'I'm just borrowing it for the evening.'

He doesn't even like this school jumper. Anna has to sweet-talk him into it every morning. He prefers the weird, wacky, rainbow-coloured concoctions that Anna knits for him. When he was going through his Teletubby phase he had four – purple, green, yellow and red – so he could be Tinky Winky, Dipsy, La La or Po as the mood took him. Today Eggs is wearing his magenta Barney-the-Dinosaur jumper. I am immensely glad I am way past the stage of Anna making me natty knitted jumpers.

'But you'll muck it up,' Eggs wails.

'*I'll* muck it up?'

Eggs is such a slurpy, splashy eater his clothes are permanently splattered orange (baked beans), yellow (egg yolk) and purple (Ribena). I examined his sweater for spots and stains very carefully indeed before putting it on.

'You'll make it smell.'

'I won't! How dare you! I don't smell.'

'You do, you do, doesn't she, Mum?' says Eggs.

'I *don't*,' I say, but I'm starting to get panicky. I don't really smell, do I? Has my deodorant stopped working? Oh God, does everyone back away from me with wary expressions and pinched nostrils and I just haven't noticed?

'Ellie doesn't smell,' says Anna.

'She does, of that yucky powdery sweet scenty

stuff. I don't want my school sweater ponging like a girl,' Egg insists, tugging at the jumper. I swat his hands away as best I can.

'Stop him, Anna, he'll rip it!'

'Yes, give over, Eggs. Though it is *his* sweater. Honestly, for years and years you wore your dad's extra large T-shirts that came way past your knees. Now you want to wear Eggs's teeny weeny little sweaters. When are you going to wear anything that fits?'

I don't ever borrow Anna's clothes. We have a very different style, even though she's only fourteen years older than me. And we're a very different shape too. She's skinny, I'm not. But I've decided I'm not going to let that bug me any more. I went on a seriously intense diet last term and started to get obsessed about my weight. But now I'm getting back to normal.

To prove it I eat a toasted cheese sandwich with Anna and Eggs even though I'll be munching at McDonald's later.

'What time shall I get Dad to come and pick you up?' says Anna.

'I don't need Dad to pick me up, I'll get the bus back.'

'Are you sure? I don't like the idea of you coming back on your own when it's getting dark.'

'I won't *be* on my own. I'll be with Nadine all the way on the bus, and as far as Park Hill Road.'

'Tell you what, you travel back to Nadine's house and give us a ring when you get back there. Then Dad can drive round and give you a lift, OK?'

'OK, OK.'

I smile at Anna and she smiles back as we acknowledge our compromise. We never used to get on, but it's weird, now we're kind of friends.

'It's not OK. Tell her to give me back my school jumper, Mum!' Eggs yells, kicking at me.

I will never be friends with Eggs. He's still wearing his school lace-ups and he's really hurting my shins. I might be wearing combat trousers but they're totally ineffective against weapons of war.

'Don't get me all hot and bothered, Eggs, or I might have to go and spray myself with perfume to cool down,' I say. 'I *might* accidentally dowse your dopey old sweater.'

'No, no, no! Don't you dare!'

'Stop teasing him, Ellie,' says Anna, sighing. She's digging in her handbag. 'How much pocket money have you got left?'

'Absolutely zilch. In fact I owe Magda, she paid for me to go swimming last Sunday.'

'And you already owe me for that pair of tights from Sock Shop.'

'Oh God, yes. Help, I'm bound for the debtors' prison.'

'Can't you kind of – budget?' says Anna, unzipping her purse.

'I try, but Dad's such a meany. Magda gets twice what I get for her allowance.'

'Don't start, Ellie.'

'But it's not fair.'

'*Life* isn't fair.'

I'll say. Still, the minute I'm fourteen, I'm all set to get *some* kind of paid work – you name it, I'll do it – then I'll be able to keep up with Magda and Nadine. Well, halfway up.

'Here you are.' Anna hands me a fiver.

I feel a bit mean. Anna hasn't got a job either. She's been looking hard since Eggs started school but there's nothing going. She has to cadge cash from Dad too. Marriage certainly isn't fair. Catch me ever getting married. In fact I'm not too sure I want anything to do with boys at all.

Magda is totally boy mad. Nadine isn't quite as crazy, although last year she went out with this total creep called Liam who treated her like dirt. I had a sort of boyfriend then too. Well, a boy who was a friend, rather than a *boy*friend. He certainly wasn't a dreamboat but he seemed to be dead keen on me. He wrote me all these love letters and couldn't wait to see me. He declared true love for ever and ever. But then his letters fizzled out and it turned out he had met this other girl and now he's declared true love for ever and ever to her. As if I care. She's welcome to him. I don't want him any more. I don't want a boyfriend at all. Really.

So anyway, I rush round to Nadine's place and she is in the middle of an argument with her mum. She's mad at Nadine because she wants her to go to this line dancing class with her and Natasha. It's a truly sad session where lots of mums go with their daughters. Nadine's mum is dead keen on line dancing and has made herself a denim skirt with matching waistcoat and she wears a pair of white fringed cowboy boots. Natasha adores her baby cowgirl outfit. She loves line dancing too and is already the little star of the class. Nadine's mum bought enough blue denim to make another matching set for Nadine. She would willingly pay for another pair of white cowgirl boots. Nadine

374

would rather *die* than go line dancing in a blue denim outfit and white cowgirl boots – especially with her mum and her loathsome little sister.

'I sometimes feel you're not part of this family at all,' says Nadine's mum.

'I sometimes wish I *wasn't* part of this family,' Nadine says defiantly. 'I'm going down to Flowerfields with Ellie.'

'Flowerfields! What's the matter with you? Only this Saturday you made such a fuss because I wanted you to come shopping in the Flowerfields Centre with Natasha and me and what did you say? Only that you couldn't stick going shopping, *especially* in the Flowerfields Shopping Centre.'

Nadine rolls her eyes, already extra expressive with their thick outline of black kohl.

Nadine's mum sighs. 'Are you as insolent to your mother, Ellie?'

'Well, it's different,' I say diplomatically. 'I mean, Anna's my stepmother but she's more my age. We're more like sisters. It's not like she's really a mum figure.'

'I wish I didn't have a mum figure,' says Nadine when we finally escape. 'God, she doesn't half go on. And Natasha's driving me nuts too. Just think, I've got four or five more years before there's a chance of breaking free. How am I going to survive?' She clenches her fist dramatically then wails, 'Oh *bum*, my nail!'

Nadine spends the next five minutes mourning her broken nail. I eventually divert her by planning out our blissful life in the future when we're eighteen and have fully served our life sentences with our families.

We'll both go to Art College, me to do graphics, Nadine to do fashion. We'll get our own little flat. We'll get up when we want and eat when we want and go out when we want and hold a party every single Saturday.

We plan it all out on the bus into town and we're still busy negotiating over the interior decorating when we meet up with Magda at the Flowerfields entrance. We're momentarily diverted. Magda looks stunning in a skimpy little pink lacy top that shows off every single *pore*. My heart beats enviously under its pad of paper tissue. If only I had Magda's confidence!

'You've got that new top!'

'And new trousers,' says Nadine, eyeing them up and down. She darts round Magda's back and pulls at the waistband. 'Wow, DKNY! Where did you get them?'

'Oh, my Auntie Cath came round at the weekend. She bought the trousers in Bond Street weeks ago, meaning to go on a diet to fit into them but she hasn't lost a pound, so guess what, I got lucky.'

'Why haven't I got a lovely auntie?' says Nadine. 'Did she give you the top too?' She fingers it enviously with her one-tenth defective long nails.

'She bought it for me as a present, yeah. Do you like the colour? You don't think it clashes with my hair?'

'Everything clashes with your hair,' I say, ruffling her amazing crimson curls.

'I want to get a lipstick the same pearly pink,' says Magda. 'Come on, girls. *Shopping* time!'

We spend hours and hours and hours circling the

make-up stands in Boots while Magda anoints her wrists with pink stripes in her attempt to find the perfect pink. Nadine is happy enough playing with make-up samples and experimenting with black lipstick and silver blusher but I get a bit fed up. I'm not really into make-up actually. I mean, I've got some and I shove it on if I'm going out anywhere special, but I always forget and dab my eyes and smear it or wipe my mouth and end up with lipstick on my chin.

Then we spend hours and hours and hours at the nail varnish stands. Nadine ends up buying a nail lengthening kit, one of those fun sets where you can paint on false nails all different patterns and add little sequins and beads and stuff. Magda buys one too but I know I'd forget and nibble mine off. I'm going to stop biting my nails *one* day, but at the moment my teeth have a beaver-like will of their own and gnaw my fingers ferociously.

'Come on, you guys, the shops will be shutting soon,' I moan – and eventually they let me drag them up to this art shop on the top floor. They get fed up after the first few seconds and hang around outside while I finger the fat white sketchpads and lust after the huge shiny tins of rainbow felt-tips. I'm only in there a minute but Magda and Nadine keep putting their heads round the door and yelling at me. I try out the pens, writing 'I am Ellie and I like to draw'. I do so, squiggling a little elephant with a wavy trunk with an 07 point and a weeny 03 point and a mean green and a flamboyant pink and after *more* moans from outside I end up buying the 05 black pen I always choose and a little square black sketchbook that I simply can't resist. I haven't got too much money left. I'm going to have to beg a few chips off Magda and Nadine or go hungry – but I'm happy.

The three of us link arms and wander round the rest of the shops, trying on high heels in Office and staggering around like drunks, and then we spend ages in the HMV store listening to the latest Claudie Coleman album. Magda, Nadine and I have entirely different musical tastes but we are all united in our admiration for Claudie. Magda likes her because she sings songs with very powerful, positive lyrics. Nadine likes her because her music is very cool and hip. I like her because she's got long, wild curly hair a bit like mine but much lovelier and she's not a bit fat but she is much curvier than your average rock chick. So she's kind of my role model.

The HMV store is crowded. Magda automatically stands wherever there's a clump of likely looking boys. They all stare at her appreciatively and three of them start chatting her up. Nadine and I sigh and slope off. This is a familiar situation and it sucks.

'Three boys, three girls, and all three want to be the one who gets Magda,' says Nadine. She is too nice to point out that she is always second choice. It's easy enough to work out where I come – last!

'Hey, wait for me!' says Magda, scurrying after us. The boys call after her but she doesn't take any notice.

'You stay with them if you want,' I say.

'Yeah, we're going down to McDonald's but you can catch up with us later,' says Nadine.

'I'm catching up with you now,' says Magda. 'This is our girl-time, right? Hey, *look* at the time! It's getting late. Come on, let's eat.'

378

Magda is sweet enough to insist on buying me a burger and fries. I draw her portrait on the first page of my sketchbook, picturing her doing a little twirl in her pink top and designer trousers with lots of adoring weeny guys milling around her ankles. Then I draw Nadine. First of all I tease her and kit her out in Rhinestone Cowboy gear, but after she's clobbered me I appease her by drawing her as a glamorous witch with nails like jewelled claws and in one elaborately manicured hand she's holding a little doll, the image of Natasha, stuck all over with pins.

I'm really into drawing now so I peer round for someone to sketch. And then I see the strangest thing. There's a boy the other side of McDonald's. *He's* not strange. He's quite good-looking with dark eyes and long, floppy hair. He's wearing Halmer High School uniform. A lot of the boys who go there are either Hooray Henrys or the twitchy nerdy type. But this boy's different. Guess what he's doing! He's got a pen and a little notebook similar to mine and he's sketching . . . *me*?

It can't be me. No, of course, it's Magda. She's the one all the boys stare at all the time. But when he looks up he's staring straight at me – and when Magda goes to get another straw for her milkshake he doesn't turn his head. Then it'll be Nadine. Yes, he's drawing Nadine with her amazing long hair and big dark eyes. Though Nadine is lolling back in her chair and I'm not sure he could see her properly now.

It's me he's looking at. Looking up at my face and down at his book, up and down, up and down, his pen moving rapidly across the page. He must see I'm staring at him but it doesn't put him off.

'Why have you gone pink, Ellie?' said Nadine.

'Oh God, I haven't, have I?'

'Shocking pink. What *is* it?'

'Nothing.'

'Who are you looking at?' says Magda, coming back with the straw. She peers round and susses things out straight away. 'Are you flirting with that Halmer High guy?'

'No.'

'*Which* boy?' says Nadine, peering.

'Don't! He's staring at us.'

'So we'll stare at him,' says Magda. 'What's he doing, writing?'

'I think he's sketching,' I say.

'What?'

'Me!'

Magda and Nadine look at me. They both look a little surprised.

'What's he drawing you for?' says Nadine.

'*I* don't know. It feels . . . weird,' I say, as his eyes flicker up and down again.

'So you draw him,' says Magda. 'Go on, Ellie.'

'It'll look silly.'

'No it won't. Go on. He's drawing you, so you draw him. Even Stevens,' says Magda.

'All right.' I start sketching the sketcher. I try a jokey portrait, making his eyes extra beady, his hair a little too long, his stance ultra alert. I draw the sketch-book in his hand with a small picture of me. In this picture I am crouched over my own sketchbook drawing a minute portrait of him.

'It's good!' says Magda.

'So you're drawing him drawing you drawing him

380

'. . . it's making my brain buzz thinking about it,' says Nadine.

'Hey, he's coming over!' says Magda.

'What?' I say, looking up. She's right, he's walking this way, still staring at me.

I shut my sketchbook up quickly, and slide it onto my lap.

'Hey, that's not fair. I want to see what you've drawn,' he says, standing at our table. He smiles at me. 'I'll show you mine if you show me yours.'

Magda and Nadine burst out laughing.

'That's an invitation you can't resist, Ellie,' says Magda.

'Ellie! Hey, you're not Ellie the Elephant, are you?' he says.

I stare at him. Ellie . . . the Elephant? Why is he calling me my old nickname? Does he think I'm that fat?

All my old anorexic loopiness overwhelms me. I feel like I'm being blown up like a balloon. Roll up, roll up to peer at the fat lady in McDonald's.

'Ellie the Elephant?' I whisper in a mouse's squeak out of my gargantuan head.

'Yes, I was in the art shop upstairs just now, you know?'

'Does she know?' says Magda. 'She only spends half her life there.'

'Half *our* lives,' says Nadine.

'Me too, me too,' he says. 'Anyway, I was buying this new pen and I went to try it out and someone else had been writing all across the pad, and there was this name, Ellie, and a cute little elephant with a wavy trunk.'

'Oh! Yes, I *see*. That was me,' I say, shrinking back into my ordinary-size self.

'So have you been drawing lots of little elephants, eh?'

'I hope not,' said Magda. 'Seeing as she's supposed to have been drawing me.'

'And me,' says Nadine. 'And also you!'

'Me?' he says eagerly.

'Shut up, Nadine,' I say.

'Oh come on, let me see. Look.' He opens his own sketchbook. 'Here's you.'

I peer at it, my heart thudding. I've never seen my portrait drawn by anyone else. Well, I suppose Eggs has included me in his shaky crayonings of MY FAMILY, but as he represents me as two big blobs, four stick lines and a wild scribble of hair, his portraits are not very flattering.

This boy's portrait of me is . . . amazing. He's brilliant at art. His pen is the same as mine and yet he's got it to swoop and spiral with such style. He's obviously a fan of Aubrey Beardsley. He places his figure on the paper with that kind of confidence, a bold outline, and immense detail with the hair, the features and texture of the jumper. My hair, my features, my jumper (well, on loan from Eggs). He's drawn me looking the way I'd *like* to look, intelligent and absorbed, drawing in my own sketchbook. Drawing him. And the picture me is drawing a minute portrait too.

'Wow!' says Nadine. 'Look, he's drawn you drawing him drawing you and you've drawn him drawing you drawing him.'

'You're burbling, Nadine,' says Magda. 'Here, Ellie, show him.'

She snatches my sketchbook and shows him my portrait of him. He laughs delightedly.

'It's great.'

'It's *not*, nowhere near as good as yours.'

It's annoying, I'm not really desperately competitive, and I couldn't care less about coming top at school or winning at games and stuff like that, but the one thing I suppose I've always taken for granted is that I'm good at art. Better than anyone else in my class.

'What year are you in?' I ask.

'Year Eleven.'

It makes it a little easier. Maybe in two years' time I'll be as good as that. Maybe.

'What year are you in, Ellie?'

'Year Nine, we all are.'

Nadine raises her eyebrows at Magda, and they both sigh, irritated at me for giving away our age. I suppose they could both get away with making out they were Year Ten. Maybe even older. But I'm smaller than them and with my chubby cheeks and dimples I could easily be mistaken for some little kid of eleven or twelve. Apart from my chest. I wriggle in my chair. I'm *not* sticking my chest out. I'm just sitting up a little straighter.

'I'm going to get myself another coffee, can I get you girls anything?'

'Well, we were just going,' I say.

'No we weren't,' says Magda. 'Sure, coffee would be great.'

He smiles and goes off to the counter, leaving his sketchbook on the table.

'I haven't got any more money,' I hiss. 'I already owe you, Mags.'

'He can pay. He'll have stacks of cash seeing he's a poshnob Halmer's boy,' says Nadine. 'He really fancies you, Ellie.'

'No he doesn't!' I say quickly, blushing again. 'He's just being friendly, that's all.'

'Oh yeah, like he trots round the whole of McDonald's buying everyone coffee?'

'It was just because I was drawing. Anyway, it's probably not me he's interested in. It could be you he fancies, Nadine – or Magda.'

'Do you think so?' says Magda, twiddling her hair and licking her lips.

'You wish, Mags,' says Nadine. 'He's only got eyes for Ellie.'

He comes back with the coffee and then he sits down beside us. Beside me.

'So what else have you been drawing, Ellie? I'm Russell, by the way.'

He holds out his hand. I blink at him. I think he's being incredibly formal and wants to shake my hand. He looks surprised when I hold out my own hand politely.

'I was reaching for your sketchbook, actually.'

'Oh!' I feel myself blushing scarlet and try to snatch my hand away.

'Let's shake anyway. That makes us friends,' says Russell, giving my hand a little squeeze.

Nadine gives Magda a triumphant nod. She's right. I can't believe it. I feel like I'm suddenly rocketed on to Romance Planet. Things like this don't happen to me.

'Let's see the sketchbook,' he says. He looks at my jokey portraits of Magda and Nadine.

'They're really fantastic,' he says, grinning.

'No they're not. They were just quick sketches anyway. I can draw a bit better than that,' I say. 'But I'm nowhere near as good as you.'

'No, I think you've got a real gift, Ellie. Do you want to do Graphics later?'

He's treating me like a serious person. *He's* a serious person. The only boyfriend I've ever had thought that you spelt it graffix and reckoned it was a stick of glue.

'Yeah, maybe,' I said casually.

'There's supposed to be a very good Graphics course at Kingtown Art College,' says Russell.

'I don't really fancy going there. It's where my dad teaches,' I say.

'Oh, right. I know the problem. My mum teaches in the juniors at my school and it was seriously weird putting my hand up and calling her Miss. I rather hoped she might make me teacher's pet and top of the class but she kept picking on me.'

We get launched into this whole long conversation about schools. Magda says something about her embarrassing enormous packed lunches when she was at junior school. Her mum and dad run a restaurant and if they are fond of anyone they want to feed them up. They're very, very, very fond of Magda. Most people are. But Russell hardly seems to notice her though he nods politely. Magda gives up.

'Shall we buzz off home, Nadine?' she suggests.

'Good idea,' she says. 'Bye, Ellie, see you tomorrow.'

'No, wait, I'm coming too,' I say.

'Can I come as well?' says Russell. 'Which way home do you go, Ellie?'

'I go on the bus with Nadine.'

'Oh, that's great, so do I,' says Russell.

'You don't even know which bus.'

'Your bus.'

Magda and Nadine roll their eyes. I giggle stupidly. I feel my cheeks with the back of my hand. They're hot enough to fry a couple of eggs. At least I cool down a little outside. Magda waves goodbye and goes off shaking her head, still a little bemused. I trot along awkwardly between Russell and Nadine, trying like mad to think of something intelligent to talk about. I want to ask Russell all sorts of stuff about art but I don't want to leave Nadine out of things. Yet if I start chattering to Nadine about French homework and what combination of colours she is going to paint her nails then it'll seem rude to Russell.

I glance nervously from one to the other. Both of them catch me looking. Nadine rolls her eyes at me. Russell smiles. He clears his throat. He hums a little tune. Perhaps he is lost for words too. This is surprisingly reassuring.

'Have you got their latest album?' says Nadine.

I stare at her blankly but Russell responds. He was humming this song by some cult hip band Nadine is nuts on. I've never even heard of them. Russell and Nadine burble on about them.

'What do you think of Animal Angst, Ellie?' Russell asks.

I blink at him. I wouldn't know Animal Angst if it howled in my ear. 'Oh, OK,' I say cautiously.

Nadine gives her eyes another roll, but she doesn't betray me. I resolve to read the *New Musical Express* every week.

We stand waiting for the bus. There's a big poster for a horror movie over the road. *Girls Out Even Later*.

'Great,' says Russell. 'It's coming out on Friday. The gory special effects are meant to be superb. Did you want to see it, Ellie?'

I dither helplessly. Does he mean – do I want to see it *with him*?

I want to go out with him, yes please! But I hate horror movies. I have to hide my eyes at all the scary parts. I can't even listen to creepy music or I come out in goosepimples. I've only ever seen horror movies on video. It would be much much scarier on a huge screen. I'd probably make a right idiot of myself with Russell and end up cowering right under the seat. If I ever got *in* as it's an eighteen. I haven't got a hope in hell of convincing anyone that I'm eighteen.

Russell is looking at me, waiting for a reply.

'Mmmmm,' I say eventually, fully aware that this reply is not worth the wait.

Nadine launches into a long rave about the director's last horror movie. I stand and stare into the middle distance. Russell seems fascinated. He's obviously realizing that he has been hitting on the wrong girl. He and Nadine are soulmates.

'What did you think of *Girls Out Late*, Ellie?' he asks.

'OK,' I mumble.

'Did you like it?' Russell presses me.

'Mmmm.'

I seem to have taken to talking in initials: O, K and M.

'Did you like the creepy bit in the multi-storey car park?' says Russell.

I look at Nadine for help.

This time she betrays me by bursting out laughing. 'Ellie never got that far,' she says. 'She started to watch it round at my place but had to hide her eyes before the title sequence was over. She only got ten minutes into the movie proper before running right out of my bedroom and refusing to come back.'

Russell grins. 'So you find horror movies a bit scary, Ellie?'

'Ellie's the type of girl who'd find the Noo Noo scary,' Nadine giggles.

My face is certainly Po red. Russell must take me for a right idiot. He's laughing at me.

'Then *please* come to the movie with me, Ellie – you'll be snuggling right up to me in no time,' he says.

I manage to laugh too, though I still feel a bit foolish. I glance at my watch. Talk about girls out late! It's nearly ten.

Still, the bus is coming, I'll be home soon. At least, that's what I *intend*.

# Chapter Two

# Time To Go Home

# Chapter Two

I don't know who to sit next to on the bus. Nadine gets on first and rather pointedly spreads herself out on a double seat. I make for the seat opposite but I suddenly feel mean. Nadine's been my best friend since we were both five years old. I've known Russell less than an hour, for God's sake. I spin on my heel and nudge up next to Nadine. Russell sits opposite. He leans forward to try to continue the conversation but this old lady huffs and puffs so he contents himself with smiling.

Nadine and I can converse OK.

'Gee whizz, I thought Magda was a quick worker!' Nadine mutters. 'I've obviously underestimated your pulling power, Ellie.'

'It's nothing to do with me!' I whisper.

'Rubbish, it was all your come-hither looks, staring at him all the time in McDonald's.'

'I was drawing him! I had to look at him. And,

anyway, he drew me first. He was the one who started it.'

'So, what happens now? Are you going to go out with him?'

'I don't know. I don't think he'll ask me. He was just being friendly because of the art thing.'

'*Ellie!* Are you being deliberately irritating? He's obviously nuts about you.'

'Do you really think so?' I hiss, delighted.

Nadine sighs. 'Look, when I get off the bus I'll clear off down Weston Avenue and go that way home, OK? I don't want to play gooseberry.'

'You're not!'

'Oh, yeah, well I'm not going to stand and file my broken fingernails while you stand snogging on the doorstep.'

'I'm not going to snog!' I forget to whisper. Nadine nudges me. Russell is staring at me. Oh God, did he hear what I said?

'Of course you'll snog,' says Nadine.

'I don't think I want to.'

'Don't you fancy him?'

'I . . . don't know,' I say stupidly. 'What do *you* think of him, Nad?'

'Well, he's OK. I mean he's not really my type.'

'Do you think he's good-looking?'

'Sort of. Well, he's not totally nerdy, but it's hard to tell when he's wearing that awful uniform.'

'Nadine, when you snog – like now, first time – are you supposed to do the tongue thing?'

'If you want to.'

'I don't know *what* I want.'

It's true. I always dreamt of a romantic encounter

391

like this – and yet now it is happening it's so over-
whelming I'm kind of scared. I almost wish Russell
had gone after Magda or Nadine. No, I don't really
wish that. I wish Russell had never started sketching
me, and that now I was going home on the bus with
Nadine after a perfectly normal girls' night out.

'Come on, it's our stop,' says Nadine.

'Maybe he'll stay on the bus,' I say.

'You're mad, Ellie. Look, he's getting up too.'

'Nadine, don't go down Weston Avenue. Come
my way. Come via my house. *Please*, I don't want to
be on my own with him,' I hiss urgently.

'Grow up, Ellie!'

That's the trouble, I'm not sure I want to grow up.

We get off the bus, Russell, Nadine and me.

'Well, cheerio, you guys,' says Nadine.

'Nadine!'

'See you tomorrow, Ellie.' She nods at Russell.

'Bye, Nadine, nice meeting you,' says Russell.
Then he turns to me. 'Which way do we go?'

'We can go Nadine's way,' I say.

But Nadine is already running off, clonking a little
in her new Shelley shoes.

'We'll go your way,' says Russell. 'Or thereabouts.
Shall we go for a little walk first?'

'Well . . .' I've got matching silver bangles jangling
on my wrist instead of my watch – but I know it's
getting late. Not just getting. It *is* late. I am a Girl Out
Late. I've got to get home. He can walk me to my
door and then I will give him a quick little kiss on the
cheek and then I'll scoot indoors. That's what I'll do.
That's what I want.

It's not what he wants.

'Come on, Ellie!' He's looking all around. 'Is there a park round here? Come and show me so that I can imagine a chubby little Ellie feeding the ducks.'

'No duck pond, no ducks. Swings.'

'Swings are better. A little swing in the park for five minutes. Ten at tops. Yes?'

My head nods automatically. We walk towards the park. Russell edges nearer to me. He reaches out. He takes hold of my hand.

Oh God, I don't know what to do with my fingers. They're crooked uncomfortably but if I fold them over they may stroke his palm in a suggestive way. My hand starts sweating, or is it *his*? If only it was the bitter cold winter and then we'd be wearing gloves.

But it's spring and I'm getting uncomfortably hot inside Eggs's tight sweater. What am I doing? I want to go *home*, and it really is late. I'm going to get into trouble.

'I'll have to get back soon, Russell, really.'

'Sure, well, so will I.'

'Where do you live?'

'Oh, around here.'

'No you don't, not if you don't even know where the park is!'

'It's . . . over there.' He gestures vaguely with his free hand.

'Totally wrong. Come on, where do you live specifically?'

'Near the park.'

'Lies!'

'OK, near *a* park, Pembridge Park.'

'That's *miles* away!'

It's also the posh part of town, with huge great

Victorian houses. I once went to a party there and I remember being astonished by the stained glass windows in the hall – I went into the living room expecting pews and an altar. Some of the grandest houses surrounding the park certainly seem as big as churches and induce a similar feeling of reverence. And I'm hand in hand with a Halmer's boy who lives there.

'A big house?' I say.

'It is, but we just have a basement flat. Well, it's called a garden flat but the garden is outside and we only have a fifth of it. The house is all split up. So are my family. I live with my dad now and my sister lives with my mum. There is also my dad's girlfriend, but the less said about her the better. I hope she fades out of the picture soon. I certainly don't fancy her as a stepmother.'

'I've got a stepmother. She's OK, though. We didn't used to get on but now we're friends.'

Anna won't be friends any more unless I go home *now*. She'll worry.

'I'm never ever going to be friends with Cynthia. Honestly, what a classic name – my stupid besotted dad is sinning with Cynthia. I don't know what's up with him. We used to get on great, Dad and me, sort of us two guys together – but now she's there all the time. It's pathetic. So I try not to hang out too much at home now. Who wants to be cooped up in the living room with his dad and his girl snogging on the sofa like teenagers?'

'In front of you? That's a bit gross.'

'Well, whenever I go out of the room. Then they spring apart when I go back in. It's like I'm the parent. So I mostly clear off to my bedroom, draw and do

394

homework and stuff. But sometimes it really gets to me, stuck there like someone in solitary confinement – so I push off by myself.'

'Don't you have any friends?'

'Oh, yes, heaps. No, don't get the impression I'm this poor sad guy without a social life.'

'I didn't mean that!'

'It's just, well, I'm OK at school, there's this little mob I go around with. But out of school – well, there's two types at Halmer's, there's the really intense anoraks and they just swot away and come top in everything and their idea of a big social thrill is accessing some porn on the Internet. Then there's the other really hip set, the ones that go to all the parties and get all the girls and drink and take drugs – and I'm a bit too wet and weedy to join in.'

'You're not a bit wet or weedy,' I say.

'But it's kind of different for boys anyway. You have mates, but you're not really *close* to them. Unless you're gay, which I'm definitely not, in spite of all the tales you hear of infamous encounters behind the Halmer's bike sheds.'

I giggle. Magda was once chatted up by this Halmer's boy in Year Eight and he swore half the Year Elevens were at it – behind the bike sheds.

'It must be great to have friends to go round with, like you and those two girls.'

'Nadine and Magda. Yeah, they're both my best friends.'

'Which do you like best?'

'Both.'

'You don't ever fall out?'

'Well, we have arguments sometimes. And last year

Nadine had this ultra creepy boyfriend so we didn't see much of her then – but we're like this now.' I cross my fingers on my free hand.

We are still clasped, albeit a little sweatily. We're nearly at the park now. A minute or two, then maybe one quick swing and then *home*.

'Does Nadine have a boyfriend now?'

'No.'

'I bet the other one does, the bubbly one with the red hair.'

'Magda? No, she doesn't have a boyfriend either.'

'And what about you, Ellie?'

I pause. I shake my head.

Russell smiles. 'Great, so . . . will you come out with me sometime?'

'I *am* out with you.'

'No, I mean for a pizza or to see a film or something.'

'OK.'

'Tomorrow?'

'If you like.'

'Seven o'clock. I could meet you at that shopping centre place. I'll be the guy sketching in case you forget what I look like.'

'Yeah, so I had better be going home now. It's ever so late.'

'No, it's not, look, some of the kids are still out playing.'

There's a little bunch of them whizzing around on the roundabout in the dark, sharing crisps and swigging Coke.

'Well, I know it's not *late*-late but I was supposed to be home ages ago.'

'But we haven't had a swing yet. Come on, Ellie. One quick swing.'

'OK, one quintessentially quick swing and then I must *go home*.'

'Promise. I love the way you talk, Ellie. You're so different from other girls.'

We walk over the tufty grass towards the play area. I'm glad I'm not wearing my high heels. I'm wearing shabby red trainers, the rubber treads worn right down – but I feel I'm bouncing on springs. It's really happening. I'm Ellie and I'm walking hand in hand with this boy who likes it that I'm different. He likes *me*, he likes *me*, he likes *me*.

We get to the swings and I think of all the times I've been here in the past. First with my mum, and there's a sad little tug of my heart even now because I still miss her so much and she'll *always* come first with me. Then there were the times Dad took me, pushing me so high on the swings I'd get scared I'd loop the loop right over the bar at the top. Nowadays Dad pushes Eggs, who once fell right off and nearly lived up to his nickname and scrambled himself. Magda, Nadine and I sometimes hang out in the park in the summer too and have long long long discussions about clothes and make-up and hairstyles and rock stars and *boys*.

And now I'm here with a boy, and he's swinging and I'm swinging, kicking right up high until my trainers point higher than the tops of the silhouetted poplars edging the park. I put my head back and make it feel even speedier but I start to get giddy and when I slow down and jump off the park suddenly tips sideways and spins by itself.

'Whoops,' says Russell, and he reaches out and steadies me. 'Are you OK, Ellie?'

Then before I can answer he bends his head and kisses me. It's just a little kiss, our lips gently bumping. We break away. I blink behind my bleary glasses.

'Oh, Ellie,' says Russell, and he kisses me again. A proper kiss. A real pressed–up–close, mouths working, meaningful kiss. I never thought it would feel so strange, so special. I feel even giddier. I cling to him and he holds me even closer.

There's something spraying in my hair. Is it raining? And little flaky things land on my shoulder. *Snowing?*

Laughter.

I push Russell away. The kids are surrounding us, deliberately sprinkling us with Coke and crisps.

'Snog snog snoggy snog!' they jeer.

'Get lost, you lot,' says Russell.

He has a crisp sticking up in his hair like a little ribbon. I remove it – and we both start giggling.

'Let's find somewhere a bit more private,' says Russell, taking my hand. 'Over by the trees?'

'No, I must get back, really.'

'Oh, come on – please, Ellie.'

'I'm sure it's time to go home.'

'Like Andy Pandy. Did you ever see that *Watch With Mother* video? I love little kids' programmes.'

'Me too! I used to like *Sesame Street* best.'

'And me. I used to draw them all with my felt-tip pens. All my little buddies in the nursery class wanted one of my special Big Bird portraits.'

'You'll have to draw the Cookie Monster for me, he's my favourite.'

'Did you like *Art Attack* when Zoë Ball was on it, ages and ages ago?'

'Yes, I *loved* it.'

'There's this guy in my class crazy about Zoë Ball, and he paid me a fiver to do a special portrait of him with his arm round her.'

'Hey, that's a great idea. All the girls in my class are nuts about Leonardo DiCaprio so maybe I'll do heaps of portraits of him and make my fortune.'

'Some people say I look a bit like Leonardo DiCaprio – you know, my hairstyle and my features. Do you think so, Ellie?'

I mumble something politely. He doesn't look *remotely* like Leonardo DiCaprio. I'm glad Nadine and Magda aren't here or they'd hoot with laughter. We've left the kids on the swings far behind. We're over by the trees where it's really dark.

'Oh, Ellie,' says Russell.

This is obviously a signal for another kiss. I'm ready this time, my head tilted so that my glasses don't get in the way. I love the way he kisses. Dan and I used to kiss but it was just silly awkward kids' stuff. This is real and adult and exciting.

This is getting too real and adult and exciting. His hand is wandering over my shoulders towards my front.

'Russell, don't.'

'Please. Just . . . *please*.'

His hand is stroking the wool of Eggs's jumper insistently. I love the way it feels. It's not like it's anything too terrible. I don't want him to think me totally uptight and pathetic. So shall I just let him go this far?

Oh my God, I've suddenly remembered the tissues! The ones I stuffed down each bra cup so I wouldn't show too much in the tight sweater. I'll die if he finds himself with a handful of paper tissue.

'Please, Russell. No, come on, I *have* to get home.' I push him away very firmly.

'Ellie!'

'I mean it. What's the time?'

He looks at his watch. 'Oh dear, I can't see the face in the dark.'

'Russell, *please*!'

'OK, OK. It's only just gone eleven.'

'*What?* You're kidding!'

'Ten past.'

'Oh, my God, what am I going to do?'

'Hey, hey, don't panic. Look, it's really not late at all. Ellie! Wait for me.'

'I've got to run.'

'Well, I'll run with you. I'll take you right home. I'll explain to your folks that it's all my fault.'

'And you'll say what? That we went for a walk in the park and started kissing and lost all sense of time?'

'Well, *some*thing along those lines.'

'To my *dad*?'

'Is he a really fierce old-fashioned kind of *father* dad?' said Russell. 'Maybe I won't come *all* the way home with you.'

'Don't, then! Look, you go off back to Pembridge Park. It's going to take you ages. I don't even know if there's a bus at this time.'

'So I'll take a taxi. No problem. And I was *joking*, Ellie. Of course I'm not going to let you go haring off on your own. I just wish you wouldn't walk so quickly. I can't keep up with you. I'm useless at running.'

'So am I!' I have to slow a little because my heart is pounding and I can hardly breathe and sweat is trickling down my back. Oh God, please let my deodorant keep working, please please please. Don't let him think of me as *Smelly* Ellie.

'So you're not a sporty girl. Not jolly hockey sticks?'

'I *hate* hockey. Mags and Nadine and I still do our best to slope off sharpish whenever there's a match.' I take a huge gasping breath. 'I'm going to have to start running again, Russell. That's quarter past striking. How did it get so *late*?'

'You were in amazing company, that's how,' said Russell. 'Hey, will your dad be seriously cross, Ellie?'

I don't know! I've never really been out late like this before. I didn't ever go out on proper dates with Dan – and *no* dad would worry about what I was getting up to with Dan anyway. Dan had total nerd written right through him, like a stick of seaside rock. He used to turn peppermint pink whenever he came up close to me. If he'd ever kissed me like Russell he'd have gone magenta and exploded. Like the girl's head in *Girls Out Late*. And I'm a girl out later than late and Dad and Anna must be seriously worried. They'll worry even more if I tell them the absolute truth. Right, I'll spin them a little story. I'll say I went back to Nadine's and she showed me her favourite horror video *Girls Out Late* and it was so compulsive we just couldn't stop watching and lost all track of time. It's not really a lie. I *have* watched part of *Girls Out Late* at Nadine's. They'll understand. They'll be cross of course. They'll wonder why I didn't phone. OK, OK, I'll say I *tried* to phone but I couldn't get through. No, Nadine's phone was out of order – even her dad's mobile. How about little green aliens landed at Nadine's and they abducted all of us and sabotaged the telephones???

We're nearly at the top of my road now.

'You go, Russell, please.'

'But I want to help you out, explain to your dad.'

'No, I'm going to tell him I was with Nadine,' I say. 'Go on, Russell, you go home.'

'OK then. Well, after one more kiss. Come on, you're this late, another second isn't going to make much difference.'

He takes me in his arms. I'm out of breath to start with – and this last kiss is so amazing I stop breathing altogether. When he eventually lets me come up for air, I'm gasping like a goldfish.

'Oh, Ellie!' says Russell, reaching for me again.

'No! I must go. Bye, Russell – bye!' I wrench myself away, and start running again. Running and running and running right down my road to my house. Oh God, what am I going to say? Think, Ellie, think. Take a deep breath. It might be all right. They might have gone to bed early or something. Who am I kidding? The lights are blazing downstairs.

I put my key in the door – and before I can even get it out, Dad wrenches open the door. *He* is blazing.

'Ellie! Where the hell have you been?'

'Oh, Ellie, we've been ever so worried!' Anna pushes past him and gives me a hug. She clings to me as if she's really really glad I'm safe. But then she pushes me away again, almost as angry as Dad. 'Why

402

didn't you *phone*? The shops close at *nine*.'

'I'm sorry, I'm sorry – it's just we went to McDonald's after, Nadine and Magda and me,' I say.

'And?' says Dad.

'And we just got talking, you know what we're like.'

'I don't know what you're like any more, Ellie,' says Dad. 'I never thought you'd start behaving like this. You've no idea what you put us through.'

'I'm *sorry*. Look, I'm really tired now, can we all just go to bed?'

'No we can't. We're going to have this out now.'

'Look, maybe we should all go to bed and discuss it in the morning,' says Anna.

'For God's sake, you're the one who has been in tears for the last hour!' says Dad.

I stare at Anna. Her eyes are red.

'Why were you *crying*?' I say. 'I mean, I can see why you're cross, but there was no need to get *upset*.'

'Our thirteen-year-old daughter out God knows where, nearly two hours late home. Come *on*, Ellie!' says Dad. He goes into the kitchen and puts the kettle on. He reaches for the coffee mugs, slamming them hard down on the table – as if he'd like to slam me down hard too.

'Look, I don't know why you're getting so shirty with me, Dad. OK, OK, I'm late home, but it's not that heinous a crime, is it? You're often ever so late home yourself.'

'Don't get smart with me, Ellie. Now, tell me, where have you been?'

'You know where I've been, at Flowerfields – and then McDonald's. You're acting like I've been popping pills all night at some rave, for God's sake.'

'Where did you go *after* McDonalds?'

'Well, we were there ages.'

'Who's we?'

'Dad! Magda, Nadine and me, honestly.'

'And then what did you do?'

'Well, Magda went home, and I went back on the bus with Nadine – and I just popped in her house to see some stuff and she started showing me this really creepy video *Girls Out Late* and I suppose I stayed a bit late watching it, goodness knows why, because you know I hate horror movies and this one is really truly *gross*.'

Dad and Anna are staring at me. I burble on and on, making stuff up about the movie. The kettle boils. Dad looks as if he should have steam spiralling out of his ears likewise. He makes the drinks, stirring so fiercely coffee slops all over the place.

'So you were at Nadine's?' he says.

'*Yes*.'

'Oh, Ellie,' Anna says.

My heart is thumping. This is all going horribly wrong.

'And then where did you go?' Dad says.

'Home.'

'By yourself?'

'Well, it's only a few streets.'

'You know you're not allowed out after dark by yourself.'

'Yes, well, I didn't think it would really matter, just from Nadine's home to here. I suppose I could have rung you.'

*Oh no!* I suddenly remember. I told Anna I *would*

404

ring from Nadine's. I look at her and she shakes her head sadly.

'We waited for you to ring. And then we rang Nadine's – and Nadine's mother said Nadine had come home on her own,' Anna says.

I swallow. 'What did Nadine say?' I whisper.

'She came out with a whole load of stupid evasions and downright lies,' says Dad. 'She couldn't seem to see how badly we needed to know where the hell you were.'

'So you've been bullying Nadine too,' I say.

'Ellie, nowadays you can't just have a thirteen-year-old out late by herself – not without going out of your mind with worry. Surely you can see that?' says Anna.

'And *eventually* Nadine tells us you've gone off with some boy you picked up in McDonald's,' says Dad.

'I didn't pick him up! He talked to me first,' I say indignantly.

'A complete stranger! And you went off on your own with him. Are you mad?'

'He's a Halmer's boy,' I say.

'Well, they're the worst. They're famous for it. Picking up silly little girls and seeing how far they can go,' Dad thunders.

'Don't, you're making all this horrible. Russell isn't a bit like that. He likes *art*, he was sketching and I was sketching, that's how we got talking – and then he came on the bus with Nadine and me and then after-wards we just had this little walk. We were talking about all sorts of stuff, that's all.'

'That's all?' says Dad. 'You've got your make-up

smudged all over your face, Ellie. It's obvious what you've been up to.'

'I haven't been up to anything! Stop it! I don't know why you're being like this, spoiling everything.'

'Your dad doesn't want to spoil anything, Ellie. He's just been so worried wondering if you were all right. He's over-reacting. I am, too. It's just this is the first time this has happened and we're obviously getting het up over nothing,' says Anna. She takes a sip of coffee then tries to smile as if this is a normal conversation. 'This Russell sounds really nice. Are you going to see him again?'

'Tomorrow.'

'No you're not,' says Dad.

'Dad! Look, what *is* this? I thought you were really cool about any kind of boyfriend stuff.'

'It's not about boyfriends, it's about you lying to us.'

'I'm sorry, I just said the first thing that came into my head.'

'It's frightening, you seemed so plausible. I just can't believe it of you, Ellie. And I *hate* the idea of you going off on your own with the first boy that beckons in your direction, letting him slobber all over you in the dark.'

'Shut up, Dad. Who are you to talk anyway? You've done enough slobbering yourself, as you so charmingly put it. I remember all those girls you went out with after Mum died, before Anna. Maybe *after* Anna too.'

'How dare you!' says Dad.

'I do dare. I'm sick of you. Why is there always one

rule for adults and another for teenagers? What gives you the right to tell me how to behave?'

'Stop it, Ellie,' Anna says sharply.

'Why should I? And why should I do what *you* say anyway? You're not my mother.'

I push past both of them and run upstairs. Eggs is standing in his pyjamas on the landing.

'You're in big trouble, Ellie,' he hisses.

'You shut up,' I say and go into my bedroom and slam the door.

I flop down on my bed and burst into tears. I hate them all. Why did they have to spoil what was the most magical evening of my life?

# Chapter Three

# Rhyme Time

# Chapter Three

Breakfast is terrible. Dad and I aren't speaking. Anna talks enough for both of us, chit-chatting to try and pretend this is a perfectly normal morning. Eggs is intrigued and delighted by all of this, and asks endless idiotic questions about 'Ellie's Boyfriend'.

'He is *not* my boyfriend. He is just a boy in Year Eleven I happened to meet yesterday and we had a good long chat about art.'

'And a good long encounter in the park afterwards,' says Dad bitterly, breaking his silence.

'Please!' says Anna, nearly in tears. 'Don't talk to Ellie like that.'

'I'll talk to her how I damn well please,' says Dad, pushing his plate away and standing up. 'She's still a child, and she is going to have to learn to do as she's told. She's not staying out till all hours.'

'Dad, I was home at twenty past eleven. Heaps of

girls in my year stay out till way past midnight.'

'I don't care what anyone else does, although from my conversation with Nadine's parents last night it was all too humiliatingly clear they were obviously appalled. It was evident that Nadine would never behave like that.'

This is so infuriating! If only they knew! Last term when Nadine had this thing with this total creep, Liam, she sneaked off and saw him all the time and she lied her little head off to her mum and dad, forever making out she was round at my place or Magda's. But obviously I can't tell Dad this because I don't want to tell tales on Nadine. So I just sigh deeply and tap my fingers on the table, acting like I'm too bored for words.

This winds Dad up so much he starts really yelling at me. Eggs stops thinking it's funny and hunches down in his chair, sucking his thumb. I start to feel scared too. Dad's acting like he really can't stand me. I just don't get it. Why does he have to be so *horrible*? I try to stare him out and act like I'm not even listening but my throat hurts and my eyes have gone all blurry behind my glasses.

'Will you please *stop it*,' says Anna, standing up too. 'You're frightening Eggs. Dear God, you're frightening all of us. Now *please* – go to college. We'll talk about it tonight, when we've all calmed down.'

'I'm out tonight, there's a faculty meeting,' says Dad. 'I'll have a sandwich at work and go straight on to the meeting. I'll be back around ten.'

I shall be out too, seeing Russell.

Dad's staring at me – and it's as if his mean

411

narrowed eyes can laser through my skull and see what's in my mind.

'*You're* not allowed out, Ellie. You do understand that? You're completely grounded.'

'Oh please! What a stupid expression. *Grounded!* It's like something out of prep school.'

This is a clever diversionary tactic. It's always the easiest way to score points off Dad. He likes to act like this ultra lefty alternative guy and yet Grandma and Grandpa are ultra strait-laced and right wing and posh and Dad got sent right through the public school system. It's something he's very embarrassed about. He does his best to talk down, but the odd little phrase creeps into his conversation every now and then and betrays him.

'You might find the expression stupid, Ellie – but I trust you understand what it means?'

'I'm not allowed out, right?'

'That's right.'

'Not at all?'

'Not at all.'

'Oh great, I can't go to school then, can I? So I'll just go back to bed for a nice long snooze.'

'Ellie, acting like a six-year-old is not going to convince me that you're old enough to stay out half the night with strangers,' says Dad, and he walks out of the kitchen.

He doesn't say goodbye to me, he doesn't even say goodbye to Anna and Eggs. He just stomps out of the room, still acting like some Victorian control freak dad, like he's Mr Barrett of Wimpole Street and I'm poetic Elizabeth. Only I'm not reclining on a sofa, I'm on a hard kitchen stool – and I'm not about to elope with my romantic Mr Browning. Russell and I are hardly at the eloping stage. I don't know whether he writes poetry or not. I don't even know his second name. But I'm going to find out. I'm meeting Russell tonight if it kills me. And Dad very likely *will* kill me if he finds out.

I don't tell Anna my plans. She might well ring Dad up at work and tell on me. She's acting like she's really upset.

'Don't mind your dad too much, Ellie,' she says anxiously.

'I won't, don't worry!'

'That's not what I meant! Oh Ellie, I wish I knew what to say. It's so awful. I can see everyone's point of view. I think your dad over-reacted – but you were very very rude.'

I open my mouth and she shakes her head.

'Don't say any more, Ellie, please. You've said more than enough.'

I feel mean. I know I shouldn't have put in that cheap dig last night about Dad playing around. A while ago, Anna did get ever so worried that he might be having an affair with one of the students at the Art College. I suppose it's not surprising she worries because Anna was once at the Art College herself. That's when she met my dad. He *is* out an awful lot, though he's always got some excuse, like this meeting tonight. If I were Anna I'd really have it out with him – but she always likes to pretend everything is perfect. She doesn't stand up to Dad the way she should. *I* haven't always stood up to Dad either. But now I've shown him he can't bully me!

'I'm sorry I said some of that stuff last night. I didn't

413

mean to hurt you. It's just *him*,' I say. 'He can't treat me like that, giving me his orders.'

'You are his daughter, Ellie.'

'That doesn't give him automatic ownership of me! You might let him walk all over you, Anna, but I'm not going to let him do it to me.'

And with that Supergirl swoops out of the kitchen and gathers up her schoolbag.

'You haven't finished your breakfast.'

I grab my toast and say I'll eat it on the way to school.

'I'm in a hurry,' I say and dash off.

I'm not in a hurry to go to school. I'm in a hurry to see Nadine and Magda and tell them everything.

But by the time I make it to school the bell has already gone and Mrs Henderson, our form teacher, is in a right mood this morning. When I get Magda and Nadine in a corner and start my story she tells me to stop gossiping and get down to the gym in double quick time.

Mrs Henderson is also the P.E. teacher, worst luck. I positively *hate* P.E., whether it's hockey or netball or athletics or rounders. You get hot and sweaty and people yell at you and you feel stupid. Well, *I* do. Nadine's pretty hopeless too – and though Magda can be quite nippy and she's good at ballwork she generally hangs around with us and doesn't try, just to be matey.

So the three of us get into a little huddle in the changing rooms and I start for a second time, but Mrs Henderson hounds us again, telling us to cut the cackle and get changed or we'll be for it.

'Oh, Mrs Henderson, I'm having a really heavy

period. Can I be excused Games today because of my stomach cramps?' I wail, clutching my tummy.

'Ooh, me too, Mrs Henderson,' says Nadine. 'It's really bad.'

'And me too, Mrs Henderson,' says Magda, determined not to be left out.

Mrs Henderson puts her hands on her hips. 'So you are all three having your periods?' she says, eyebrows raised.

'It's a very strange but true phenomenon that women living in close circumstances menstruate at exactly the same time,' I say. This is a fact. I've read it somewhere, anyway. Even though it doesn't actually apply to Nadine and Magda and me. It would be kind of creepy. And what if you found you needed to do everything else in unison too, so you all woke up at exactly the same time and had to make a dash for the loo simultaneously?

'It's a very strange but true phenomenon that lazy schoolgirls will concoct any silly excuse whatsoever to get out of Games,' says Mrs Henderson. 'I don't care if you three girls are about to have *babies* – you are still going out on the games field and you will take *exercise*.'

We are forced to take so much exercise that I can't even speak the rare times I stagger near Magda or collapse beside Nadine. I just gasp helplessly like a goldfish.

Mrs Henderson keeps us hop, skip and jump-jump-jumping until the bell goes, which is incredibly mean because we have to charge back to the changing rooms and shower and shove on our clothes in a frantic rush as we only have a five-minute changeover period and it's Mrs Madley next lesson. A double period – just enough to give everyone stomach cramps! Mrs Madley takes us for English and it's my second favourite subject (Art first, of course) but Mrs Madley is mega-strict and the one thing she really gets mad about is if we're late for her lesson, which we are.

She rants on as if it's all our fault, and when Magda explains we were still dashing around the athletics field in our P.E. kit when the bell went Mrs Madley says that's no concern of hers, *her* concern is her lesson and we are late, and that is inexcusable. She wastes a good ten minutes telling us we can't afford to be late because we've got so much to do, and when she eventually starts the lesson it's *poetry*. I like a good story, not airy fairy poems. Especially as she wants us to concentrate on nature poetry. It is not in *my* nature to like nature. It sucks. I should have 'townie' tattooed on my forehead. We have this awful mouldering holiday cottage halfway up a mountain in the wettest part of Wales and every hour I'm forced to spend there seems to last as long as a week.

Mrs Madley glares at our groans and reads us examples from the Romantic Poets. I perk up a little at the word Romantic but it doesn't mean *romance*. I don't know what romantic countryside these Romantic Poets tramped through but *I* never stand transfixed on my little Welsh hill and admire the fair musk-rose blooms or mellow fruits – there's just a lot of rank vegetation and mud everywhere.

Then she swaps to modern poetry and she reads a Sylvia Plath poem about blackberrying and I suddenly sit up and listen because I like it, it's so sharp and

416

strange, but then she starts another poem called *Wuthering Heights* and the first line says something about horizons ringing her like faggots and we all collapse and Mrs Madley gets very narked indeed and says we're all utterly pathetic and then she says *we* all have to write a poem now. Straight away. At least twelve lines. On Nature. And any girl who fails to do so will get a detention and double English homework.

I struggle.

I think of Wales. I think hard.

Mud, mud, horrible mud.

It's like that old hippopotamus song.

*If you slip in the mud.*

*You fall down with a thud.*

I think Mrs Madley requires a more passionate response to Nature.

I try again.

*Up in the mountain*

*Through the glen*

*You will always wonder when*

*You can clear off*

*Home again.*

I peer round the room. Help! Everyone else seems to have got stuck in straight away. Nadine rolls her eyes at me and Magda sticks out her tongue, but their eyes are vague. Concentrating on their poems. The entire class is looking serious. I daren't do something silly and jokey. But how can I act like I *care* about the countryside? Hang on. Nature doesn't stop bang at every town boundary. I could write about Nature here. I peer out of the window. It is a grey dreary day. The privet hedges of the suburban gardens over the road are cut into ugly arcs. The bedding plants are crude poster paint colours, set out in unattractive repeating patterns, like wallpaper. The trees have all been pollarded so their branches don't wave in the wind. Suburban nature is not a pretty sight.

OK. What about in the dark? In the park. Me in the park with Russell, and the moon above and the poplar trees? *Yes.*

I write. I forget this is my English lesson and Mrs Madley is in a mood and my tights are all skew-whiff because I pulled them up too quickly after P.E. and my hair has gone even wilder than usual so it's spiralling up and out like there's been a minor explosion in my head.

I'm not here at all. I'm back in the park with Russell, and the key words form on the page, my hand writing as if it's got a will of its own.

'Time's up, girls,' says Mrs Madley. 'Right, you've all been very busy. I hope the fruits of your labour are mellow. Who's going to read first?'

Oh no. She wants us to read them out *loud*! I sit, heart thudding. She picks Jess first and she reads out this neat little poem about flowers, simple and safe. Then Stacy gets chosen and she gushes on about the sea, the wild white horses and the flying foam until she's practically foaming at the mouth too. It is a totally phoney poem with Absolutely Awful Annoying Alliteration but Mrs Madley goes a bundle on this too. She picks poor shy Maddie next, who blushes and says hers is rubbish and then she whispers it so we can barely hear. Stuff about mills and fields and harvests and yields. Mrs Madley doesn't look impressed but says very good, dear. Then she picks Nadine.

'Mine's about night, Mrs Madley,' says Nadine.

It's good too, very Gothic, a total stormy night with bats flying and cats stalking and trees tapping on windows and flashes of lightning like spears from hell and the crash of thunder as the devil rides out.

'You've really tried hard, Nadine. Well done,' says Mrs Madley. 'Now . . . *Ellie*.'

Oh God. My eyes flash over the page. No, I can't.

'Ellie?'

'Er – mine's about the night too. It's similar to Nadine's. It'll be so repetitious, night after night. Can't we have a day poem instead?'

'Ellie, I'm used to you girls being repetitious. Now start reading.'

'*Night in the park*
*The pale moon bare*
*Luminous above the poplar trees –*
*Tall thin dark*
*A giant feather frieze*
*Surrounding the soft square.*'

I stop and swallow. I feel my face going red.

'Go on,' says Mrs Madley. 'It's good, Ellie.'

'That's it,' I say. 'I've finished.'

'No you haven't. I can see there's another verse. And I stipulated a bare minimum of twelve lines. I can count, Ellie.'

I take a deep breath.

'*Hold me in the park*
*Your pale face intent*
*Luminous above mine*
*Tall, thin, dark*
*Around me twine*
*Surrounding, savouring, spent.*'

There's a gasp and then the entire class explodes. Mrs Madley stares at me, and then she sighs. Heavily.

'Quieten down, you idiotic girls. Eleanor Allard, what did I ask you to write?'

'A poem, Mrs Madley.'

'What sort of poem?'

'On Nature.'

'Did I ask for adolescent soft pornography?'

'No, Mrs Madley.'

'That's right. It seems to me unbelievably stupid to waste your poetic talent and my valuable lesson time on such nonsense. You will do double homework. An essay on Nature Poetry and another nature poem – and on Monday you will read it out aloud and if anyone so much as titters at the content you will start all over again. Do I make myself plain?'

As plain as a pikestaff. What *is* a pikestaff? Some sort of weapon? *She's* a deadly weapon. A member of staff with the features and ferocious nature of a pike. It's so unfair. I wasn't trying to be insolent – I just got carried away thinking about Russell and me in the park. And it was a poetical comment, contrasting Nature with *human* nature. Mean old bag!

Nadine and Magda are mouthing messages at me but I daren't respond with Mrs Madley in this mood. What's the matter with all the teachers today? I can't stick school. I go off into a private dream about when I'm grown up and I have my own little studio flat and I can draw all day. Maybe it could be a *big* studio flat with two desks. I could work at one end of the studio, Russell at the other . . .

I am mad, I've only just met him and already I'm thinking about living with him. I wonder what it would be like spending all the day with him. And then all the night too . . .

I jump when the bell goes, startled right out of Russell's arms. Magda and Nadine pounce on me the moment we're outside the classroom.

'Tell us what happened with Russell, Ellie!'

'Your poem! God, you really spelt it out. How could you read it out in front of the entire *class*?'

'I didn't want to. She made me.'

'But you wrote it in your English book, you idiot.'

'Yes, well, the words just came.'

'Like Russell!' says Magda, and she and Nadine hoot with helpless laughter.

'So you actually did it with Russell?'

'I can't believe it when you've only just met him.'

'And you lectured me like crazy about not going too far with Liam.'

'You were careful, weren't you, Ellie?'

'What was it *like*?'

'Tell us absolutely every little detail.'

I stare at them like they've gone bananas.

'OK, OK, he kissed me. Once. Several times.'

'*And*?'

'And that's it.'

'But you made it out in your poem you did it.'

'No I didn't.'

'You did, you did. Here, give us it.'

Magda snatches my English book and fumbles for my poem. She reads the last line – and she and Nadine curl up laughing again.

'What?'

'You put *spent*.'

'Yeah, I know it sounds a bit odd.'

'I'll say.'

'But, I wanted an s word to make it alliterative, right, seeing as Mrs Madley's so hot on it – and it had to rhyme with intent and it was all I could come up with.'

'Can you believe it, Nadine!' says Magda, sighing and raising her eyebrows.

'Oh *Ellie*! You mean you didn't *mean* "spent"?'

'I meant – well, we spent time together, the evening was spent – it was the end. What else could I mean?'

'It sounded like you and Russell – you know. So then he was *spent*.'

'Oh my God, I didn't mean *that*. No-one thought I meant that, did they?'

'That's what we all thought you meant. Including Mrs Madley.'

'No wonder she's given me all this extra home-work.'

'So you and Russell didn't really do anything,' said Nadine, sounding disappointed. 'The way your dad was creating you'd have thought you'd both eloped.'

'I'm sorry, I feel awful about him harassing you.'

'No problem. I just wish I could have invented some satisfactory excuse for you. I didn't know what to say.'

'Neither did I. He's still really mad at me. He says I'm not allowed out at all now.'

'What – *ever*?'

'For the foreseeable future. Of course I'm not taking any notice. I'm seeing Russell tonight.'

'Really! Wow, he must be keen.'

'So are you just going to walk out or what?'

'Well, Dad's not going to be at home so it's simple.'

'What about Anna?'

'Oh she's no problem,' I say lightly – hoping it's true.

'You're so lucky, Ellie. My mum's my *big* problem,' says Nadine.

'So you're really stuck on Russell?' says Magda.

We're sitting down in the canteen by this time, eating school pizza. Magda's licking up her melted cheese strands. Her little pink cat tongue is very pointed. Her tone is a little pointed too.

'Well . . .' I shrug. I wish I knew what Magda and Nadine think of him. I don't want to act like I'm going overboard if they think he's a total upper-class anorak. On the other hand, if they're dead impressed and envious then I want to act like I'm really enthusiastic, that *he's* ultra keen. And he is – isn't he?

What about me? I wish I knew! Sitting here eating pizza in my gungy school uniform I feel almost like I made him up. I'm glad I've got Nadine and Magda as witnesses to the fact that he actually exists.

I can't quite conjure his face up now. I know longish hair. I know brown eyes, but that's about it. I'm not even a hundred per cent sure of his voice. Is he really posh or just sort of ordinary? There's one thing I do remember vividly. The feeling of his mouth on mine.

'Ellie! You're blushing.'

'I'm not,' I protest foolishly, though my face is red hot.

'Are you *sure* you didn't do anything else but kiss?' says Nadine.

'Sure!'

'What's he like at kissing?' asks Magda.

'Good!'

'Mmm – that sounds heartfelt. Better than Dan?'

'I'm sure *Eggs* is a better kisser than Dan.'

Dan was never a real boyfriend anyway whereas Russell . . . Can I call him a boyfriend yet? I know one thing, I simply have to see him tonight – and there's nothing Anna can do about it.

It's hard all the same. Anna has a lovely little snack of fruit bread and soft cheese and plums waiting for me when I get back from school. We have a little munch together while she tells me all about Eggs's new little girlfriend in Year Three – an older woman! Eggs gollops down half a bag of plums and smiles smugly whenever Mandy's name is mentioned.

'It was a bit bold of you to chat her up, seeing as she is in the juniors,' I say.

'*She* was the one who chatted *me* up,' says Eggs, biting into another plum. 'She thinks I'm sweet. She wants me to play with her every day.'

'She won't think you're sweet tomorrow when you're stuck in the boys' bogs with terrible diarrhoea after eating all those plums,' I say.

'It's Saturday tomorrow, so I won't *be* at school, ha ha ha,' says Eggs and he puts an entire whole plum in his mouth.

'Eggs! Don't be so greedy and disgusting. Oh God, you'll choke,' says Anna, leaping up and bashing him on the back.

The plum flies out of Eggs's mouth and lands with a messy *phut* on the kitchen floor.

'My plum!' Eggs protests, about to pick it up.

'It's all grimy now,' says Anna, whisking it away quickly.

'So is Eggs,' I say. 'Look at him, he's *filthy*.'

'He had finger-painting today,' says Anna. 'Only in Eggs's case it was more like entire-body-painting. Shall we give you a bath, little chap?'

'Oh, I want a bath,' I say quickly.

Anna looks at me. I usually have my bath late at night. I only have a bath early if I'm going out. She hesitates. We haven't even referred to the tempestuous events of last night and this morning. I can see her struggling, not wanting to spoil our friendly time unless it's absolutely necessary.

I whizz out of the kitchen before she makes up her mind – up to the bathroom, where I wash hurriedly, glad that the hot bath has steamed up the mirror. After my stupid anorexic bulemic blip I'm trying hard to accept my body the way it is – but the way it is is P–L–U–M–P. When you're about to go out on your first serious date you'd *so* much rather look skinny! I pull on my best trousers and a lacy top, decide they look way too tight (why did I have three slices of fruit bread?), put on my baggy trousers and a shirt, decide I look too casual, put on a dress, which looks much too *dressy*, stand in my knickers and search my entire wardrobe, and *eventually* shove my best trousers and lacy top back on.

Time is tick-tocking faster and faster. I do my make up, doing a serious cover up job of every weeny snippet of a spot. I outline my eyes to make them look big and beguiling and put mascara on my lashes so I can flutter them provocatively. I leave the lipstick out altogether as I don't want to smear it all over Russell. Then it's hair raking time. I flex my muscles, brandish my fiercest hairbrush, and do my best to tame it – though it's curlier than ever from getting damp in the bath. I still hate the way I look when I've finished, but I looked *worse* yesterday and yet I was the one Russell sketched. Not Magda, not Nadine. Me.

That's still so amazing I can hardly take it in.

'Me me me me me!' I sing, sounding like an opera singer warming up.

Then I go downstairs, steeling myself. I *could* just charge up the hall and out the front door without saying anything. Maybe it would be easier all round?

'Ellie?' Anna calls. She comes to the kitchen door. 'You're going out!'

'Bye Anna,' I say, trying to act perfectly normally.

'Ellie! Your dad says you're not allowed out.'

'I know, but he's not here.'

'Oh for God's sake, don't do this to me! Ellie, you *can't* go out, not after last night.'

'You know Dad overreacted.'

'Maybe he did a bit, OK – but if you go out now he's never going to back down over this.'

'He won't know. I'll be home long before him.'

'I should tell him.'

'But you won't, will you?'

'*I* don't know. Look, Ellie, can't you invite this Russell round here? That way you could still see him and not defy your dad.'

'I don't know his phone number. I don't even know his second name. That's why I have to go and meet him, Anna. If I don't he'll just think I've stood him up and then I'll never see him again.'

'And you really like him?'

'Yes! Oh Anna, please. I've got to go and see him.'

426

'I *can't* just let you go off with him. What if anything happened?'

'What could happen? Look, we're meeting at Flowerfields. I expect we'll go to McDonald's. Or maybe for a pizza, I don't know. I'll explain that I have to get back early – really early. By nine. Well, nine thirty say. Please, Anna. Please let me go. I *promise* I'll get back by nine thirty. I won't let you down. Please trust me. *Please.*'

'Oh go on then, you bad girl,' says Anna and she even gives me another fiver.

I throw my arms round her and give her a big kiss. 'You're a darling,' I say, and I rush off.

I'm so thrilled she's let me go that I bounce up the road. It isn't until I'm on the bus into town that I start to get nervous. I wonder what I'm going to say when I see Russell. 'Hi Russell,' I mutter to myself, grinning and giving little waves. Oh God, someone's staring at me. They'll be wondering about the mad girl sitting muttering and waving to herself. I am starting to get very hot inside my lacy top. It's quite cheap lace so it's itchy. I'm scratching myself with both hands. Now everyone will think I've got *fleas*.

I must keep still when I meet Russell. No more grins, mutters, waves and definitely no more scratching – otherwise he'll sketch me as a monkey.

The bus is taking for ever. I'm scared I'm going to be late, and he'll think I'm not coming. Oh Russell, of *course* I'm coming. I've braved my dad, I've bullied poor Anna – I've chanced everything to see you.

I leap off the bus as soon as it gets into town. I run wildly all the way to Flowerfields Shopping Centre. I pull up, panting, with one minute to spare. I'm *first*.

And last. This is why.
I wait.
Russell is late.
I wait and wait and wait.
Russell is very very very late.
I wait until eight.
And then I trail home, trying not to cry.

# Chapter Four

## Doom and Gloom Time

## Chapter Four

'Oh Ellie, thank goodness. You are a good girl! But you didn't have to come back this early,' says Anna.

Then she sees my face.

'Ellie? Oh dear. What happened? Wasn't he so nice this time? Did he do anything to upset you?'

'He didn't do anything. He didn't turn up!' I wail, and then all the tears inside me gush like the waters in *Titanic*.

Eggs is in bed, thank God, and Dad is out of course. So it's just Anna and me. She puts her arms round me and I howl on her shoulder. She's wearing a new pale blue sweater her friend Sara gave her and I'm wearing a lot of mascara.

'Oh God, Anna, I've got black splodges all over your sweater. I'm so sorry,' I burble.

'Never mind. I don't actually like this sweater anyway – simply because Sara shows off so much about designing her own-label clothes. She thinks I'm dotty about her stuff but I only bought it to be polite.'

'I'll have it off you if you don't like it.'

'I wonder why you want to wear everyone *else's* sweaters,' says Anna, mopping at my face with a tissue.

'I draw the line at Dad's,' I say. 'Oh Anna, don't tell him Russell didn't turn up, will you?'

'Of course not. I'm not even telling him you went out! I'm so sorry, Ellie – but I'm so relieved you're OK. I *shouldn't* have let you go out. Not because of your dad. It's really not safe for a girl your age to go out by herself.'

'Yes it is. All too safe. No-one wants to have their wicked way with me. Certainly not Russell. Oh Anna, it was so awful waiting there. All these girls were hanging around and they kept looking at me and giggling. It was totally obvious they knew I'd been stood up.'

'You're sure it was tonight you were supposed to be meeting?'

'Yes, the time, the place, everything. He obviously didn't mean it. Dad was *right*. He wasn't the slightest bit interested in me. He just wanted to try it on.'

'Did he?' Anna asked, alarmed.

'No. We just kissed.'

I think about Russell's kisses – and how special they were to me and yet he obviously doesn't want to kiss me ever again. I cover my face and sob.

'Poor old Ellie. Don't take it to heart. I've been stood up before. So has everyone. Don't get so upset. Look, why not phone Nadine or Magda? Have a good moan to them.'

But for just about the first time in my life I can't face talking to my two best friends. I know they'd be sweet to me, but it would be just so humiliating, especially after showing off about Russell so at school and writing that stupid poem . . .

I can understand why Nadine would barely talk to me when she was so cut up about Liam. He was a hateful pig who just wanted to have sex with her – but at least he went out with her lots of times and made her think she was really special. Russell couldn't be bothered to go out with me *once*.

I go upstairs to bed very early, wanting to be well out of the way before Dad comes home. In my bedroom, I take out my sketchbook. I look at the portrait of Russell. Then I take my fattest blackest crayon and scribble all over it, again and again until it's just a black crumpled mess. Then I pull it out of the book and tear it into tiny little shreds and empty them out of my window. They flutter into the night air like black confetti.

Right, I've torn him up. Now I shall forget all about him. He's not worth another thought.

I know this. But I do think about him. Half the night. I have a lie-in until really late in the morning, huddling right down under the covers so I can't see the daylight. I dimly hear the telephone ringing. Then Anna's light footsteps.

'Phone for you, Ellie.'

For one lunatic second I wonder if it could possibly be Russell ringing to apologize – and then I remember he doesn't know my number, he doesn't even know my full name.

It's Magda.

'Were you still in *bed*? So you had a seriously late night with the divine Russell, right?'

'Wrong,' I mumble.

'What? Oh, is your dad around?' says Magda.

Dad's actually out at the swimming baths with Eggs. Thank goodness.

I mumble something even less intelligible to Magda.

'I can't *hear* you! Look, just answer yes or no if your dad's ear-wigging. Did you have a good time with Russell?'

'No.'

'Oh, so you had a *bad* time with Russell?'

'No.'

'Well, make up your mind!'

'Look, I can't talk about it, Mags.'

'Well, meet me this afternoon, OK? And Nadine?'

'I'm not allowed *out*. Dad won't let me,' I say, and I put the phone down.

'Your dad *will* let you go out with Magda and Nadine,' says Anna.

'I don't feel like it anyway,' I say, and I droop back up the stairs.

'Are you going to have a bath?' Anna asks.

I don't feel like having a bath. I don't feel like getting dressed. I don't feel like having breakfast. I don't feel like having any communication with the outside world ever again. I don't even want to talk to Anna any more.

I go back to my rumpled bed and huddle up, my knees under my chin. I wish I still had my old blue special elephant. I wish I was a really little girl again. I wish I still thought boys were stupid mucky

433

creatures who picked their noses and ate it and yanked the arms off Barbie dolls. I wish Eggs didn't exist and Dad hadn't met Anna. I wish my mum was still alive.

My throat aches and my eyes burn and I start crying because I suddenly miss Mum so much even though she died long ago. I cry under the covers for ages. When I eventually crawl out at lunchtime my eyes are sore and swollen. I come downstairs to have bacon sandwiches. Anna has obviously said something to Dad and Eggs. They both stare at me but after one fierce glance from Anna they start nattering on about swimming. Eggs demonstrates his version of freestyle so wildly that his sandwich crusts go flying and he nearly pokes me in the eye. Dad tells him to calm down. Eggs gets wilder. Dad gets cross. Anna intervenes. I let it all wash over me. As if I care about any of this stuff. As if I care about anything any more. It's not like I'll ever have a family of my own. It's obvious no boy is ever going to want to go out with me, let alone form a proper partnership. My first boyfriend Dan was a total nerd. Anorak Boy with a capital A, and yet even he fell out of love with me. And Russell couldn't even be bothered to turn up on our very first date. I am going to lead a totally solitary unloved uncherished life.

A tear drips down my cheek.

'Oh Ellie,' says Dad. 'I can't bear to see you so miserable. Look, I'm *sorry* I wouldn't let you meet up with this boy yesterday.'

I glance at Anna. She raises her eyebrows a fraction. I decide it's safer to say nothing.

'Ellie's crying,' says Eggs, unnecessarily.

'Just finish your sandwich, Eggs, and leave Ellie alone,' says Anna.

'I feel like I've overplayed the heavy father role,' says Dad. 'You do understand, Ellie, it was just because I care about you.'

No-one else cares about me. No need to worry about Russell going too far with me, Dad. Russell doesn't want to get anywhere *near* me.

I don't say any of this. I simply sniff.

'Anna says you told Magda I wouldn't let you meet up with her this afternoon. Ellie, I'm not that mean. You can go out with your girlfriends, for goodness' sake.'

I just shrug and shrink back into my bedroom.

But Magda and Nadine don't give up on me that easily. There's a knock at the door ten minutes later. Magda. And Nadine. Dad answers the door and walks right into it.

'Oh, Mr Allard! Look, we've come round to plead with you,' I hear Magda say.

'We know you're cross with Ellie. I'm sorry I didn't tell you what was going on straight away. It's partly my fault,' says Nadine.

They badger and flirt and flutter. Dad is clearly enjoying the situation and lets them carry on for ages. Then he pretends to weaken.

'Well, girls, I'd hate to spoil your afternoon. OK, you've persuaded me. Ellie can go out with you.'

They squeal gratefully then come bounding upstairs. Magda clatter-clatters in her platforms, Nadine bounce-bounces in her trainers. They barge into my bedroom like two knights in armour rescuing a princess. I feel more like the loathsome monster.

They show off about their supposed victory and I try to act grateful.

'Though actually I don't really feel like going out,' I protest weakly.

I pretend it's because I've got a bad period. They are as suspicious as Mrs Henderson. They are both peering at my sore eyes and blotchy face.

'Come *on*, Ellie,' says Magda. 'Tell us about Russell. Oh God, didn't he turn up?'

'You've got it,' I say, and I start sniffing again.

'Oh Ellie, what a creepy mean rotten thing to do. How long did you wait for him?' says Nadine.

'An *hour*!' I wail.

I tell them all about it. Magda puts her arm round my neck and Nadine puts her arm round my waist and they both pat me sympathetically. Nadine says she thought his eyes were too close together and he had this really seriously shifty look which should have been a warning. But then she's not one to talk, looking at her and Liam. Magda says he seemed awfully juvenile for his age anyway, just wanting to show off about himself, but she's no-one to talk either, she went out with Greg who had all the sophistication of Dennis the Menace.

I start to feel a bit better. Nadine goes to the bath-room, comes back with my flannel and bathes my eyes. Magda whips out her own make-up bag and powders them deep grey and outlines them in black and I now have new eyes and old friends and I feel a *lot* better.

'Coming out now?' says Magda.

Nadine gets my jacket, and off we go, the three of us. I start to wonder why on earth I was so upset over

Russell. Boyfriends are OK, but they aren't a patch on girlfriends who've stuck by you and care about you for ever.

We go down the town to Flowerfields and I actually manage to be funny about a sad little ghost of Ellie still standing waiting there. We wander round the clothes shops for a while, trying on different stuff and hooting with laughter.

'There! I knew you'd cheer up if we took you out,' says Magda. 'Forget Russell, forget all boys. They're not worth it.'

At that precise moment her eyes are following three boys in tight jeans fooling around outside the HMV shop. They disappear inside.

'I'm wondering about buying that new Best Ever Love Songs compilation album,' says Magda. 'Can I go and have another listen?'

Nadine catches my eye and we have a giggle.

We saunter into HMV and Magda eyes up the boys while Nadine and I have another flip through our current favourites, playing the If-I-had-a-hundred-quid-to-spend game. The Claudie Coleman album is high on both our lists.

'Hey, look!' says Nadine, pointing to a Claudie Coleman poster above the counter. 'She's singing at the Albert Hall next month.'

'Oh wow, let's go!' says Magda, actually distracted from the boys. 'I'd love to see her in person, wouldn't you?'

'Well, the tickets would be seriously pricey,' I say cautiously, wishing I wasn't always so strapped over cash. 'But maybe Anna would help me out.'

'Look, I'll help you out if needs be – and you too,

Nadine,' says Magda. 'But us three girls have simply *got* to go and see Claudie, right?' She's scribbling down the phone number for the ticket office. 'I'll get my dad to book them on his credit card the minute I get home, OK?'

We take it in turns singing along with Claudie at the listening station. There's one particular tune that I can't get enough of. Claudie's singing very close up, soft and breathy, like she's whispering in your ear.

*'Don't even think about him*
*He's not worth it, worth it, worth it.*
*Who needs a man to feel a woman?*
*You're doing fine without him, girl.'*

I replay it till I know it off by heart and we sing it as we go all around Flowerfields. I sing it as a duet on the bus with Nadine. She's bought the album, lucky thing, but she's promised to do a tape for me. Then I hum a solo version as I walk back from her house.

Who needs Russell? Who cares about Russell? *Don't even think about him.*

'Ellie, guess who came calling round here this afternoon?'

I stand staring and wait.

'Guess,' says Dad.

'*I* don't know,' I say, shrugging.

'A certain young man.'

I miss a beat.

'*Which* young man?'

'With floppy hair. Rather full of himself. Sketchbook tucked slightly pretentiously under his arm.'

'Russell!'

'The very one.'

'But how did he know where I *live*?'

'Ah. That was my question too. And he had a rather impressive answer. He knew vaguely the area, so he'd worked his way up and down several roads describing a certain young lady called Ellie – and eventually someone somewhere recognized the description and suggested he call at our house.'

'Oh my God! Are you *serious*, Dad? Russell really did come round?'

'He did indeed. He was very worried about last night. Russell's dad kicked up merry hell because the lad was late back on Thursday night. Apparently he hadn't deigned to tell his dad he was going walkabout after school and when he sauntered home at midnight he was so angry with him he wouldn't let him out at all yesterday, even though young Russell begged and pleaded and moaned and groaned. So he couldn't meet you at your special trysting place – which is just as well because you were similarly shut up by your equally outraged parent. Yes?'

'Yes, yes, right! So what else did Russell say?'

'Not a lot. He seemed a little dismayed by my reaction. I was extremely angry with the young man. He had no right to purloin you and whisk you off to the park.'

'You didn't really get cross with him, did you, Dad? I can't *believe* this. He didn't stand me up? He really couldn't help it? And he went all over the place trying to track me down this afternoon just to explain?'

'*Just* to explain?' says Dad. 'He needed to explain until he was blue in the face. Positively ultramarine.'

'Oh, Dad, you weren't really heavy with him, were you?'

'You bet I was. That young man won't dare so much as blink in your direction without my say-so. And I say *no*.'

I stare at Dad, desperate to suss whether he's serious or not. I think he's teasing me, but I can't be sure. I just wish Anna was here and she could sort him out for me. Why did Russell have to come round when I was *out*, for heaven's sake! But imagine – going from house to house asking for me. That sounds like he's really serious about seeing me!

'So what exactly did he say, Dad?'

'I told you, I did nearly all the talking.'

'And how was it left?'

Dad shrugs. 'I think he sees the error of his ways.'

'*Dad*. I wish you wouldn't be so annoying. I mean, did Russell say anything about . . . seeing me again?'

Dad shakes his head. 'Certainly not, seeing as I'd expressly forbidden it.'

'You didn't! Really, truly, you said I couldn't go out with him?' I'm still pretty sure he's winding me up but I can hear my voice getting shrill all the same.

'Really, truly . . . possibly!' Dad says.

'Did he suggest seeing me or not?'

'You always insist you're a liberated young woman. Maybe *you* should make the running. If I were to allow you out again, which I doubt.'

'So how can I make the running, Dad? Did Russell tell you his address?'

'Nope.'

'He really didn't?'

Dad shakes his head but he's still got that irritating grin on his face.

'So how can I get in touch with him? Do I have to go on an equivalent quest all around Pembridge Park?'

'You could,' says Dad. 'Or he could have jotted it down in this letter.' He brings out an envelope from his pocket and waves it in the air at me.

I snatch it and tear it open. My eyes skitter down the page. 'See you – I *HOPE*! Russell.' And a little picture.

My heart is thudding.

'Well?' says Dad.

Aha! It's his turn to be curious.

'Yes, he's very well,' I say, smiling.

'And you are now, too, I take it?' says Dad.

'Yep.' I dance off to the kitchen and make myself a cup of coffee, reading Russell's letter while the kettle boils. Then I read his letter again while I drink my coffee. And again and again.

*Dear Ellie,*

*I'm so so so so extra sorry. I felt so bad about not being able to make it on Friday night. And kind of humiliated too, because my dad went completely off his head and wouldn't let me out simply because he got fussed last night.*

*I can't believe his attitude – and it's bloody hypocritical too, going on about what I'm getting up to when he's smooching all over our house with his girlfriend. But anyway, he can't keep me locked up permanently. Will you meet me after school on Monday – at McDonald's? I'll be there as soon as I can make it – around twenty to four. I'll wait for you and hope very*

441

*much that you'll come. I'll be the one looking stupid
and saying sorry over and over again.*
   *See you – I HOPE! Russell.*


He's done a small sketch of himself – floppy hair,
earnest expression, pencil in one hand, sketchbook in
the other. There are little initial letters on the sketch-
book, so tiny I have to hold them up to my eyes and
squint. R L E. Rule? Role? No, Russell. R for
Russell, E for Ellie? L? L? L? L? L? L? L? L? L?
   *Russell Loves Ellie.*
   I feel as if I'm on a giant switchback, swooping up
and over, up and over, up and over.
   'Aren't you making your old dad a cup of coffee
too?' says Dad, coming into the kitchen.
   'Sure.' I shove the letter quickly into my pocket.
   'Nice letter?'
   'Hmm.'
   'He wants to see you again?'
   'Sort of, yeah.'
   'So what are you going to do? Your dad expressly
forbids it.'
   'What?' I stare at Dad. 'Are you serious?'
   Dad is trying to frown but his eyes are twinkling.
'Sort of,' he says. 'Look, Ellie, I got seriously panicky
about Thursday night. It's the first time you've ever
been out after dark like that and I couldn't stand it.'
   'I bet you went out with girls when you were
my age.'
   'Maybe that's why I panicked. I remember all too
clearly what I was like when I was Russell's age. It
makes me cringe now. I didn't treat girls like people.
I was trapped in this awful stuffy boys' school so I

never knew girls properly. They were just amazing exotic creatures and we were struck dumb in their company and it was like this sick competition seeing how far you could go with them—'

'Dad!'

'I know, I know. And then we'd boast about it afterwards to our mates – exaggerating obviously, saying all this degrading stuff.'

'Look, Dad, that was way back when boys were like Neanderthals. Russell isn't a bit like that,' I insist, though I feel myself getting pink in the face, remembering the way we kissed.

'I know, I know,' says Dad. 'As soon as I met him I could see he's just a nice decent kid who wants to be friends with my daughter. He told me you had this long intense conversation about art. He showed me his sketch of you, by the way, and it's *good*. His style needs a bit of fine-tuning but for his age he's got a great sense of line. Anyway, I felt like a total prat. I believed he was a sex-crazed loony slobbering all over you when all the time you were having this totally platonic artistic discussion.'

'Yeah, that's just the way it was, Dad, I told you,' I say, still pink in the face. 'So, as you realize times have changed, is it OK if I go out with Russell? To do some sketching together!'

'That's the thing, Ellie. Times *have* changed. When I was young I stayed out till really late as a teenager and no-one turned a hair. Even when Anna was young she went out to local discos and youth clubs when she was thirteen or fourteen. But now there aren't any harmless little discos, it's all wild raves. And you know I don't want you going anywhere near

Seventh Heaven again after they did that drug raid there.'

'OK, OK, I promise we won't *go* to Seventh Heaven.'

'I don't feel happy about you and Russell going anywhere, Ellie, not after dark. The town is attracting a whole load of yobs who just want to roam around picking fights and getting into trouble. I'm not surprised Russell's dad was really worried about him being out late.'

'Russell can look after himself, Dad. He's not some sad little wimp.'

'He could be Mr Muscles Macho Man. It wouldn't make any difference if a whole gang started in on him.'

'You're getting totally *paranoid*, Dad.'

'Maybe. I don't know. But how about if you and Russell met up after school and then he went back home around nine?'

'Dad! We're not *Eggs's* age!'

'I know, I know – but you're as precious to me as Eggs and I don't need another night like Thursday. Look, you're still supposed to be in the doghouse for that. I'll let you see Russell, but I'm going to stick to this nine o'clock curfew for the time being. I think that's more than fair.'

'I don't!'

'Well it gets dark by nine – so you couldn't do any sketching then, could you?' says Dad, smiling.

I smile back weakly. I don't know who's bluffing who. But at least I can see Russell – even if it's only in daylight!

I go up to my bedroom and read his letter again.

Several times more. Then I go downstairs and ring Nadine and tell her that it's all OK and that Russell walked round and round the town looking for me, practically knocking at every house door.

Nadine isn't quite as impressed as I'd hoped. She's got her Claudie album playing full blast (her family are obviously out) and she's singing along instead of concentrating fully. I need to ask her something.

'Nadine, do you really think Russell looks seriously shifty?'

Nadine herself sounds as if she's doing some serious shifting the other end of the phone. 'No, no, Ellie, not at all. I was just, you know, saying stuff to comfort you. I don't think his eyes are too close together either. I think it was just his intense expression when he was sketching you.'

I let it go at that. I ring Magda next. She's got some great news for me first – her dad has booked three tickets for us to go and hear Claudie next month! 'There, aren't you pleased, Ellie? Claudie will cheer you up. He's not worth it, worth it, worth it, right?'

'Well, maybe he *is* worth it after all, Magda.'

I fill her in on all the details, massaging the facts even more impressively, so that I have Russell practically trekking round the entire country looking for me.

I wait for Magda's comments. There's a little silence on the end of the phone.

'So it shows he didn't just stand me up,' I say.

'Sorry, Ellie, I'm not quite clear. You mean he stood you up because his dad wouldn't let him go out?'

'He didn't stand me up, he wanted to come.'

'But Daddy wouldn't let him.'

I don't like that Daddy bit. I pause. 'I take it you still think Russell is awfully juvenile, just wanting to show off about himself?'

I can hear Magda swallowing.

'No, no, well, not Russell in particular. Just most boys in Year Eleven. I mean, they're better than the pathetic creeps in Year Ten, not to mention Year Nine, but they're still not exactly . . . mature.'

'So you think that Russell is *im*mature?'

'Oh Ellie, stop being so prickly. I think all boys are immature, full stop. But your Russell is great . . . for a boy.'

I agree happily, and tell her to thank her dad for ordering the tickets. Some time I am going to have to tackle *my* dad about coughing up the cash, but maybe it might be better to wait till tomorrow seeing as we have already spent so long negotiating today.

I decide to put myself in a good light by making him another coffee, even though it's nearly teatime. I wonder where Anna and Eggs have got to. I have to make sure I get Anna on her own to get her to promise to keep quiet about my sneaking out to meet Russell on Friday night. If Dad knows I deliberately disobeyed him then maybe he'll stop me seeing Russell altogether. And I *have* to see him!

I think about him going round all those houses asking for me. It's like a fairytale. He's the handsome prince on the loopy quest: knock three times on every house in this street and the next and *then* you will find the princess and get to kiss her . . .

I go into a happy little daze in my bedroom and

don't resurface until I hear the front door.

'Is that you, Anna?' I shout.

'No it's just me,' Dad calls. 'I was looking down the road to see if there was any sign of them. I don't know where they've got to.'

'Where were they going? Shopping?' I peer over the banisters at him.

'Ellie! As if Anna would go shopping with Eggs. You know what a pain he can be. No, Nadine's mum phoned her up.' Dad pulls a face.

I giggle. Nadine's mum is one of those women who seem to spring from their bed fully made-up, hair lacquered into a helmet, armed with a J-Cloth and a Dust Buster.

'Don't you dare laugh! She's still very much looking down her pointy nose at me because you were out so late on Thursday, and she doesn't want you to be a bad influence on her Nadine.'

'Oh God, she wasn't going on about it *again*, was she?'

'For a while, yes. But she was also telling Anna about this local photo shoot she's dragging that showy little sister of Nadine's to this afternoon – and she wondered if Anna wanted to take Eggs.'

'What? *Eggs!*'

'I know, I know, I can't really see the little guy prancing around in front of a photographer myself, but apparently this particular company wanted to find a little boys who *look* like little boys – that is, filthy dirty and fooling about. It's for this washing powder where a little girl is all dressed up in a pristine party frock—'

'Natasha!'

447

'And all these little boys come along and get her to play football with them and then push her over and get her all muddy.'

'Ah, Eggs might be good at that!'

'That's what Anna thought. He seemed to relish the idea too. And you get paid! So that's where they went. Only they've been gone hours and hours.'

'Eggs probably got too enthusiastic and completely coated Natasha in mud. They might have to hose her down and dry her off and pretty her up again for each take – that would take ages.'

'And meanwhile we've got rumbly tummies. I suppose I ought to mosey out into the kitchen and get something started for supper.'

Dad sounds totally lacking in enthusiasm. He understands the concept of the New Man but has all the laziness and lack of inclination of a very *old* man.

'I'll rustle something up, Dad,' I say cheerily, determined to keep in his good books so that he might just extend this ludicrous nine o'clock curfew.

I rustle – and hustle and bustle – and we sit down to burnt omelettes and soggy chips.

'This is delicious,' Dad says determinedly. 'But the thing is, Ellie, I'm starting to get really worried about Anna and Eggs, so I've sort of lost my appetite.'

It's only partly an excuse. He does look a bit tense and twitchy.

'They'll be all right, Dad. This shoot thing will have just gone on for ages. Look, I'll phone Nadine again and ask her how long these things take.'

I phone Nadine, but this time Nadine's mum answers. She doesn't sound too thrilled when she hears my voice.

448

'Oh, it's *you*, Ellie. I hope you've done your best to show you're sorry for your behaviour last Thursday night. Your poor parents were in a terrible state. And I wasn't at all happy about you involving my Nadine in your little deception.'

She rants on in similar vein for ages. I hold the receiver away from my ear, sighing. Eventually there seems to be a little pause.

'I'm really sorry, but anyway, I just wanted to ask—'

'No you can't talk to Nadine just now, she's having her supper. You girls! You're on the phone every two minutes and yet you see each other every day. What? No, Nadine — go back to the table! What's that, Natasha, pet?'

'Have you and Natasha just got back from the photo shoot?' I gabble quickly.

'No! No, we've been back since five o'clock. It was a reasonably quick shoot — *no* thanks to your little brother, who ran wild and wouldn't behave sensibly at all. So much so, they didn't even *use* him in the end.'

'So where are Eggs and Anna now?' I ask.

'*I* don't know.'

'But didn't they come back with you?'

'No. I offered them a lift in my car but Anna had got talking to some strange man and they went off with him.'

'Anna went off with a strange *man*?' I say.

Dad comes rushing to the phone. He grabs it from me and starts asking Nadine's mum all sorts of questions.

'I keep telling you, Mr Allard, I don't know who

this man is, or anything about him. I was busy looking after my Natasha. I don't know if he was another parent – although he didn't seem to have a child with him. He wasn't on the main photographic team because I've got to know everyone involved. I suppose he could have been representing the washing powder company – but he didn't look the type. He was wearing a black leather jacket. He seemed a bit rough, like a biker. I was a little surprised to see your wife going off with him.'

'So why didn't you try to stop her?' Dad shouts.

'Well, really! *I'm* not responsible for your wife's behaviour. Nor your daughter's behaviour either. I'd be grateful if you'd stop phoning me up and acting as if it's my fault if one or the other goes missing.'

She puts the phone down on us. Dad and I stare at each other.

'Don't look so worried, Dad. Don't take any notice of her, you know what she's like.'

'But she's not a liar. She said she saw Anna go off with this strange man. Eggs too. Dear God, Ellie, what's happened to them?'

'Maybe Nadine's mum made a mistake,' I say, though Nadine's mum is like one of those meerkats, all beady-eyed and extended neck, seeing absolutely everything. She isn't the sort of woman who ever makes mistakes. But then Anna isn't the sort of woman to disappear with a strange biker either.

'Anna wouldn't ever go off with a weirdo stranger – especially not with Eggs,' I say.

'I know,' Dad says wretchedly. 'That's what makes it worse. Oh Ellie, maybe she knows this man.'

'What?'

'Maybe – maybe he's a friend of hers. More than a friend.'

'Oh, *Dad*.'

'Well, I suppose I'm not the easiest man in the world to live with. And – and sometimes I enjoy a little harmless flirt with some of the students. It's nothing serious, I swear, but perhaps it preys on Anna's mind. Then on Thursday night you turned on me and practically accused me of having a girlfriend on the side.'

'Dad, I was just trying to *get* to you.'

'I know, and it worked too. And I *haven't* got a girl-friend. I maybe mightn't have always been squeaky clean in the past but I hope I've grown up a bit now. I know I've got a really wonderful wife—'

'You've had two,' I say, suddenly fierce.

'Yes, I'm sorry, Ellie. No-one can ever replace your mum. We know that. It's been hard for Anna. I don't really treasure her enough. I forget how young she is. She used to be so different when I first met her—'

'Dad, don't.'

'You don't think this guy in the leathers is some boyfriend of hers? Someone she met at her Italian class, maybe?'

'Of course not,' I say firmly, but Dad's in such a state he's almost got me wondering. There's a part of me that knows perfectly well that this is totally crazy and my own kind, sensible stepmother isn't going to hit the road on a Harley with a secret lover – certainly not with Eggs along too – but then it seems so unlike Anna to be so late and not even phone.

451

Maybe this strange man was just giving her a lift – but then they had an accident. A crash.

I let myself think just for a second what it would be like if Anna never ever came back. And it's so weird. For years I didn't like her. I felt she *was* taking my mum's place and I just wanted her to get out so it could be Dad and me, even though we were half a family without Mum. But now – Anna's part of this new family. She can be an old ratbag sometimes when she has a nag about homework or the state of my bedroom, but most of the time she's like a special big sister to me.

And what about my real little brother. Heavens, would I actually miss *Eggs*???

'Oh, Dad, they've got to be all right,' I say, and he puts his arms round me and holds me tight.

'Of course they are, take no notice of that stupid stuff I said. I'm just ranting rubbish. Of course they're all right. There's obviously some perfectly ordinary explanation. They'll be here any minute now, you wait and see.'

And then suddenly there's a key in the door and Eggs calling and they *are* here and the waiting is over.

'Hi! Did you wonder what had happened to us?' Anna says cheerily, while Dad swoops Eggs up in his arms and gives him a huge bear-hug.

I feel so relieved that they're safe, so ridiculous for getting worried, so angry that Anna's got me all churned up like this.

'Where have you been? You could have *phoned*!' I say furiously.

Anna stares – then she bursts out laughing.

'What's so funny?' I growl.

'Talk about role reversal! You sound just like a mum,' Anna laughs. She looks at Dad, expecting him to join in the laughter.

'We were really worried, Anna,' says Dad, releasing Eggs and putting him down on the carpet. 'Why didn't you phone? What were you playing at?'

'I'm sorry. I didn't realize you'd be so worried,' says Anna, going into the kitchen. 'Have you two had your tea? Oh dear, who burnt the frying-pan? Hey ho. Eggs, what would you like? Boiled eggs or scrambled?'

'Scrambled me please,' says Eggs, shrieking with laughter, as if this is the most original joke in the entire world, though he's told it every time he's eaten an egg for the past couple of years.

He seems even more full of himself than usual, puffing out his chest and beating it like a little gorilla.

'I'm going to be famous, Ellie,' he says.

'I thought you were pretty useless at the photo shoot, not doing what you were told and being silly to Natasha. They didn't even use you,' I snub him.

'How did you know?' says Anna, startled.

'Because I phoned Nadine's mum,' I explain.

'Oh dear! Yes, she wasn't best pleased with us. She felt we were mucking up Natasha's big moment. I must admit, though, when I saw that child prancing and pouting in front of the cameras I was awfully glad I had an ordinary mischievous little kid like Eggs,' says Anna, whisking eggs. 'Anyone else want any eggs? Apart from Humpty Dumpty here.'

'Do an eggy Humpty jumper, Mum!' says Eggs.

'Hey, yes, that would look *great*. Maybe Humpty

could be sitting on the wall on the front and falling off and in pieces on the back,' Anna says, giving Eggs a kiss on the nose.

'And it's my woolly jumper, isn't it, Mum? They're all my jumpers and Ellie can't ever ever borrow them, can she?'

'As if I'd want to!' I say witheringly.

'Well, I know you've always thought my funny jumpers are awful, Ellie – but they might just prove popular,' says Anna, stirring eggs. She catches sight of Dad, who is still staring at her. 'What?'

'What the hell do you mean, "What?"' Dad explodes. 'I just can't believe this. You disappear with our son for almost the whole day. You're hours and hours late home, you were seen by that dreadful woman going off with this weirdo biker—'

'Biker?' says Anna, looking mystified.

'A man in a black leather biker jacket.'

'*Oh!*' says Anna, giggling.

'It's not funny!' Dad thunders. 'For God's sake tell me what you've been up to.'

'OK, OK. But a *biker*!' Anna splutters again. 'That was George, and the biker jacket is actually an Armani masterpiece that's only seen the inside of his new silver Audi.'

'So who the hell is George?' says Dad – and now he sounds *really* worried.

'George is the editor of a new family magazine. Not the tea-cosy and telly type, this is ultra hip and designer-orientated, right?'

Anna sounds like she's talking a new language. She almost looks like a new person. Her face is glowing, her eyes are big, her hair is a little ruffled in a chic sort of way, her whole stance is different, chin up, chest out, confident. It's as if this George is a fairy godfather and changed her into Cinderella at the ball.

Then she remembers the eggs, rescues them and serves Eggs his tea.

'So what about this George?' I say. 'Oh Anna, has he offered you a job on his magazine?'

'Yes! Well, on a freelance basis, so there's no problem about being here for Eggs,' says Anna, dipping toast into Eggs's eggs and nibbling.

'But you don't know the first thing about journalism,' says Dad.

'I know. He's offered me a job as a designer,' says Anna. She looks at me triumphantly. 'It's my jumpers, Ellie! He saw Eggs and asked me where I'd bought his sweater. I said I made it myself so he asked about a pattern and I explained that I sketch the picture out in crosses first and then I knit it up hoping for the best and he was really interested. Then after the shoot (and dear God it was Eggs who needed shooting, he was *so* naughty), George asked if we could go to the magazine offices to talk things over.'

'And you did? On a Saturday? Surely it would be all locked up?'

'Darling, George is the *editor*. He can go into his own office whenever he chooses,' Anna says.

'You were still a bit reckless agreeing so easily. He could have been spinning you a line,' says Dad.

Anna shakes her head at him. 'It's not like he invited me back to his *house*. It was a beautiful state-of-the-art office in Bloomsbury.'

'You went all the way to London with him?'

'Yes, I rode in his car and he had his own

PlayStation and he let *me* play with it and I got to the third level,' says Eggs, his mouth all yellow froth.

'Don't talk with your mouth full, Eggs. Do you want some yoghurt now? *Anyway*, George and I talked things through at length—'

'While *we* were sitting here at home wondering what the hell had happened to you. Why didn't you phone?' Dad demands.

'Because I didn't think it would look particularly professional if I said "Excuse me, I have to phone my husband to stop him worrying about me",' says Anna. She folds her arms and faces Dad. 'I'm sorry you and Ellie got worried but I feel I behaved perfectly responsibly. I don't see why you have to give me the third degree now. I thought you'd be thrilled for me. It's the chance I've been waiting for. I was so envious when Sara started designing her clothes. I felt I'd wasted all my art school training. You've no idea what it's been like never having a job.'

'I thought you were happy looking after me and Ellie and Eggs,' says Dad.

'I *am* happy – but I don't see why I can't have a career as well, especially now Eggs has begun school.'

'And now George really wants Anna-jumpers?' I say.

'He got me to sketch some of the ones I've made already. Of course some of the characters have their own trademark so we can't use them – but I roughed out some new animal ones for him, pigs and piglets in little stripy shirts, a funny cow milkman driving an orange milkcart, a granny sheep knitting a jumper, a chicken painting a Fabergé-type egg. He wants all those designs properly drawn out with the knitting instructions and the jumpers knitted up, of course. He says I can use a professional knitter or two if I don't have time myself, as it's obviously the designs that are important. Then we've talked about sweaters in football colours and a set of weather jumpers, a light silky cotton jersey with a sun, a thick double-knit sweater with a snowman, a rainbow-striped sweater with the sun on one side and raindrops on the other. It was weird, once I got started I couldn't stop, all these ideas came tumbling out – and you'll never guess, he's paying me five hundred pounds per design, can you imagine, and that's just for starters, there might be all sorts of spin-offs—'

Anna seems spinning herself, circling way above our heads. Dad is staring at her as if any minute now she'll whizz out of the window and up into the wide blue yonder.

# Chapter Five

I can't concentrate at school. I've got one word whirling round every little squiggle and twist of my brain. R–U–S–S–E–L–L. I wonder if he's thinking about me???

I think about him particularly hard in the last double lesson, ART. We've got this new young ultra hip Art teacher, Mr Windsor. I like him a lot and I love all the stuff he tells us about the history of art and women painters and the changing ways women have been portrayed. I normally hang on to his every word and try to impress him, but his voice today is like background buzz on a radio. I can't even get interested when he shows us some Blake watercolours and Picasso paintings of mythical creatures. Magda and Nadine like the Blake triple Hecate of three young women huddled together. Mr Windsor says she's a goddess of the Underworld, and then he flashes lots more Greek gods at us and amuses us with muses.

'Now, I want you all to draw yourselves as a mythical creature. Be as inventive as possible,' says Mr Windsor, handing out paper. 'You can use black ink and watercolour, like little Blakelets, or paint like Picasso.'

Magda and Nadine want to sellotape our papers together and do a joint Hecate.

'We can all draw her together,' says Magda.

'Ellie can do the bodies as she's the best at drawing and then we'll each do our own heads,' says Nadine. 'You sit in the middle, Ellie, right?'

I hesitate. I don't really want to join up with Magda and Nadine and do the Hecate. I rather fancy the muse theme.

'Ellie?' Magda's staring at me.

'Ellie?' Nadine's staring at me too.

They're both looking bewildered.

I feel mean. I don't want to hurt their feelings.

'Right, right, who's got some sellotape then?' I say quickly.

Luckily Mr Windsor isn't keen on mutual effort art either.

'No, you three. I know you're inseparable, but I'd sooner you each made a solo attempt,' he says.

I pretend to be disappointed like Nadine and Magda, and settle down to my muse. I get so caught up in it that I don't chatter to the others. I don't even look to see what they are doing. Mr Windsor comes and has a wander round just before the bell goes to see how our paintings are progressing.

'I like it, Nadine,' he says, laughing.

I stop and peer at Nadine's painting. She's drawn

herself as a mermaid, her long black hair discreetly veiling her bare top, her jade-green tail wittily tattooed with little navy sailors and anchors and ships.

'What do you think of mine, Mr Windsor?' Magda asks eagerly, looking up at him and batting her eyelashes. She flirts with any guy, great or small, old or young, gross or gorgeous, but she's always thought Mr Windsor *seriously* special.

He looks at her painting – and then looks at her like she's seriously special too. I crane my neck to see it properly. I know Nadine is nearly as good at art as me but Magda's only fair-to-middling. Her drawing isn't that good, I suppose – it's just the idea. She's drawn herself as a phoenix, with a fluffy head of feathers just like her own flame-red curls and she's flying right out of a fire.

'What a great idea, Magda,' says Mr Windsor. 'I'm truly impressed. You two didn't just copy an idea like most of the others. You invented your own. We'll have both of these up on the wall. Now, Ellie, let's see what you've been up to.'

He stands behind me and is quiet for rather longer than usual.

'How strange,' he says at last.

'Strange?' says Magda, coming over to have a look. 'Oh, Ellie, it's ever so good. I wish I could draw like that.'

'You look just like you – and the artist looks just like a certain boy we all know,' says Nadine, giving me a nudge.

'Don't you like Ellie's painting, Mr Windsor?' says Magda. 'I *wish* I could draw like her.'

'It's . . . interesting,' says Mr Windsor.

He looks closely at my picture of me posing self-consciously while Russell sketches me. It's very similar to the Picasso he showed us but his model was naked and I'm obviously not going to portray myself without a stitch on. Come to think of it, the artist was naked too, but I'm certainly not drawing Russell starkers. I suddenly wonder what he looks like bare and start blushing.

'Why did you draw yourself as a muse, Ellie?' Mr Windsor asks.

I wonder what he's getting at? Does he think I'm pathetic for imagining I could ever be a muse figure? Perhaps he thinks it deeply sad that a plump plain girl like me could ever inspire anyone to create worthwhile art?

'I know muses are meant to be kind of beautiful,' I mumble. 'It was just a bit of . . . artistic licence.'

'Muses can look any way you want them – but *you're* the artist. You should be the one clutching the paintbrush, not the model staring into space empty-handed.'

I think he's paying me a compliment. I suddenly slot back into my senses. I turn my paper over and for the ten minutes left of the lesson I do a quick sketch of Magda and Nadine and me as Hecate – me wearing my glasses and looking earnest, Magda with her head on one side in a flirty fashion and Nadine gazing dreamily into the distance. Magda and Nadine have a happy giggle and Mr Windsor grins.

'We'll put that one on the wall, OK?' he says, as the bell goes. 'Hometime! Off you go, girls.'

He doesn't need to tell me twice. I can't WAIT to see Russell. Nadine's eager to be off too but Magda's

463

hanging about, watching as Mr Windsor gathers up his stuff and fumbles for his car keys.

'Oh *sweet*! I like your Teletubby key-ring, Mr Windsor!' she says. 'Tinky-Winky! Whoops, where's your handbag?'

'You're a cheeky girl, Magda. It's a good job I'm such a laid-back, tolerant teacher,' says Mr Windsor, trying to shoo her out of the classroom.

'You're not like a *teacher* at all. Well, not like Mr Prescott and Mr Daleford and Mr Pargiter. I can't imagine them with Teletubby key-rings.'

'It's not exactly the coolest of icons,' says Mr Windsor.

'Are they your favourite telly programme then, Mr Windsor? Do you watch it again and again?' Magda asks.

'I'm telling you again and again – it's time to go home.'

'You're quoting that little Andy Pandy now. My nan used to watch him,' says Magda. 'And my mum loved the Clangers. Do you have little kids who like the Teletubbies then, Mr Windsor?'

'Little kids! I'm not even married. Now, buzz off the lot of you.'

Magda buzzes at last. She practically skips out of the art room and out into the playground.

'Did you hear that, you two! He's not married!'

'Magda! Are you crazy?'

'Magda, you can't go after *Mr Windsor*!'

'Why not? How old do you think he is? Only twenty-something. That's not really old, is it?'

'You *are* crazy!'

'Anyway, I've got to run,' I say quickly. 'I'm seeing

464

Russell at McDonald's and I can't bear to be late or he'll think *I've* stood *him* up.'

'Oh dear, I'm starting to feel a bit left out here,' says Nadine. 'First there's you blowing hot and cold over this Russell, Ellie, and now Magda suddenly gone totally bananas over Mr Windsor. I'm the only sane one left.'

'Cheek! Look at the way you were with Liam!' I say. Nadine flinches a little. I bite my lip, wishing I hadn't said it.

'Sorry, Nadine,' I say guiltily, giving her hand a squeeze.

'That creep Liam is history,' says Magda firmly.

But there at the school gate is Liam himself.

He's standing looking our way, ultra cool in his black clothes, his hair flopping sexily forward, his dark eyes gleaming.

Nadine is always pale but now she goes so white I'm scared she's going to faint. She takes one wobbly step, then I grab her by the elbow, Magda the other.

'There, Nadine. Don't worry. We've got you,' I say.

'The cheek of that creep!' says Magda.

'What's he doing here?' Nadine whispers.

'He shouldn't be allowed to hang round our school,' I say indignantly. 'We ought to tell Mrs Henderson.'

'Yeah, you know what a fierce feminist she is. She'd take aim with her hockey stick and give him a swift crack right where it hurts,' says Magda, chuckling.

Nadine certainly isn't laughing.

'Do you think he wants to talk to me?' she says.

'Well, you're not talking to him!' says Magda. 'Don't worry, we'll walk you straight past him.'

'Don't even glance in his direction,' I say.

But Nadine can't seem to take her eyes off him.

'You don't *want* to see him, do you?' I say.

'Oh God, Nadine, think about the way he treated you. The way he treats all the girls he's been out with,' says Magda.

'I know,' says Nadine. 'OK. We'll walk straight past. Quick!'

We start walking across the playground. Nearer and nearer. Liam is looking straight at us. His blue eyes are boring right into Nadine.

'Take no notice, no matter what he says,' Magda hisses.

'Remember Claudie? Don't even think about him. He's not worth it, worth it, worth it,' I sing softly.

Nadine takes a deep breath and walks on. She doesn't make a sound but her lips are moving. I think she's muttering Claudie's song under her breath.

We draw close, swinging sideways out the gate, the three of us marching in unison, like we're joined at the hips, a walking manifestation of Hecate.

'Hi, Nadine,' says Liam. He ignores Magda and me, like we're Nadine's walking sticks. We do our best to prop her up.

She doesn't say a word. She doesn't even glance in his direction. We walk her past him and hurry her up the road.

'He's still staring after us,' says Magda. 'Let's hurry!'

We practically sprint to the corner. Magda peers back breathlessly.

'It's OK, he's still standing outside school. The nerve! Mind you, I do get what you saw in him, Nadine. He's gorgeous. Look at his bum in those jeans!'

'Magda, stop being ridiculous,' I snap.

Nadine still says nothing.

'Naddie? Are you all right?'

She gives a little nod.

'You don't *still* have a thing about him, do you?'

'He's history, like Claudie sings,' Nadine insists.

'Isn't it good my dad got tickets,' says Magda, quickly steering the subject away from Liam. 'They were very nearly sold out too. It's on the 29th. That's the Friday night. We'll have a great girly night out.'

'Yeah, it'll be fantastic. I can't wait,' I say.

'Claudie wouldn't waste her time on any guy who used her,' Nadine mutters.

'Too right she wouldn't. She wouldn't waste her time.' The word 'time' makes me glance at my watch. 'Oh help! I can't be late. Look, I have to charge off to McDonald's to see Russell. Is that OK?'

'Don't worry, Ellie. I'll go back to Nadine's with her,' says Magda. 'We can do our homework together, right, Naddie?'

'Oh no, it's Maths! Can I copy off you two tomorrow morning before school?' I beg.

'You could always ask Russell for help,' says Magda. 'Seeing as he's the seriously brainy type.'

I'm not so sure I appreciate this remark. I like it that Russell's clever. It's a huge bonus he's so gifted at art too. But I wish Magda thought he was gorgeous like Liam.

Do *I* think Russell is gorgeous? I try to conjure him

467

up in my mind as I rush off towards the town centre. It's weird, I've thought about him constantly all day and yet now when I'm about to meet him I can't really think what he looks like. I just keep seeing my own portrait of him instead.

Then I catch a glimpse of myself in a shop window and I start to worry what *I* look like. If only I'd thought to bring some other clothes with me to school. I look so stupid in my horrible old school uniform. The skirt's so short and my legs are so fat. My hair's standing on end like I'm Shock-Headed Peter and I've got yoghurt slurp all down my school sweater. I put down my schoolbag, struggle out of my blazer, and start pulling my sweater over my head. There's a chorus of piercing wolf whistles from a stupid little gang of Year Seven Allen's boys.

I stand my ground and sigh disdainfully, even though I can feel myself going red.

'Hey, girlie, all your blouse is undone – you can see your whatsits!' one yells.

I struggle. I know it's a joke. But I can't be sure. What if . . . ?

I look down. My blouse is buttoned. They all shriek with laughter. I say farewell to dignity, make a very rude gesture at them, grab my gear and hurry on. I'm not at all sure about wearing the blouse without the sweater. The buttons do come undone sometimes. It's too tight so that it bunches across my chest. It doesn't look remotely inviting, it just looks like I've got a couple of unwieldy bags of sugar stuffed down my shirt front. What if I've got all sweaty with the rush and the hassle with Allen's idiots? If only I'd taken my deodorant to school. Oh God, if only I could rewind and start again – but I really need to fast forward because the journey's taking longer than I thought.

Maybe he'll give up on me or think that Dad never passed on the letter? Maybe I almost wish Dad *hadn't* given me the letter. What's the matter with me? I've been looking forward to seeing Russell all day but now I'm dreading it! My hands are clammy, my blouse is sticking to me, my tongue is tingling, my tummy's clenched. I'm dying to go to the loo and my brain is going *bleep bleep bleep*. I can't think. What shall I say when I see him?

Hello, Russell. Hi there. Fancy seeing you. Sorry I'm late. Remember me? Hallo hallo hallo. Knock knock, who's there?

Oh God, I'm really going crazy. I'm going into the Flowerfields Centre, it's just down the escalator and I'm outside McDonald's and *bang bang bang* my heart beats because I can see him there, peering all round, looking for someone, looking for me.

He sees me and starts waving – so eagerly he knocks his cup of coffee flying. I go up to him, grab a couple of paper napkins and get mopping.

'Typical!' says Russell. 'I was sitting here practising the coolest way of saying hello and then I see you and spill my coffee all over myself. Not exactly the coolest action in the world.'

'It's possibly the hottest way of saying hello,' I say, discarding one soggy napkin and starting with the next. He's got coffee all in his lap too but I can't really dab at his trousers.

'Good job it's lukewarm because I've been here ages,' says Russell.

'I'm sorry I'm a bit late. Did you think I wasn't coming?'

'I wasn't sure. Your dad was really mad at me at first but he didn't seem like the kind of guy who'd hang on to my letter. Though I didn't know if you'd want to come. You must feel I'm totally pathetic – not allowed out by my stupid father. Talk about humiliating.'

Russell raises his eyebrows in mock despair and mops his sketchbook dry.

'The coffee hasn't gone on your sketchbook, has it?'

'I don't think so. Maybe it's added a sepia tint or two! I didn't have it open. I didn't want to look too posey, sketching again, even though it's what I like to do best. Well, second best.'

'So what's *best* best then?' I ask.

'Kissing you,' says Russell.

We both blush violently.

'I'll get you a coffee – and me a replacement,' says Russell. 'Do you want anything to eat?'

We end up sharing French fries, taking turns chip by chip.

'I can't get over you practically combing the neighbourhood for me,' I say.

'I'm sorry, it was a kind of desperate needy thing to do.'

'I think it was seriously romantic,' I say.

'Yeah, like it's seriously romantic not even to be allowed to ask you out just now because my father's such a stupid mean old fart,' says Russell. 'Well, he can't physically stop me going out and doing what I want. I mean, I'm stronger than him for a start. But

470

he says I can't live there if I don't accept his ground rules. I don't want to go back to living with my mum either, because she and my sister have this all-girls-together thing and all they seem to do is slag off Dad and if I do any totally normal bloke thing like leave the toilet seat up then they go on about me being just like my father which makes me so mad. It's like there isn't any ideal *home* home. When Mum and Dad first split up I used to shuttle between them, one week with Mum, then I'd pack my little suitcase and go and have one week with Dad.'

'I read a book about a girl like that,' I say sympathetically. 'It must have been really hard on you, Russell.'

'Maybe I'm just exaggerating my situation to get you to feel sorry for me.'

'OK, you're allowed to do that, just so long as you let me bang on about *my* problem family.'

I have a good moan, though I feel a bit mean as Anna has been so sweet to me recently, Dad seems to have taken off his unreasonable Ogre head, and even Eggs has seemed quite cute the last couple of days, drawing lots of pictures of monsters and monkeys and lorries and trucks and fire engines, claiming he's helping Anna with her jumper designs.

'I suppose my family aren't *too* terrible,' I wind up eventually. 'But I can't wait until I'm eighteen. Nadine and Magda and I all want to share a flat. Maybe we'll all go to Art College. *Not* my dad's. Hey, show me what you've been drawing.'

I'm hoping there are sketches of me. There are *several*! Me arm in arm with Magda and Nadine, me chatting on the bus, me walking hand in hand with

Russell in the park. He's glamorized me considerably. He's defrizzed my hair and pencilled it in as flowing curls, pared down my weight, added several inches to my height and given my outfit a designer edge. He's set about improving his own image too, adding to his stature and muscle tone until he looks like an Olympic athlete bulging out of his uniform. He's made his hair more sexily floppy and he's given his features a full Leonardo DiCaprio make-over so he could get a job as his double for the movies.

'I wish. You wish,' I say, laughing.

'What?' Russell sounds a little peeved.

'We don't look like that.'

'Yes we do. Well, *you* do.'

'Rubbish! And the park certainly doesn't look a bit like that. You've drawn it like a romantic rose-strewn bower.'

'OK, maybe I used a bit of artistic licence here and there. Tell you what, let's go to the park now and I can sketch it like it really is.'

'Oh yeah. So it's not "Come up and see my etchings." It's "Come out and watch my sketchings!"'

'You can sketch too. Come on, Ellie, finish up the chips and let's get cracking.'

'But you've got to go home and so have I. Look at all the trouble we both got into last time.'

'It's not even half past four! I told my dad I was going to this art club – I do sometimes stay on, we've got a great Art teacher. Anyway Dad and Cynthia don't get back from work till half past six so he's not to know, is he?'

'My dad is back from Art College by five some nights. And Anna will be home with Eggs.'

'Can't you say *you're* at an art club?'

'I suppose. Mr Windsor was talking about starting one the other day. He's great too. My friend Magda's developed this serious crush on him. She was having this terrible flirty conversation with him today – and he seemed to be enjoying it terribly.' There's a little pang to my voice. *I've* had a little bit of a crush on Mr Windsor since he came to our school. I suppose I've always thought of him as *my* Mr Windsor because I'm the one so nuts on Art. But he's never chuckled at me the way he did with Magda.

'Everyone always fancies Magda like mad,' I say.

'I don't,' says Russell.

'Don't you?' I say, ever so eagerly.

'No, not a bit. I mean, she's fun, she's pretty and all that, but—'

'But?'

'Well. She's a bit obvious. All that giggly wiggly stuff.'

'Hey, Magda's my friend,' I say – but there's a tiny wicked bit of me that is thrilled.

'I know, I know. You and Magda and Nadine, the Unholy Trinity.'

'What do you think of Nadine? She's not giggly and wiggly.'

'Yes, but she's sort of weird and stuck in her own world. She's OK, Magda's OK, but you're the one that I want, Ellie.'

It's a supremely magical moment – but his words remind me irresistibly of John Travolta. Russell grins, on the same wavelength.

'You're the one that I want,' he sings.

473

'Oooh oooh oooh!' I sing back, and we both collapse.

We have this long involved old-movie conversation all the way on the bus, comparing our special favourites. Sometimes we differ. He's a total *Star Wars* freak while I find it all a Big Yawn. He wanted to vomit whilst watching my beloved *Little Women*. I get scared telling him my number one favourite film is *The Piano*. I won't be able to bear it if he sneers. The relationship between Flora and Ada is just the way I remember it between my mum and me. But Russell says it's one of his favourites too because it's so strange – those poke bonnets and crinolines and the piano on that bare beach are such haunting images. Russell is obviously into film theory. He's predictably a Tarantino fan. He starts the little riff about McDonald's in Europe and he's impressed when I chant along with him. Then we rewind to the start of the movie and do the Stick Up scene. We get a bit carried away and this little old guy at the front of the bus jumps up like it's *really* a stick-up, and a fish-faced middle-aged lady tells us to Mind Our Language.

It's just as well it's my stop next. We're still giggling when we get to the park. We're both hoping it might have turned into the magical glade in Russell's sketchbook, but it's just the scrubby old park, totally unromantic in the daylight, with toddlers howling, mums shouting, an old vagrant muttering, torn Magnum wrappers flapping in the breeze and dog dirt in the grass.

'*Not* a haunting image,' I say.

'We'll go over by the trees,' says Russell.

But there's a little group of guys, one with his hood

474

up, several looking shifty. There seems to be an exchange of hard cash for equally hard drugs.

'Maybe going over by the trees isn't such a good idea,' says Russell. 'So where *can* we go?'

We end up walking out of the park and down by the old allotments. Someone has planted cabbages. Their sour reek fills the air. We stand looking at each other, breathing shallowly. It's hard knowing how to start kissing in broad daylight, especially as there are several old chaps and a girl in dungarees digging their allotments. Russell glances round and then closes in on me. His eyes morph into one as his lips touch mine. His head is at a slightly awkward angle so my glasses get pressed into my nose, but then the kiss takes over and my eyes blur and the cabbages turn into great green roses and the shouts and yells sound sweet as birdsong.

'We're going to lose track of time all over again,' I say, when we eventually draw breath.

'Who cares?' says Russell, and kisses me again.

'I care,' I say eventually. 'I don't want you to get into any more trouble with your dad.'

'I care too,' says Russell. 'I don't want you to get into any trouble either. So we'll go now. Well, in a minute. One more kiss.'

We do go . . . after quite a few more kisses. Russell sees me right to my front door and we arrange to meet tomorrow. Same time. Same place. Same boy and girl. Same love story.

I waltz indoors, sure that Anna will take one look at my wild hair and shining eyes and flushed face and swollen lips and start to create. But Anna is busy with her own creating, crawling round on her hands and knees on the living-room carpet matching up pieces of sweater, while the kitchen table is covered in potential designs. Eggs is sitting cross-legged in a corner, a huge toffee in his mouth clamping his teeth together. He is also creating, with needles fat as crayons and scarlet triple-knitting wool.

''ook, 'ook, Ellie,' he says, dribbling toffee-slurp down his chin. 'I c'n *knit*!'

'Good for you, Eggs.'

'I wish *I* could knit,' Anna says. 'Dear goodness what have I taken on, Ellie? I must be mad! You wouldn't be an *angel*, would you, and help me come up with one or two more designs?'

'How about an angel design then? An angel motif on the front, little gold lurex halo, wings in some fancy overstitch to look like feathers – and then a little devil on the back with silver lurex horns and hooves?'

'Oh Ellie, that's brilliant!'

I help Anna all evening, the good-girl daughter with ultra amazing original ideas. Dad comes home, pats me on my unruly head and delicately enquires if I've had a brief tryst with Russell.

'In McDonald's, yes,' I say.

'Ah! Love amongst the Big Macs,' says Dad. 'Well, just so long as you're home for tea. Good girl.'

I am enjoying this new role no end. Maybe I've finally sussed out a way of having a great time *and* being a Good Girl.

Magda and Nadine seem intent on being Bad Girls. At school the next day they listen to my detailed account of My Meeting in McDonald's with My Boyfriend Russell, but they both seem gently distracted. I'm all set to show off just a little weeny

476

bit at going home time because I have another date with Russell but neither Magda or Nadine seem interested. They have Other Plans.

Magda hangs back when the bell goes, telling us she has 'things to do' and suggests we hurry on homewards without her. We blink at her.

'*What* things?'

'What are you up to, Magda?'

Magda looks shifty. 'OK, OK, I'm just going to hang around here until Mr Windsor materializes.'

'Oh Magda, you are a fool.'

'He's a *teacher*.'

'I'm not a fool. I seriously think I could be on to a good thing. And it's great that he's a teacher. Who wants to waste their time with schoolboys?' Then she catches my eye. 'Sorry, Ellie! I wasn't getting at you and Russell.'

'I know, I know,' I say. Though I rather think she was.

Nadine and I can't persuade her to come along with us.

'She's mad,' I say crossly. 'She's making a complete fool of herself. As if Mr Windsor would seriously consider a little fling with Magda! He'd lose his job for a start.'

'Mmm,' says Nadine.

She isn't really concentrating. We go out into the playground. Nadine starts. I suddenly realize what's preoccupying her. Liam is waiting by the gate again.

'Oh-oh,' I say. 'Don't worry, Naddie. I'm here.'

She's not even listening. I look at her flushed cheeks. Maybe she doesn't *want* me here!

'Nadine, don't look at him. Come on.'

477

'What's he *doing* here?' says Nadine.

'Well, it's obvious. He's hanging around trying to get you to go out with him again.'

'I loved him so much,' Nadine says softly. 'He was so gentle, so romantic at first.'

'Yes, but look what he was really like. Nadine, are you crazy? Stop looking at him!'

She suddenly gasps.

'What is it now?' I take hold of her arm. She's trembling.

'He's not here to see me,' Nadine says. 'Look!'

I turn – and see Liam waving to someone. A little blonde girl in Year Eight is rushing across the playground towards him.

'Oh my God,' I say. 'He's the absolute pits. Come *on*, Nadine.'

But she pulls away from me, still staring at Liam and the little Year Eight girl. He's kissing her now. He is *disgusting*. He's doing it deliberately to hurt Nadine. And it's working. She's looking absolutely stricken.

'Please, Naddie. Come away.'

'I've got to see him,' she says.

'*What?* You're mad!'

'Let me go, Ellie.'

'Don't be so stupid. Just come with me. Please. I'm begging you.'

'He's not going out with her,' says Nadine.

She starts walking towards them.

'Nadine!' I yell at her, furious she can be such a fool.

She turns, shakes her head at me, and then goes on walking Liam-wards. I can't stand it. How can she be such a total idiot?

I ought to go after her. I should haul her away from that creep and keep her locked up until she comes to her senses. But she won't listen. And I'm already late. I've got to go into town to see Russell.

I try one more time.

'Nadine, *please*!'

It's a waste of breath. She doesn't even turn round this time. So I tell myself there's nothing else I can do. I go off into town to meet Russell – but my heart's thumping all the time and inside my head there's this horror video playing of Nadine and Liam leaving the sad little Year Eight girl and going off alone together . . .

Why do I feel so guilty? It's not my fault. I'm not going to think about Nadine any more. Or Magda. I'm just going to concentrate on Russell.

He's waiting for me in McDonald's.

He's already bought French fries and arranged a few on a napkin so that they spell out *Hi! X X X*. He leans over towards me and I wonder if he's going to give me those three big kisses here in McDonald's – but there are some other Halmer High boys over by the water fountain and Russell quickly veers away from my lips and nods his head at me instead. I nod back. Russell nods again gratefully, like we're both auditioning for Little Noddy. Then I slide into the seat beside him and snaffle chips and start telling him all about Magda and Nadine and how they've both suddenly gone crazy. Russell listens for a little while but then he starts fidgeting.

'Never mind Magda and Nadine. Tell me about you, Ellie.'

So I tell him stuff and he tells me stuff, and we

compare the craziest things like our favourite outfits when we were little kids. I had these terrible pink girly leggings with a pink flowery little top that I pretended was my special ballet dancer outfit! Russell had a favourite pair of jeans that he wore every day for months until they fell apart.

Then we talk about our favourite places. He likes fairgrounds and I like beaches and we both love Whippy ice-cream. As I've snaffled more cash from Anna I treat us to McDonald's ice-cream with chocolate sauce. Then we get on to the wondrous world of favourite chocolate bars, swopping passions. It's as if we're best friends, not just boyfriend and girlfriend. It's just great.

After a while Russell gets a bit fidgety and indicates that it would be even greater if we could enjoy another Love in the Allotment session. I don't want to look too eager so I demur a bit – but I'm quite keen for us to be alone together too. The park is overrun with little kids playing footie but this time the allotments are empty, apart from a homespun scarecrow who waves his stick arms at us. We take no notice. We take no notice of anything else but each other. I don't even think any more. I just feel.

Then I *do* have to start thinking, because it's feeling so good that I'm losing all common sense.

'No. Russell. Stop it.'

He does stop, though he tries hard to persuade me to carry on. I suddenly think of Nadine and Liam and wonder if they're currently involved in a similar scenario. It makes me a little more understanding, though I'm sure Liam is just using Nadine. Then I wonder if Russell is just using me.

'What's up, Ellie?' Russell says, kissing my neck.

'Nothing. Well. I was just thinking about Nadine—'

Russell sighs. 'You're always thinking about Nadine. Or Magda.'

'No I'm not,' I say, although I've gone off on a Magda tack now and I wonder if she's followed Mr Windsor all the way home and asked herself in for a coffee. Maybe *they* could be similarly entwined on Mr Windsor's sofa. The thought is so bizarre I burst out laughing.

'What's funny?' says Russell, trying to draw me even closer.

'Nothing. It's just Magda has this thing about—'

'Magda!' says Russell. 'See, I'm right. Magda Magda Magda. Nadine Nadine Nadine. You and your girlfriends!'

'Did your last girlfriend have special best friends too?' I ask.

'Mmm,' says Russell. He hesitates. 'Well, if I'm absolutely truthful . . . No, you'll laugh at me.'

'No I won't!'

'You're my first girlfriend.'

'Really!'

'Yeah. I mean, I could have gone out with various girls – and then there's the school discos, I've *danced* with heaps of girls there. Hey, Ellie, there's a special big dance coming up because it's the school centenary. They're trying to make it like a June ball at university. You know, a meal, two bands, a bouncy castle, maybe fairground rides. Will you come?'

'Sure! Though what if you're still grounded?'

'Oh it's not till the end of the month. Dad will have

calmed down by then. And we're all expected to go, partner or not. But it would be simply great if you'd be my partner, Ellie.'

'Do I have to wear a ball dress, all low cut with a sticky-out skirt?'

'Oh, no. Well, feel free to go for a little low-cut number. You'd look really terrific. But no sticky-out skirts, just something maybe . . . slinky?'

*Me???* I can't stuff myself into a slinky little number, I'd look positively obscene. I mentally rifle through my entire wardrobe and start to panic. I'll have to see if Anna will fork out for something new. But *what*?

I ponder long and hard, though it's difficult to concentrate while Russell is kissing me. After he's walked me home I'm supposed to be settling down to my homework, but I design and discard a dozen different outfits instead. Anna looks over my shoulder.

'They're great designs, Ellie, but they're all far too sophisticated. The jumpers are very much for the under-tens.'

Anna is living, eating, and breathing jumpers. It's as if her brain is three-ply cable twist. She's wrapped up in her own woolly world and even when she's talking to Eggs or Dad or me you can see the *click click* of knitting needles flickering in her eyes.

I ring Magda to ask her advice about outfits for Russell's dance, but she's out. Her mum becomes anxious. She thought she was round at my place.

I ring Nadine, but she's out too. Her mum becomes annoyed. She thought she was round at my place.

Help! I have unwittingly got both my friends into serious trouble. And what on earth are they doing out late? What's *happened*? Is Magda really having a passionate encounter with Mr Windsor? And what about Nadine? Oh God, I should have tried harder to stop her going off with Liam. What sort of friend am I?

I'm starting to get really worried. Our phone goes halfway through the evening. I rush to answer. It's Russell.

'Russell!' I say, surprised. I *nearly* say 'I hoped you were Nadine/Magda' – but this would *not* be a good idea.

'Dad and Cynthia have gone out for a drink so I've got the place to myself,' says Russell. 'I'm supposed to be doing my Maths homework—'

*I've* still got last night's Maths homework. I'll have to copy off Magda again. And then there's French and I didn't do last night's either . . .

'But I thought I'd much sooner talk to you.'

'That's great.'

'I wish we were still in the park together, Ellie. I love it when we're together.'

'Mmm. I do too.'

'You don't sound very certain!'

'It's kind of awkward right now,' I say.

The phone is in the living room. Dad is staring at me, ear-wigging every word, even though Eggs has the television up so loud I can barely hear myself. Even Anna has stopped crawling round the carpet and has her head on one side, watching me.

'Awkward?' says Russell. 'Oh! You mean you've got Magda and Nadine round?'

I don't like his tone. So what if I *did* have Magda and Nadine round?

'No Magda. No Nadine. But Anna and Dad and Eggs are all in the living room,' I say.

'What, listening right this minute?'

'You've got it.'

'Can't you use the extension?'

'We haven't *got* one.'

'Tell you what. I'll e-mail you a message. Can you commandeer the computer?'

'Russell, we haven't joined the real world. Dad's old Apple Mac isn't up to e-mail.'

'OK, OK. I know! I'll write you a sweet old-fashioned love letter. How about that?'

'That sounds great.'

'And you'll write me one too?'

'OK.'

'And we'll swop them tomorrow? In McDonald's?'

'Right.'

'See you then.'

'Yes.

'Bye for now.'

'Bye.'

'Bye, Ellie, it's been great talking to you.'

'And you.'

'You don't mind my phoning?'

'No. Not a bit.'

'Tomorrow then?'

'Yes.'

'Bye.'

'Bye.'

'Oh per-lease, put the phone down!' Dad hisses – but he's smiling.

I do put the phone down – and smile back. I feel this great glorious grin flash across my face.

'He's very keen,' says Anna.

'Mmm,' I say happily.

'I still don't approve at all,' says Dad, but it's obvious he doesn't *really* mind.

Eggs is the only one looking mutinous.

'I don't like this new boyfriend,' he declares.

'You haven't met him, silly,' I say, picking him up and turning him upside down.

I used to be able to shake him like a beanbag but now it's a real struggle. Eggs is still skinny but he's growing rapidly. It's a weird feeling that maybe one day he'll be towering over me, and there might be enough muscle in those matchstick arms to pick me up and turn *me* upside down.

I get a flash of what it might be like for Dad. He's so used to me being his funny fat little Ellie. It must be so weird for him now I've started going out with boys.

'I don't want to meet him!' Eggs gurgles, going beetroot red. 'Put me round the right way, Ellie!' He kicks at me and struggles.

'Ellie! He'll be sick in a minute,' says Anna.

I right him quickly. I've had Eggs puke all down me before and it's not a pleasant experience.

'I like Dan,' Eggs says, harping back to this other boy I used to know.

'Russell is a hundred times better than Dan,' I say.

'Do you love him then?' asks Eggs. He stares at

me. '*Do* you? Why have you gone all red? Ellie?'

I retreat rapidly to my bedroom. I let the French and History homework go hang. I worry a bit about Nadine and Magda – but most of the time I lie on my bed and dream about Russell.

Do I love him?

I think I do.

I do. I do. I do.

# Chapter Six

# Bad Timing

# Chapter Six

I get to school very early. I wait for Magda. I wait for Nadine.

They don't come in early. They're both very late, after the bell. Nadine is very pale, with dark smudges under her eyes. Magda is flushed and jittery, hardly able to keep still. And *she* hasn't done her Maths homework, so we're all in trouble.

There's no way we can talk about yesterday evening under the watchful eye of Mrs Henderson so I pass them both notes.

'Nadine – *what happened with you and Liam??? Tell me – in detail. Are you OK? You're not cross with me, are you? Love Ellie. X X X*'

'Magda – *what happened with you and Mr Windsor??? Tell me – in detail. Are you OK? You're not cross with me, are you? Love Ellie. X X X*'

For five very long minutes I don't think either of

them is even going to bother to reply. Then Nadine starts a note in her Gothic script and Magda writes her little round scribble.

'*Ellie – I could kill you for ringing my mum like that! I am VERY CROSS with you. I don't want to write stuff about Liam. It was so upsetting and horrible last night. I'll tell you and Magda later. Love Nadine.*'

'*Ellie – I had a terrible time making up excuses to my mum because you were daft enough to ring up. And I wasn't in the mood. Don't ask about me and Mr Windsor. It was awful. I'll tell you and Nad as soon as poss. Love Magda.*'

I can't wait to get them round by the Portakabins at break where we can be private.

'Magda! What happened last night?'

'Nadine! What happened last night?'

'You tell first, Magda,' says Nadine.

'No. You tell,' says Magda.

'I had to go and talk to Liam,' Nadine starts. She sees me shake my head. 'Don't look at me like that, Ellie. Honestly! You think I'm mad, don't you?'

'Yes! She is, isn't she, Magda?'

'I don't know. Maybe I'm the mad one,' Magda mumbles.

'Well, *I'm* not mad,' says Nadine. 'I don't love Liam any more. I hate him. All right, when I saw him outside school I couldn't help feeling a bit funny, especially when I thought he was waiting for me. But then when I saw him with that Year Eight girl – she's called Vicky and she's so *sad* – I just felt boiling mad.'

'How dare he treat you like that, deliberately kissing that girl in front of you,' I say.

489

'How dare he treat *her* like that. She's only just thirteen. He is so sick. He was thrilled too, when I went storming up to him. He looked at me like, *See*, Nadine, look what you're missing. It made me want to slap his stupid face. But I started talking to Vicky, telling her I needed to talk to her privately. She just thought I was making trouble, that I was jealous. Liam tried to make me clear off. But I just stood there in front of them, telling Vicky all this stuff about Liam and how he just uses girls. I came out with all these lovely secret romantic things he once said to me – and of course it turns out he's said exactly the same things to her.

'So then she started to wonder whether I *was* just trying to make trouble like Liam said. I asked her to come for a walk with me so we could have a proper talk together. Liam got very angry then and said I was just jealous because I'd blown my chances with him. He said he wouldn't want to touch me now if I was the last girl in the world. He said holding me in his arms was like holding a marble pillar because I was so stiff, so cold, so unresponsive. He said no boy would ever want to kiss me because I'm so boring.'

'How *dare* he, the filthy creep!' I say.

'Don't take any notice of that jerk, Nadine. You're beautiful and all the boys want to go out with you. You didn't take him seriously?'

'Well, it was horrible, him saying all that,' says Nadine, her voice shaking. 'But it worked for Vicky. She started staring at him in horror, seeing him in his true light at last. So we went off together. We left Liam just standing there. He started yelling stuff after both of us. Vicky started crying. I did too, actually. We went back to her house – it was OK, her mum

490

works late, so we had the place to ourselves, and we could have a good heart to heart. It turns out she was all set to do whatever he wanted because he'd got her convinced it was the way to prove her love. I know, I know, it's so sad – but I nearly fell for that old line too.

'Anyway, I stayed really late at Vicky's, because she needed a lot of looking after. I thought I'd tell my mum I was round at your house, Ellie, to save complication.'

'Oh oh. I kind of complicated things more,' I say.

'I'll say! When I eventually got home my mum went bananas. She's convinced I'm seeing this secret boyfriend. It's crazy. All the time I was seeing Liam she didn't suspect a thing, but the one time I'm truly just round at a girl's house she goes nuts and I'm in deep trouble. She's not going to let me out again in a hurry. She even started on about the Claudie concert, but I *think* I can still go OK, seeing it's with you two.'

'I can't wait to see her on the 29th,' says Magda. 'The tickets came this morning. The one good thing. At least the post got me out of bed. I wasn't going to get up today. I certainly wasn't coming to school. Not ever again, actually.'

'Because of Mr Windsor?'

'Mmm,' says Magda.

'He didn't do anything really awful, did he?'

'I can't believe it. I always *liked* Mr Windsor.'

'He didn't do anything. And *I* like him. He's lovely. Oh God, I made such a complete idiot of myself.' Magda hides her head in her hands.

'What did you *do*?'

'Tell, Magda! Come on. *I* told,' says Nadine, blowing her nose.

'Mags! You've got to tell us. We tell each other everything,' I say, pulling her hands away.

Her face is as red as her hair.

'OK, OK, I'll tell. I followed Mr Windsor home yesterday. I stayed back after school and we had a little natter about this and that. I made out I was really getting into Art and how much his lessons mean to me. He seemed dead chuffed about it. I didn't *mean* it. I know you're stuck on Art, Ellie, but it's just a bit of fun to me. Anyway, Mr Windsor and I seemed to be getting on like a house on fire. The way he was looking at me with those big dark eyes of his it was practically Great Fire of London time! I didn't just want to leave it when he sloped off to his car. I wondered about asking him for a lift but I thought he'd be a bit uncomfortable on the school premises, anyone could be watching. So I thought, OK, cool it for a bit but maybe . . . sort of turn up at his house!'

'Wow! Magda, you really flipped!'

'Tell me about it!' says Magda, shaking her head.

'You didn't *go* to his house?'

'I did. Well, his flat. It's fabulous too, just the way you'd imagine, this big airy loft space in one of those converted warehouses near the river. It's not fair! Why does everything about him have to be gorgeous?'

'How did you know where he lives?'

'You couldn't have run along behind his *car*!'

'How do you *think* I found out where he lives? I looked him up in the telephone directory at home. And I changed out of this ropy old uniform and wore my black lacy top—'

'The see-through one!'

'Well, I had my bra on – and my black trousers, the brilliant ones that kind of show off my bum, and my red sandals with the high heels to show him I don't have to look like a boring little schoolgirl.'

'I'll say!'

'I made out to Mum that you'd set me up with this double date, Ellie, with your Russell and some mate of his. I warned her I might be late back and then I got the bus over to the river—'

'Your mum didn't mind you going out late?'

'Your mum didn't mind you going out all tarted up and glamorous?'

'Mum's reasonably cool about it. She's always trusted me – until *you* phone up, Ellie, and blow the whole thing.'

'I wasn't to know, was I? But I'm sorry all the same.'

'I know. Anyway, I found the right block for Mr Windsor and there's this entryphone thing. I hung around for a bit wondering how I was going to announce myself. To be absolutely truthful I very nearly chickened out at that stage. If only I had!'

'Magda, I just can't believe you had the nerve!'

'I must have been completely crackers. OK, I announced myself over his answerphone, sort of "Hi, it's Magda here". And then I waited. Mr Windsor says on the intercom, "Magda who?" which didn't exactly help my self-esteem. But then I thought he was maybe acting dumb deliberately to be cautious. After all, there aren't that many Magdas around. I said I was Magda from school. He just said "Oh!" sounding amazed. I mean, we'd been chatting away only an hour or so before. I wondered if he was ever going to invite me in so I spun him this story about some dodgy-looking guy I thought might be following me, so he buzzed the door release.

'I went rushing up the stairs and there he was, standing by his front door, looking really anxious. He asked all about the dodgy guy and I said it was OK, I'd maybe been imagining it, but could I come in and wait for a bit just to make sure he was gone?

'He still hesitated, looking like he hardly recognized me. I suppose he's so used to seeing me in my dreary old school uniform. He asked what I wanted. I said I wanted to talk to him. He said maybe I'd better talk to him at school and I said I really needed to talk to him now, so he let me in, though he sort of edged round me and kept well away, as if I had a filthy cold and he was scared of catching it.

'I was really bowled over by his flat. It's ultra cool, polished bare boards, very minimal chic, not much furniture at all. He had one of those bashed-about metal sculptures in a corner. The walls were the only crowded bit. Paintings. All his.'

'What were they of?'

I couldn't help envying Magda terribly. I'd give anything to see Mr Windsor's flat – especially his paintings.

'I don't know. Women, mostly.'

'What, portraits? Full length? Nudes?'

'Ellie! As if it matters! Get on with the juicy bit, Magda,' says Nadine.

'It matters to me!' I say. 'What style, Magda?'

'Sort of realistic but a bit splotchy,' Magda says vaguely.

'What kind of colours?'

'Darkish. I think. I don't know. I made out I was looking at this one painting – a woman in a blue dress, OK, Ellie? – and I said stupid stuff about it being a happy picture and it made me think of the seaside. It was just because the woman was wearing a sundress and she looked like she had a tan, but it turned out it was a lucky guess because he'd painted it on holiday. He burbled on about the quality of the light, bla bla bla, but I just wanted to know who the woman was, but I didn't like to ask in case it sounded crass. I wish I had, then I could still have got out of there without looking a total fool.'

'What did you *do*? I'm going nuts with the suspense,' says Nadine.

'So I sit down on the sofa while Mr Windsor's still nattering on about his old painting and gradually his voice trails away and he asks me why I've come round. So I say, ever so casual, that I was meeting someone else later, but I'd been told he lived in these flats down by the river so I thought I'd just pop by. Like you do.

'He still seemed a bit fazed by this and asked *who* had told me where he lived so I just laughed and wouldn't tell him. Then he asked who I was going to be meeting and I laughed some more and said I didn't want to tell him that either. He went off at a bit of a tangent then, asking me ever so seriously about who I was going out with. I thought he was maybe a teeny bit jealous, which was simply great, so I hammed it up a bit, and he got even more serious and seemed to think that I'd come round to discuss this mythical boyfriend with him. He said perhaps I was getting more involved than I really wanted and though he was flattered I wanted to discuss it with him maybe I'd do better talking things over with some other teachers – like Mrs Henderson! Dear God, imagine discussing your love life with Mrs Henderson! So I said – I said – Oh God, I said . . .'

'*What* did you say?'

'I said I wanted to discuss my love life with him. Because *he* was my love life,' Magda mumbles, ruby-red.

'You didn't say that!'

'You're kidding, right?'

'I wish I was. But I did say it. I must have been barking mad. Woof woof,' Magda says. 'It was just I thought we'd be pussyfooting around all evening. Oh help. First it's dogs, now it's cats. I'm going completely batty. There you are. Bats.'

'Magda. Calm down. Take a deep breath. And now tell us what Mr Windsor said!'

'He didn't say anything for a full minute. He just gave me this awful astonished appalled look. Then he kind of paced round the room saying nothing at all while I sat on his sofa wanting to sink straight through the cushions because I could see I'd made this *huge* mistake. Then he went out into his kitchen and I thought this was a signal to me to go so I was just about to make a bolt for his front door when I heard this tinkle of glasses and a pop of a bottle opening and he came back with a Coke for me and a glass of wine for him. He gave me my drink and then he sat down on the sofa too, but right up the other end. Then he says, "Oh Magda," shaking his head. And I take a little sip of Coke, shaking so much my teeth go clink against the glass. I managed to stammer out "Oh Mr Windsor" and then we both have a silly giggle. Then Mr Windsor says – oh God, he was so lovely which kind of makes it worse – he says "I'm very flattered that you've taken such an interest in me, Magda, especially when I know you could have your pick of all the boys."'

'He said that?' I ask enviously. 'Those exact words?'

'Yep. And he went on, "You don't want to waste your feelings on a boring old teacher like me." So I dared pluck up the courage to tell him he was the least boring man I'd ever met, and he said I was a very sweet girl to say so, but by next week or the week after I'll be totally fed up with him and I'll just look back on this as a fleeting crush. I said I didn't think so – and then I asked him to tell me why he wasn't interested. Was it just because of the school thing or didn't he like me at all? And he said he liked me a lot, but probably not in the way I meant. He said I was way way way too young to be involved with a guy in his twenties and certainly he'd never be unprofessional enough to have any liaison with any pupil, even in the sixth form, and *then* he said, "And my girlfriend wouldn't be too happy about it anyway."'

'He's got a girlfriend?'

'They live together. It's actually *her* flat. She's in advertising and I think she must make a lot of money. He showed me this photo of her. It's not fair, she's gorgeous, this black girl with a face like Naomi Campbell and the most amazing long hair. She's called Miranda and when he says her name his face

497

goes all soft and it's obvious he's crazy about her.'

Magda sighs.

Nadine sighs.

I sigh.

'He suggested I stay and meet her. He even asked me to have supper with them but I couldn't face it. So I made out I really did have this date with a boy from Halmer High and then I apologized for making such an idiot of myself. He said, "Don't worry about it, Magda. We'll both forget this ever happened." But how *can* I forget? How can I ever face him? Every time we have Art I'll have to skulk in the toilets for the whole double lesson.'

The bell goes and we go back into school – and there's Mr Windsor coming along the corridor towards us!

'Oh no!' says Magda. 'Quick, hide me!'

We can't drape ourselves around her or squash her up small in our schoolbags so there's obviously no way we can hide her. I link into her arm on one side, Nadine does the other, and we carry on walking up the corridor. Mr Windsor saunters along like he hasn't a care in the world. When he draws near he gives us all his normal cheery smile.

'Hi Ellie. Hi Magda. Hi Nadine,' he says, and then he strolls off.

'Phew!' says Magda, breathing upwards so sharply she ruffles her fringe.

'What style!' says Nadine. 'He acted like it never happened.

'Maybe it *didn't*,' says Magda. 'Maybe last night was just a mad delusion on my part. Perhaps I dreamt it all.'

'I wish my evening was only a dream,' Nadine says sadly.

'But you acted wonderfully. You looked after Vicky and you stood up to Liam and showed him just what you thought of him,' I say, giving her a hug.

'You don't think I am all cold and boring, do you?' Nadine says.

'Of *course* not!'

'And boys will like kissing me?'

'Nadine! You just wait and see. I'm sure you'll meet someone very special really soon,' I say. 'I predict it!'

'Predict someone special for me too, Ellie,' says Magda, sighing.

'OK, someone special for both of you. Now cheer up, right? Big smiles!'

Magda bares her teeth at me.

'It's all right for you, Ellie. You've got Russell,' says Nadine.

'Yeah, right, I've got Russell. But he's nowhere near as important to me as you two,' I say – and I mean every word.

But when I meet up with Russell in McDonald's after school I forget all about Magda and Nadine. Russell's bought me a little present! It's in a little black box. A jewellery box???

I open it, my heart hammering.

'Don't worry, it's not a seriously heavy commitment present. It's not like a ring or anything,' Russell says quickly.

It's two little pearly daisy-shaped hairslides very delicate and utterly delightful.

'I hope you like them,' Russell says. 'I thought

they'd look good in all your lovely curly hair. But don't feel you have to wear them if you don't want to.'

'I *do* want to! They're wonderful.'

'You honestly like them? I spent ages looking at all this hair stuff. The girl in the shop kept giving me these weird looks like she thought I was shopping for myself and rushed off to Madame Jo Jo's of an evening. Here, shall I help you fix them? I just love your hair, Ellie, it's so springy.'

'Kind of exploding mattress springy – but I'm ever so glad you like it. I've always hated there being so *much* of it, all frizzy curls. I've always wished I had hair like Nadine's, smooth and glossy and gorgeous, but of course mine couldn't ever go like that. I *could* try having it very short like Magda. Do you think it would suit me?'

'You don't want to look like Magda or Nadine. You want to look like you,' says Russell firmly, clipping the slides into place. 'There! They really suit you, Ellie. Will you wear them to the centenary dance?'

'You bet! In fact I've got this pearly-grey silky top, I could wear that. It's *sort* of slinky.'

'Sounds great! I got the extra ticket today. My dad coughed up the cash. He's mellowing considerably. I've told him all about you. Well, I made out my Art teacher is a mate of your Art teacher and they were both comparing notes on the brilliance of their pet pupils, etc., etc. I thought it would go down better than saying we met here. Dad has a seriously weird problem about me hanging out at McDonald's. Anyway, we're all set for the dance on the 29th.'

'The 29th,' I repeat.

Why is that date so familiar? Why do I suddenly feel anxious?

'The 29th,' I say yet again. 'That's not a Friday, is it?'

'Yes. Why?'

Oh God. I know why.

'I'm supposed to be going to a Claudie Coleman concert on the 29th!'

'Oh Ellie! Can't you go another night?'

'I think she's only doing the one gig.'

'Claudie Coleman – the singer with the red hair? Yeah, I like her too. But she's always doing concerts. Couldn't you go another time? Please, Ellie.'

'Well, it's just . . . You see, Magda's dad got the tickets specially.'

'Magda again.'

'Don't say it like that, Russell, please. Look, I can't really back out now and let her down.'

'I bet Nadine's going too.'

'Yes, she is.'

'So, Magda and Nadine can go together. It's not like you're leaving one on her own.'

'Yes, but, well, we were all three going to have this girls' night out.'

'Oh. So they're more important than me and my dance?'

'No! No, of course not.' I'm starting to panic. I was so happy just seconds ago, loving my beautiful pearly hairslides, thrilled to bits that Russell had bought them specially for me. Now I feel the slides are digging directly into my head and I can't think straight.

I take Russell's hand, though I'm extremely conscious of all the kids milling round us in McDonald's.

'Russell. You're *much* more important. You know that.'

'Then come to the dance with me, Ellie. I've spent the whole day showing off to everyone that you're coming. I'll look such an idiot if I have to say you'd sooner go off to some concert with a couple of girlfriends.'

'It's not just any old concert. I've loved Claudie for ages and I've never had the chance to hear her sing live before. And Nadine and Magda aren't any old girlfriends either. They're my best ever friends.'

'But I'm your boyfriend, aren't I?'

'Well . . . yes, of course.'

'And you're my girlfriend and I need you to come to this dance with me. *Please*, Ellie.'

'OK, OK! Of course I'll come. I'm sure Nadine and Magda will understand.'

Russell gives me a quick kiss right there and then in McDonald's.

Nadine and Magda don't understand at *all* when I phone them both in the evening. Nadine listens while I tell her about Russell and his dance.

'You don't mind too much, do you, Nadine? You do understand, don't you? You'd probably do the same, wouldn't you? Nadine?'

Nadine says nothing at all though I can hear the sound of her breathing on the other end of the phone.

'Nadine, speak to me!'

'I don't want to speak to you,' she says, and puts the phone down.

I ring Magda and tell her. Magda says plenty.

'I can't *believe* you could be so amazingly un-grateful! We decided to go to the Claudie concert specially for you, because Russell had stood you up.'

'Yes, but he hadn't *really* stood me up, he wasn't allowed out.'

'Yeah, yeah, Daddy wouldn't let him out – which if you don't mind my saying so always sounded a totally pathetic excuse, but that's not the point. The *point* is that my dad got us those three tickets—'

'I'll still pay for my ticket, Mags!'

'My dad got those tickets as a *present*. We were going to have this big girly night out.'

'I know, but you and Nadine can still go.'

'You bet we'll still go.'

'And I can come next time Claudie sings.'

'Unless Russell asks you out on a pressing date – like a Big Mac and a large order of French fries.'

'You're not being fair, Magda. It's this very special centenary dance at his school. He's told all his friends he's taking me.'

'I'm sure he has. I've heard the way those Halmer High boys talk about girls. Well, if you want to go and be exhibited as the latest notch on Russell's belt you go for it, Ellie.'

'You'd do the same, Magda. You in particular. You're boy mad.' I can't stop myself. 'I think that's half the problem. You've had a down on Russell right from the start, because he went after me instead of you.' Oh God, what have I said? I take a deep breath. 'I'm sorry, Mags. I didn't mean any of that,' I say – but she's put the phone down on me.

I can't believe it. Both my girlfriends have stopped speaking to me.

I sniff hard and make for the stairs. Everything is a blur. I suddenly encounter something small and bouncy on the stairs – and scream as a large dagger pierces my ankle. The something screams too, at the top of his lungs.

'Ooow! Ellie, you hurt me! You walked straight into me! You did that on purpose and now look what you've done! You've made me drop all my stitches.'

'Look what *you've* done. You attacked me with your knitting needle. Look, I'm bleeding! And you've laddered my best tights too, you little moron.'

'Hey, hey, what on earth's going on?' says Anna, running into the hall, a ball of knitting wool caught comically round her ankles.

We both start talking at once, Eggs wailing over his rapidly unravelling scarf and me hopping on one leg staunching the trickle of blood.

'Do calm down, both of you. Eggs, stop that noise! I'll pick up your stitches up for you, easy peasy. Why did you barge straight into him, Ellie? He was sitting on the stairs as good as gold. I really *can't* stop now, I'm right in the middle of working out this really tricky design and I'm seeing George tomorrow. Look, you're not crying, are you? It's only a little scratch.'

'You wouldn't care if I had needles skewered all the way up and down my legs! Why do you always have to take Eggs's side over everything? It's not fair! Why doesn't anyone understand what it's like for *me*?' I shout, and I rush up the stairs and slam myself into my bedroom.

I have a good long howl into my pillow. When

I've got to the choked-up, gulping, badly-in-need-of-tissues stage Anna comes into my bedroom with a box of Kleenex and a cold flannel.

'You could at least knock,' I grumble, but I let her mop me up. Then she sits down beside me and puts her arm round me. I hold myself stiff for a moment but then relax and lean against her.

'OK, Ellie, tell me,' Anna says gently.

'Nadine and Magda aren't speaking to me!' I sob.

'What's happened? Come on, don't cry so. Don't worry, you'll make it up with them. You'll always be best friends.'

'Not any more,' I gulp, and I tell her everything.

'Poor old Ellie. This is big problem time,' Anna says, when I've gone through the whole thing. 'Choosing between girlfriends and boyfriends is always very very tricky.'

'It's not fair! Why can't they *all* be friends?' I wail. 'I thought Magda and Nadine would understand. I mean, this is a very important dance for Russell. It would be pretty magic to go. And he bought me these little pearly hairslides, look.'

'Yes, they're lovely. And Russell sounds lovely too. And, after all, he asked you to the dance first.'

'Well. No. Actually he didn't. I arranged to go to the concert first.'

'So why didn't you tell him about the concert when he started telling you about the dance?'

'I didn't take in the date. You know what a dilly dream I can be about stuff like that.'

'You're telling me! So what are you going to do?'

'I don't know. I didn't realize how horrid it would feel, Magda and Nadine turning on me like this. It's

505

not fair, they *both* put boyfriends first. Nadine did when she was going out with horrible Liam and Magda did when she went out with that creep Greg.'

'Ah,' says Anna. 'So what does that tell you about boyfriends and girlfriends? Boyfriends aren't usually permanent, even though you might be crazy about them at the time. Nadine and Magda and you have a very special friendship. I think that's maybe why all the boys get threatened by it.'

'So you think I should turn Russell down?'

'I don't know. It's difficult. I don't think there are any rights or wrongs. Which do you really want to go to, Ellie, the concert or the dance?'

'I want to go to both!' I say. 'I want to keep in with Russell and please him. I know the dance means a great deal to him. But on the other hand Magda did suggest going to the Claudie concert to cheer me up – and now she's the one who needs cheering up, and Nadine too. Oh Anna, I *can't* go to the dance with Russell. Do you think he'll ever understand?'

'No! But you'll just have to try to make it up to him in some way,' says Anna.

She sees my expression.

'Not *that* way!' she says, and we both burst out laughing.

# Chapter Seven

# Dangerous Times

# Chapter Seven

It is sad being in the doghouse. I feel as if I've been smacked on the nose, had my bone snatched away and been banished to my kennel. Magda and Nadine don't fall on me with open arms when I tell them I can come to the Claudie concert after all.

'Per-lease. You're not doing *us* a favour,' says Magda.

'You'd obviously far sooner go to this dance with the Walking Sketchbook,' says Nadine.

I have to breathe deeply and take it. I tell myself that they are my very special girlfriends and their love and support and companionship is of supreme importance to me – even though right this moment I want to slap Magda's smug face and pull Nadine's long witchy hair. But I keep my temper – and their own temper improves. By the end of the day things are nearly back to normal, and we've all started to plan exactly what we're going to wear to the Claudie concert and how we're going to get there, though we're not quite clear which dad is going to be roped in to do the ferrying about. I give both Magda and Nadine a quick hug when we say goodbye, and they both hug me back hard.

I feel enormously relieved that we're all three best friends again. But now I've got to tell Russell.

That is even worse.

There's no real way of getting round it. And it's awful, because the moment I see him at McDonald's he starts chatting excitedly about the dance and how sad it is that half his mates can't get any girls to go with them and how great he feels that he can go with me.

'Don't feel too great, Russell,' I say sadly, my tummy a tight knot. 'In fact, get ready to feel ultra small. And seriously mad at me into the bargain.'

'What's the matter, Ellie? Oh God, you can still come, can't you? Don't tell me your dad's put his oar in. He's *got* to let you come.'

I see a glimmer of a good way out.

'I'm so sorry, Russell. I'd give anything to come to the dance with you. But you're right, it *is* Dad.'

'Oh no! But he seemed to get to like me after the first sticky ten minutes. *Why* won't he let you?'

'I think he can remember *his* school dances and the sort of things that went on,' I lie smoothly. 'He's been so strict with me recently, Russell. I've tried and tried but there's no way he'll budge.'

Oh Dad, I'm sorry. I feel so mean, but it's the only way to smooth things over with Russell.

'How about if I go to see your dad and try to talk him round?' Russell suggests.

'No! No, I think that would only make him worse. And he doesn't know I've been seeing so much of you. No, please don't, Russell,' I say, panicking. 'Then he'll really clamp down and stop me seeing you altogether. He's already got this total ban on me going out at night.'

'But he was going to let you go to that concert,' says Russell, eyes narrowing. 'Are you sure this isn't all just a mega-excuse to get out of the dance so you can go off with your beloved girly-friends.'

'No! Russell! I don't tell lies,' I lie, looking hurt.

'But you *are* still going to the concert?' says Russell.

*Why* did I ever mention it to him???

'Well, maybe,' I hedge. 'After all, Magda's dad got the tickets. It would be silly to waste it. And my dad doesn't mind because – because he'll drive us there and then drive us back so he can keep an eye on us all the time.'

'How about if he drives you and me to the dance and then drives us back? Then he can keep an eye on us,' says Russell.

'I don't think that's quite the same.'

'No, things aren't quite the same,' Russell says – and I don't like the way he says it.

He doesn't suggest we go to the park. He doesn't suggest we go anywhere. We sit in McDonald's for half an uncomfortable hour and then Russell looks at his watch ostentatiously.

'Gosh, is that the time? I'd better get back. I've got heaps of homework to do tonight.'

'You're mad at me, aren't you?' I mumble.

'No, really. It's OK. I understand,' he says – sounding like he doesn't understand at all.

'I feel so mean letting you down.'

'Well.' Russell shrugs his shoulders. 'Maybe I'll find someone else to go to the dance with me.'

I feel as if he's slapped me in the face. I stand up, feeling sick.

'Right,' I say. 'Well. See you.'

'Yes. See you,' says Russell.

We both know what this means. We *won't* see each other. Ever again.

I try to tell myself that if he can be so mean and petty just because I can't go to his dance then he's really not worth bothering about.

'He's not worth it, worth it, worth it.'

That's right. I shall go to the Claudie concert with my two best girlfriends in all the world and we'll have a great time.

It's no use. I wish I hadn't said no to Russell. He *is* worth it. I care about him. I love him.

I go straight home.

I go straight home from school the next day too. There's no point going to McDonald's. Nadine and Magda are sisterly and supportive. It doesn't really help.

In afternoon Art the next day Mr Windsor is still into Myths and Legends. I draw a sad silly Psyche drooping miserably because she can't see Cupid. Mr Windsor is very complimentary but for once this doesn't mean much. He admires Nadine's Circe too but barely glances at Magda's Venus, mumbling 'Very good' and edging past quickly. Magda does her best to maintain her cool but her face is as red as her hair.

She rushes out of class without waiting for us.

'Don't you rush off too, Ellie,' says Nadine. 'I need you to be there just in case . . . well, you know. If Liam's there.'

'Oh Naddie,' I say, giving her a little pat.

But it isn't Liam who's waiting at the gate. It's Russell – and he's talking to Magda.

I feel dizzy. Maybe he's always liked Magda. Everyone else does. Maybe he's asking her out instead of me. Maybe he's asking *her* to the dance!

I grab Nadine's arm.

'It's OK, Ellie,' she says, peering over at the wall where Liam used to wait. 'He's not there.'

'Russell *is*,' I hiss urgently. 'Only he's chatting up Magda. Hang on to me tight, Nadine. I want to walk right past as if I haven't even noticed them. Nadine, stop staring!'

But I can't help staring too. Magda's smiling at Russell. She's looking right into his eyes and he's looking back eagerly, *hungrily*, like she's the juiciest ice-lolly in the freezer and he wants to lick her all up.

'I can't believe it,' I say. 'How *could* he?'

'How could *she*? She doesn't even like him. She told me she was amazed you were so dotty about him. She said she thought he was a snotty little creep,' says Nadine.

'He's *not* a snotty little creep!' I say, outraged. Then I see him smile at Magda and my stomach turns over. 'Yes he is!'

'Look, take my arm, Ellie. Come on, we'll whizz past them quick. You hold your head up high. Don't say a word to Russell – *or* Magda. We're not going to speak to her at *all*. And she's supposed to be your friend!'

Nadine leads me across the playground although my legs have turned to jelly. I wobble all over. I try to set my face in a mould but as we get close up everything threatens to melt and run.

'Ellie?'

It's Russell – smiling at *me*!

The nerve! I walk past, my head high.

'Ellie!'

It's Magda, and she's smiling too.

My eyes sting. It's bad enough that Russell could betray me, but I can't bear it that my best friend Magda could do this to me, and so blatantly too.

'Ellie, stop. Wait! I want to talk to you,' Russell says, hurrying after me.

'Well, *she* doesn't want to talk to you,' says Nadine, elbowing him out of the way.

'Ellie? Nadine? What's up with you two?' says Magda, dodging round the other side.

'What's up with *you*?' says Nadine. 'How *could* you, Magda?'

'How could I what? Here's me doing my best to act like Cupid, helping these two idiots get it together again, and you act like I've done something dreadful!'

I stop. Nadine stops. Magda stops. Russell hovers, while we three girls stare at each other.

'What are you on about, Magda?' says Nadine.

'Russell stopped me as I came out of school and asked me how Ellie was and whether she was still mad at him. He'd hung around McDonald's for hours yesterday and she didn't show, so he wanted to know if she might be willing to make it up or had he blown it for ever. I said I thought she was still crazy about him and pretty miserable at the moment and that she'd be more than willing to make it up – but then you two sweep past with your noses in the air, not even speaking. I can't work out *why*. I mean, don't speak to Russell if you don't want to, Ellie, but don't take it out on me.'

'Oh Mags,' says Nadine. 'You'll never guess what Ellie thought!'

'You thought it too!' I say, weak with relief.

'You thought *what*?' says Magda.

'Nothing!' I say quickly, because Russell is in earshot. I turn to look at him. He looks at me. I feel like I'm the ice-lolly now. Melting.

'Go on, you two. Go and enjoy your romantic reunion. Have a happy little snog in McDonald's,' says Magda.

'French kiss over the French fries.'

'Blush amongst the burgers.'

'Cuddle over your Cokes.'

'Sauce the ice-cream with your sweet talk.'

'Froth the coffee with your feverish embraces.'

'Shut *up*, you two,' I say – but fondly.

They're such sweet friends. And so is Russell. When we get away by ourselves at last he says he's really sorry he said he'd take someone else to the dance.

'I just wanted to hurt you, Ellie. It was stupid. You didn't believe it, did you?'

'Of course I didn't!' I insist. 'Oh Russell, I'm still so sorry I've let you down over the dance.'

'Well, it's not like it's this super-cool ultra great social date. It's just a school dance. It'll probably be a totally sad embarrassing occasion, so maybe it's just as well you're not coming.'

'Maybe we could go to some other dance together?'

'Sure. That would be great. Though actually I can't dance very well. I sort of fling my arms and legs around and look like a total prat. Maybe if you saw me you'd go off me instantly. Always assuming that you're *on* me, of course.'

'You're the one who went off me. You were really mad at me last time.'

'You were the one who didn't turn up at McDonald's. I waited *hours*.'

'You didn't suggest meeting there. I didn't think you'd go. I didn't think you wanted to see me again.'

'I do.'

'I do too. Want to see you.'

'Oh, Ellie.' Russell suddenly pulls me close, right there in the street.

I don't care who's watching. I fling my arms round his neck.

There's a toot on a car horn.

'Eleanor Allard!'

Oh my God! *Mrs Henderson* is leaning out of her car window.

'Put that boy down at once!' she calls, and then she winds up her window and drives off.

'Oh oh!' says Russell sheepishly. 'Who was that? One of your mum's friends?'

'Mrs Henderson's my form teacher,' I say, hoarse with shock.

'Your *teacher*? Wow, she's a good sport.'

'I suppose she is,' I say.

But the next day Mrs Henderson gives me a half-hour lecture about decorous behaviour out in the street in school uniform. I am very glad she didn't come across Russell and me later on by the allotments!

'So you're all lovey-dovey with the Walking Sketchbook again?' says Nadine.

'Don't call him that, Naddie, his name's *Russell*,' I say, nudging her. I give Magda a nudge too. 'What's all this about you calling Russell a snotty little creep?'

'*Me?*' says Magda, all outraged innocence. 'Look, I'm the Cupid who brought you two together again.'

I can't believe how good it feels to *be* together again with Russell. And with Magda and Nadine.

'I'm so h-a-p-p-y, hippy hoppy happy,' I sing in the shower on the day of Claudie's concert. It's this silly little song she's tacked on to the end of her album. It goes on: '*I don't need the love of a good man, I don't need the love of a bad man, I don't need the love of a-n-y man at all – 'cause I'm so h-a-p-p-y,* etc., etc.' But that's not the way *I* sing it. I invent my own version: 'I *do* need the love of a good man, though I don't need the love of a bad man, I do need the love of MY man Russ-ell – cause I'm so h-a-p-p-y, hippy hoppy happy . . .'

The shower is full on so I don't think anyone can hear me. I am wrong.

'I'm so d-i-r-t-y, dippy dotty dirty,' Dad bawls from the other side of the bathroom door. 'I *do* need the scrub of a good soap, I do need the the scrub of any kind of soap, I do need the scrub of a-n-y soap at all – 'cause my daughter's in the shower and she won't let me in so I'm so d-i-r-t-y, dippy dotty dirty!'

'*Dad!*' I say, emerging blushing in my bath towel. 'Do you have to listen?'

'*Ellie!*' says Dad, gently pulling a lock of my wet hair. 'Can I *help* listening when you're singing fit to bust, o Daughter Diva of the Shower Stall. But hey, I'm glad you're happy. Now what are the plans for the concert tonight? Is Nadine's dad driving you or Magda's? I'm sorry I've got this stupid meeting at the college.'

'Magda's dad's taking us,' I say.

'Poor guy,' says Dad gratefully. 'I owe him.'

But when I get to school Magda says her dad can't manage it after all because the wheelshaft went on his car last night and it'll need to be in the garage for a couple of days.

We look expectantly at Nadine.

'Oh help,' she says. 'Dad always takes Natasha and Mum to their loopy line dancing on Friday nights.'

'Well, my dad's got this meeting and needs the car so Anna can't drive us. She's stuck with Eggs and she's knitting nine hundred and ninety-nine stupid sweaters every evening anyway,' I say.

We ponder.

'Tell you what,' says Magda. 'We'll take ourselves. Train and then tube. Couldn't be simpler.'

'Couldn't be *harder*,' says Nadine. 'My mum won't let me.'

'I don't think Anna will either,' I say. 'Well, getting there's OK. It's coming back late at night. Won't your mum mind, Mags?'

'Sure. But she won't know. She thinks your dad's taking us, Ellie. Your folks think Ellie's dad's taking us too, Nadine. And Ellie, you can say *my* dad's taking us. Then they don't have to worry and we can push off and have fun.'

517

'Great,' says Nadine, though she looks worried.

'Perfect,' I say, though I'm fussed about having to tell a whole load of lies all over again.

'So it's all settled,' says Magda. 'We'll meet up at six, right? At the railway station. Don't worry about cash, Ellie, you can borrow off me. It'll be fantastic. A *real* girls' night out.'

So that's exactly what we do. Nadine's at the station first, looking great in black, with new black shoes with huge heels so that she's taller than ever.

'I'm going to have to carry a little collapsing ladder and clamber up it every time I need to talk to you,' I complain. 'You make me feel littler and dumpier than ever.'

'Don't be daft, Ellie. You look great,' says Nadine.

I've certainly done my best, trying on half my clothes before plumping (horribly ominous word) for my black trousers and silver grey top. I suppose I *do* look plump. If *only* I was lithe and long and lean like Nadine. But at least Russell doesn't seem to mind. He phoned me when I was getting dressed.

'I'm just phoning to wish you a good time at the concert,' he said.

'If I ever get there. I can't decide what to wear. I'm half in and half out of my trousers at the moment.'

'Oh help. You'd better not tell me any more, you're dangerously inflaming me.'

'Calm down, Russell, it's not a pretty sight.'

'You're a *very* pretty sight. I think you look wonderful in your trousers – and even more gorgeous *half* in them. *Which* half?'

'Oh shut up. Though you're very sweet. I'm

wearing your hairslides. They're really great. You're really great, Russell.'

There was a sudden totally disgusting mock-vomiting sound. Eggs had crept up behind me and was groaning and gagging.

'Ellie? Are you OK?' Russell sounded alarmed.

'I am fine. However, my little brother Eggs is going to be minus his head in a millisecond,' I said. 'Anyway, enjoy the dance, Russell. I'm really really sorry I'm not going with you.'

'I know exactly where you're going to go with me to make it up to me,' he said, chuckling mysteriously.

'I'll go anywhere with you, Russell,' I said – provoking Eggs into such an orgy of mock-vomiting he nearly made himself really sick.

I didn't tear his head off his shoulders. I felt so great I just laughed at him.

I feel great now. I don't care if I *look* great (as in enormous).

'I'm so h-a-p-p-y,' I sing again and Nadine harmonizes with me. We're not feeling quite so harmonious after another ten minutes have gone by. Magda still hasn't turned up – and she's got the tickets for the Claudie concert.

'Why is she *always* late?' I say.

'Maybe she's got distracted chatting up some boy,' says Nadine. 'You know what she's like.'

'How about you, Nadine?' I ask gently. 'Are you over Liam once and for all now, ready to do some chatting up yourself?'

'Sure,' says Nadine firmly – but when a boy with dark hair and wicked eyes comes sauntering out of the station, his arm round some girl, Nadine's head jerks and she turns white.

I look at the boy too.

'It's not Liam,' I say.

'I know. I just thought it might be,' says Nadine.

'Oh, Naddie. You know exactly what he's like now. You've got to forget about him. You'll meet someone else soon.'

'I don't think I'll ever meet anyone like Liam,' says Nadine. 'Not that I'd want to, of course.'

I hope Nadine means it. She looks a bit down, so I change the subject.

'Where *is* Magda?' I say. 'Why does she always do this to us?'

'Hi, you two!'

It's Magda, running wiggle-waggle up to us in her high heels, coyly waving to two grinning boys who are eyeing her up and down.

'Sorry! Am I a bit late?' Magda asks infuriatingly. 'It was just Warren came round to borrow a tie from one of my brothers and you know I've always had a bit of a crush on him – he used to be at school with my brother, right? – hey, you should see his hair, he's got this totally cool new haircut so he looks a total dish, and this evening when he saw me all dressed up to go out to the concert it was like he'd suddenly seen me for the first time. I wasn't just this silly little schoolgirl. And you'll never guess where he's going tonight! Would you believe he's got this scholarship to Halmer High sixth form and he's going to the dance. And guess what again – he broke up with his girlfriend a couple of months ago and so he was all set to go by himself but when we got talking, Warren and me, he asked if *I'd* like to go to the dance by any chance! Get that! I was ever so tempted actually.'

'*What?*' I say.

Magda grins. 'But then I thought to myself, it wouldn't be sisterly. I explained I couldn't possibly let my girlfriends down. He was ever so disappointed but said he understood. And guess what yet again – he's asked me out tomorrow night. A real date, a special meal out, at the Terrazza, you know, that Italian place. It's ever so posh. Bit of a change from a burger in McDonald's, eh?'

'Lucky old you,' I say a little sourly.

'Yes, you don't have to go *on* about it,' says Nadine. 'Have you remembered the Claudie tickets?'

'Of course I have. Cheer up, you two! It's our girls' night out, right?'

We do cheer up on the train, messing around and singing Claudie songs. We get on the wrong tube at Waterloo and have to catch another tube back to where we started, and then we bump into some silly middle-aged business blokes and get a fit of the giggles, and then we're not quite sure where to go when we get out of the tube station and we wander round for a while until Magda chats up a policeman and he escorts us all the way up the road.

Time is getting on and we're all starting to worry we might miss the beginning of the concert. I want Magda and Nadine to run but it's like they're both on stilts with their high heels so we don't make much progress. We turn into the main street and see lots of people wearing Claudie T-shirts which is reassuring – until we realize they all seem to be walking *away* from the concert hall.

'What's up? Where are you going? Isn't the Claudie concert this way?' Magda asks a group of girls.

'She's cancelled it,' says one girl miserably.

'What? Why? Is she sick?'

'Sick in the head, more like,' says another girl, looking angry.

'What are you on about?' says Nadine.

'What's the matter with Claudie?' I ask.

'She's got this boyfriend, right? It was all over the papers last month. Some yobby football player not good enough to kiss her fingertips,' says a third girl, pulling at her Claudie T-shirt in distress so that Claudie's image lengthens into a comical grimace.

'So? It's not a crime to have a boyfriend. It's Frankie Dobson, isn't it? I think he's pretty tasty myself,' says Magda.

'Oh right, so I suppose *you* think he's just being all masterful now he's told Claudie she has to quit singing,' says the T-shirt girl.

'She has to *quit*?'

'Because *he* says so?'

'But *why*?'

'He went to her concert in Manchester last night and it was a big success. One of my friends was there and she phoned me up and told me all about it. The hall was packed out with fans, and Claudie sang all her most popular numbers, the really stirring stuff. Everyone cheered their heads off. This stupid Frankie couldn't take it. He thought all the songs were an insult to him because lots of them are about independence and women not needing men, so he gave Claudie an ultimatum. If she didn't pull out of her concert tour and stop singing all her very best songs he'd leave her.'

'So why didn't she tell him where to get off?' says Magda.

'Exactly! But astonishingly she said he meant so much to her that her career wasn't anything without him.'

'Claudie wouldn't say that!' I protest. 'She's a total feminist icon. It would go against absolutely everything she's ever sung about.'

'That's what *I* thought – even though it was front-page news in the tabloids this morning. So we came along to the concert hoping it was all some stupid rumour, even a publicity stunt. But it's true. The concert's off. She's pulled out the whole tour, just like he said.'

I still can't believe it. We go to the concert hall to see for ourselves. There's just little stickers on every Claudie poster saying 'Cancelled due to illness'.

'Perhaps she really *is* ill,' I say, because Claudie is my heroine and I'm word perfect in every song and I've taken on board everything she's ever said and I feel as if she's deliberately let me down.

But when Magda goes to the ticket office to try to claim a refund the guy behind the desk confirms everything those other girls said.

'You'll have to write in for your refund. Claudie's left us in the lurch and we haven't got enough cash to give out to everyone. The girl's crazy, wrecking her career for that Frankie. He can't leave the girls alone. He'll be off with some new trophy blonde before Claudie has time to turn round and then where will she be?'

'How can she do this to herself?' I say, practically in tears.

'Cheer up, Ellie. We'll find you someone else to go crazy about,' says Magda.

'What are we going to do now?' says Nadine. 'I want to listen to some music. There must be something else on somewhere.'

'How about coming to listen to us?'

We all spin round. There's a group of boys looking at us, reasonably hip guys, though one's very Gothic, with long black hair and chunky silver jewellery. Nadine stares at him, dazzled.

'So, like . . . you're a band?' Nadine says.

'Sure.'

I'm *not* so sure.

'Come on, Nadine,' I say – but it's a waste of breath. Magda's smiling too, her head on one side.

'A band, eh?' she says. 'What are you called?'

'Well, we've gone through a lot of changes. We're just this little indie band at the moment. We've toyed with the name Indie, because I'm Dave and he's Ian and he's Ewan so we're almost there with our initials. I'm lead guitar, he's bass, and Ewan's the drummer. We just need to find some guy called Neville or Neil or something to be the lead singer.' He looks at Nadine. 'Or a girl, of course. Called Nadine.'

Yuck! I can't *believe* his corny old chat-up line – but Nadine seems to be falling for it. She's tossing her hair and looking up at him through her long eyelashes.

'Are you really looking for a singer?' she says.

'Sure! So why don't you come back to my place and have a little jam session with the band?'

'I can't sing!' says Nadine.

Too right she can't. I stand next to her in singing lessons so I should know.

'I can sing OK,' says Magda.

'So you come too, Scarlet,' says the fair guy, Ewan the drummer.

'What's your singing like then, babe?' says Ian, the bass guitarist, looking at me.

I can't stand guys who call you *babe*, like you're the pig in that sweet little kids' film. Ian looks a bit like a pig himself, with a snub snouty nose and a bit of a belly.

'We've got to get home,' I say firmly. 'Come on, Magda. Come on, Nadine.'

Magda shrugs and waves at the guys – but Nadine is still staring awestruck at Gothic Dave.

'I like your rings,' she says, nodding at the big silver skulls.

'Do you want to try one on?' he says, offering it to her.

'Wow! It's wonderful. I'd give anything for this sort of jewellery,' says Nadine.

'I've got all sorts back home, crosses and stuff. Come and see. And we could try out your voice. You certainly *look* the part, doesn't she, you guys?'

Nadine looks pleadingly at me. 'Shall we, Ellie? Just for a little while?'

I shake my head at her, astonished.

'Go on. Our van's just round the corner.'

'My van,' says Ewan, as if he thinks we'll be impressed. He looks hopefully at Magda. 'Dave's gaff is only ten minutes away. You'll come, won't you?'

Magda's starting to see sense now. 'Maybe not,

525

fellows,' she says. She links into my arm and jerks her head at Nadine. 'Come on, Nad.'

Nadine looks at us. She looks at Dave. She nibbles her lip, hesitating. She looks down, her long hair falling over her face.

'Nadine!' I say.

'You do what your mates tell you, do you, Nadine?' says Dave, and he gently pushes her hair back so that he can see her face.

'Not always,' says Nadine, going pink. 'I'll come to your place then, Dave.' She stares defiantly at Magda and me. 'How about if I meet you back at the station at eleven, OK?'

We stare at her as if she's gone completely crazy. Is she really serious? She's willing to go off with these three complete strangers in a van???

'Nadine, please,' I hiss – but I know just how stubborn she can be. And she's always been so mad about weird indie bands. I suppose this is like her dream come true. Only she can't see that it could easily turn into a nightmare.

'We can't let her go off in this van on her own,' Magda whispers to me. 'She's totally nuts. We'll have to go with her to make sure she's all right.'

'Oh Mags, this is crazy.'

'I agree! But if we can all stick together we should be OK. Well, sort of.'

'Magda!'

'It's kind of a chance of a lifetime though, isn't it? I mean, suppose they eventually make it big. And Nadine gets to be the lead singer. Or . . . or me.'

I don't know what to do. They've both gone completely loopy. Nadine's already walking off with

Dave Skull and Magda's smiling at Ewan drummer, asking him where his van is parked. I ignore Piggy Ian and slope after the others miserably.

The van is an awful old thing, really bashed-in and filthy dirty. Magda looks a bit put-out and even Nadine wavers. I grab her quickly.

'Nadine, we can't go in that van with them. We haven't got a clue who they are,' I hiss at her.

'We do know who they are. They're these guys in this band,' says Nadine.

'They're probably making it all up. And even if they have got a band they'll never let you sing in it, idiot.'

'I don't see why not,' Nadine says, looking hurt. 'Anyway, I want to see all Dave's stuff. Isn't he fantastic? I'm crazy about him.'

'You've only been talking to him two minutes!'

'Look, Ellie, you were the one telling me I'd meet someone special soon! You predicted it!'

'Yes, but I didn't predict you'd let yourself get picked up by a complete stranger!'

'You did. With Russell.'

'That's different. *He's* different.'

'Exactly. He's a silly little schoolkid. These guys are amazing,' says Nadine.

I don't know how to get through to her. What little brain she has seems to have shrunk to pea-size, rattling round in her obstinate skull like the silver ones grinning on the Dave guy's fingers. He's got hold of Nadine now.

'Come on, babe,' he says, and he holds open the back door of the van for her.

She smiles up at him – and climbs inside.

Magda shakes her head up at me. 'We'll have to go too,' she says.

'I know. But it's mad. *We're* mad if we go.'

'Come on, Scarlet! In you get,' says Ewan, brushing his fair hair out of his eyes. I suppose he's quite good-looking if you like that type. Magda's starting to look like she does.

'Maybe it's time to live a little dangerously,' she says, and she gets in the van too.

So I follow them and get in the van, though I know this is a BIG mistake.

# Chapter Eight

# Running Out Of Time

Chapter Eight

Dave doesn't live ten minutes away. Ewan drives for at least half an hour. I haven't got a clue where we are. I can't believe this is happening. Magda is reasonably OK because she's sitting in the front of the van with Ewan and he's got to keep at least one arm on the steering-wheel. But I'm in the back with Ian and Nadine and Dave.

Nadine and Dave start acting like a couple almost straight away. Nadine's proving she's no marble pillar. I don't know where to look. I definitely *don't* look at Ian.

He doesn't seem very interested in me – and yet when I fall against him as Ewan rounds a corner too sharply he hangs on to me, trying to pull me close.

'Don't!' I say, trying to wriggle away.

'What's up with you? I only want to be friendly,' he says.

'I don't want to be friendly! I'm in a relationship already,' I say primly.

'So? I am too. Come on. Let's get cosy, eh?'

'No thanks!'

'OK. Be like that. You're just a silly little kid. Why can't you be more like your mates? At least they're having a bit of fun.'

What a *pig*! I imagine his snout rootling in the mud, his big pink pig-belly smeared all over.

Magda isn't having fun anyway. She laughs at stuff Ewan says but then she looks suddenly outraged and flounces away from him, as he's obviously gone too far.

Nadine's starting to look worried too. She keeps trying to wriggle free.

'Where on earth are we?' she says desperately. 'We've been driving ages.'

'We're very nearly there. Just around the next corner,' says Dave Skull.

And the next and the next and the next. And then eventually Ewan slows down and we drive slowly through a seedy council estate with boarded-up shops, overflowing dustbins and a few scraggy boys sucking on cans of lager like babies with bottles.

'We're here,' says Dave.

'Here?' says Nadine, staring out, dazed. 'You don't live *here*, do you, Dave?'

For the first time in her life she sounds just a little bit like her mum.

'What's up, sweetheart? Don't you like life when it's a little on the wild side?' says Dave. 'Come on, out you get.'

Magda and I look at each other, trying to work out

531

what on earth to do now. Nadine is whiter than usual, her lipstick smeared all over her chin.

'Oh help,' she whispers. 'Maybe this wasn't such a good idea after all.'

This is the scariest place I've ever been. The boys drinking lager yell ugly stuff at Magda when she wriggles out the van. She reacts with her fingers but this just encourages them.

'Hey, clear off, you berks,' says Dave Skull. Well, that's *approximately* what he says. He's got hold of Nadine again so she can't run away. He can see she's having second thoughts. Third, fourth, fifth thoughts.

'I didn't realize it had got so late,' Nadine says. 'I'm sorry, but I think we really ought to get back now.'

'We'll take you back. Later on. Let's go and play a little music, eh?'

'I can't sing at all, actually,' says Nadine.

'Never mind. I'm sure you can dance. I'd like to watch you dance, Nadine.'

'Yeah, sure you would,' says Magda. 'Look, we have to get back. Now.'

'Keep your hair on, Scarlet,' says Ewan. 'We'll take you back. Later. Come and strut your stuff first. We want to hear you sing too.'

'I'm not in a singing mood any more,' says Magda.

'Then we'll have a little drink first. Loosen you up. Yeah, we'll have a little party, right, Dave?'

'You bet.'

'You're on,' says Pig Ian.

We look at them. They look at us.

'OK, just one drink,' says Magda.

'No!' I hiss. 'Let's just run off, please!'

But Magda's looking round at the guys, at the

532

boys drinking lager, at the bleak stone walkways.

'If we try to make a run for it now they'll catch us and then they might get really ugly. We'd better go with them and then clear off as soon as we can,' Magda mutters.

'I'm sorry,' Nadine wails. 'It's all my fault.'

'What are you girls whispering about, eh?' says Dave. 'Come on. Follow me.'

So we do, because there doesn't seem to be any other alternative. They take us in a stinking lift up to the top floor, swooping up so fast I feel sick. It's a relief to step out into fresh air but the view over the balcony makes me dizzy. I hold the rail tight, little flecks of rust embedding themselves in my palms. The buildings below don't look real. I feel I could jump from roof to roof as if they were stepping stones.

'Quite a view, isn't it?' says Ian Pig, standing close behind me.

I try to shuffle away from him, pressing against the cold concrete. Space whirls in front of me. I look down down down at the tiny toy world below. The pig rootles nearer. Blood starts drumming in my head. My knees won't lock to hold my legs straight. He puts his damp hands on my shoulders, gripping tight. I give a little squeak.

'Scary, eh?' he says. 'Don't worry, I'll keep you safe.'

'You let her go!' says Nadine, looking wretched.

'He's only teasing,' says Dave Skull. 'In you come, then.'

I suppose we were hoping it might be better inside. Maybe painted black like Nadine's own bedroom, with Gothic decorations and silver candlesticks and weird posters. But it's just a bleak bare wreck of a flat, smelling of drink and cigarette smoke.

'Hey, no-one pretended it was House Beautiful,' says Dave, seeing our faces. He's picking up a ropy old guitar – but his strumming doesn't sound very skilled.

'Are you going to sing, Nadine?' he says.

She shakes her head nervously.

'How about you, Scarlet?' says Ewan, sitting on the sofa and slapping his knees as if they were a drum kit.

'Somehow I'm not in the singing mood,' she says.

'Sure – but we'll fix that,' says Dave, nodding at Ian. 'Get us all a drink, eh?'

'Just one,' says Magda. She's looking at the door, obviously wondering if it might be better to make a dash for it as I suggested.

Dave Skull sees she's looking at the door too. He stops strumming, strolls down the hall, takes out his key – and double-locks the door. Then he puts the key in the pocket of his jeans, grinning.

So this is it. We're really trapped now. Nobody knows where we are. Our families think we're at the Claudie concert and we're being driven home afterwards. They won't worry about us for hours. And what can they do when they eventually phone round and find out we're missing? How can anyone ever find us? *We* don't even know where we are.

I still feel sick. I wonder if I'm actually going to throw up. I mutter something about needing the loo and find the right door. I flop inside the dank little room, desperately trying to think what to do. If only we were at Claudie's concert enjoying our girls' night out! This is all a crazy nightmare and it's getting worse and worse and worse.

I join the others in the dingy living room. Ian Pig has got his guitar now but they're certainly no real band. They've opened up some cans of beer. Magda and Nadine are clutching a can each.

'Come on, girls, drink up,' says Dave Skull. He tosses me a can of beer too. I hold it helplessly.

'What's up? Don't you like the taste?' he says. 'I know what you might like more.' He brings a bottle of vodka out of a cupboard. 'Here, have a little swig of that. It'll help you relax.' He passes it to me.

'I don't drink, actually.'

All the boys laugh unpleasantly.

'This one doesn't do much,' says Piggy Ian.

Ewan tries to pull Magda on to his lap. She bats him off fiercely.

'Maybe this is a big mistake,' he says. 'They're just silly little schoolgirls.'

'My Nadine's cool, aren't you, babe?' says Dave. 'Hey, you want to see the rest of my jewellery? Come through here.' He gestures towards the bedroom.

'I think I'm OK here, thanks,' Nadine says in a tiny voice.

Dave hands the vodka to her and she takes a little swig and then chokes.

'I'll have some too,' says Magda, taking the bottle.

She doesn't drink a drop, keeping her lips tightly closed as she tilts the bottle up in the air. 'There!' she says, wiping her mouth as if she's just downed a triple measure. 'That's better. Hey, how about you guys putting some music on your CD player? Then we can all play and sing along, and we won't feel so self-conscious.'

It helps a little to have the music blaring. The three guys down their beers and pass the vodka round. We pretend to swig from the bottle too. Magda's doing her best to lighten things up. Nadine keeps trying to edge away from Dave Skull.

'Hang on,' he says, going to his bedroom. He brings back a little bag. Oh God. Drugs.

'Yeah, great idea,' says Nadine.

I stare at her in horror – but she gives me a little wink. It's just a quick flicker of her eyelid but it's enough. Magda's watching too, and gives a nod. We watch while Dave Skull and Ewan Drum and Ian Pig start rolling special cigarettes. Dave lights his, takes a deep drag, and then passes it to Nadine.

'Cool,' she says, getting up. She wanders over to the window. 'This is such a great view,' she says, turning her back as she stares out. She seems to be taking a deep drag but I think she's bluffing. Magda joins her at the window.

'My turn,' she says, pretending to take a drag herself.

Before I can join them Pig Ian is by my side.

'Don't say you're into a little light relaxation, Miss Priss,' he says.

I giggle foolishly, trying not to antagonize him.

'Here, I'll show you how to do it,' he says, taking the roll-up from Magda and waving it in front of me.

'Sure. Great. In a minute,' I say, jumping up. 'I've just got to go to the loo.'

'You've only just been. What's the matter with

you?' he says, taking a long drag himself.

'I've got a little bug,' I say. 'I'll be right back.'

I go out into the hall and stand in the loo again, trying to think of some way we can get out. I look up at the window. It's too high up, too small. Much much too small. I could stand on the toilet but I could only get my arm out of the window. My head wouldn't fit through, let alone my body. But . . . maybe we could get out of another window?

I creep out of the loo and tiptoe across the hall to the kitchen. There are two large windows above the blocked sink. One hitch up onto the draining board. I could make it. And Nadine. And Magda.

I think.

I run the water tap. I splash it on my face. I throw cold water over my lovely pearl grey shirt. Then I take a deep breath and call.

'Magda. Nadine. Can you come out here and help me a minute?'

Pig Ian comes out. 'What's up with you, Little Priss?' he says blearily. 'What are you yelling for?'

'Oh please, don't look at me. I've been sick,' I say. 'It must have been the vodka. I don't want you to see me like this, not till I've cleaned myself up. I need my friends. They've got tissues and stuff.'

'God, you really are a kid,' says Pig Ian disgustedly. 'OK, OK, I'll get your mates.'

He goes – and Nadine and Magda come running.

'Have you been sick, Ellie?' Magda says.

'This is all my fault,' Nadine weeps.

'Sh! Quick! Shut the door. We'll get out of the window,' I hiss.

'Wow!'

'Great thinking!'

'Easier said than done,' I gasp, hooking my leg way up onto the draining board and trying to heave myself up after it.

Magda gives me a push, Nadine gives me a shove, and I'm suddenly up on the draining board. I grab hold of the window handle. The whole window frame is rotting and at first it sticks. I pull and tug at it, hurting my hand, and then take off my shoe and give it a last desperate bang. It moves – and the window opens.

Nadine is already up beside me, and she helps haul Magda up.

'Oh help!' I say. 'It's a long way to jump. We're all going to break our legs.'

'I'd sooner break my *neck* than stay locked up with those creeps,' says Magda, and she jumps first. She lands like a little cat, not even tottering in spite of her high heels. Nadine goes next, arms and legs kicking out wildly. She ends up on her bottom but manages to scramble up again unhurt.

My go. Oh God. I stare straight out into empty space. What if I misjudge my jump, leap a little too far, and hurtle right over the balcony?

I clench my sweaty fists.

'*Quick*, Ellie,' Nadine hisses.

'Jump like Mrs Henderson says. Bend your knees and spring,' Magda calls.

I jump. I bend. I don't exactly spring. I stumble and hobble and trip. But I'm down, safe on the cold concrete walkway.

'Right, let's get out of here,' says Magda, pressing the lift button.

'At least they're all pretty wrecked. It'll take them a while to react,' says Nadine.

'Come *on*, lift,' I say, jabbing at the button. Nothing happens. We keep peering round desperately at their door. They'll be after us any minute.

'I think we'd better make a run for it, down all the stairs,' I say.

So we run along the walkway, making for the staircase. Something feels funny. I'm all uneven, hobbling sideways. Did I twist my ankle? Then I realize.

'My shoe! I left it in their kitchen!'

'Well, we're not going back for it now,' Magda gasps.

'They were my best shoes from Shelleys,' I moan.

'I'll save up and buy you a new pair, Ellie,' Nadine puffs. 'And I'll buy you some too, Magda. Name your pressie! Anything to make it up to you.'

'Shall we try the lift again on the next floor down?' says Magda.

'But what if they've got into it up at the top?' I say.

'Help, yes! OK, well, down we go.'

Down and down and down and down. My tights are already ripped. My foot gets sorer each time it slaps down on the cold concrete. My knees ache, my chest hurts, I'm gasping for breath and we're not even halfway down. Down and down and down and down. I'm wet with sweat, my hair hanging wildly, one pearly hairslide dangling loose. I snatch it up, terrified of losing it. I think of Russell. Down and down, unable to breathe, my foot hurting so. What if they're coming after us? What will they do to us now if they catch us?

'Quick!'

'Can't go any quicker!' Nadine gasps.

'I'll never go to another step class again,' Magda moans.

Down and down and down and down – and then suddenly we round the last corner and we're there, out into the courtyard, on ground level at last.

'This way!' says Magda, forging forward.

'No, wait. Keep to the edges so that if they look down they won't see us,' I say.

We skirt round the sides of the tower block, legs still wobbling after all those hundreds of stairs.

'Which is the way we came in?'

'Can't remember.'

'It doesn't matter. Let's just get *out*.'

We scuttle on, ducking through an archway, round a corner – and then suddenly stumble upon the lager lads.

'Hey, look! It's them stupid stuck-up birds.'

'There's the one that gave me the finger. I'll have her.'

'I'll have the one with the big whatsits,' says another, making a grab at me.

My hand flies out, hitting his face. He screams and staggers, clutching his head. His mates stare at him in astonishment.

'Quick,' I say, and we start running again. We run right round the estate before we spot an exit, and then we're right out in the road at long last.

'Where now?' I gasp.

'We'll make for the nearest tube,' says Magda.

'You certainly gave that guy a brilliant punch in the face, Ellie!' says Nadine.

'It wasn't a punch, it was a jab,' I say, showing them my hairslide.

'You should have jabbed the guys in the flat too!' said Magda.

'No, they could have got really really nasty,' says Nadine.

'Hey, none of this seems real, does it?' I say. 'I mean, we should all be watching the Claudie concert, not wandering unknown streets with mad drunk druggies in hot pursuit.'

'Don't!' says Nadine, looking nervously over her shoulder. 'I can't believe I could have been so stupid. Thanks so much for sticking with me, you two.'

'That's what girlfriends are for,' says Magda. 'Hey, where on earth *are* we?'

'Maybe we're not *on* earth. Maybe we stepped into alternative time just before the Claudie concert. I mean, does it seem real that Claudie would give up her whole singing career for some inadequate boyfriend? No, in real time she's singing away and we're all singing along with her in the concert hall, right? But now we're stuck in *this* spooky time on a dead-end planet and we're going to be lost for ever, meeting up with all these threatening creepy guys—'

As I'm saying these very words a couple of drunk men come lurching out a pub door and bump right into us. We all shriek.

'Hey, sorry, girls!'

'Didn't hurt you, did we?'

'Had one too many.'

'A few too many.'

'Where are you off to, eh?'

'Shouldn't be out late by yourselves, nice little girls like you.'

We don't need to be told this. They seem relatively harmless but we don't want to take any risks. We run for it.

'I feel like I've been in a twenty-four-hour marathon aerobics class,' I puff, when we're right down the street and round the corner.

'Mrs Henderson would be proud of us,' Nadine gasps.

'Mrs Henderson would be deeply *ashamed* of us because we seem to have been behaving like ninnies all night,' I say, slowing down. 'Look, it's daft just wandering. Let's ask someone where the tube is.'

There's a late-night video shop on the corner so we dodge in and ask. The man behind the counter shakes his head.

'Sorry, girls. There's no tubes round this area. You could get a bus into Central London, but I'm not quite sure of the times. And there's been a lot of rowdy behaviour on the buses when the pubs come out. I wouldn't like a daughter of mine to be on one.'

'Oh help, what shall we do now?' says Magda.

'Maybe we're going to have to phone our dads,' I say.

'My dad will kill me,' says Nadine.

'And mine,' says Magda.

'Mine too,' I say. 'But we can't wander the streets all night long, can we?'

'What about getting a taxi?' says Nadine. 'Only I haven't got any spare cash.'

'Neither have I,' I say.

We both look hopefully at Magda.

'I haven't got enough for a taxi right across London and all the way home,' she says. 'But maybe we could get a taxi back into town to the nearest tube – and we've got our train tickets.'

'What time does the last train go?' I ask anxiously.

'I don't know. But it must be quite late,' says Magda.

'*We're* quite late already,' says Nadine.

'We're *always* late in this alternative reality,' I say.

'Shut up, Ellie! It's spooky enough without you making stuff up,' says Magda.

'At least we've got each other,' says Nadine, linking arms with both of us.

'Only there are replicants in this alternative world. Maybe one of *us* is a replacement!' I say. 'Maybe it's you, Nadine, and you were deliberately plotting our downfall with those creeps. Or maybe it's you, Magda, and you're going to jump in a taxi by yourself and abandon Nadine and me. Or maybe it's *me*?'

'You're a one-off, Ellie. They could never program a replicant as weird and wacky as you,' says Magda, and then she suddenly starts jumping up and down and waving her arms in the air.

'*I'm* wacky?' I say.

'It's a taxi!' Magda shrieks.

We all jump up and down and wave our arms in the air and it stops and we jump in.

'I'm terribly afraid we haven't got much cash on us,' Magda starts.

'Well, *I'm* terribly afraid you'll have to pile straight

out my cab again,' says the taxi driver, but his eyes are twinkling. 'You crazy girls. Right, how *much* cash – and how far do you need to go?'

Magda waves a five-pound note and Nadine and I come up with a few coins.

'That's a fair kitty,' says the taxi driver, but he whistles in alarm when Magda tells him where we live. 'No way, girls. I wouldn't take you that far even if you *had* the cash.'

'Just to the nearest tube station?' Magda asks.

'Now you're talking. And then will you get the train from Waterloo?'

'That's what we're hoping. Do you know what time the last train goes?'

'I'm not too sure. I'd better step on it, eh, girls. You've got train tickets already, have you?'

'Oh yes,' I say, and then panic when I can't find mine in my pocket.

'Help, where is it?' I say, rummaging around.

'You seem like the forgetful type,' says the taxi driver. 'I couldn't help noticing you've forgotten one of your shoes!'

I wiggle my poor cold foot in its tattered tight.

'Well, I didn't exactly *forget* it,' I say.

'It was all my fault,' Nadine sighs.

'You girls haven't been in any real trouble, have you?' the taxi driver asks.

'Well, *nearly*,' I say. 'But we escaped in the nick of time.'

'I don't know. You girls nowadays! How old are you? Fifteen?'

We preen and don't put him right.

'You're all allowed out so late now. And I know

you think you know it all, but you act so nutty some-times. Look at you, Miss Curly! What are you going to do? No train ticket and no cash.'

'Aha!' I say, finding my ticket scrunched up at the very bottom of my purse. 'Found it!'

'You're a very lucky girl,' says the taxi driver, laughing.

We're all three very lucky girls because the taxi driver insists on taking us all the way to Waterloo. He stops his meter when it gets to five pounds and won't even take our spare change.

'You keep it to telephone your dads when you get off the train,' he says. 'I hate the thought of nice girls like you wandering the streets in the middle of the night.'

We don't have to telephone our dads. You will never guess who we meet up with on the last train home! Mr Windsor – and his girlfriend, sitting snuggled up together.

'Good Lord! Ellie. Nadine. And Magda,' says Mr Windsor.

He looks wonderful in a V-neck long-sleeved T-shirt, black jacket and black trousers – ultra cool.

'This is Miranda,' he says.

Miranda looks just as wonderful – long black hair, fantastically plaited, big brown eyes, slinky figure in tiny stripy top and black jeans.

'Hi! Are you Guy's students?' she says, giggling.

Guy!!!

We giggle too, though Magda's giggle is a little shrill.

'What are you three doing out so late?' says Mr Windsor.

'It's a long story,' I say. 'We set out to go to a Claudie Coleman concert. She's this really great singer—'

'We know,' says Miranda. 'I'm her number one fan. Guy and I were going to the concert too. But when she cancelled we trekked round half London to see if there were any other likely gigs – and ended up at this amazing *country* do, with some sad blonde doing a Tammy Wynette impersonation – *Stand by Your Man*. I ask you! And they even started doing *line dancing*.'

Nadine winces.

'So what did you girls do as a Claudie alternative?'

We hesitate. We shrug. Nadine looks embarrassed. Magda *already* looks embarrassed. It's down to me.

'We had a girls' night out,' I say, and then I rapidly change the subject and start talking about Claudie and her songs. I can usually talk about Claudie all night long but it's pretty heavy keeping the conversation going for the entire journey, especially as Magda and Nadine remain monosyllabic.

We all get out at the same station. Mr Windsor hesitates.

'How are you girls getting home? Is anyone meeting you?'

'We're fine,' I say.

Mr Windsor nods, but Miranda narrows her eyes.

'Does that mean you're being met or not?'

'Not,' I admit.

'OK. So maybe we'd better do a little taxi service,' says Mr Windsor, sighing.

'We're not little kids,' says Magda.

'Of course not,' Miranda says soothingly. 'But it

can get a bit dodgy round the station late at night. I know I always wimp out if I've been up in town with *my* girlfriends and get Guy to pick me up from the station. So come on – *please* let us give you a lift. Especially as you've only got five shoes between the three of you.'

Magda has to give in graciously. I really feel for her. It's bad enough Mr Windsor having a girlfriend, but it's extra painful that Miranda is a) extremely pretty and b) extremely nice. I look her over several times to try to find *something* to be catty about tomorrow with Magda but draw a total blank. I stare at Mr Windsor instead, hoping to see sudden signs of senility so I can convince Magda she's better off without him, but his hair looks as dark and lustrous as always and his shoulders stay square, not stooped.

He asks us all our addresses and drops us off in turn. Logically Magda should be last but he does a little detour so that she is taken home first. Maybe he's not quite as cool about everything as he makes out. He doesn't seem to have mentioned Magda's surprise visit to Miranda.

'What a sweet girl. I love her hair! But she seems ever so shy,' says Miranda, as Magda ducks out of the car and dives for her front door.

Nadine and I nudge each other in the dark. That's the first time Magda's ever been labelled *shy*!

'Does she say much in class, Guy?' Miranda persists.

'Oh, Magda has her moments,' he says. 'Right, Nadine, you're next.'

Nadine gets delivered. She gives my hand one last squeeze to say sorry.

I'm left in the car with Mr Windsor and Miranda.

'So, how do you enjoy Guy's art classes?' Miranda asks me chattily.

'Miranda!' says Mr Windsor.

'They're great,' I say truthfully.

'Really?' says Miranda. 'He was *so* nervous that first week of term. What year are you, Ellie?'

'Year Nine.'

'Aha! He was *particularly* scared of Year Nine. He thought you'd give him a really hard time.'

'Shut up, Miranda,' says Mr Windsor.

'Oh darling, no need to be bashful! Anyway, he came rushing home full of the joys of spring saying it had all gone splendidly after all. In fact he still raves about you Year Nine girls. You're a very talented bunch by all accounts.'

'Miranda, I'm pressing my ejector seat button right this minute,' says Mr Windsor, but he's laughing.

'There's one really talented girl – she specializes in all these crazy cartoons but she's great at serious portraits too. Now, I wonder what her name is?' says Miranda.

'Who??'

They both laugh. At me.

'You must realize you're Guy's star pupil, Ellie. He's always going on about you.'

'Oh wow! I mean – cool,' I say, totally flustered but thrilled to bits. Star pupil! I'm twinkling all over the back seat. It's surprising the entire car isn't illuminated by my stardust.

I'm still sparkling when I let myself in at home. In spite of all the adventures of the evening I am actually back a minute before midnight, my Cinderella curfew.

I kick off my remaining shoe in the hall and try to compose myself before going into the living room. Dad's sleepily watching television and Anna is still twitching over a complicated teddy jumper with a little knitted teddy attached on a woolly string.

'Did you have a good time at your Claudie concert, Ellie?' she asks, experimenting with the dangling teddy.

I hesitate. It's simpler just to say yes. So I do.

'And Magda's dad picked you up OK after the concert?' says my dad.

'Sure,' I say. 'Anna, that teddy looks as if he's hung himself. He's too droopy.'

'I know, I know, but I can't work out how else I can attach it. If I try to put in a pocket it'll throw the whole design out of sync and I've got to get it finished by tomorrow.'

'It's mad you taking on all this work,' says Dad, yawning. 'Well, I'm off to bed. Come on, Anna, sort it out tomorrow, you're exhausted.'

'No, I've got to fix it. Somehow,' says Anna.

'Hey, what about a bit of velcro? Then you could stick the teddy to the jumper.'

'Yes! Oh, Ellie, you're a genius,' says Anna, giving me a kiss.

'I'm not sure I'd go *that* far,' says Dad, giving us both a big bear-hug. 'But you're a good girl, Ellie. I'm pleased you're being really straight with us now. No more silly lies, right?'

'Right,' I say, practically swallowing my black tongue.

But it's all right. They'll never know.

\* \* \*

Famous last words!!! There's an item in Saturday's newspaper all about Claudie Coleman and her cancelled concert.

Oh help!

'Ellie!' Dad thunders.

I am in for a stormy time. I try to explain. Over and over again.

It gets me nowhere.

Magda rings. Her mum spotted the newspaper article too.

Nadine rings. Ditto *her* mum.

We were supposed to be meeting up to go shopping in the afternoon. We are not allowed. We are not allowed out anywhere apart from school for a *very* long time.

Russell rings.

'Hi Ellie! How are you? Enjoy the concert? My dance was totally dire. I'm rather glad you weren't there, it was just so incredibly stupid and stuffy. In fact I left early because it was so boring standing there with a whole lot of other sad guys without girls. Not that I'd have wanted any of the girls who *were* there. There was no-one remotely like you, Ellie. So anyway, I got home early, like I said, and my dad was pleased and said he's glad I'm behaving like a responsible human being at last – so I'm not grounded any more. We can go out on our first proper date. Tonight! Remember I said I knew where I wanted to go? How about the 7.30 showing of *Girls Out Even Later*? It's still on at the Rio.'

'There's just one problem, Russell.'

'Don't worry about it being scary. I'll hold your hand tight, I promise. Everyone says *Girls Out Even*

*Later* is a really great film. Well, not great art, just great fun.'

'Russell—'

'But don't worry. We don't have to see it if you really think it might upset you. We'll go anywhere you want.'

'I can't go to *Girls Out Even Later.* I can't go out late myself. Or early. Oh Russell, I'm in big trouble. *I'm* not allowed out for ages now.'

I explain. Russell listens. Groans. Tells me off for taking crazy risks. Moans that we can't go out after all.

'So it's back to secret after-school trysts in McDonald's?' he says.

'It looks like it.'

'Ah well. I suppose it can't be helped. We'll have our big night out *one* day, right?'

'You bet.'

'Good. Because you mean a lot to me, Ellie.' There's a little pause. I hear him swallow. 'Ellie . . . I love you.'

I swallow too. I glance around quickly to make sure Eggs isn't lurking.

'I love you too,' I whisper, and then I put the phone down.

I pick it up again. Who shall I phone first, Magda or Nadine? I can't wait to tell them what Russell's just said!

# ABOUT THE AUTHOR

JACQUELINE WILSON was born in Bath in 1945, but has spent most of her life in Kingston-on-Thames, Surrey. She always wanted to be a writer and wrote her first 'novel' when she was nine, filling countless Woolworths' exercise books as she grew up. She started work at a publishing company and then went on to work as a journalist on JACKIE magazine before turning to writing fiction full-time.

Since 1990 Jacqueline has written prolifically for children and been awarded many of the UK's top awards for children's books, including the Smarties Prize in 2000 and the Guardian Children's Fiction Award and the Children's Book of the Year in 1999. Over 8 million copies of Jacqueline's books have now been sold in the UK and approximately 50,000 copies of her books are sold each month. An avid reader herself, Jacqueline has a personal collection of more than 10,000 books.

She lives in Surrey and has one grown-up daughter.

'A brilliant young writer of wit and subtlety whose stories are never patronising and are often complex and many-layered' *The Times*

'Jacqueline Wilson has a rare gift for writing lightly and amusingly about emotional issues' *Bookseller*

'Wilson writes like a child, and children instantly recognise themselves in her characters. The tone of voice is faultless, her stories are about the problems many children face, and her plots work with classic simplicity . . . a subtle art is concealed by artlessness, and some might call that genius' *Daily Telegraph*

# ABOUT THE ILLUSTRATOR

NICK SHARRATT knew from an early age that he wanted to use his artistic skills in his career. He went to Manchester Polytechnic to do an Art Foundation course, followed by a BA (Hons) in Graphic Design at St Martin's School of Art in London. Since graduating in 1984, Nick has been working full-time as an illustrator, with his work much in demand for magazines and children's books. He has also designed and illustrated packaging for confectionery.

His famous collaboration with Jacqueline Wilson began with *The Story of Tracy Beaker*, published in 1991 and he has illustrated every one of her bestselling books published by Doubleday/Corgi since then.

Nick also illustrates full-colour picture and novelty books such as *Eat Your Peas* (Bodley Head), written by Kes Gray, which won the 2000 Children's Book Award. He also writes his own books, including *The Cheese and Tomato Spider* (Scholastic) which won the 1997 Sheffield Children's Book Award.

After living in London for thirteen years, Nick moved to Gloucestershire and then to Brighton, Sussex, where he now lives. When he is not working, he loves to eat – he says that food is a major part of his life!

## GIRLS IN TEARS
Jacqueline Wilson

Ellie, Magda and Nadine are back – but they're not very happy!
Ellie's glorious romance with Russell is teetering on the rocks.
Magda's lost her pet and is desperately upset (though the others
didn't even know she still had a hamster!). And Nadine is fed up
with the other two lecturing her about the dangers of meeting
someone on the Internet – her e-mail boyfriend *sounds*
wonderful!

Buckets of tears are wept and hundreds of tissues sniffled into. Can
the girls' friendship survive these testing times?

A superb fourth instalment in the GIRLS series, following GIRLS
IN LOVE, GIRLS UNDER PRESSURE and GIRLS OUT
LATE. A perfect read for older fans from the bestselling author,
Jacqueline Wilson.

DOUBLEDAY

DUSTBIN BABY
Jacqueline Wilson

*April Showers.*
*That's my nickname now. It's better than April Fool.*
*It's much, much better than Dustbin Baby.*

April started out in life as a dustbin baby – unceremoniously
abandoned in a rubbish bin on 1st April. Now she's turned 14,
April's determined to find out where she came from. If only she
could remember her birth mother – or, maybe, even find her . . .

It's not going to be easy but can April forget the old labels and
discover who she really is?

Another unforgettable story for older readers from award-
winning and bestselling author, Jacqueline Wilson.

'Jacqueline Wilson at her compassionate best' *Guardian*

'This is a book that will resonate with many teenage girls'
*Daily Telegraph*

DOUBLEDAY/CORGI BOOKS

THE ILLUSTRATED MUM
Jacqueline Wilson

*Star used to love Marigold, love me, love our life together. We three were the colourful ones, like the glowing pictures inked all over Marigold.*

Covered from head to foot with glorious tattoos, Marigold is the brightest, most beautiful mother in the world. That's what Dolphin thinks (she just wishes her beautiful mother wouldn't stay out partying all night or go weird now and then). Her older sister, Star, isn't so sure any more. She loves Marigold too, but sometimes she just can't help wishing she were more *normal* . . .

A powerful and memorable tale for older readers from Jacqueline Wilson, the award-winning author of *The Suitcase Kid*, *Double Act*, *Bad Girls* and many other titles.

'Disturbingly perceptive and provocative' *Guardian*

'A marvellous, poignant tale . . . Jacqueline Wilson's best yet' *The Telegraph*

WINNER OF THE 2000 BRITISH BOOK AWARD (NIBBIES)
WINNER OF THE CHILDREN'S BOOK OF THE YEAR AWARD
AND THE GUARDIAN CHILDREN'S FICTION AWARD.
HIGHLY COMMENDED FOR THE CARNEGIE MEDAL.
SHORTLISTED FOR THE WHITBREAD AWARD AND FOR
THE 2000 BLUE PETER BOOK AWARDS.

SECRETS

Jacqueline Wilson

*'I keep a diary,'* Treasure said.
*'I keep a diary, too,'* said India, *and then she blushed.*
*'You girls!'* said Nan. *'Well, I* don't *keep a diary. I'm not confiding my secrets to anyone.'*

India lives in a large, luxurious house with a mum she can't stand and a rather distracted dad. Inspired by her heroine, Anne Frank, India keeps a diary full of the secrets she observes all round the house.

Treasure lives in a council flat with her nan, whom she adores. But she's scared of having to go back to live with her mother and brutish stepfather. She keeps a diary of ways to punish her stepfather, The Terrible Terry Torture Manual.

A chance meeting sparks a great friendship between the girls. When Treasure has to run away, India has an idea for an amazing hiding place, based on the life of her favourite author. And that gives the girls their biggest secret ever.

A superbly moving novel from the bestselling author of *The Illustrated Mum*, winner of the Guardian Children's Fiction Award and *Double Act*, winner of the Smarties Prize.

DOUBLEDAY

VICKY ANGEL
Jacqueline Wilson

*'You look as if you've seen a ghost!'*

Jade is so used to being with and agreeing with Vicky, her larger-than-life best friend, that when a tragic accident occurs, she can hardly believe that Vicky's no longer there. But Vicky's a sparky girl who's not going to let a small thing like being dead stop her from living life to the full. Whether Jade is in lessons, out running or tentatively trying to make new friends, Jade is making her presence felt . . .

CORGI YEARLING BOOKS

For all dedicated Jacqueline Wilson fans, visit her website at www.jacquelinewilson.co.uk for news on the latest titles, forthcoming events in your area, TV and film adapations, reviews, quizzes and fun. And join the fantastic on-line Official Jacqueline Wilson Fan Club!